Thread

of Souls

Ashley Roepel

Always seek adventures! Ashley Roepel

Book I

Phantom

Five

To my husband, Scottie. We built this world together.

And to Ben and Sean, who started the adventure with us.

Jade's Map of Corventos

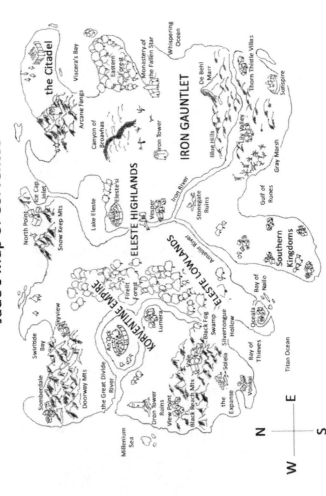

Prologue

UNOLÉ

.

.

.

  The field of tall grass, bronze in the harsh sunlight, slapped across Unolé's skin as she ran. It tugged at her legs, threatening to trip her. But she pushed on. She had to. At least until she and her sister found somewhere to hide. All that mattered now was keeping the little girl at her side safe.

  Her vision was a blur of grass with flashes of blue sky. The pounding of her heart in her ears almost drowned out the shouting of the man behind them. The man they'd come to steal from. It was not supposed to be a dangerous contract. The Shadow Guild didn't often send members as young as Unatchi on deadly assignments. Perhaps that was why Unolé had let her guard down. The staff they'd been sent to steal had been guarded by arcane wards. It had alerted the owner to their presence. And then everything went wrong.

  She couldn't fathom why someone who appeared to be a farmer would possess a magic staff the Shadow Guild had interest in. Not this far outside of An'Ock. They were so far away from the capital that it was hard to make out the skyline of the rising castle. Farmland stretched as far as the eye could see.

  "Unolé!" Unatchi gasped at her side, her small boot caught in the weeds.

  Unolé spun around, her tail lashing out to help keep her balance. She crouched, desperately trying to untangle her sister. The weeds cut at her hands but she didn't feel the pain. She could hear the man running closer, shouting, "Demons! *Unholy*! Get off my land!"

The words had long since lost their sting. It was nothing she hadn't been called so many times before.

As she ripped the last tangle free, and Unatchi let out her breath in relief, the man was on them. He was silhouetted against the sun, staff raised high.

He shouted again, "*Demons*!" Then he swung the staff in a wide arc at their heads.

Unolé grabbed her little sister and threw them both backwards, avoiding the blow. There was a flash of green light in the air, blinding, and then they landed hard on the ground. Unolé wrenched her dagger free from its sheath and held it in front of her protectively. She glared up at the man, and made sure to bare her teeth. The pointed incisors had always been useful for intimidation. But he wasn't looking at her. He stared at her sister with his mouth open in shock.

Unolé's head whipped around to the side, and saw her sister unmoving, eyes gazing sightlessly up at the sky. There was a rustle of movement as the man ran off, vanishing into the grass. But Unolé hardly noticed. The world around her locked.

"Unatchi?" she whispered, laying a hand on the girl's arm. Surely the magic had only paralyzed her. Stunned her. She would be better in a minute. She searched those large eyes for life. They were beautiful, a light purple, the same as her own. Unatchi's hair was black, tied into pigtails. Unolé's hair was very different, a stark white, despite her twenty-four years of age. Staring at her sister there, waiting for something to happen, made her realize again how young she was. The horns on either side of her head were small and brown, unlike Unolé's that had grown to a graceful curve on both sides of her face. Surely the man would not have killed someone so innocent looking.

"Unatchi?" she asked again, her voice hoarse from all the running.

A huge shadow passed overhead, eclipsing the sunlight. Unolé flinched, head snapping up to look at the sky.

A black beast with wings. It circled the farmland and then made a lazy turn, heading in her direction. Panic seized her. She had no idea what this monstrosity was, but it was huge. She scrambled backwards in the grass, working her way into a muddy hole that offered better cover. Crouching low, she watched the beast warily.

Its black wings flapped, sending a burst of wind that momentarily scattered the grass. Then it landed with a heavy thud that shook the ground. A raven-like head swiveled from side to side, observing the land around it. Now that Unolé had a closer look, she could see it was very bird-like. She would have thought it was a great eagle or roc if it hadn't been for its four legs that ended in talons as long as swords.

She held her breath. Was this something the staff had conjured? She'd lived in this area all her life and had never once seen this beast.

Its head turned to where her sister lay.

No! she thought, horror turning her blood to ice. She hoped it couldn't see a girl so small. Hoped it wouldn't be interested.

A great flap of its wings sent another blast of wind that made her eyes water. Relief washed over her. It was leaving. But just as it lifted a couple feet from the ground one of its talons shot out and picked up Unatchi. Another thunderous flap and it took to the sky, turning around to fly off.

Unolé leaped up, racing after the beast. Her legs shook and her breath came out in raspy gasps. She was so tired from all this running. But her sister needed her. Pursuing the beast, she pushed her body to its limits, struggling to keep up. But the creature was too fast. Soon it was gone. She stumbled to a stop, breathing heavily. Her mind spun. The world was soon to follow. She lost her balance and dropped to her knees, gasping.

It had taken Unatchi. It had taken her sister. Was her sister . . . dead?

Her mind just couldn't wrap around this. And so as she sat there, shaking, she noticed drifting from the sky four black feathers. They landed a few inches from where she knelt. Unolé reached over and picked them up. They were silky and nearly a foot in length.

She held them in her hand. And stared at them until the sun set.

.

.

.

PART I

ZOK

.

.

.

Zok struggled to worm his way through the crowded tavern. The patrons were either too drunk or too excited to notice him, making his journey more difficult. Feet stomped, cheers sounded, beer was raised high into the lantern-lit air. Gold coins jingled as they passed from hand to hand. Bets taken, changed, and raised against the two brawlers in the fighting pit. From this vantage point Zok could not see them, but he could hear them all too well. Even over the din in the Arrowed Knee Tavern. Grunts, slaps, punches, howls of pain. And deep laughter. His friend, Sen, fighting again.

A small smile crept over Zok's face as he pushed further in. It was a wonder anyone still challenged Sen to fight. If not from his appearance alone, certainly from his reputation as the undefeated brawler of the tavern. He normally didn't come to see his friend fight. The temple certainly wouldn't like it. But it wasn't the first time he was in a gray area with his oath and he was sure it wouldn't be the last.

Another push got him to the inner circle of spectators, and now he had a clear view of the fighting ring. There was a soft rub against his leg. He didn't need to look down to know it was a red fox. Smiling, Zok gave the animal a scratch behind the ears. Happy to be noticed, the fox led him along the ring of people. He followed at a slower pace, dodging waving hands and spilling beer. His clothes were a bright, clean white. He wasn't about to get them dirty here, of all places.

Looking up, he spotted the bright red and orange feathers tucked behind a pointed ear. "Jade."

She turned and waved at him as her fox took his place again at her side. "Zok, glad you made it."

"How is he doing?" he leaned against the metal railing alongside his friend. "There is a lot of anticipation for tonight."

The Wild Elf smiled, lantern light gleaming in her dark green eyes. "It is never much of challenge for him."

Zok turned his attention to the fighting. The ring was wooden, the floor stained with old blood and cracked from heavy falls. A man was there, shirtless and sweating. His fists were up to protect his face, which already had some bruising. The man was big, but who he faced down was bigger. Standing over seven feet tall of solid muscle covered in red scales, Sen the Dragonborn had a lazy grin over his lizard-like face. His heavy leather boots stomped around the ring as he dodged and struck, landing blows and deflecting others. Even when one of the smaller man's fists managed to strike Sen in the gut, he didn't seem to feel it.

The red fox stood up on his hind legs, resting his front two paws on the rail to mimic his owner, eagerly watching the combat. Jade absently pet the animal, an amused smile on her tan face as she watched the fight.

The two danced back and forth in the ring, the Human more and more desperate while the Dragonborn sauntered after him. One punch, another, and then a third finally knocked the Human from his feet. He didn't get back up, instead holding up a hand in surrender.

The crowd burst into cheers, the noise rattling the wooden walls of the tavern. Jade and Zok clapped, laughing at the way Sen strolled the ring. The Dragonborn shook his fists to the sky, flexing muscles. His deep voice boomed through the room as he shouted, "The next round is on me!"

Thunderous applause followed. The barkeep hopped over the rail and into the ring, holding a piece of paper. He cleared his throat to get the crowd to settle some before

7

reading, "The Arrowed Knee Tavern would like to commemorate this day, the fifteenth of Morivaec, as the day Captain Sen won his hundredth fight over exactly one hundred days." More cheering followed. "From this day forward, Sen drinks free!"

Over the crowd Sen roared, "Party on my ship tonight! Everyone is invited!"

It took several minutes for the tavern to clear out and fans to finish congratulating Sen. By the time Zok and Jade were able to make their way over there, the Dragonborn was lounging in a chair and putting all the gold rings back on his fingers. He adjusted the black bandana that was tied around his head, but other than his bright purple pants he was bare.

Seeing the two approach brought him to his feet. "Jade! Zok!" He scooped them both up in a hug with one arm, the other holding a massive tankard of rum. He sat them down and pet the fox that bounded around his legs. "Good to see you, too, little Foxy."

"Congratulations," Jade said.

"One hundred is an impressive feat," Zok added. "Maybe you and I should spar one day. You could teach me some things, I'm sure."

Sen gave a deep laugh. "I don't think your little Half-Elven body could handle it, my friend, but I'm always up for embarrassing you." He took a drink and then asked, "Are you two coming to the ship tonight? It will be a wild party."

Jade chuckled. "Wild parties aren't really my thing, but I'll certainly be there to honor your victory over the sad brawlers here in Somberdale."

The Dragonborn winked one eye. "I may have to find a new favorite port for some fresh blood in the fighting rings."

Zok smiled. He knew Sen was jesting. Somberdale had a charm. A remote port village far to the northwest in the Korventine Empire, it drew little notice from the law while still being considered a safe harbor for families. Sen's often illegal excursions at sea made it too risky to make port closer south towards the capital city. Zok found the temple here to be a welcome home. One where he could have peace and where his contributions went far. It had been a surprise, years ago, when he'd first come to Somberdale to see Jade here. He knew she was a nomad, and they'd crossed paths many years ago in the Elven town of Vesper. She was a good friend. The three of them had grown quite close in this small village.

They headed out of the tavern and into the night. The stars shone brilliantly over Somberdale. A pleasant wind blew Zok's shoulder length brown hair from his face. Street lights illuminated the houses, shops, and roads that were some parts stone, some parts dirt. One tall tower rose up over the other buildings, the home of a local eccentric wizard. The ocean could be heard rushing on and off of the beaches. And against the night sky the masts of ships large and small swayed and creaked. A light blossomed on one ship in particular as the patrons of the tavern boarded for a long night of partying. Already a banjo was playing a lively tune.

The three headed down the central road of the town, Foxy trotting along beside Jade. Zok looked up at his large friend. "One hundred fights, Sen. That is truly something."

"And many more on the high seas and in various tavern brawls," the Dragonborn chucked. "What can I say? I'm like a barbarian."

Zok knew the Dragonborn was deadly with his giant fists. But Sen was even more deadly with the weapon strapped to his back. A massive two-sided axe. It was never far from him. The edges were stained with old blood, the wood of the handle sturdy but weathered from life on the seas. Even in arms as powerful as Sen's, it required two hands to wield.

Zok chose to use an iron hammer to defend himself. One that could be swung with both hands or one if he had his shield with him. He typically dressed in the formal armor of his order. All shining gold and white. But not tonight. Tonight was a celebration, one where he could shed his formality and be with his friends. But he still kept the hammer strapped to his back, and a dagger on his belt. Somberdale was considered safe, but the surrounding lands were not. Danger lurked in the expansive Doorway Mountains. Feral animals and creatures that preyed on unsuspecting travelers. There was also the danger of enemies coming in from the ocean. But despite carrying his weapons, despite usually wearing his armor, and despite training daily, Zok had never run into any danger inside the town.

Jade carried no weapons on her, but Zok knew she was never unarmed. She was a spellcaster. Her magic always took the form of nature and of the elements. She referred to herself as a Druid. He wasn't entirely sure what that title entailed, but he knew she had other Druids she kept in contact with and they helped protect the wild lands.

Sen asked, "Would either of you two ever fight in the pit?"

Zok shook his head. "The temple wouldn't allow it. Fighting for gold in a crowd of drunkards is not considered honorable."

Sen waved a hand dismissively. "You and your honor. What about you, Jade?"

A smile spread across her face. "They couldn't handle me."

The Dragonborn gave a hearty laugh at this, patting her on the back more roughly than intended, making her stumble. But she laughed along with him as they walked.

Conversation quieted down. There was a moment of solitude, where they three were the only ones in the town center, before a man in a dark cloak could be seen further ahead, rushing in their direction. His form was small and hunched, and Zok did not pay much attention until the man drew closer, making it clear he was coming at them. Ragged breathing sounded as he scuttled up. Once he was within fifteen feet he shouted, "Help! *Help!*"

The three gave a start. "What's wrong?" Zok asked, taking in the man's elderly and lined face. A small silver beard was visible. He was thankful for his Half-Elf blood in times like this as it helped him see in the dark. He wasn't thankful for it in any other aspect of his life. It wasn't something easy to hide. He had pointed ears but a full brown beard. Elves couldn't grow beards, and so the Human side of him was easily given away.

The old man regarded him with sharp eyes. "My son! My boy! He fell. Tripped in the dark. Couldn't see where he was going."

Zok stole a glance at his friends. Sen seemed interested, Jade seemed skeptical. Her face slightly scrunched in a frown, crinkling the red band tattoo that crossed from ear to ear.

"Where did he fall?" Zok asked.

The old man pointed to the well just off the street. "In there. I'm too old to climb down. Could you three help him?" His eyes darted over to Sen. "You're big and strong."

Zok touched the medallion he wore around his neck. A golden symbol of an eye. "The Temple of the Holy Dragon is happy to assist. We will get your son out shortly."

The three jogged over to the well, looking down as the elderly man hung back. "I got this," Sen stated, pulling a length of rope from his thick belt and tossing it over the side. One hand still holding his drink, the other tied the rope off against the well. He gestured with one massive hand towards Jade. "After you."

Jade glanced over her shoulder at her animal. "Stay here, Foxy. We'll be right up." She gracefully moved over the side and slid down along the rope, her brown hair flowing out behind her.

Sen went next, making a great deal of noise as he climbed over the edge of the well and hopped onto the rope. Some rum splashed out of his glass and onto the Wild Elf below. Jade's voice sounded up, "*Sen!* I'm still climbing."

Zok looked back at the old man. "I could wait here with you?"

The man waved his hands frantically. "No, please go! Your friends may need your help." His eyes flitted over Zok, taking in the formality of his clothing. "Paladin."

11

Something didn't feel quite right. But the Half-Elf couldn't be sure what it was. Touching the symbol of his deity for guidance, he leaped over and onto the rope, making his way after his friends.

It was a long way down into darkness. The muscles in his arms tensed as Zok slowly lowered himself. He immediately was suspicious. He should have hit water by now. But instead the rope kept going through air. He peered down with his darkvision. He could see a stone bottom. Sen and Jade had just landed and were taking in the area. As he reached the end of the rope it dangled about ten feet from the ground. Zok landed lightly, his feet splashing in a few inches of water. Curious it wasn't fuller. He had expected to be searching for a drowning boy. But if a child had fallen this distance, he would be seriously injured.

"What is this?" Jade asked, her voice echoing slightly.

The room was wide and square, the stonework damp. It was completely dark other than a ring of symbols in the center. They glowed with light, each a different color. Zok approached them cautiously. "I don't understand the language."

Jade knelt down, getting a better look. "It's not a language. They are arcane symbols. Be careful, magic could-"

Sen jerked back from where he'd touched one of the symbols, a burst of electricity rippling over him. He roared with pain and then a slew of profanity came from his mouth, ending with, "Those are dangerous."

Jade gave him a heavy frown. "You know I'm better with magic, Sen. Let me investigate things first."

"You are a Druid," the Dragonborn stated. "This is not a plant. Best way to tell what it does is touch it."

The Wild Elf gave her friend a glare as she stood. "Your recklessness is going to be the death of you one day, pirate."

Sen laughed. "I certainly hope so."

Zok began to walk the length of the room. "I don't understand. Why would magic be down here? What purpose-

" He broke off as the stone wall at the far end cracked, the noise echoing throughout the room. A gray hand emerged from the crack, then an arm, and then a full body. Rubble tumbled to the floor as a man made of stone tore itself free from the wall. Its body was badly damaged and cracked, and two blue lights shone in place of eyes. A golem controlled by magic.

"Alright, a fight!" Sen reached over his shoulder and unhooked his weapon. The heavy two-sided axe shone in the light from the arcane symbols. With a great roar he sprang forward, coming down towards the golem.

A stone hand struck out lightning fast. It caught Sen in his side and sent him flying into the wall. He hit roughly and fell to the ground with a splash. The golem then turned its head towards Zok and charged. From beneath his white cloak the Paladin unhooked his iron war hammer. He wished he had his armor on as he ducked under a swipe from the golem. He swiveled around and swung his hammer as hard and heavy as he could to its side. A crack splintered off from the impact, but that was it.

Zok only had a moment to see a stone fist coming towards his face before a green vine ripped free from the ground and caught its wrist. The golem struggled against the binding, and its head swiveled over to where the Druid stood, her hands outstretched from the spell she'd cast.

The golem grabbed the vine with its free hand and snapped it in half, then lunged at Jade. She spun out of the way, but the back of her foot caught one of the arcane symbols on the ground. She cried out as a burst of fire erupted, catching at her brown and green clothes. She dropped to the watery ground and rolled to put it out.

Zok ran up behind the golem and swung hard with his hammer again. His arm vibrated from the impact as his weapon struck. More cracks splintered along the golem's body. Its hand reached behind at an impossible angle and grabbed hold of his tunic. Zok's cry echoed through the room as he was pulled from his feet and tossed.

He hit the stone hard, the breath forced from his

lungs and his hammer from his hand. He slid across one of the arcane symbols and burning cold spread across his shin. As he came to a stop, groaning from the pain, he looked down to see ice incasing his leg. Just as quickly as it came it melted away, leaving a lingering ache.

The golem loped towards him and then Jade ran in between, standing her ground as her hands filled with fire. She aimed her fists forward and the fire shot out in two bolts, hitting the enemy with enough force to stagger it to a stop.

With a great shout Sen rushed in from the side, hitting the golem with his shoulder. It was knocked from its feet, and one arm broke off as it landed roughly. The Dragonborn hefted his axe and came down with a heavy swing. The golem rolled out of the way, getting back to its feet in a smooth movement. It kicked out and caught Sen in the stomach. The Dragonborn wasn't used to an opponent with so much strength behind its attacks. He braced himself to absorb the blow and instead was sent sliding back, barely keeping his footing.

Zok scrambled up, his clothes now heavy with chilly water. He ran the distance to pick up his hammer just as the golem was on him, its punch aiming for his head. He deflected the blow with his weapon, grunting from the effort. The impact reverberated in the room.

Zok then twisted around and swung his hammer at the golem's midsection. He hit, more cracks spiderwebbing through its body. A stone elbow came at his head and the Half-Elf jumped backwards, barely avoiding the blow. The golem then turned on him again, the cold fire in its eyes staring him down.

With a thunderous shout Sen leaped through the air, enormous axe held high overhead. Zok had barely enough time to jump out of the way as the Dragonborn crashed down on the golem, his axe splitting it completely in two.

There was a pause as the two halves stood on their own. And then they fell to the floor, crumpling in a pile of rubble. The head fell with a splash and the lights in its eyes went out.

The echoes died down to silence as the three regarded the broken stone man. The arcane symbols on the floor flickered and then faded out, plunging them into darkness.

.

.

.

JADE

·

·

·

"There is no child in here," Jade said angrily, looking about in the dark. Zok did a final search of the room, his white cloak trailing out behind him.

Jade approached the golem and knelt down beside it. Now that she had a closer look she could tell it was shoddily made. Or being sealed under the well had damaged its structure. Whichever the case, it hadn't been a golem at full strength. There were no runes on it to give details of the enchantment. No markings from the maker, either.

The Druid sighed. "There are no clues on this golem to tell us why it was down here."

"I don't understand," Zok muttered. "If there is no child, why would that man send us down here?"

"Let's find out," Jade turned to the Dragonborn who patiently waited against the wall, unable to see without a light source. "I'll help you, Sen."

She grabbed her friend's huge arm, leading him over to the rope. She made sure to hand him the drink he'd sat down as well and he climbed up with one arm. She and Zok shared a worried look. It didn't make any sense. She'd used water from this well only this morning. It couldn't have gone dry within a day. And who would have put a golem underneath Somberdale? Unless it was from ages past, she couldn't see any logic behind it.

The three climbed out of the well, fresh air hitting their faces. The elderly man still stood where they'd left him, but this time the fear was gone from his face. He stood tall with a wide smile, his arms crossed.

That was enough to set Jade off. "What in the Hells?! Was that some kind of joke to you? We could have been

16

killed."

"It was all in good fun," the man chuckled. "I knew three capable warriors like you could handle it."

"Then what was the purpose?" Zok demanded, the night breeze ruffling his hair. "Who are you? I've never seen you here before."

The man's smile widened. "I'm sure you'll see me again." He drew a symbol in the air with his fingers and whispered the words of a spell, then vanished.

Jade growled in frustration.

"You know," Sen said thoughtfully, taking a sip of rum. "I used to have an uncle. A grouchy old Dragonborn named Jenkins. He liked to play pranks on the younger generations, usually involving some level of danger to see who was the strongest of our bloodline. Kinda barbaric, you know? Never sat well with the rest of the family. He died a very unpopular guy. This old man reminded me of Jenkins."

"So you think he was just a prankster?" Zok questioned. "Just a traveler looking to entertain himself at the cost of others' pain?"

Sen shrugged one massive shoulder. "Some people are just like that. Let's go party now."

Jade gave her friend a smile. Ever the optimist. The party would be a good distraction from what happened. Still, something did not feel right. She had been alive a long time, and had encountered many people across Corventos. Most who engaged in such acts were harmless. Just looking for a quick laugh. But others were much, much worse.

Zok nodded. "I'll be right behind you. I'm going to inform the temple about what has happened to the well. Perhaps some of our more powerful spellcasters can fix it."

Jade felt a pang in her chest at that sentence. There was a time she could have fixed it. But that was long ago, now. She wasn't as powerful as she used to be.

They spent most of the night on Sen's ship, the Scarlet Maiden, enjoying frivolities with the crew and some residents of Somberdale. It wasn't until many hours later that one of the Clerics from the Temple of the Holy Dragon approached them and said the well had been investigated. But it was found to be full of water, with no golem and no magic inside.

.

.

.

Morning sunlight awoke Jade, coming through the trees. She opened her green eyes, gazing up at a maze of branches and leaves. She could see the tips of some leaves turning red and orange. It was halfway through the month of Morivaec, the first month of autumn. She knew further south in Corventos the trees would be showing more. She remembered fondly the southern edges of the Firelit Forest during autumn. She and her Druid master Galen would walk among the trees and feel their spirits settling in for a winter slumber.

It was her favorite season. She knew many Druids preferred the spring. Life awakening again in every plant, animals coming out to frolic in the greenery and sunlight. But she liked the relaxed feeling of the autumn months. The sunset of nature before a cold night of winter. It was only fitting that the first day of Morivaec held the Festival of the Tamer and Dusk. Elven gods of nature celebrated in a month named in honor of the Elves. Jade worshipped these two gods in everything she did. She felt her Druid magic, at its core, was a worship of them.

She sat up from the bed of grass she'd slept on. She preferred to sleep outside rather than in a tavern. Not only did it make her feel closer to nature, but it was also simply something she was used to. She grew up in a nomadic tribe of Wild Elves. Sleeping on the ground felt natural to her.

Foxy stretched, coming out of her lap. She stroked him and stood up, heading over to a creek. Its water trickled over smooth gray stones. Jade cupped some of the cold water in her hands and washed off her face. Her fox drank beside her, fur shining an illustrious red in the morning light.

She took some time to pray to her two gods before getting ready to go into Somberdale. She put small braids into her chest-length brown hair. Brown boots were pulled on, outer layers of her clothes attached, and her red and orange feathers tucked behind one pointed ear.

Satisfied, Jade and Foxy made their way towards Somberdale. It was only a twenty minute walk. She heard the noises of the village before she crossed into its border. Residents went about their daily business, and ships came and left from the docks. Snacking on a breakfast of fruits from her pack, the Wild Elf made her way towards the beach. She needed to gather more ingredients for her healing balms. Magic was certainly useful for sealing up wounds, but nothing could replace the usefulness of plants for long-term healing. It was also a good way for her to make money. She tried to live as coin-free as possible. There simply wasn't much use in gold for a person who lived off the land. But, needs still arose and so some form of income was always necessary. It was a side business she had done for many, many years.

The ocean was aquamarine in the morning light as Jade made her way onto the beach. The area she ventured to was mostly empty. A family with a few children played in the waves. Much further down she could see the busy docks with their workers and stalls. And out on the Millennium Sea fishing vessels bobbed with the waves, catching lobster and shrimp that would be sold along the wharf later. Jade searched the sand, looking for a specific kind of seaweed that would wash up. She was so caught up in her concentration that a male voice had to repeat the word "Miss?" a few times before she turned around.

"Oh, I'm sorry," Jade apologized, taking in a young Human that was dressed in the garb of the tavern employees. "I wasn't paying attention. Can I help you?"

He held out a letter that fluttered in the ocean breeze. "You've got a guest at the Arrowed Knee Tavern wishing to speak to you. He paid me to deliver the message to you."

Jade took it with a frown. "Thanks." The young man lingered, looking at her expectantly. She passed him a gold coin and he took it with a smile, heading off. That irritated her. She didn't understand the concept of tipping. The materialistic ways of urban life could even worm their way into a town as small as Somberdale, it seemed. Opening the letter, she read:

Jade,
It's been too long since we've chatted. I find myself in Somberdale and would enjoy catching up with you. Please meet me at the Arrowed Knee Tavern at your earliest convenience today. I will wait for you.
Sincerely,
Therond

A smile broke across her face. Tucking the letter into her bag, she and Foxy left the beach and quickly headed for the tavern. The name Therond warmed her heart. It had been over a decade since she'd last seen him. She missed their conversations. She barely took in the beauty of Somberdale as she passed back through, mist lifting off the mountains that bordered the town. She wound her way down the cobblestone streets, passing under the shadows of trees that clustered at each corner. The market had just opened, stalls selling all kinds of fish, brightly colored fruits, bandanas, and shell jewelry. After another turn she came upon the Arrowed Knee Tavern, its outer white paint peeling in the wind and the sun. She headed inside.

It was much darker inside the tavern, but open windows allowed shafts of sunlight to fall in like waterfalls and create pools on the floor. Her eyes scanned the mostly empty space until they found the blond High Elf at a table in the corner. He raised his hand in greeting, smiling.

Jade crossed the space to him, her brown boots making barely any noise on the wooden floor. She sat down at the table, and her fox curled up underneath the chair. "Therond! It's been far too long."

"It is so good to see you," he grinned. "This is rather far west for you to be living now, isn't it? I thought you preferred Eleste."

She chuckled. "Well, it's a port town. I thought I would spend some time getting to know new people. What brings you to the coast? Surely it's not just to see me."

His blue eyes twinkled at that. Though Therond was two hundred years her senior, his face still held the smoothness of youth that all Elves were blessed with. Even Elves towards the end of their lives barely showed their age. The hair only lost its color, and some of the agility and grace with which the Elves moved slowed. His longer blond hair had traditional braids weaved through it. And his clothes, while functional for traveling, still had all the splendor and fine quality of a High Elf from Eleste'si.

Therond answered, "Part of it is to visit my old friend, of course."

Jade raised a brown eyebrow. "The rest is business for the Queen?"

"It is. Which I'm sure you're not interested in."

"I am not. But do tell, how is her all-mighty Highness?"

Therond couldn't maintain the disapproving frown he was trying for, amusement cracked through into a small smile. "She is fine. But you did hear that the King passed away, correct?"

"Oh." Some shame from her attitude clenched her stomach. "I did not. How long ago?"

"About fifteen years now, I believe."

"I'm sorry to hear that. What happened?"

"His age just caught up with him. He died peacefully in his sleep."

Jade sighed heavily. "Well, I'm sure he will be missed."

He glanced her over. "Are you still going by Galanodel or should I refer to you as Jade Moontide around here?"

A small smile passed her lips. "This far out it is safe for me to introduce myself as Jade Galanodel. However, I try to remain on a first name basis with as many as possible. I know what family name I choose in my heart. That is all that matters."

"Certainly."

"How was your trip west? That is quite the distance to travel."

"Fairly uneventful until I arrived in the Doorway Mountains." He made a gesture to the windows, indicating the mountain range outside. "I got attacked by goblins in the middle of the night. I don't pride myself on my fighting capabilities, but I was able to defend my life and my belongings until they scattered. They did steal one pack, unfortunately."

"Ugh, goblins are disgusting. What did they steal?"

"The pack didn't contain anything important in it. Extra gear for traveling, a change of shirt. But during the fight one did manage to take my ring off." He rubbed the finger where it had been. "That was difficult to lose. Not only was it of familial value, it was highly magical."

"It was enchanted?" Jade did not know this about her friend. "What did it do?"

"It had anti-divination magic. It prevented me from being the target of a scrying spell. As someone who does many errands for the Queen, it's been irreplaceable as a means of secrecy."

"I could get it back for you," she offered, leaning forward. "I've traveled all over that range. To make income while here in Somberdale I've been acting as a guide for travelers across the Doorway Mountains. If you could give me the general location I'm sure I could track it down." She reached into her pack and pulled out a map. It was a bit wrinkled and the edges were torn from use, but the ink still held clear and black as she spread it over the table. It was a map of all of the Korventine Empire, the Eleste Highlands and Lowlands, the Southern Kingdoms, and the Iron Gauntlet. Many of the places she'd travelled. Other details had been acquired through research.

Therond smiled, his blue eyes gazing over it. "Still making maps, I see. Beautiful craftsmanship."

Her eyes meet his. "Somebody has to help educate

all the generations of Humans, Dragonborn and Half-Elves what the world looks like. They certainly don't live as long as the rest of us. Maybe one day I'll be able to travel the rest of Corventos and verify my information."

His finger traveled over the lines of the Doorway Mountains until he stopped at a location. "It was around here."

Jade brought her own finger up, tapping on the area. "That is less than a day's journey. I know there is a cavern system in that area, that is probably where the goblins went." Her finger looked so dark next to his pale skin. She was a Wild Elf, her race known for living close to nature, brown of skin and hair. But he was a High Elf, living in the luxury of the Elven capital city, Eleste'si. Pale skin, blond hair, and blue eyes marked his kind. Despite everything the Elves had in common: their beauty, their dexterity, and their long lives, they were a deeply divided group. When Jade had lived in Eleste'si, it hadn't always been easy. The city was dominated by High Elves and she wasn't always welcome. She'd heard that far underneath the city the malevolent Dark Elves lived, often creeping out at night to kidnap citizens who would never be seen again. Slavers and torturers that dwelled in the lightless tunnels of the Deep Hollows, performing vile rituals to their spider goddess.

Therond had always been kind to her, however. This line of thought made her offer a sad sigh. "I do miss your friendship. I wish I could go back to Eleste'si. But I can't. Not just because of what happened while I was there, but it's too hard now. The memories are still too fresh."

"I understand. I don't think you should go back, either."

They both sat back as the map curled in on itself. There was a moment of silence. Then she said, "Somberdale is a nice place, truly. I don't know if I'll stay here for too much longer, though. If this place does not provide answers, I will have to move on."

"Answers to the visions you've had?" His tone was serious. Her family had dismissed her concerns. But Therond had taken them seriously.

"Yes," she replied. "I feel that time is running out. But the trade of information here is good with all the ships coming to and from the port. I'm remaining hopeful that one day the answers I need will reveal themselves."

"I certainly wish I could help. I will remain alert, as I always do. Keep my network open. If I hear of *anything* related to your visions, I will find a way to get in contact with you."

"Your network? I forget how fancy you are, Therond."

His eyes twinkled in amusement. "Well, perhaps that was an ambitious promise. The Greycastles of An'Ock are forthcoming. But the Dwarves of De Behl Marr are less communicative. And the gods only know what it would take to get the Citadel to divulge any secrets. I always will try, though."

"Thank you, my friend."

"Of course. I appreciate you going after my ring. Will you go alone? Surely a wanderer like yourself has some brave and noble adventurers to take with you." He smiled.

Jade grinned back. "I don't know about those adjectives. But I do know two I can convince to help."

.

.

.

The mountain peaks were all too familiar to Jade as she led Zok and Sen along the difficult terrain. Foxy bounded ahead of her, happy to be out in the wild. She smiled at the red animal as his bushy tail twirled with each leap. She'd gotten the fox not too long ago in the Firelit Forest. She'd found him as a baby in a hunter's trap. After freeing the fox she'd dispatched of the hunter. It wasn't her proudest moment, but it was a dark time in her life. One she hoped to never revisit again.

She glanced back at her friends. "The sun is setting soon; we can make camp and enter the caverns in the morning."

The two certainly didn't move quietly. Sen lumbered through every weed and bush, carrying a bottle of rum at his side. Zok had his full Paladin armor on, the white and gold sparkling in the lowering sun. It clanked with his movements and made him shine like a beacon in this world of greens and browns.

Well, at least they were good fighters.

"You blend into your surroundings," Sen said to Jade. "Don't go too far ahead or we might never find you again."

She laughed. Her clothes were the colors of the forest, and the beads that were woven into her braids and on her clothes were the colors of autumn. She'd always felt a special connection with nature. The Elven gods of the wild had blessed her with a unique relationship to the world around her. It was what led her to pursue training as a Druid. A spellcaster who specialized in nature, animals, and the elements. The three of them certainly made an interesting adventuring group. Her with her magic, Sen with his axe and fists, and Zok who was a warrior for the Temple of the Holy Dragon, the god he worshipped. Jade didn't know much about the order other than the inductees had to take an oath to do good. She didn't like rigid structure and routine. That life could never have been for her.

They hiked for another half hour before Jade found a good spot to make camp. It wasn't far from where she knew the caverns were, but it still offered protection. Trees grew thick in the area, and the ground was even and soft. They ate some food they'd brought along, breads, hard cheeses, and jerky. They didn't light a campfire so they could keep their location hidden.

"Who is this Therond, again?" Sen asked, tearing into his meat with sharp teeth.

"And old friend," she replied. "An old friend I met on my many travels. He's helped me in the past, so I think it's only right I return the favor."

"You've been far more places than I have," Sen stated. "How old are you, anyway? Don't Elves live like thousands of years?"

She chuckled. "We don't live over a thousand, typically. I myself am 406 years of age."

Sen spit out the meat he was chewing. "Incredible! And you've spent that whole time traveling?"

"Most of it. I grew up in a nomadic tribe. I've stayed in different cities for a few decades. But the wild calls to me." She glanced out into the darkness of the mountains. "To be among the trees is to be at peace." She looked over at Zok. He stared at his hands, his blue eyes far away. "Are you alright, Zok? You've been really quiet."

He blinked, his attention returning to the moment. "I am fine. Just tired today."

"Well," she said, "I do appreciate you both coming to help me. And I know Therond will be grateful to get his ring back."

Sen clenched one hand into a fist, punching it into his other open palm. "You never have to ask me twice for a rumble! Someone my size against goblins hardly seems fair, maybe I'll fight them with only one hand."

A smile did pull at Zok's somber face then. "One goblin is never a threat. That's why they travel in groups. So they can overwhelm and out-maneuver with their numbers. That being said, I still would like to see you fight with one hand."

The Dragonborn laughed. "Clearly I've never told you of the time my crew clashed with some other pirates at sea. They came upon us in the middle of a party. I fought the entire time with a tankard of rum in one hand."

They listened to Sen's tale as the night grew deeper. And eventually it was time to rest. They slept in bedrolls on the ground. Jade loved sleeping in the forest. The smell of bark, the sound of leaves, the life of insects and animals hummed around her. Foxy curled up against her torso, her arm draped over him. She knew Sen preferred the sway of his ship and Zok a bed, but the hike had been long and strenuous and the three fell asleep quickly.

Hushed whispering awoke Jade. She couldn't quite make out what words were spoken. She stirred, eyes blinking open in dawn light. The sun hadn't risen yet, but color slowly seeped back into a world of grays.

She turned her head towards the noise, Foxy's fur soft against her neck. Movement was beside Sen. Two small figures going through his pack. Goblins? No, they were too petite. Just as she began to lift a hand to wake her friends up, Sen's yellow eyes snapped open and his fist swung across his body, punching one of the small forms in the face. There was a high-pitched yelp of pain and the two fell back, crying and cowering.

"How dare you go through my things!" Sen roared, getting to his feet.

Zok started awake at this, sitting up quickly with his hair at crazy angles. "Wha-?"

Jade scrambled to her feet, holding her hands up to cast any spell necessary. But then she got a good look at the intruders. It appeared Sen did as well, for his demeanor immediately shrunk, his fists falling to his side.

Two Halflings cowered upon the grass. Standing only three feet tall and dressed in simple clothes, they stared up at the big pirate in horror. One held a hand to his nose where blood trickled out. "We're sorry! We were only looking for weapons."

A look of disbelief crossed Sen's face. "You thought you could possibly use a weapon meant for *me?*" He gestured to his muscular arms.

Jade sighed, stepping up next to her friend. As the sun broke the horizon, she could see the Halflings had short blond hair and dirty clothes. Their ears were pointed but were short and wide, not long and narrow like hers were.

They said, "We figured between the two of us we could wield one of your weapons. We're sorry! We just need to rescue our friends."

"Rescue them from what?" Jade asked.

"Goblins," one spoke. "We were crossing the

mountains yesterday and were attacked. They took three of our friends. We got away."

Jade turned back towards Zok as he got to his feet. They exchanged concerned looks. Goblins were always dangerous to unskilled warriors and unsuspecting travelers, but kidnapping people? She'd never heard of that before. Unless they had developed a taste for Halfling flesh.

"You're in luck," Sen said. "The three of us are going goblin hunting today. You can come along if you can hold your own."

The one that had the bloody noise sniffled. "I'm in a lot of pain."

Jade knelt in front of him. "I can help with that. Move your hand." As he did, he revealed a severely broken nose. She sighed. "*Sen.*"

The Dragonborn shrugged. "I hit first and ask questions later."

Jade held her hand in front of the Halfling's face and closed her eyes. She hadn't done healing magic in a long time. At first she worried it had been too long. That it was yet another thing she'd lost. But as she opened her mind, listened to the sounds of the forest around her, she felt magic spark inside her. Like the start of a fire, the crash of a wave, or the call of a hawk.

She whispered her spell in Elvish, "*Naturātā cho ë gan'etu cho.*" And the wound closed up, the nose righting itself again.

"Incredible!" the other Halfling gasped.

The one she'd healed felt his nose and then exclaimed, "Thank you! Thank you! We're sorry we tried to steal from all of you."

Jade stood with a smile. "Ask for help first. There are still some good people left in this world." She turned to her two friends. "Let's go rescue the others."

.

.

.

SEN

.
.
.

The temperature dropped quickly upon entering the cavern system. Sen lit a torch that cast their shadows on the rocky walls around them. He led in the front, Zok and Jade following, and then the two Halflings at the back. He didn't like to travel with those who couldn't defend themselves. It was like having an extra crew member on his ship that knew nothing about sailing. But he'd rather bring the Halflings along so they could be reunited with their captured friends immediately. It was better than worrying about their safety in the mountains.

He wasn't a big fan of the mountains. Everything felt too closed in. On the ocean, you could see for miles. The only mountains you would find were waves during a storm. He'd ridden so many of those out, grasping the wooden helm of the *Scarlet Maiden,* laughing into the wind and the rain. But underground he disliked most of all. *Things* lived underground. Things that didn't like the sunlight, or the ocean, or fresh air. And that he just couldn't understand.

His size dwarfed his two friends behind him, but he knew they were formidable fighters. He'd seen Jade shoot fire from her hands. And he'd seen Zok sparring with hammer and dagger on the temple grounds. He'd rather have those two fighting alongside him than any Dragonborn that had never seen battle. Not that there were too many Dragonborn in the world. Draconic bloodlines were running out. It had been nearly sixteen-hundred years since actual dragons roamed the world. Perhaps one day there would be no more Dragonborn at all.

The tunnel sloped downwards, and he shuffled his

heavy boots along the ground to avoid losing his balance. Jade was silent behind him, Foxy trailing. But Zok's armor and the Halfling's heavy breathing destroyed any chance of stealth. A few tunnels branched off into different directions. Sen glanced at the choices curiously.

"This path is well-worn," Jade pointed to the one on the left. "And by creatures with a small gait."

Sen couldn't truly tell the difference. The texture was different, certainly, but he couldn't decipher its meaning. Glad at the Druid's expertise, he led the group down the corridor. It narrowed and widened, curved left and right, and gradually went down.

He slowed as the tunnel opened up ahead. Sliding against the wall, he and the others peered out into the large cavern beyond. A few torches were mounted in the walls, giving off a red glow. Stacks of loot were set to the side. Bags, small boxes, clothes. And along the far wall there were three dungeon cells. The iron bars were dirty and rusted. One cell held three other Halflings, huddled together in the far corner, looking beaten and bloody. The other housed a man in red robes with a long silver beard. He appeared to be in some kind of meditation, kneeling on the ground.

"I don't see any goblins," Sen whispered to the others. "Should I go break down those cell doors?"

"Let's see if we can locate a key first," Jade advised. "If they don't know we're here, we want to keep it that way."

The group carefully crept into the room. But the approaching torchlight drew the jailed Halflings' attention. They cheered in happiness as they saw their two friends come to rescue them. Just as Zok gave a quick *shush* to the group, shrieking echoed down the connecting tunnels.

Sen dropped the torch he was holding, taking out his huge axe with both hands. "It's fighting time!"

"Go hide!" Jade shouted at the two Halflings, who scurried behind boxes.

It took mere seconds before a group of six goblins came rushing into the room, swords and spears in their hands. They were small, nasty creatures. Their skin was shades of brown and green, stretched tight over bony faces. They wore dirty rags for clothes, and kept very poor hygiene. Rotted, sharp teeth protruded from their mouths, and their nails curved into claws.

Two bolts of fire erupted from Jade's hands, sending bright light and heat streaking across from the room before impacting one goblin. It screamed, its skin blistering and clothes burning. Zok swung his war hammer in a wide arc, tossing one creature back where it came from. Another hurled a spear at him but it bounced off his armor with a resounding *clang.*

Sen laughed as he rushed the opponents, his axe slicing through the air. He gored one goblin straight through, blood splashing across the rocky floor. Another swung at him with its sword but he danced away, then brought his axe back down again, killing a second.

Jade twisted her hand in the air and a long vine erupted from the ground. It lashed around one goblin and slammed it into the ceiling, crushing it. Then she turned and shot another bolt of fire at an enemy that Zok came and finished off. A few more vicious swings of Sen's axe and the last of the goblins were dead.

All of the Halflings cheered.

Sen snorted with a sharp-toothed grin across his face. "That wasn't so hard."

More screeching came from the tunnels, echoing around them.

Zok spun his hammer, taking out his shield that was emblazoned with the golden eye of the Holy Dragon. He readied his stance. "Round two."

A wave of ten more goblins came rushing in, weapons raised high. They crashed upon the group like a wave, their cries piercing the air. Sen swung his axe as wide as he could, sending two flying back. Pain flared across his leg where a goblin's sword cut him. He kicked with his other leg, feeling bones break beneath his foot as he sent the creature to the ground.

Zok ducked behind his shield as three arrows

bounced off. He swung his hammer at one goblin that came up behind him, attempting to gore him with its spear. It fell at the bone-crushing impact. Another goblin attempted to climb up over his shield, a dagger brandished. With a grunt of effort, he brought his shield down hard into the ground, forcing the opponent to let go. Another downward swing of the hammer and the goblin was no more.

Jade backed up to protect the two cowering Halflings, the green vine dancing before her. It moved in sync with her hands, disarming goblins and sending them flying through the cavern. It grabbed others and squeezed, slamming them into the floor and walls.

Sen spun around, axe glinting with blood and torchlight. Adrenaline pumped through him, making him a raging beast of battle. He laughed as one by one the goblins fell before him and his friends. And just as it looked like victory was secured, a bright glow approached from one of the tunnels. He lifted his axe again, watching the tunnel guardedly.

The glow grew brighter until what appeared to be fire moved into the cavern, lighting the whole area in reds and oranges. But as Sen squinted, looking closer, he could make out more details. Its body was humanoid, almost in the shape of a Dwarf. And it wielded a spiked hammer of flame. Immense heat filled the room at its presence, and he heard the Halflings squeal in terror.

The fire creature turned to Sen, the closest threat. And it attacked. The Dragonborn backed up, avoiding the quick strikes of the spiked hammer. He blocked one attack with his own axe and was surprised to hear the clang of metal on metal resound around them.

Jade leaped forward and the vine she'd conjured looped around the creature. Its flames burst out brighter and hotter, burning the vine away. With a cry Zok jumped into the fray, swinging his hammer down. The fire creature parried with its weapon, then made a quick jab at the Paladin who blocked with his shield, stumbling back from the force of the blow.

"What is this thing?" Sen shouted, still backing up as the enemy pursued him. They exchanged quick but heavy blows. The temperature was beginning to hurt his heat-resistant scales. He could only imagine how hot it was for his two friends.

"Some kind of fire elemental," Jade said, fending off two more goblins that attempted to flank her. "Its core is still vulnerable, aim there!"

Zok came at it from behind, but its flames sprang up wildly, forcing the Paladin to back off, sweat sticking strands of brown hair to his face.

Sen made a quick strike, going for the form he could barely make out through the flames. The creature blocked again, countering with a quick thrust at Sen's shoulder. The weapon impacted, piercing his scales and burning. He cried out in pain, taking one large step back to avoid a second strike from the weapon. He glanced up at his friends. They finished off the last of the goblins, thin cuts on their bodies.

The Dragonborn steeled himself. His scales were red, which meant the blood of ancient red dragons flowed through his veins. Dragons that brought terror from the skies and reigned fire on the lands below. He would not be intimidated by a being made of that same fire.

With a growl Sen launched himself forward, going on the attack. His axe swung hard and fast, forcing his opponent to start backing up. He ignored the scorching heat, going in closer to put more and more muscle behind each strike. And finally, he got the opening he needed. Knocking the fire creature's weapon wide with a fierce strike, its core was open and vulnerable. He slammed his axe forward, the blade sinking into something beneath all the flames. The creature writhed but made no noise. The flames burst up once more, licking at his scales and singeing him, before the whole thing dissolved into ash.

Breathing hard, Sen looked over at his friends. "Are you two alright?"

"We are," Zok nodded. "Are you? I've never seen anything like that."

"I've seen things similar," Jade replied as the three drew closer together. "It's not native to this plane, that is for certain. Goblins could not possess magic strong enough to summon a fire elemental. Something else is going on here."

"Please help us!" the three Halflings in the cell cried. "It's so scary here!"

"Let's get you out," Zok stated, putting his hammer away and locating a set of keys on the wall.

As he approached the cell Jade searched through the loot until she found an Elven satchel as well as a silver ring. She swung the satchel around her shoulder and put the ring on for safe keeping.

Sen kicked through the bags and boxes until he heard one jingle with gold. Grinning, he picked it up and hooked it on his belt. A good pay for good work.

Zok unlocked the cell and the three Halflings raced out, embracing their two friends. There was the noise of a throat clearing and the bearded man in the other cell said, "Please, release me as well."

"Of course," the Paladin hurried and unlocked the door.

The man stood up, dusting off his red robes. As he walked out he said, "Thank you for your assistance. It was quite dirty in there."

"How long were you captured?" Jade asked.

"Oh, just a couple hours. I came into this cavern to do some investigating and got a bit more than I bargained for." He wandered over to the bags and boxes, shifted through a few things, and then pulled out two books. One was brown and the other red. "Aha! I certainly need this." He tucked the brown one into his robes, then looked at the others. "Are you from Somberdale?"

"We are," Jade answered.

"Good, good! I found this tome inside the cavern system," he held out the red book. "I fear I cannot read it and was hoping you could take it to Tymus. Do you know him?"

The Wild Elf nodded. "He's the wizard that lives in the tower. I've never met him before but I can take it." As she grabbed it she turned it over in her hands. "What is it about? It's locked."

"Magically so," the man in red nodded. "But Tymus can handle it. I need it translated. Tell him Rowland the Wizard sent you."

Sen frowned. "You're a wizard? How did you end up in a cell? I thought all wizards were super powerful."

Rowland chuckled, stroking his beard. "Sometimes patience brings us more answers than rash action. And besides," he patted the book in his robes, "I had lost my spellbook. Now, I appreciate your help, and I shall be on my way." He turned and began heading further into the caverns.

"Wait," Zok said. "You're not leaving?"

"Oh, goodness, no. I still need answers. I'm looking for a –" He was cut off by a roar deep within the tunnels, so loud and deep it shook the walls. The Halflings cried out, huddling together. "Oh, yes, that would be what I'm looking for."

"What in the Hells was that?" Sen asked, holding his axe up. An unfamiliar feeling ran through him. Fear. The sea was a dangerous place and he'd faced each challenge with unlimited courage. But the roar of something so large so deep underground put his nerves on edge.

"The Hells is a good guess," Rowland replied, seeming unfazed. "It seems a demon has gotten loose from the Hells. Or a place far more sinister. It is making its home on this plane of existence, now. It's been making the goblins bolder. I am afraid myself and the little Halflings were captured to feed it, and I doubt we were the first. The Citadel sent me to return it to its home."

There was another ground-shaking roar. "Do you need help?" Jade asked.

Rowland took a moment to look over the three of them. "I see fear and uncertainty in your eyes. That will not do against a foe such as this. But do not worry, I can undoubtedly handle myself." He smiled. "Safe travels, may we meet again."

Then he vanished down the darkness of the tunnel.

Zok turned to the others. "Should we help him?"

Sen shook his head. "As much as I enjoy fighting, I do *not* want to get involved in any kind of planar magic. That stuff is unnatural."

The Dragonborn turned and headed off, followed by the scared Halflings. In his peripheral vision he saw Zok and Jade hesitate, then turn and follow him. He knew they liked to help others. But the warning from Rowland seemed to shake them. Sen wished the old man well. The Citadel was a familiar name, but he couldn't quite place where he'd heard it before. All the same, Rowland had seemed completely confident. Sometimes it was best not to bring fists to a magic fight.

He'd heard of things able to cross into other planes of existence. Of portals and experiments and summonings. Of places where undead dwelled and places where fey creatures roamed wild. He was happy to keep himself in this world, where he knew the waters, the coasts, and could celebrate in a tavern at the end of every day.

.

.

.

UNOLÉ

.
.
.

The tears had dried up a long time ago, leaving her eyes red and aching. As she sat at the edge of a pond, hidden amongst the reeds and rocks, she felt hollow inside. All of her emotion had been spent in the last couple days searching for her sister. She'd found nothing. And now nothing was all she could feel.

It was twilight, the sky bathed in shades of orange. In the far distance she could see the silhouette of An'Ock. Its high city walls ringed a tall castle. And she could just barely make out the shimmer of the river that surrounded it, rendering it nearly impenetrable. She'd grown up in that city. She and Unatchi had only had each other. There were no parents, no other siblings, no friends. Who would want to take in two Half-Fiend children?

Unolé wished she knew who her parents were. She wasn't mad at them for creating her and her sister, even if it was into a world that hated and feared them. She just wished she knew why they had been left alone. Unolé had grown up in an orphanage. And strangely, when she was twelve, another baby Half-Fiend had been dropped off. Unatchi. All she was told was that this was her sister. They had been inseparable ever since.

She leaned forward and studied her reflection in the water. Her skin had a yellowish tone to it, making the deep red of her lips stand out. Her dark clothes had always helped her blend into the shadows and avoid being noticed if she needed to. She was good at sneaking. By all accounts, her basic features were very Human. But then came the horns. Dark brown ones that curled on either side of her face. She had the tips adorned with gold. Her pointed incisor teeth, purple eyes, and short white hair also marked her as foreign. But the tail most of all stood out. It, too, was a dark brown and came to a triangle tip. She had it lined with rings of gold and red cloth. She could always hide her appearance under hoods and cloaks, but beneath it all she was unashamed.

She noticed she still had her mask on. A deep, blood red mask that went over her eyes. It was trimmed with gold. She wore it when on contracts for the Shadow Guild, just to further protect her identity and the Guild's. She didn't bother removing it. It helped hide the redness of her face from crying.

Unolé had barely eaten since her sister was taken by the four-legged flying beast. She'd searched the farmlands over and over, trailed the walls of An'Ock, and even asked travelers if they'd seen a creature matching the description she gave. But she found nothing.

Unolé drew her gaze from her reflection to the black feathers she clenched in her hand. It was proof what she'd seen had been real. And she wasn't going to lose them. Not until she found Unatchi.

Maybe there is no point, a thought intruded. *She is dead. You saw it. There was no life in her eyes.*

But she refused to give into such thoughts. Not until she knew for certain.

A part of her knew she needed to return to the Shadow Guild. She needed to tell the leader what had happened. The Grandmother would not be pleased at the loss of the staff. Delaying returning would only make it worse. But how could she go back, pretending everything was normal, when her world had just been torn apart? What was the point of anything, anymore? If she didn't have Unatchi, she had no one. She was alone.

She squeezed the feathers hard, another sob escaping her. As the sun dipped below the horizon, something shimmered on the edge of pond. She looked up, eyes going wide. An upright circle hovered just above the water, about two feet out from the shore. It looked as if it was made from moonlight, glimmering in the air. It made no sound, had no smell. But it gave off light that reflected on the gold adornments she wore.

Unolé slowly approached, her black boots dipping into the water. She tucked the feathers away in her pack, making sure to lock it securely. The water came up to her knees as she stopped in front of the circle. Unolé reached a hand out and touched it. The tips of her fingers passed through. She felt no sensation. Frowning, she pushed her arm further in, up to her elbow. Still there was no pain, no heat, no cold. Nothing that felt dangerous.

She didn't know what this was. She didn't know if answers lied within or if it was a shortcut to her death. But at this point, doing something was better than sitting and crying. So, she gathered her courage and stepped through.

A world of white greeted her beyond. It was like she stood in a thick cloud of fog, but brighter. Like some sunlight was trying to break through. She could make out shapes. White trees, their branches bare. Rocky ground that she stepped on. Bodies of water that dotted the landscape, most no more than ten feet across. And ahead, a long bridge. She couldn't see the other side due to the fog in the area. A quick glance behind revealed the portal she'd stepped through was gone.

Where is this? she thought.

Unolé slowly approached the bridge, her hands hovering at the two daggers strapped to her belt. She also carried a silver whip hooked against her lower back. It bounced against her hips with each step.

As she neared the bridge she saw it was intricately designed. The sides had swirling patterns of great complexity. She trailed her hand along the railing as she crossed. Looking over the side, she saw the bridge spanned a wide silver river. It flowed tranquilly underneath, barely making a sound.

Crossing to the center of it, she saw a black ring lying on the ground. Kneeling down for a closer look revealed it was in the shape of a curled feather. She picked it up and put it in her pocket. As she stood again she could see the other side of the bridge. A gazebo made of white sat at the end, rising a few steps up. And hovering in the middle was some kind of serpent creature. It was about a foot and half in length, no legs but two wings. Its head was snake-like in shape, with large round eyes. It was covered in feathers. What made it stand out the most were its brilliant colors. Its feathers were light purple, aqua, and a soft green.

"Hello?" Unolé asked, slowly approaching it.

The mouth did not move, but a deep, kind voice in her head said, "Hello."

She started, surprised. "How did you do that?"

Again, the voice spoke in her head while the eyes gazed at her, "That is just my way of communicating. What is your name?"

"Unolé. And yours?"

"Teshuva." His wings flapped gently to keep himself in the air. "It is a pleasure to meet you. How did you find your way here?"

She shook her head. "I don't know. This portal just appeared in the air where I was. So, I stepped through."

He chuckled. "A curious one, I see. The magic of the black feathers, perhaps?"

She frowned. "How do you know about those?"

"Our meeting is not chance. I was sent here to aid you in the search for your sister."

Unolé's heart skipped a beat at that, excitement rushing through her. "Really? Who sent you? Who knows about my sister?"

"I serve the Silver Dancer."

"I've never heard of her. Is that another Guild?"

What appeared to be a smile tugged at Teshuva's mouth. "No. She is a goddess." At Unolé's frown he asked, "Do you not have faith?"

"I've never thought about it, honestly. I've seen the temples in An'Ock to deities. I remember a Holy Dragon, a Raven Mother, Elven gods named Tamer and Dusk, and another called the Sheppard. There were others. Silver Dancer doesn't sound familiar."

"Mm, I would be surprised if it was. But she is whom I serve. And I am here to help."

"How can you help?" Unolé asked. "Do you know where we can find the beast that took her?"

"Unfortunately, I do not. But I believe we are dealing with an interplanar being and therefore, we must explore other planes."

"Other planes?" The idea seemed ridiculous. Fantastical. And yet, what other choice did she have? Go back to the pond and cry? "Do you have the power to travel between worlds?"

"With the help of your black feathers, I can. The magic in them is powerful."

Unolé took a step closer, studying Teshuva intently. "What kind of creature are you?"

"I am a coatl. A winged serpent."

Unolé went up the steps into the gazebo. She glanced around at the white world. "Where is this place? Is this another plane?"

"It is between the planes. It takes many forms. There is never just one way to get to a place, after all." He nodded his head towards her pocket. "That ring you picked up. Left behind by someone careless. It should serve you well. Go ahead and put it on."

Unolé didn't know why she obeyed. She rarely trusted anyone. Even the other members of the Shadow Guild were dubious at times. But she trusted Teshuva. There was something about his voice, his words, his gaze that was otherworldly. Powerful. And kind. So, she slipped the ring on her finger. She felt magic pulsing in it. She'd never handled anything enchanted before, but she could immediately feel the tether of magic. And so it was only with a bit of concentration that she activated its power.

A pair of black, raven-like wings sprouted from her back in a rush of feathers. She flinched, gasped, and then smiled. "This is amazing! Can I fly now?"

Teshuva chuckled. "They are not permanent. Enchantments only have so much magic to expend each day, after all. But in a tight spot, it will be helpful for both of us to fly."

She stared in awe over her shoulder, letting the wings expand. They felt like a natural extension of her, as easy to control as her own arms. There was a grace and a beauty to them. She was tempted to take off into the air, fly around this strange place, and try out this new magic. But she didn't want to expend it too quickly. She might need them later this day.

Unolé concentrated and released the magic, the wings disappearing. "Thank you. But . . . why would you help me? Why would this . . . Silver Dancer help me? I have nothing to give. I am nobody."

Teshuva smiled. "In this great and intricate web of life, souls of nobodies meet, intertwine, and shake the fates around them. Perhaps your soul will also rise, Unolé."

She couldn't help but beam at that. It was a nice sentiment. That she was meant for something larger than stealing for a Guild in the underbelly of a city. Perhaps this coatl was right, perhaps not. But if traveling to other planes meant a better chance at finding her sister, she would jump right in. "Where to first?"

"It is not a very kind place," he warned. "But it is one where living and dead souls alike end up when they've been taken. This will require courage."

She steeled herself. "I am ready." She held the black feathers out.

Teshuva flew in a circle in the air, and the feathers in her hand hummed. Then one of the small bodies of water, about thirty feet away, pulsed with light. He said, "There is our destination. The Hells."

Unolé strode down the steps of the gazebo with purpose, her eyes fixed on the portal. She would not back down from this. No matter what dangers lay ahead, she would face them and rescue her sister. Bring her back home. She crossed the distance to her destination, passing other dormant pools of water. Stepping up to the edge, Unolé took a moment to lift her chin and square her shoulders, the coatl flying at her side. Then, she leaped into the portal.

There was a spinning sensation, colors and shapes blurred around her. Momentary fear took hold but her resolve hardened her. She would do whatever it took to find Unatchi. There was no time for fear. If her sister was still alive, she must be incredibly frightened. Unolé had to be strong for both of them.

The spinning subsided, colors and shapes taking form again. There was black and red. Angular shapes of buildings and roads. And then as her feet touched stone ground, the world solidified around her.

She was in an alley between two buildings, looking out into an open street. For cover Unolé sidled up against one of the buildings but instantly withdrew, the heat from the walls scorching her skin. She noticed there was heat everywhere. It seemed to rise up from the ground, the buildings, and permeate the air.

"Your Half-Fiend blood aids you here, Unolé," Teshuva's voice said as he hovered at her shoulder. "It gives you resistance to this heat."

"Does it? It's very hot."

"A Human in your place would be exhausted coping with this environment. You are handling yourself well."

That was comforting. She didn't think there was much else to be thankful about in her bloodline. Being more careful this time, she peered around the corner to take in her surroundings. She was in a city. Buildings made of metal and stone lined streets set up in a grid fashion. Most were smaller and just one story, but others rose up higher and some were multiple-story towers. Everything appeared to have a red tinge, but Unolé couldn't be sure if it was from the heat radiating in the air or just the color scheme. The streets were gray and stone, but all the buildings were shades of black, red, and brown. The sky overhead was a straight blood red with no distinguishing features.

And there were residents here. She was surprised to see so many others that looked like her. Half-Fiends with horns and tails. But most looked even more exotic than she did, with skin of reds and purples. There were creatures as well. Tall insect-like beings that scurried about on two legs, skeletal beings with wings, creatures that looked mostly animal with hooves for feet and faces like bulls. Sluggish creatures crawled by, all fleshy and fat. She saw a humanoid male that walked a line of prisoners on chains, his whip cracking over their heads. Among the prisoners she made out Humans, Elves, and one Dwarf. At first she feared anyone not of this plane would be immediately unwelcome, but then she did notice two Humans chatting with one shadowy creature and exchanging coins.

"This is not a pleasant place," she whispered to Teshuva, glancing about.

"No," he agreed. "But it is a good starting point to search for answers. I will remain out of sight. I have Celestial blood, which is rare and valuable. I don't want to bring undue trouble on us."

She nodded. "Good idea. Where will you be?"

He did a graceful flip in the air and then dove into her hood.

Oh, Unolé thought. *Well, that works.*

She tucked the black feathers away again and, steeling her nerves, she stepped out into the street. It was fairly busy, with all manner of monstrosities coming and going. The air smelled of sulfur and burnt flesh. There was a general chatter, some in languages she did not understand, others in ones she did. She found there was a peculiar dialect many of the devils were using that she was sure she had never heard before but she could still understand it. There were also cries of pain and the cracking of whips every few minutes. It made her realize many people were here against their will.

Glancing over the buildings, she found one that looked like a tavern.

A good place to find information, she thought.

She headed over, the heat making her sweat a little. The inside was unremarkable. The walls and floor were mostly black, and the tables had certainly seen better days.

Instead of lanterns on the walls, there were skulls with candles set in them. She could make out the elegant bone structure of Elven skulls, smaller ones perhaps belonging to Gnomes, and a few that looked dragon-like. The patrons were all of the devilish variety and fairly terrible to look upon. Except for one red-skinned man with small horns that was sitting in a back corner. He gave her a long look as she walked in. Unolé made certain that the two daggers on her belt were visible as she went over to the bar.

Behind the bar was a woman in a black dress that left very little up to the imagination. Dark hair was pulled back in a messy bun. She had pointed teeth and two bat-like wings came from her back. Unolé couldn't be entirely certain, but this woman did remind her of drawings she'd seen of a Succubus.

"Where can I go for information?" Unolé asked, resting her gloved hands on the bar.

The woman gave her a slow grin. "It depends what information you're seeking, darling."

"I'm looking for someone who was taken. I think she may have ended up here."

The Succubus chuckled. "No information is free. But that man in the corner-" she pointed to the red-skinned man "-he might be able to help for the right price."

Unolé glanced back once to see the man still looking at her. She returned her gaze to the bartender. "Have you ever heard of a winged beast that looks like a raven but has four legs?"

The woman's eyes narrowed. "No information is free here."

Unolé sighed. "How about for two gold?"

There was a scoff. "No less than five gold coins!"

"Three."

"*Four* and I'm being generous."

Unolé held her gaze for a heated moment. "Three gold coins and five silver coins."

The Succubus glared at her. "Fine. Hand it over."

Unolé reluctantly drew out the coins as promised,

passing them over. She was glad her currency still held value here. She crossed her arms expectantly.

The Succubus replied, "I've never heard of such a beast. And I've never overheard any of the patrons here talking about it. As you can see, the skies are clear. If one was flying around, I'd know it."

"You're no help at all," Unolé griped. She turned from the bar and headed over to the red-skinned man. As she approached his table he smiled, revealing all pointed teeth. "I was told you can provide information."

He leaned forward and spoke in a thickly accented voice. "Perhaps. What kind of information are you seeking?"

"I'm looking for someone I think may have ended up down here."

He considered for a moment. "I do have connections. I can find out about recent slave trade and new prisoners brought in. Who would I be looking for?"

Unolé swallowed her tight throat. Saying the words out loud hurt. "A little girl that looks like me."

He nodded. "I will check with my contacts. Come back here tomorrow evening and we will make an exchange."

Unolé narrowed her purple eyes. "And what do you want in exchange for this information?"

His smile was shrewd as he replied, "We will discuss tomorrow depending upon how valuable I think my information is."

"Listen, I just paid the bartender money for no answers to my questions. I'm not doing the same with you."

His eyes grew darker. "Careful, demon-girl. I don't take threats lightly."

They glared at each other for a few seconds, and then Unolé walked away. She headed out of the tavern and onto the street again, the heat instantly hitting her skin. Pausing to let a line of monstrous, slug-like beings cross, she made her way across the street. She didn't know where to go, she just knew she needed to talk to Teshuva in private. Picking out a narrow alley that was out of sight from the tavern, the Half-Fiend deftly ducked into it. Not wanting to draw attention to herself, she crouched down into the shadows.

Teshuva slithered slightly out of her hood, regarding her with bright green eyes. "That was well done."

"Do you think so? It's just so frustrating. Every day that goes by it will be harder and harder to find my sister."

"I understand, but we must be patient. If your sister was brought here and sold into slavery we can rescue her." He paused. "You're doing well. I expected planar travel, especially to a place as inhospitable as this, to be more trying for you."

She gave a short laugh. "It many ways it reminds me of the Guilds in An'Ock. If it wasn't for all the devil beings and slaves walking about I would think I'm back home."

Teshuva chuckled. "You have a strong heart. But let us not only rely on the word of one resident here in the Hells. I think we should search more on our own."

Unolé stood. "I agree."

And she stepped out again into the streets.

.

.

.

TALIESIN

.
.
.

The Deep Hollows were not a safe place to travel. Far from the borders of Berenzia now, Taliesin knew he was alone. When – not if – he ran into danger there would be no one to help. But with each passing step through the dark and twisting tunnels, his confidence grew. He could handle himself. After what happened a year ago, it's not like the other Dark Elves would help him, anyway. He could have lain out in the middle of the city, bleeding, and no one would have given him a second glance.

It'll all be different soon, he thought. *Once I'm successful I can come back and return to my place in society.*

He knew he would be successful on his quest. He had to be. There was no other alternative. How could he return empty-handed after running off in the middle of the night? There would not be forgiveness. He stole a glance over his shoulder. Four hours had passed since he'd snuck out of his home. He needed to put as much distance between himself and the city as possible. He didn't want to run into any other Dark Elves that he knew.

But he knew better than to move quickly through the Deep Hollows. Stealth was his friend here. His clothes were nearly entirely black, helping to hide him in the lightless underground tunnels. He did not need light. Yellow eyes flicked back and forth to keep constant vigil.

The tunnels went up and down, branched off, narrowed and widened. An interlocking network of roads. He passed only one sign, pointing to his right for Balum Guar. A city of Dark Dwarves. This intersection was worn from trade traffic.

Move fast, move fast, he encouraged himself.

Trailing a gloved hand along the wall, he scurried forward. He hoped it was too early for trade traffic. That the businesses which catered to those traversing the tunnels were not yet open. If he hurried, he could-

"Wanna buy something?"

A surprised cry escaped him and he staggered back. A small Gnome had set up shop in an alcove, shaved bald with skin that was a dark blue. Enormous eyes stared up at him, approachable, but the axes on his belt served as a deterrent for thieves and trouble makers.

The Dark Gnome chuckled. "Sorry to startle you, little Dark Elf. Whatcha doin' so far from the city?"

Taliesin hadn't realized he'd brought his hand over his pounding heart until he could feel its beat through the silver scale breastplate he wore. He dropped his hand to his hip, fixing the man with a frown. "'Little' is a rich adjective coming from you, *Gnome*."

The Gnome grinned. "Fair enough. But I know a baby Elf when I see one. I didn't expect anyone to be out on the trade routes this early, but I got most of m'shop out. Where ya headed? Some of this stuff could be useful." He waved his hand over the small table he had sat before him with wares.

Taliesin took offense to that statement. He was ninety-eight years old, which was considered the edge of adulthood for Dark Elves. Though he knew Gnomes lived long lives, as well. The two-foot tall man before him was probably a few hundred years his senior. He dropped his gaze to the table. Rope, food, empty vials, a few old knives, some bandages. He had packed fairly well for his journey, he was certain. But a basket of fresh fruit caught his eye. "Where did you get this fruit? The Surface?"

The Gnome drew himself up proudly. "I stole it myself. For the effort and puttin' meself in danger, they are a gold coin a piece."

Taliesin had no idea if that was a fair price or not. But he had enough money with him. Fetching a coin from his bag he placed it on the table with a *clink*. "Sure, I'll take one."

The Gnome's long grin revealed pointed and dirty

teeth. "Pleasure doin' business with you, mister Dark Elf." He tossed the small, yellow fruit over. "Nothin' else for your journey? Where you goin' all alone?"

Taliesin fixed him with a disapproving look. "Mind your own business, *little* Gnome." He turned and headed onward. But the Gnome's words did shake his resolution slightly. He *was* all alone, after all. This was dangerous in the Deep Hollows, and even more dangerous for his destination. The Surface. A place any Dark Elf would be mad to venture except for a few hours for business, to steal items, or capture people for enslavement. But none of those were his purpose. And he would be gone much longer than a few hours.

He truly didn't know much about the Surface. Only what he'd read in books and had been taught in school. He knew, in this region of the Deep Hollows, there was only one exit that led above ground. Supposedly it led out into a city called Eleste'si. A place full of High Elves. He had seen plenty of this race before as slaves in Berenzia. His mother and the priestesses of his city always stated that the Dark Elves were a superior race. The other races of the Deep Hollows, Dark Dwarves and Gnomes, were tolerable. But even worse were the races of the Surface. Most especially Humans, Half-Elves, Wild Elves, and High Elves. He would need to be careful on the Surface. It was best to stay out of sight.

He ate the fruit as he walked, and it was delicious. He was sure he'd tire of the hard, dry rations he'd brought along for his travels. Any chance to eat something with more flavor would be worth it. A couple more hours passed as he wandered the caverns. He consulted the map he'd brought along a few times. He'd never been to the Surface before, let alone this far from Berenzia. Getting lost in the Deep Hollows meant certain death. Things lived down here that dropped from the ceiling on their victims, that ate minds, that could snuff out magic with a single glance.

As his thoughts wandered to his family, wondering how long before his parents and his sister realized he was actually gone, he heard scuffling up ahead. Taliesin slowed his pace, his black cloak lined with white trailing out behind him.

He pressed himself against the rough rock wall and crept forward. The sounds got louder. Animal growling, snapping. The noise of steel. A cry of pain.

He moved faster up to an outcropping. Peering around, he saw four large, hairy animals attacking one prey that they had backed into a corner. The animals moved on four legs, but seemed able to use their front two paws for slashing as well. Their snouts were short and they were covered in a grayish fur. His gaze moved to their victim. It was hard to see through the beasts but he could make out a mass of wild, fiery hair, brown leather, and two flashing swords. There was another cry of pain from the prey.

I'd better help out, he thought. A thrill of excitement went through him. It had been awhile since anyone had needed his healing magic.

Taliesin spun around the outcropping and fired a silver bolt of magic from his hand. It pierced through the back of one animal's head, dropping it instantly. He shot another one but this time the animals were aware of him. His target dodged and sprang onto him, knocking him back. There was a flare of pain as claws dug into his shoulder. He reached up and grabbed the beast's neck, keeping its teeth from his face. He could feel the matted fur and straining muscles against his exposed fingertips. Necrotic magic flared from his hand and the animal cried out, blood seeping from its nose, mouth, and ears. It dropped over, dead.

Pushing the heavy body off of him he saw the distraction had given the prey an opening. Dual swords flashed through the air and killed the last animals. He then locked eyes with their victim. A female Dark Dwarf, with a very thick beard. She was bleeding profusely from various bites and scratches on her. The fire in her green eyes dulled and she slumped backwards.

Taliesin sprang to his feet and ran over to her. Dropping to his knees again, he said, "Hold on, hold on. I can help." He grabbed her arm and muttered his healing spell. *"Moza di dziakuj bainha dabro zakalu razam"*. The magic flowed through him, like a river. His other hand grasped his medallion. A chain hooked to a spider made of silver. The symbol of his deity. Closing his eyes momentarily helped him concentrate on maintaining the spell. As it neared completion he opened them again, looking at his handiwork. The wounds were closing up. The last words came from his lips and he sat back, sighing in relief. "There you go. No problem at all."

The Dark Dwarf sat up straight, looking over her body, eyes wide in amazement. He took a moment to study her. Her skin was a deep, charcoal gray like his, but hers also had a strong bluish tint to it. Characteristic of the Dwarves that lived in the Deep Hollows. They were also known for their red hair, but hers was more colorful than usual. Bloody red, to flame orange, to an ashy gray, and then to white at the ends. Braids weaved through it and her beard. Her clothes were made for hard travel. And curiously there was a huge wooden barrel strapped to her back.

"You're welcome," Taliesin prompted.

She looked over at him. "Thank you. I mean, I had it under control. But the healing is appreciated." Her Dwarvish accent was thick.

He smiled, tucking some longer strands of white hair behind his ear. "I *am* a good healer."

She stood up and sheathed her swords. "Well, you saved my life. My honor decrees I must repay you. So . . ." she crossed her arms. "What do you want?"

Taliesin stood as well, dusting off his black pants. "It's fine. I don't need anything. Just wanted to help."

She frowned. "I gotta do something for you. To return the act in kind."

"Like what? Like *you* save *my* life?" He laughed.

"You watch your attitude, *Dark Elf*," she warned. "I am good with my blades. I can guard you to your next destination. We're in wild Deep Hollow territory, here. It's dangerous."

"Well . . ." He hesitated, glancing her over. "I could use the help. I'm heading to the Surface on a research mission. I don't know how long it will take, but I need answers before I return here. Help me on my research until your debt is repaid."

Her face set into a deep scowl. "The *Surface*? I've never been up there before. Our kind isn't welcome, you know. "

He winked. "Which is why I'll need your protection."

She gave a heavy, drawn out sigh. "*Fine.* Just until I save your life. Which I'm sure won't be long. I mean, *look at you.* You're so skinny."

"You're welcome, again, for healing your numerous and deadly wounds."

She regarded him in exasperation. Then held out a gloved hand. "My name is Ruuda Drybarrel."

He took it. "I am Taliesin Ostoroth." They shook.

"So, Taliesin, do you know where to go from here?"

He pulled out the map and double-checked his path. "I do. Let's keep moving."

They walked in silence for a while, both of them nearly soundless through the caverns. Taliesin found his spirits lifted by the company. She could help take notes on his research while he focused on the bigger picture. Powerful Dark Elf Houses, like his family's, kept slaves to do basic and routine tasks. Slaves that were captured during raids to the Surface. Taliesin had been too young to participate in these raids. And once he got old enough, well, that's when everything fell apart. It was good to have someone serve him. It was almost like being back home.

"So, why are you going to the Surface?" Ruuda asked.

"Have you noticed the spiders have disappeared?"

She gave him an incredulous look. "No . . . I haven't . . ."

"They're gone. They have been for nearly a year now. At least, that's when I started noticing. No searching or research here in the Deep Hollows has provided any answers. So I'm heading to the Surface to see if the spiders are gone there, too."

"And why do you care about the spiders?"

"They have religious significance to us."

"Strange. We'll have to be careful up there. We are not well-liked. At least, that's what I've heard."

He bit his lower lip with a sly smile. "It is probably because we make slaves of their people."

Ruuda chuckled. "You Dark Elves and your power systems. We Dwarves don't rely on slaves for menial tasks. We build things with our own two hands." To illustrate she clenched her fists, the leather of her gloves crinkling. "The Dwarves that disappoint are the ones who must suffer."

"We, too, punish Elves that get out of line. Sometimes their crimes are so severe they get sacrificed to our goddess." He paused. The conversation made him uncomfortable. "Why are you carrying a barrel?"

"Don't ask about it. It's personal."

"Is it full of wine?"

"It's *empty* and *never* wine. Only beer."

He scrunched up his nose at that.

"Ay, don't make that face! My family brews the best beer you've ever tasted."

"Do you have some with you to try?"

Her gaze dropped. "Maybe later."

Silence enveloped them again as they traveled the rest of the day. It didn't take long for Taliesin to realize Ruuda was an excellent navigator. She used his map, expertly guided them over the terrain, and had sharp ears for creatures in the area. Often they had to sneak past a tunnel where she was sure something lived. A couple times Taliesin caught the movement of shapes, things with arms that were too long, things with tentacles, things with too many eyes. Ruuda was also good at checking the ground for tracks or fresh blood. This helped them avoid anything dangerous they came across.

As the hours dragged on Taliesin could feel weariness pulling at his body. It was time to rest. "I think we should sleep and start again tomorrow. It's been a long day."

She nodded, rolling up the map. "We've got to find somewhere we're not too exposed."

They searched for thirty minutes, wandering the

tunnels for some form of shelter. At last they found an alcove that went a foot deep into the wall and then made a sharp turn, going in another few feet. It was small and cramped, but it was out of sight. Ruuda gestured to it proudly.

"What in the Hells is that?" Taliesin demanded, arms crossed. "There is not enough room to lie down."

"No. We'll have to sleep sitting up."

He eyed the alcove uneasily. It looked incredibly uncomfortable. "I suppose I can endure one night of this. For safety."

"By all means," she waved her hand towards the open tunnel, "you're welcome to sleep out there like a buffet. It'll help repay my debt faster if you're dead in the morning."

He glowered at her and marched past into the recess, keeping his head low to avoid the rocks. He sat his pack to the side and propped his blanket up to cushion him as best as possible. Then he slowly sat down, wiggling himself into a curled position in the corner.

Ruuda allowed him to get comfortable before she squeezed in as well. He watched as she unstrapped her barrel, opened the lid, and pulled a bedroll from it. She made her corner comfortable as well and sat her swords across her lap. Her eyes closed for a moment, settling in, before looking at him. "Not so bad, is it?"

Well, he felt his personal bubble had undoubtedly been breached. Their feet pressed against each other's, and her shoulder was a mere foot from his. But that wasn't what had caught his attention the most. "You keep a bedroll in your barrel?"

A momentary look of panic passed over her face before she quickly got it under control. "I enjoy camping. So yes, I always keep one with me."

He didn't believe her. She was leaving. Where and why were a mystery, but having that bit of information satisfied him for the present. "You're from Balum Guar, I presume?"

"Aye. And my guess is you're from Berenzia?"

"Yes."

"Never been there," she settled back more snuggly into the wall.

"My mother runs a trading business," he said conversationally. "Your city is a major point of trade for us. I hear its name quite a bit. Jewels, ore, metal for our weapons."

"If your kind would drink beer our families could have traded." Her tone was sarcastic, but a real smile tugged at the corners of her mouth.

After a moment of quiet he asked, "Should we take turns keeping watch?"

She shook her head, her eyes drifting shut. "We are out of sight. Unless something that can smell really well passes by."

That thought did not comfort Taliesin. But his legs were sore and his stamina was low from walking all day long. And so despite the cramped and rocky sleeping quarters, he quickly drifted off.

.

.

.

Pressure on his legs woke Taliesin. A heavy weight on his thighs and shins. He was disoriented. A hard surface dug into his back, and his joints were stiff and sore from sleeping in one position for too long. The smell hit him next. Rotted meat, sewage, filth.

He gagged, waking completely with a start. His yellow eyes flew open, looking to the source of the pressure.

It was an enormous rat. Its long, bulging body covered the entire length of his legs, sharp claws digging in. A pale tail draped heavily on the rock floor. Red eyes stared up at him, an open mouth revealing sharp, stained teeth.

And it wasn't alone. Two more were behind it, creeping up silently. A fourth climbed over Ruuda's barrel in an attempt to get to her.

"Ruuda!" Taliesin shouted, just as the rat on his legs made a bite for his stomach. Teeth scraped against scale-mail, not having enough force to penetrate the armor. It then went for the bit of exposed flesh it could find: his throat. His hands flailed out and managed to catch it in midair, the immense weight behind the bloated creature straining his forearms.

Ruuda cried out as she awoke, grabbing a sword and swinging it wide. The small space made this difficult, and the blade sliced across the walls before sinking into the side of the creature atop her barrel. It screeched as she wrenched the blade free, flinging its dead body to the ground with a wet *thump.*

The giant rat in Taliesin's hands made a swipe for his face, coming up short. Hot anger flared in him and he focused his energy. His hands hummed with necrotic power that pulsed into the creature. It shrieked and blood dripped from its mouth, nose, and ears. Then it went limp.

The Dark Dwarf got to her feet, scooping up her second sword. She brought both down in an arc, cutting a rat into three pieces as it attempted to race past her. The final made a jump for her head, its screech splitting the air and echoing off the tunnel walls.

Taliesin's hand shot out. The magic energy that had been humming in him flew down his arm and out of his fingertips in a slice of silver light. It went straight through the rat in midair, leaving behind a bloody hole in its chest. The body dropped limp to the ground.

For a moment the only noise was their breathing. Then Ruuda spun her swords once and sheathed them. "Damn ugly beasts. We must be close to the Surface to have those things sniff us down."

The Dark Elf felt a shiver of repulsion go through his body. "Disgusting. They smell horrid."

Ruuda kicked at one with her thick leather boot. "Yeah, I've run into them once before. *Ugh.*" She rubbed her face, blinking tired green eyes. "Well, I feel like I've gotten most of an eight hour rest. We could press on?"

Taliesin let out his breath heavily, tightening the leather cord that tied his hair back. He'd been growing it out for a while, but strands that were too short to be tied back fell on either side of his face. Longer hair was favored amongst the Dark Elves, stark white against their rich gray skin. "That sounds good. I don't want to spend another night traveling alone down here."

They packed up quickly and left the corpses of the giant rats behind. They ate breakfast while walking, a meal of jerky made from fish, with edible moss and mushrooms in a bowl. Afterwards Ruuda kept the map out, directing them through the twisting and branching tunnels. They began to see a few other travelers. A pair of Dark Dwarves passed carrying bags full of wine that had obviously been stolen from the Surface. A female Dark Elf hurried past but went down a separate tunnel, not sparing them any glance.

Taliesin hoped this meant the Surface was not far ahead. But the hours still dragged on. They passed through a narrow tunnel full of fungus that glowed with soft blue light. Then on into an enormous cavern that had several narrow bridges spanning it on multiple levels. They could see other travelers above and below them, going about their daily business. Bats flew by overhead, the noise of their flapping wings reverberating around the chamber.

"Dark Dwarves built this, you know," Ruuda commented as they crossed a stone bridge that was nearly eighty feet long. "It's stood for hundreds of years."

Taliesin glanced at some of the columns carved into walls and standing at the ends of the bridges. He could see now the artistic style of the Dwarves in the thick, angular lines, the blocky patterns, and even the reliefs of stern, bearded faces.

Once on the other side they reached an area more traveled. The steep slopes had stairs carved into them. There were more signs directing to different trade posts, an underground lake, land forms of note, and, finally, a sign for the Surface. A few hours passed and eventually they took a break for dinner, eating the food Taliesin had packed along. Ruuda revealed she had a small amount of supplies and food hiding in her barrel, as well.

All the while Taliesin kept an eye out for any spiders.

But he found none. None alive, none dead, and no webs. It only confirmed his belief that something big was happening. Had they all been wiped out? Or had they all gone somewhere?

Time dragged on as they continued their journey. But at last they were heading up. Stone steps led higher and higher in the Deep Hollows. The air had a different quality. It felt lighter, and carried more scents with it. And finally, after another full day of travel, they came to a set of stairs that led to a wooden door marked 'The Surface'.

The two shared a look of anticipation. Ruuda slowly rolled up the map, handing it back to Taliesin who tucked it away in his bag. The moment stretched out as they regarded the door.

"This is big," the Dark Elf breathed, his heart hammering in his chest.

"It is," she agreed.

After another moment's hesitation, Taliesin opened the door. With a loud creak it revealed a tavern. Lanterns dimly lit the area in an orange haze. A swell of noise hit them. Patrons that mingled about the bar, that lounged at tables, and that leaned against walls were all chatting with each other in a variety of languages. Some of it seemed friendly and personal, but most seemed business-oriented. Papers were exchanged, goods were traded, information was swapped. Some tables had card games going. Food and drink filled the area with rich smells. There was an assortment of people inside the tavern. Dark Elves, Dwarves and Gnomes mostly. There was one lady of red skin, with two large horns and a pointed tail that was doing business with two Dark Elves.

"Whoa," Taliesin gasped, taking it all in. He noted there were no windows, but instead a set of wooden stairs that went up. They were in a basement.

"We could get some food here for the road," Ruuda suggested.

He nodded and they wandered up to the bar, weaving between the patrons. No one paid them any attention. The barkeep turned to them, a female Dark Elf with a low-cut blouse and curly white hair. She flashed a red smile at them. "What can I get for you two?"

"We're headed out into the city and looking for some food to take with us," Taliesin supplied. "Whatever is worth . . ." he fetched some coins from his pack and set them on the bar, "five gold."

"I'll get you fixed right up, handsome. Wait here." She turned and sauntered off.

The two of them leaned against the bar, looking out over the room. Taliesin was glad to see no one he recognized. Anticipation ran through him. The thrill of the unknown, of adventure. And the fear of it. He had no idea what to expect once they went up those stairs and out into Eleste'si. He knew it was a city of High Elves, and that other races were not easily welcome there. It would be best to avoid being seen, to stick to the alleys and dark roads. To travel at night and hide during the day.

On that thought, he had no idea what the difference between night and day would be like. Only what he heard in stories. About a sun too bright to see in. And a night that had a high ceiling full of white spots that were called stars. It all seemed . . . fantastical. And ridiculous. Was the Surface really all that different from the Deep Hollows?

The barkeep returned with a pack of food. Taliesin took note that it was all food from the Surface. Cheese, leafy greens, breads, and some varieties of meat. After putting it away the two headed up the wooden steps. Ruuda's footfalls were heavier than Taliesin's as they wound their way up. They were only passed by one Dark Dwarf scurrying down. The noise quieted as they reached another wooden door.

Taliesin carefully opened it, finding a storage room on the other side. Barrels, boxes, and bags lined the walls, a small lantern illuminating the area. A few baskets of brightly colored fruit set about. Taliesin had to blink a few times when he took the fruit in. He didn't even know what some of those colors were.

Ruuda pointed at another door to their left. They

quietly crept through, finding themselves on the first floor of the tavern. It was nearly completely empty. A man in a hood sat in the far corner, chewing on some bread. Dust gathered on the tables and the heavy chandelier. A woman worked at the bar, cleaning off some glasses. She looked to be a High Elf, with long blonde hair and pale skin. But when she saw them her image shimmered and the illusion dropped, revealing herself to be a Dark Elf. "Are you two headed out?" She gestured with her head to the door.

"Yes," Taliesin answered. His nerves made his throat tight, his reply coming out hoarse.

"It's night currently so you should be safe," she answered. "Is this your first time out? I don't recognize either of you two."

"It is our first time," he admitted.

"Well, keep a low profile," she advised. "Stick to the narrow, darker streets. There is one other tavern in the city friendly to our kind, if you need a place to sleep. It's called the Tranquil Grail and is closer to the outskirts. There is a passphrase for both taverns to get inside. It is *Sanctuary.*"

"Thanks for the information," Taliesin said.

The barkeep nodded and resumed her illusion of a High Elf again.

The two crossed the empty room to the door. As they paused before it Taliesin pulled his hood up to better hide his identity. He glanced down at Ruuda. She watched him expectantly. His hand hovered over the handle. For a moment, the gravity of his decision fell on him. He was leaving everything he ever knew behind. The comfort of his wealthy House, the familiar roads and food of Berenzia, his family. But part of him knew this nostalgia was a fantasy. A dream. From a time in his life when he didn't fully understand his status. When he hadn't fully comprehended the limits placed on what he wanted to achieve. There was nothing for him there anymore. His attempt to enact change and to stand up for himself had only ended in pain. If he was to return to a better life in Berenzia, he had to find out what happened to the spiders. Surely this was what the Silk Weaver wanted.

And if he could contribute in this way, and bring answers back, his life would be good again. And his voice would finally be heard, his opinions listened to, his goals attainable.

Courage welled up inside of him. Courage to face whatever was on the other side of the door. And with that he turned the handle, opened it, and they stepped out into the moonlit city of Eleste'si.

.
.
.

JADE

.

.

.

"Thank you for this," Therond stated, sliding the silver ring back onto his finger. "I hope no one got hurt in this venture."

"On the contrary," Jade replied, "we rescued a group of Halflings the goblins had taken prisoner."

Therond's eyebrows drew together in concern. It was a bright morning in Somberdale. Dew dotted the lush green grasses, and the town was stirring, going about its daily routine. The blacksmith, the leather workers, the general store, and other shops were opening. Humans, Half-Elves, and Halflings were the majority of the population in the port town. But some Wild Elves, Gnomes, and Dragonborn called this place home as well. The Korventine Empire was considered predominantly Human. The king and queen, ruling from their thrones in An'Ock, were Human as well. But being a port gave Somberdale a bit more variety in its races. Jade liked that about the town. It reminded her of her Druid Circle, such a diverse group from so many places coming together to protect the laws of nature. She needed to check in with them again, soon.

"Strange," Therond stated, "for goblins to take prisoners."

Sen nodded, he and Zok standing across from the two Elves. "They thought they were going to be sacrificed to some kinda demon that was loose in the caverns. From another plane, supposedly."

At Therond's increasing confused and worried expression, Jade clarified, "We met a wizard named Rowland inside the mountain. The Citadel had sent him to take care of the issue. He didn't seem to need our help so we left with the

Halflings and your belongings."

"Oh, well, that's good to hear," the High Elf replied. "I appreciate you going into danger for me."

"Your visit was too short," Jade smiled. "I will miss you."

Therond patted the horse that he had behind him, his packs slung over it. The saddle had beautiful curving details carved in. Swirls and leaves and light characteristic of Elven art. "Alas, I have more business to attend to on my way back to Her Majesty. My road takes me south to An'Ock where I fear I'll be forced to stay longer than I hope. Humans and their politics are tiresome."

Jade, Sen, and Therond all chuckled at that. But the Wild Elf noticed Zok was not participating in the conversation. In fact, he and Therond did not make eye contact at all. She was curious about that. She knew Therond to be, overall, welcoming of other races. Perhaps it was Zok that felt awkward. A Half-Elf in the presence of a High Elf. And not just any High Elf, but the right hand of the Queen of Eleste'si, the Elven capital city. From her throne in the north she ruled over all the Elven lands as far south as the coast Oceala sat upon. Jade had met the Queen in person and had not been fond of her. Those blue eyes had judged her Wild Elf status as being inferior to the High Elves. She could only imagine how Zok must feel. A half breed, not fully welcome in either world.

"Good luck in An'Ock," Jade said. "I have never been inside that city and hope I never do."

Therond chuckled. "The world is strange my dear friend, you never know what the next adventure may bring. Especially for a wanderer like you." He put his hand on her shoulder. "I will miss you, as well. I hope we can meet again soon."

They embraced each other. Therond looked up at Sen. "Thank you for your assistance, Sen." His eyes just briefly passed over the Half-Elf. "And yours too, Brother Zok. Farewell." With that he mounted his horse, turned it around, and took off at a relaxed pace down the road.

Sen gave a short laugh. "*Brother Zok.* Listen to that,

you've got a fancy-pants High Elf calling you by your Paladin title."

Zok seemed intent on studying the ground. "I am, first and foremost, a representative of my order."

"Is everything all right?" Jade asked.

"It's fine. We should take that book to Tymus like Rowland asked." He pulled it out of his bag, holding the red tome up. "It might take some time for translation."

The three turned to head back into the heart of Somberdale. Although none of them had ever been to Tymus' tower, the landmark was not easy to miss. The stone structure rose above the vibrant green trees, standing multiple stories tall. It made the surrounding buildings seem very small indeed. They made their way down the central road, passing stalls that sold shell jewelry, pots holding herbs such as basil and cilantro, and chickens that scurried across their path.

As they walked across the town, Foxy following, Jade reflected on the goblin caverns. It had been very odd to see a wizard from the Citadel this far west. She knew a bit about the place given her younger brother was attempting to learn magic. What came easily for Jade was a struggle for him. Nevertheless, he kept trying to get enrolled at the Citadel. Great mages were educated there, but it was more than just a school. It was the hub of magical research, law, and order. Because of its prestige it was very particular on who was allowed to join. And for many years now, her brother had always been rejected.

She wondered how Tymus and Rowland knew each other. She knew very little about the wizard that lived in the tower. That form of magic – learned through study and discipline – was foreign to Jade. Her magic came from meditation in nature, from the life force she felt in plants and animals. The ever changing moods and whims of the weather.

They came to the outer gate around the tower. It was open, and a stone path led sixty feet forward to the base of the tower.

"It's quite the construction," Zok commented as they

approached the wooden front door. "He certainly wants everyone in town to know who he is."

"I like his style," Sen nodded. "Maybe I should get my own tower."

They stepped up to the door and Jade knocked. They waited a few minutes before noise was heard on the other side. The door cracked and a young, Human male stood there. His skin was pale and his eyes were sunken. Strands of black hair hung in front of his face, and his clothes were all black as well.

There was a pause as he regarded them. Then Zok said, "We came to see Tymus. We have something the wizard Rowland wanted to give him."

The young man nodded and said in a monotone voice. "Come in."

The door opened and the three plus the fox walked inside. They found themselves in a wide, circular room that was the width of the tower. A grand staircase ran up and down along the wall. The rest of the space was taken up by shelves and cabinets crammed full of items. Bags of seeds, pots of various plants, vegetables, boxes with insects, cages with birds, clumps of fur, heavy books, candles, incense, quills, and pots of ink. Vials shone in sunlight that came from the windows, most empty but some with colorful liquid inside. A few chairs and tables were scattered about. The intent was likely to give ample seating room for guests, but the end result was haphazardly arranged furniture that was already stacked with more books, parchments, and tools. Jade took in the smell of multiple different species of plants and rich soil. And, in stark contrast to the darkly dressed youth that had answered the door, everything was exceedingly colorful.

"Holy shit," Sen uttered, taking it all in. "This place is incredible."

"Guest! Guests!" a jubilant voice called from the stairs. There was the sound of quick feet bounding down before a Gnome reached the ground floor. He spread his arms out wide. "Welcome to my tower! I am Tymus

Altawayne, and I am happy to be of service to you!"

Tymus was even more colorful than the room around him. Flamboyant clothes of multiple colors and patterns adorned his small body. His fingers glittered with rings, and his hair was dyed a bright pink.

"Hello," Jade said, unable to help but smile at all the vibrancy around her. "My name is Jade. These are my friends Captain Sen of the Scarlet Maiden, and Brother Zok of the Temple of the Holy Dragon."

Tymus eagerly shook their hands, staring up in wonder at the Dragonborn. "Goodness, you are *huge!* What is it like to tower over everyone around you? No – no, don't tell me! If I ever perfect my Potion of Growth I will find out myself!"

Zok raised one eyebrow. "You want to be taller?"

"Taller, shorter, invisible. I want to try it all! But, only temporarily, mind you. I would never want to permanently change the fantastic body I have."

Zok held the red tome forward. "Rowland sent us to-"

"Rowland!" Tymus gasped in delight. "Please sit, sit! Tell me the whole story!"

They were ushered over to the jumbled furniture. Sen moved a pile of books off of one large blue chair and lounged back, his enormous form overflowing in it. Jade and Zok sat together on a sofa, bookended by pots of plants. Foxy roamed the room and smelled everything while the darkly dressed youth watched warily.

Tymus waved in his direction. "Don't mind Jem, he's always like that." The Gnome took the book from the Paladin and plopped himself in a pink armchair with a high back. "So, you mentioned Rowland? Where did you see him? Is he coming here?"

The three exchanged glances and Jade replied, "Maybe. We were in the Doorway Mountains looking for goblins. They stole an item from a friend of mine and we went to get it back. Rowland was there, he'd been captured-"

Tymus laughed loudly, clutching at this stomach.

"The mighty and powerful Rowland captured like a common thief! I love this story already! Please, continue!"

Jade said, "We helped him out and he said the Citadel had sent him to investigate a demon that had entered from the Hells, or some other plane. He was supposed to send it back where it came from. He didn't seem to really need our help so we parted there. But, he did say he found that book and needed you to translate it for him."

Tymus eyed the lock on the book. "I think I can open this, yes. I'll definitely need a secure environment and some protective enchantments." His face grew serious for the first time as he looked up at them. "A demon, you say? Did he mention what kind?"

"No," Zok replied. "But we heard it deeper in the tunnels. It was very loud and powerful."

"He should have come to me for assistance!" Tymus huffed. "Those mountains are my backyard, after all."

"If I may ask," Jade ventured, leaning forward and resting her elbows on her knees, "how do you know Rowland?"

"We studied at the Citadel together," the Gnome responded cheerily. His eyes went distant, as if reliving long hours in classrooms. "We graduated at the same time. Rowland decided to stay and contribute to research efforts there. However, I wanted to study plants and animals for magical properties. Herbalism, potions, shape changers, magical beasts and the like. The Citadel wanted a presence in this town. When I heard about Somberdale I volunteered to go. On the coast surrounded by mountains and forest . . . it was just the spot I was looking for! We've kept in touch as best we could since then." He smiled widely. "That is good news he's coming here for the book! It will be so nice to see him again."

"What is the Citadel?" Sen asked.

Tymus drew himself up proudly. "It is a place of high honor among all mages! Promising students apply and are brought there to be educated in great uses of magic. Once you graduate from the Citadel, you are forever a part of the order. You go where they ask you and complete what tasks they require. We do a great deal of research into arcane matters, such as I am doing. Sometimes, after many years in the field, we return to the Citadel as professors to teach new generations. The laws of magic use are determined at the Citadel and enforced through a group known as the Clairvoyant Arcane. For instance, traveling between the planes is illegal. So if someone is responsible for letting a demon loose from the Hells, then the Clairvoyant Arcane will track them down, arrest them, and they will have to plead their case before the courts of the Citadel. After which their fate will be decided by the Citadel."

That made Jade uncomfortable. It sounded like the Citadel made the laws, judged those who were accused of breaking them, and acted as jury on their sentence. It was too much power in one place. She was glad she had chosen to live her life as a nomad, outside of the laws of civilizations.

"Fascinatin'," Sen nodded. "I've never been magically inclined myself. I prefer to punch things."

Tymus grinned. "We are all gifted differently." His gaze drifted to the other two. "Do either of you have any magic abilities?"

"I am a Druid," Jade answered. "I share your interest in plants and animals. The natural world is rich in its complexity."

"I have a few spells I know," Zok answered. "They were taught to me through the temple and I fuel my magic with my prayers."

"Ah, the wonder of the arcane!" Tymus cheered. "So many forms it takes. So helpful and so powerful. Used to heal . . . and used to kill. It's a good thing we have the Citadel to help navigate it all, isn't it?"

Jade did not agree.

.
.
.

Jade had been deeply sleeping for awhile when she felt a strange tug on her. It wasn't only physical, the tug seemed to be attached to her mind and soul as well. A deep-rooted pull on her very core. She had only a moment to open her eyes and take in the forest where she was sleeping, Foxy pulled close to her, when the world warped around her. Colors and shapes twisted, melded, and then reset themselves.

She was no longer in the same place as before.

Panic took hold as she scrambled to her feet. *Another vision,* she thought. *Not another vision. I can't keep seeing that destruction.*

But she quickly realized it wasn't the vision she'd been having on and off for a couple of years. In fact, it wasn't a vision at all. For Foxy sniffed curiously at the air, circling his master. She could feel the hard ground beneath her feet, feel the cold night breeze. She smelled pine and stone and dirt. Wherever she was, it was far from Somberdale.

Jade glanced around. She was in a heavily wooded area. These trees were old and thick, heavy with pine needles and creeping roots. The sky was clear overhead, a full moon lighting the area. She could make out some kind of stone structure. It was a singular story, large and square. Vines and ivy were slowly overtaking it, snaking up the walls and through the broken windows.

"What the fuck?"

Jade whirled around at the voice. She jumped, taking in the two people who were also standing there, looking entirely confused. One was a Half-Elf woman. She looked very young, perhaps early twenties. Her long blonde hair was tied in a braid, and her pale skin shone in the moonlight. She wore traveling clothes of grays and faded blues. A bow and quiver were strapped to her back. And at her feet was a large gray wolf. The wolf guarded her, emitting a low growl.

The second was a Dragonborn with bronze scales. He wasn't as large as Sen, but still taller and thicker than the average person. Red eyes took in the scene around him. He wore robes of dark blue with silver accents that came up in a hood, shadowing most of his face.

"Who are you two?" Jade asked.

The young woman gestured to the Dragonborn. "I'm not with him. I was just . . . teleported here, or something! I was just hiking."

"I was asleep at an inn," the other stated. "I have no idea what is going on."

"Same for me," Jade replied.

The wolf and fox cautiously approached each other, smelling. They didn't seem to feel threatened by one another.

"Why are we here?" the Half-Elf asked, fury in her blue eyes.

Another voice broke the silence, "Because I summoned you."

The three of them spun around. When Jade saw who stepped from the shadows, anger burned in her. It was the old man, the one Sen had said reminded him of his uncle Jenkins. But gone was the hunched back and shaky hands. He stood tall and broad, his silver beard hanging longer this time. His robes of gray and black shifted in the wind. "It's so good to see you all."

The blonde woman drew her bow and set an arrow in one swift motion, the muscles in her bare arms tensing. "Send us back."

"Shooting at me would be unwise," the old man stated, "unless you want to be stranded here. But I promise I will teleport you away from this place as soon as you help me find what I need here."

"After what you did in Somberdale?" Jade snapped. "I have no patience for your trickery, old man. I will not go along with this."

He shrugged. "Suit yourself. You can stay here. I am seeking a glass dagger set inside that old stone fortress. Get it for me and I will return you to where you came from."

The arrow from the bow loosed, aiming for the old man's arm. His hand shot up in a flash and the arrow deflected off an invisible shield. A dark smile spread across his face. Then he vanished.

Jade felt frustration boiling up inside her. A helplessness at the situation. She didn't know where she was.

71

That was a feat in itself, because she had traveled extensively over her 406 years of life. If she was more powerful, she could get out of this situation. But she'd lost that power long ago. Now, she was lucky enough to be able to produce fire from her hands.

How did I let myself stay so weak for so long? she thought. *I should have sought help. I should have done something to try and regain my magic.*

The Dragonborn began to head to the stone structure.

"What are you doing?" the Half-Elf demanded.

He shrugged. "I'm going to find the glass dagger. I want out of here."

Just as he took another few steps there was a ripping sound from the ground. Dirt churned in several places as bony hands dug their way out. Jade swore, fire lighting up around her hands as she prepared for a fight. Skeletons pulled their way up from under the ground, some gore still clinging to their bodies.

The Half-Elf shrieked. "Undead!" She backed up rapidly, headed towards the building. As she did so she notched another arrow and fired. It went through the eye socket of an approaching skeleton, going with such force through the back of its skull that the bone broke apart. The body swayed and then dropped.

Jade dropped the fire from her hands and pushed both outwards. She felt a connection with the earth, the land around her. She stretched out her inner being and linked with the life force that was the soil. A thick green vine erupted from the dirt, looping around one undead and snapping it in half. Two more raced past their fallen ally, coming at the Druid with sharpened fingers.

Foxy sprang forward and snapped at one, biting its leg bone futilely. Jade directed the vine to intercept one but the skeleton was too fast. It slashed out and ripped five bloody lines along her arm. She cried out at the pain, stumbling back against the stone structure. The vine lashed again and caught it this time, dragging it backwards. The third skeleton got free from the fox and made a leap at the Druid. An arrow whizzed by, close enough to ruffle Jade's brown hair, and split the undead's skull from the rest of its body.

The Half-Elf archer turned and fired at more approaching enemies, slowly heading towards the fortress. "We'd better get inside or we'll get overrun out here!"

The Dragonborn shoved at the front door with his shoulder. It splintered and creaked and then swung halfway open. He turned towards two undead running at him, their hands outstretched. From his sleeve he produced a black wand. Its tip lit up and four orbs of light shot out, searing the air as they passed. Three crashed into one of the undead, breaking it apart. The final one took off the arm of the second undead, but it kept running and threw itself upon the Dragonborn. The two fell back into the fortress.

Jade growled, racing for the door. She made one final sweep of her vine, knocking a few skeletons prone, before dropping the magic. The archer was close behind her as she bounded up the steps and through the door. It was very dark inside, but moonlight still spilled from shattered windows, showing a dirty stone passage.

The Dragonborn was pressed back against the wall, struggling to shove the skeleton off of him. Claws tore at robes, drawing blood. Jade felt a swell of magic inside her. The horror at seeing undead, something so unnatural, above the ground filled her with a fury. She reached into the air, and her fury turned to cold frost. A dagger made of ice crystalized in her hand and she threw it. It spun through the air before slicing clean through the skeleton's head. It dropped its grip on the Dragonborn and fell to the floor.

The Half-Elf spun around and kicked the door shut again with an echoing *bang*. "Let's hurry. They can still get through the windows."

The three ran down the hall, the wolf and fox following. They turned one sharp corner, passing by a window, as one undead leaped through it, landing on the back of the archer. She shouted in anger and slammed herself back against the stone. But it didn't let go. Her wolf jumped up and snapped its jaws around the spine of the skeleton, and with one powerful pull it came lose. As the undead clattered to the ground the Dragonborn fired the same spell from his wand, burning orbs tearing the bones apart.

They continued to run, making their way through the winding, confusing passages inside the stone fortress. They passed no doors and no distinguishing marks. They could hear the noises of more skeletons searching after them, the clattering of bones seeming to come from all directions. Jade whipped around once as they ran, firing out two bolts of fire that impacted with enough force to throw one undead from its feet.

They reached another closed wooden door. The hallway was lined with windows, and spindly shapes eclipsed moonlight as the skeletons tried to find a way inside. The Dragonborn pushed at the door, trying to force it open. It shifted on its hinges but didn't open.

"Hurry!" the archer snapped, taking a stance and notching another arrow.

Jade took a deep breath to center herself as she lifted her hands. She focused her energy and fire lit up her fingers once again, illuminating the hall in an orange glow. And then four skeletons crashed through the windows, rushing at them with jaws open.

The Half-Elf let loose an arrow. It whizzed through the air and burst into the head of an undead, sending it to the ground. Jade heard the Dragonborn throwing himself at the door again as she punched her fists forward. The fire shot from her hands with alarming speed, crashing into a second undead and shattering its spine. The bones fell to the floor with a great clamor. A skeleton got close, grappling the archer's bow. They tugged back and forth for a moment before she turned herself into a somersault, taking the undead with her and then flinging it away with the momentum. Rolling to one knee she drew an arrow in the same motion and fired, stopping the enemy that had attacked her.

There was a crack as the door burst open, the

Dragonborn stumbling into the next room from the impact. Jade lifted her fists to shoot fire at the final skeleton but the Half-Elf was faster, pivoting on her knee and taking it out with another arrow. The two of them backed quickly up into the room behind, forcing the door shut again.

Jade turned around, finding herself in a small, square, windowless room. The darkness didn't bother her, but the Dragonborn lit up a light at the end of his wand, casting their shadows behind them. The room was plain except for a wooden chest.

"There's no lock," the Half-Elf stated, crouching down and glancing it over.

Jade tried to reach out and feel any magic aura emanating from it, but she couldn't. Her power was too weak. "It could be trapped. Let's first-"

The Dragonborn bent down and popped the lid open. The inside was lined with black velvet. And the only item was a glass dagger. The hilt and blade were made of the same material, glittering dully in the wand light.

Steeling herself, Jade bent down and picked it up. Nothing happened except for a sudden quieting around the stone fortress. No more noise of scratching skeletal hands or feet.

"Did that get rid of the undead?" the archer asked.

Jade examined the weapon. "Perhaps they were placed here to protect this thing."

The Dragonborn huffed. "Is that why the old man didn't want to get this himself?"

The Druid sighed. "That sounds about right. Let's head back out."

They wound their way through the twisting stone passages, stepping over the carnage of bones they'd left behind. They exited the front door and out into the night again. The crisp air was refreshing after the dustiness of the structure.

The old man was waiting for them, a smile on his face. "Good work. The dagger, please?" He held out an expectant hand.

Jade took a moment to decide. Giving him his prize after what he put them through felt horrible. And if it was her alone, perhaps she would have fought. But there were the other two to consider. She couldn't make that choice for them. So it was with a reluctant hand that she gave him the dagger.

"Thank you," he stated.

Then he spoke a jumble of words and the world around Jade shifted. Trees spun, smells vanished, and she found herself standing once again in the forest outside of Somberdale. Foxy rubbed happily against her, panting from all the running they did. She scratched behind his ears, smiling. She would need to tell Zok and Sen what happened in the morning. But for now, she was very tired. She knew it would be difficult to rest worrying about what the glass dagger-

"What the *fuck?*"

Jade jumped, turning around. And there was the Half-Elf archer and the Dragonborn, standing there looking entirely befuddled.

The Dragonborn asked. "Where are we?"

.

.

.

PART II

Zok

.
.
.

The noise of metal clanging rang over the beach as Zok sparred with another member of the Temple of the Holy Dragon. It was a bright and beautiful morning. The waves rolled on and off the sand, white foam bubbling and glistening in the sunlight. The temple itself backed up to the beach, a white fence separating its land from the rest of Somberdale. The structure was impressive. All gold and white standing three stories tall. It was a perfect square, and mosaic windows reflected blues in the sun.

The grounds around the temple were immaculate. A tall stone fountain stood in the center of the gardens. There were a few smaller buildings set to the side for members of the temple to live in. The rooms were basic and bare-bone, but they were functional. It was good for those like Zok who devoted their lives to the service of the temple. He was not the only Paladin. There were others who took up blade and shield to protect in service of the Holy Dragon. There were also Clerics who healed the sick and injured. There were the priests and priestesses who led worship and took leadership roles. And there were new inductees that helped clean the grounds, take offerings, light candles, and burn incense.

The temple had been Zok's home since he moved to Somberdale three years ago. Now, at twenty-nine years old, he felt like he had a place he could stay forever. A place where he could find purpose. The head of the temple, High Priest Amon, had welcomed him with open arms. It was very different from the temple he'd been to previously in Eleste'si. He had not been welcomed there.

"Focus," Brother Baelfire laughed, flipping a dagger

in his hand, "you're slowing down."

Zok turned his attention from his memories and to the sparring. He and the other warrior members of the temple fought often. Practice kept reflexes quick and muscles strong. As he'd recently found out with the stone golem and the goblins, one never knew when danger would approach. He was happy he could defend his friends and other lives with his training.

The two slashed and parried back and forth, feet moving quickly over the grass and sand. Their traditional armor and more formal attire were gone. They both wore loose shirts and pants of white, the thin fabric flapping against their bodies in the ocean wind.

Baelfire's blonde hair scattered around his chiseled face as he spun and struck, moving quickly. He was Human, and had been at the temple longer than Zok had. He knew his friend to be very devout to their religion. An example of someone to look up to.

Zok blocked the next few blows, his dagger held steady in his hand. The two seemed to be evenly matched. Out of his peripheral vision he saw Sen and Jade approaching down the beach, the wind whipping at Jade's forest colored clothes and Sen's purple pants. Zok pushed on the attack, and after a few quick strikes was able to disarm Baelfire.

The Human laughed. "Nice work! That was impressive. Who are you showing off for?" He glanced in the direction Zok was looking. "Oh, for the Wild Elf? They're quite beautiful, those Elves."

He couldn't help but laugh at that, sheathing his dagger in his belt. "Don't be ridiculous, after I'm dead she's going to outlive me by five hundred years."

"You're optimistic that you will die of old age and not heroically young in battle."

"If this was a war time I'd be worried. But if the greatest threat is an old man who sends me on nonsense quests down wells, I think I'll be safe."

Baelfire shook his head, amused. "I still have a hard time wrapping my mind around that story. Are you *sure* you weren't drunk?"

"I am always sure."

Jade and Sen approached, passing through the open gate and onto the temple grounds. "Zok," the Wild Elf greeted. "Sorry to interrupt but we need to talk."

"I am *not* sorry to interrupt," Sen clarified. He nodded to the Human. "Hello there, Baelfire."

Baelfire returned the nod. "Good morning, Captain Sen. And good morning to you as well, my dear lady Jade."

"Is something wrong?" Zok asked. It wasn't unusual for his friends to come by the temple to visit him, but both of them together had never happened before.

"I believe so," Jade answered.

Baelfire patted Zok's shoulder. "I'll take my leave." With another nod to Sen and Jade he walked off towards the temple.

The three headed out further onto the beach before sitting down on the soft and pliant sand. Jade drew her knees up to her chest, resting her arms on them. "I was able to tell Sen on the way here. I think we're in trouble."

"This is a crazy story," the Dragonborn added.

Zok crossed his legs, frowning. Now he was certainly worried. "What is going on?"

The Druid began. "Last night, while I was sleeping, I got teleported. I don't know where to, but it was a ruined stone fortress in the woods. The trees were pine and I couldn't see any mountains. It was far from here, wherever it was."

"Who teleported you?" Zok asked, shock coming through in his voice.

Sen leaned forward eagerly. "It was the old Jenkins man! The one from the well."

Zok's wide blue eyes swiveled back to the Wild Elf as she continued. "It was. And I wasn't alone. There was a Half-Elf female archer there, and a male Dragonborn that was smaller than Sen."

"Everyone is smaller than me," Sen commented.

Zok gave his friend a sardonic look. "Not whatever

demon was in those goblin tunnels."

That quieted the Dragonborn down as Jade said, "None of us knew how we got there. And then the old man – I'll just call him Jenkins for simplicity – said he brought us all there to retrieve a glass dagger from the fortress. We refused, of course. The archer even shot at him but he cast a magic shield around himself. Then Jenkins vanished and undead came up from under the ground. They were endless and we were forced inside the fortress. We located the dagger and as soon as we picked it up all the undead were gone. We went back outside and I, unfortunately, had to give the dagger to Jenkins. I didn't want to risk the others' lives. He said he'd send us all back. But, once I was returned to Somberdale . . ." She took a breath before finishing, "the other two were still with me."

"They were teleported *here?*" Zok gasped. "How are they doing?"

"They are fine for now," Jade replied. "They're staying at the tavern."

"Have you learned anything about them?" the Paladin asked.

"Yes. The Dragonborn gave his name as Skar. He's a Wizard. And the Half-Elf archer is called Artemis Wolfsbane. She did, indeed, have a very large wolf with her. And," Jade leaned forward, "she is an incredible fighter! I've rarely seen someone move so fast with such skill. She's clearly not only been trained but she's seen extensive battle, I'm certain."

"Hm," Zok considered for a moment. "So, the question is: were they randomly chosen by this old man Jenkins, or a calculated choice?"

"They didn't seem to know who he was," Jade answered.

"I don't understand why he would need a glass dagger," Sen said. "He can do magic."

"We don't know the extent of his powers," Zok reminded. "But this dagger must have significance. Were there any distinguishing markings on it?"

Jade sighed, shaking her head. "None. It was all

made of solid glass and that was it."

"Does this sound like anything you've heard of?" the Paladin asked.

The Druid replied, "I know some powerful spells require certain components to cast. But I'm not familiar with anything that requires a glass dagger."

"Are they still at the tavern?"

"Yes, Sen has already met them. Let's go introduce you."

As the three stood up, Zok heard his name called. He turned around to see Priestess Liana approaching, her white robes blowing about and her dark hair pulled back from her face. He looked back to his friends. "I'll meet you two there shortly." Then he headed towards Liana.

Meeting him halfway, the Human priestess said, "I have . . . I have very sad news."

He took in the dark circles under her eyes, and the deep frown at her lips. "What has happened?"

"High Priest Amon has died. It was overnight in his sleep. Peacefully."

Zok took a step back at that, catching himself on the white fence. He knew High Priest Amon was very elderly, but his health had appeared to be in great condition. "I . . . I am very saddened by this."

Liana looked at him sympathetically. "I know he took you in when you arrived here. He was like a grandfather to me, as well. We'll be holding a funeral tomorrow, but his body will be available for viewing in his room today, if you wish."

"Thank you. I'll be by later today. It seems this morning is not one for good news."

As he began heading away from the temple, Liana called after him. "Is something else bad happening?"

He glanced over his shoulder at her. "I really hope not."

Zok made his way through Somberdale, but his mind wasn't focused. The loss of High Priest Amon stung. He had been a kind, gentle soul. A steady leader at the Temple of the

Holy Dragon. He'd given Zok a home when it felt like he'd had none.

As he approached the Arrowed Knee Tavern he touched the symbol of his deity around his neck before walking inside. He needed a clear head to figure out just what was going on here. Across the room he spotted his friends sitting at a table, along with the two Jade mentioned. He approached and held out his hand towards the archer. "I am Brother Zok of the Temple of the Holy Dragon. It is good to meet you."

She shook it, her grip firm. "I'm Artemis Wolfsbane." He took in her pointed ears and fair skin, nearly the same shade as his. While attractive, she did have a rougher look about her that he didn't equate with full-blooded Elves. Jade was right, clearly a Half-Elf. She had long blonde hair tied into a braid, and her blue eyes were sharp and alert. Clothes of blues and grays had obviously seen hard travel.

The bronze Dragonborn shook his hand next. "I'm Skar from Volcano Island." He was taller and broader than Zok. His dark blue robes might as well have the word Wizard embroidered on them. His hood cast most of his face in shadow, but two red eyes appeared friendly enough.

Zok frowned. "I've never heard of Volcano Island."

"Really? Odd."

The Paladin looked to Artemis. "And where are you from?"

She looked him over before responding, "Far south of here."

Zok pulled out a chair to sit next to Sen. It's legs creaked audibly along the wooden floor of the tavern. "I am very sorry to hear what has happened."

Artemis nodded. "Jade told us you all have met this old man Jenkins before. I certainly have not."

"Do either of you know why you were targeted?" Zok asked, looking back and forth between the two of them.

Skar shrugged his large shoulders. "I cannot think of any."

"I'm nobody important," Artemis stated.

"Well, we'd certainly like to get you both home," Zok said. "But are you able to stay for a few nights? Just until we figure out why you were teleported."

Artemis glanced around at the tavern. "I don't mind staying here. I was looking for a new place to explore, anyway." She patted the large wolf at her side. "Wolfie and I love adventure."

Zok glanced back and forth between the wolf and the fox. "So now we have a Foxy . . . and a Wolfie."

"Oh!" Skar excitedly rummaged through his robes and pulled out a small wooden box. "And I have a two-headed worm." He opened it with flourish to reveal, indeed, a small, two-headed worm inside. "I haven't named it. I suppose I can keep with the theme here and call it Wormy."

"Please, don't name it that," Zok sighed, and rubbed the bridge of his nose. "Where did you find that thing?"

Skar tucked the box away again in his robes. "I collect many things."

Sen asked, "Are you from the Citadel?"

"I am not," Skar replied.

Jade frowned and leaned forward slightly, her interest clearly piqued. "You're a Wizard who learned magic outside of the Citadel?"

The bronze Dragonborn shrugged. Then said, "I do not mind staying here. I've never been to Somberdale. Perhaps there are more things I can add to my collection!"

"Thank you," Zok said. "I'm sure we can get to the bottom of this."

He noticed Jade looking at him in concern. He was sure she could see the sadness in his eyes. She was always very perceptive. She asked, "Is everything alright with Priestess Liana?"

He looked over to her. "I received news High Priest Amon died in his sleep last night."

"Who's that?" Skar asked.

Artemis waved a hand to hush him.

"I'm so sorry, Zok," Jade said.

"Me too, friend," Sen added, patting him on the

back.

Zok gave them a half-hearted smile in response.

They finished off conversing with Artemis and Skar. The two seemed nice enough, and Zok was glad they chose to stay. Perhaps Jenkins would show himself again, and they could get answers. But for now, he would need to be patient.

After leaving the tavern he returned to the temple. He wanted to see High Priest Amon's body so he could pay his final respects in private. The funeral would be very traditional and structured. He wanted some time to just speak his mind.

The temple was quiet when he entered. The central chamber was large and round, adorned gold and white. There was a large stained-glass window that held the visage of a long dragon. Their deity. Zok had known of the Holy Dragon for as long as he could remember. He grew up outside of Sunspire, so far from here. It was a highly religious city, where many gods were worshipped and laws were strictly enforced to keep the peace. He supposed he'd always been drawn to the things the Holy Dragon valued. Kindness, honor, loyalty, honesty. Doing good to others and helping out whenever one could. He was in his early twenties when he swore his oath to the Holy Dragon and became a Paladin. And he felt his life was fuller because of it.

Zok made his way up the stairs to the top level of the temple. He went down the familiar stone hall, muted sunlight coming through the windows, until he reached what he knew to be High Priest Amon's door. He saw Priestess Liana as well as Priestess Whitney outside of it. Whitney was a rare Half-Fiend, her skin red with curving horns arching back from her forehead, and a tail with a triangle tip. He knew very little of her race except that they were usually distrusted and outcasts. But at least here, in the temple, Whitney had found a home.

"Brother Zok," they greeted.

He nodded to them. "Is it all right if I step inside to see him?"

"Please do," Liana replied. "We were just saying our

goodbyes." The two of them turned and left down the hall.

Zok took a moment to gather himself before he opened the door. Amon's chambers were simple, unexpected for a lead priest. A grand bed sat against the far wall, its four pillars in the shape of a twisting dragon. But other than some nice furnishings the room was empty. A few prayer books sat on a desk. Incense smelling of cinnamon sat beside them. There was a mirror hung where Zok could see his own reflection, looking downcast and tired. Longer dark hair and a beard framed a pale face with sad eyes. Hunched shoulders held the heavy weight of grief.

He returned his gaze to the bed where Amon lay, a silk blanket covering him to his chest. Zok approached. The face was peaceful and still, almost like he was about to smile. Short gray hair topped his head. His ears were round, a Human, but Amon had never been known for turning anyone away due to their race.

Zok sank to his knees, resting his arms on the bed and his chin on top of them. "High Priest Amon, I know you lived a good life. Your devotion to the Holy Dragon was always inspiring to me. Thank you for allowing me into this temple where I can serve others. I . . . I hope to follow your example." He then bent his head and recited his oath.

"I devote my life to follow you, Holy Dragon.
In your example I will be honest, and keep my word in all things.
I will protect others as though their life is greater than mine.
I will show mercy to my foes, but punish those who do evil.
I will obey those with just authority.
I will answer for my actions and ask forgiveness for any wrong I have done.
And in all things I will be honorable.
May you guide my steps and my voice, so I may always serve you justly."

Taking a deep breath, Zok returned his gaze to High Priest Amon. Studying the lines of his elderly face, trying to memorize the man before he could no longer see him.

And then something caught his eye. Zok leaned

forward, his toes pushing against the rug, to get a closer look. There, behind Amon's ear, was a small puncture wound. He narrowed his eyes, studying it. It was small enough to be from a needle or dart.

Immediately Zok sat back, looking around. Ensuring he was alone. The cold hand of dread slowly closed around his heart.

Did somebody kill High Priest Amon? he thought.

Zok got to his feet. He carefully looked over the room, the parchment, the books. But no other clues were left behind. His heart pounded in his chest now. He wanted to be wrong, but each time he went to check the wound was still there. His Half-Elven eyes aided him in perceiving something so small. And he was certain as to what it was.

Then another thought struck him. What if someone was listening outside and heard him looking around? Zok went quickly over to the door and opened it, nearly running into Brother Baelfire.

"Oh!" Zok gasped, pulling himself backwards.

"So sorry!" Baelfire said. "I didn't realize anyone was in here. I came to say my goodbyes." His hazel eyes grew darker as he looked his friend over. "Is everything all right?"

"I . . ." He hesitated. "I am just having a hard time accepting his death." He realized, ironically, that he'd just finished reciting his oath that enforced honesty. But if something was really going on, he didn't want Baelfire to get hurt. He looked at the other Paladin and saw his eyes were red from crying.

"I am as well," Baelfire sighed. Gone was the joy from this morning. He looked as if he'd aged ten years. "He was such an inspiration."

"Have . . . all the other members of the temple been by?"

"As far as I know. Priestesses Liana and Whitney have been busy arranging the funeral. Everyone has been informed except for Priest Jafr. No one has seen him today."

"Oh?" Zok frowned. "Does that seem . . . strange?"

Baelfire shook his head noncommittally. And Zok

could tell the man couldn't focus on much else at the moment except for the lifeless body on the bed.

"I'm sorry," Zok apologized. "I will let you have your time with him." He hurriedly ducked out of the room, closing the door behind him.

He headed down the stairs, attempting to move quickly without bringing undue attention on himself. His hand trailed the railing as he returned to the first floor. He noticed Whitney there, writing down notes in a book. "Priestess Whitney!"

Her eyes flicked up to him. "Brother Zok, may I help you?"

"Have you seen Priest Jafr? I wanted . . . to speak to him."

"I have not. We've all been so busy around here today. You should ask the squire in the stables. I'm sure he has less to juggle and knows where to find everyone."

"Thank you."

Zok crossed the round room and headed outside. It was early afternoon, but the sunlight from this morning was dulled behind clouds that slowly crept across the sky. He went around the gardens, the many flowers going dormant as autumn drew on. He went over to the stables at the side of the temple. Only a few horses were kept for use of the temple residents. He knew that was the most likely place to find the new squire, a boy of twelve named Phil.

And indeed, he saw the Human brushing the coat of a brown horse, humming to himself.

"Squire," Zok said gently, coming up.

Phil turned around. "Brother Zok, good afternoon! Can I be of service?"

"I'm looking for Priest Jafr, do you know where he is?"

The boy shrugged. "I haven't seen him much the last week. He keeps going into the tombs."

Zok stood very still at that, a frown pulling at his lips. "The tombs?"

"Yes, Brother, it's where he's been spending most of

his time."

"Has he said why?"

"No, he doesn't speak to me much. I'm sure he is a very busy man."

"Well, that will not do. Your work is appreciated here, Squire. And I know one day you will rise to be a Priest as well."

A smile lit up Phil's face at that. "Thank you, Brother Zok."

"Thank you for the information." Zok turned and crossed the grounds again, heading towards the entrance to the tombs. The tombs were a series of catacombs that ran underneath the temple, housing the bodies of all who died in service to the Temple of the Holy Dragon here in Somberdale. He had been there twice before. It was a place of reverence. But he couldn't imagine why anyone would need to go there every day for a week.

Zok came up to the entrance. A stone mausoleum, standing twelve feet high and ten feet long. Columns adorned each corner, and the symbol of the Holy Dragon's eye was carved into the door.

He reached his hand out for the handle . . . then hesitated. Was there anything inherently wrong with Priest Jafr spending time away from everyone else? Perhaps he wanted solitude. Or, another part of Zok reasoned, he was afraid for his life and was hiding. Maybe he knew who killed High Priest Amon and was scared. A darker, deeper part of Zok's mind wondered if Jafr was responsible for Amon's death. But he quickly pushed that thought away. Members of the temple killing each other just didn't make sense. And it certainly wasn't part of the oath they all took.

Zok dropped his hand back to his side. He wasn't going to go barging in there to question Jafr. It was unbecoming of a Paladin, after all. He would wait until nightfall, when most of the temple was asleep, and then come back. Perhaps he could find out what was interesting enough inside the tombs to keep Jafr returning.

And maybe it was best to bring along help. Jade's

keen eyes and knowledge of the arcane would be helpful. And Sen's company was, at the very least, a de-stressor. The pirate always knew how to make him smile.

.

.

.

Night fell over Somberdale. The clouds had fully moved in now, blocking all moonlight. Out over the ocean, the horizon line was invisible, making the world bleed off into black. There was nothing odd about walking the temple grounds at night. In his first year in Somberdale, Zok often took time to walk alone in the dark. It was a good time to reflect, and he'd spent many hours mulling over the events that had led him to this town.

But tonight he felt on edge. He constantly looked over his shoulder, even though he knew nothing they were doing was suspicious. But something was clearly wrong. How could anyone kill Priest Amon? He was going to find answers, and bring the murderer to justice.

Zok came up to the mausoleum again, the entrance to the tombs. He turned around, facing the company of warriors behind him. Jade was there, her green Elven eyes bright even with barely any light. Behind her stood the massive form of Sen, drinking some rum. And then there were Artemis and Skar. He hadn't been too sure about bringing them along. But Artemis had overheard their conversation and invited herself on the mission. After that, it had simply seemed unfair to leave Skar out. Maybe it was good for them to come. Perhaps all of this was linked to Jenkins, and their presence would uncover answers.

Nodding at them all, Zok opened the mausoleum and they entered. It was clean and mostly empty inside. The far wall had the carving of the Holy Dragon, his serpent-like body curved gracefully. His eyes stared straight through the Paladin.

"What god is this?" Skar asked, his gruff voice hushed.

"The Holy Dragon," Zok answered, crouching down.

"Those who follow him, like me, uphold the ideals of loyalty, honesty, and protecting others." He found the latch in the stone and opened a door in the floor. It revealed stairs descending into darkness. "Can we have some light?"

The Wizard illuminated the end of his wand with soft light, and the group descended. The temperature dropped the further down they went. Their steps echoed lightly around them. Zok had decided to put on his full armor and shield, just in case they ran into trouble. He was happy to see the group following were armed as well. Artemis had her bow and quiver on her back, as well as two daggers at her hips. Sen's massive battle axe was strapped to his back. He knew Jade's capabilities, and he only hoped Skar was a strong fighter as well.

After five minutes of walking they came to the bottom. A long stone passage greeted them. Unlit sconces were mounted into the walls. And every five feet the wall recessed for a coffin. A statue overlooked most of these, carved in the likeness of the person who died. Powerful faces of the men and women who served the Holy Dragon looked down at the coffins, which were also made of stone and beautifully designed.

And all of them had been ransacked.

The coffins had been opened, a few with significant force to damage them. Some of the treasures kept inside each had been strewn across the floor. Goblets, weapons, pieces of armor. In the effort to open a few the statues behind had been cracked, as well.

Zok stared at it all in horror. He drifted slowly over to one, looking inside. The skeletal body had been disturbed, its bones pushed at different angles as if someone had been searching it. "This . . . this . . ." Anger then burned up inside him. "This is an outrage! These are *my* people! Why would anyone do this?"

The others wandered along the hall, looking at the damage. Skar said, "Clearly whoever did this was searching for something. What is of value down here?"

Zok gestured angrily to the items on the floor. "All of

this has value! But it's just been left behind."

"Why cause so much damage?" Jade wondered aloud. "Surely Priest Jafr wouldn't do this?"

Zok wheeled about, his white cloak rippling from his movements. "If he's known about this, he has a lot to answer for." He then stalked further down the hall, knowing the others would follow. Out of his peripheral vision he could see Sen's eyes linger on the treasures, but he left everything alone.

The wand light glinted off the metal of more possessions scattered on the ground as they made their way deeper in the catacombs. Every tomb was vandalized, and some skulls stared out at them as they passed. Fury flared inside Zok. Fury at the disrespectful way the dead were being treated. Had Jafr done all this? Or had he known and kept it secret?

They came to the end of the hall, and an arched entrance opened up into a circular chamber beyond. Zok knew this was where the first priest of Somberdale's temple was buried. A place of high honor and respect for the legacy left behind. As he approached, he could see the coffin up on a pedestal, and a ceiling decorated with unlit lanterns made of fine metals and jewels. The lanterns would be lit on days the priest was honored.

And standing in the center of the room, staring at the now-open coffin, was Priest Jafr.

Zok stepped inside, the others filing in behind him. "Jafr, what have you done?!"

The Human turned around. He was middle-aged, with a lined face and short black hair. His white attire was stained dark with dirt and dust from spending so much time below ground. A torch was set to the side, lighting the room up and sending flickering shadows against the walls. "Brother Zok. What exactly is it you are accusing me of?"

The Paladin threw his arms wide. "All of this! Destroying the coffins, looting the bodies. What are you looking for?"

"Something that is not here," Jafr responded in a

clear, calm voice.

Zok's eyes narrowed. "Did you kill High Priest Amon?"

A smile tugged at the corners of Jafr's mouth. "These hands did not kill him, no. But they would have."

Zok pointed back to the corridor, shouting, "You will come with me back to the temple and answer for what you've done here!"

Jafr tilted his head to the side. "I am not going anywhere." Then his hands shot forward, and a thunderous burst of energy rippled out from him.

Zok felt the impact as if something massive had hit him. He was thrown back and into Sen, the two falling onto the ground and sliding back a few feet. He saw Foxy and Wolfie both slide past them, and heard the impacts of Jade, Artemis, and Skar as they slammed into the wall, still inside of the room.

Zok sprang to his feet, racing back inside as Artemis rapidly notched an arrow and snapped, "You're hopelessly outnumbered, ugly man. You cannot survive this fight."

Jafr then whispered a few words and flicked his wrists. Spectral daggers made of green mist appeared before him, shooting out at each individual. Jade pulled to the side, the dagger aimed at her hitting the stone wall and vanishing. Zok blocked with his shield, and Sen with his axe. The one aimed for Skar sliced his shoulder, disappearing after hitting but leaving behind a bloody wound. The Wizard cried out in pain. Artemis spun away from the one that flew at her, immediately shooting her arrow afterwards with barely a second to aim. The arrow flew straight at Jafr's chest, but the Human threw up a magic shield, deflecting the blow.

A vine ripped its way free from the stone ground and wound around the priest's leg, tethering him in place. As she focused on the spell, Jade said, "Stop! We don't want to hurt you!"

Skar made a gesture with his wand and four small, burning orbs shot forward, impacting on Jafr's body. The priest hissed in pain as his clothes and skin sizzled where the magic struck. He then brought out a short sword from behind his cloak and sliced through the vine holding him with one heavy chop. He made to run for the exit, sword out to cut down anyone that stood in his way.

"Stop!" Zok shouted.

But Jafr swung his sword at the Paladin, forcing Zok to block the attack and step out of the way. For a moment the two locked eyes. And Zok could see something else behind the anger. A confusion, a struggle. Something wasn't right.

"Priest?" Zok asked, reaching out to grab the man's arm.

As Jafr pushed it off, he stumbled, and just barely got out the words, "I'm sorry" before an arrow whizzed through the air and shot clean through his head, an explosion of blood scattering against the stone wall. The body paused, teetered, and then fell.

Silence stretched out as they all stared at the body. Zok looked down at his own armor, seeing Jafr's blood streaked across it. He looked up at the rest of the group. "He . . . he just said he was sorry."

Sen huffed. "Sorry for what? Trying to kill us?"

The Paladin shook his head. "No, it was something else. I saw it in his eyes. It was like he was struggling with what he was doing."

The pirate was unfazed. "A bit too late to have a crisis of conscience."

Jade stepped closer. "Do you think his actions were being controlled? Like blackmail or something worse?"

Skar nodded thoughtfully, tucking his wand away. "You mean like mind control?"

A pained look crossed Artemis' face. "Oh . . . I . . . feel kind of bad now."

Sen patted her on the shoulder, his red scaled hand massive in comparison to her smaller, Half-Elven form. "We tried to get him to stop."

Zok didn't feel anger towards the archer. He wasn't even sure what he felt. Hollow, perhaps. But he did say, "We could have questioned him."

"Or he could have killed you," Artemis stated. "You were hesitating."

Sen looked over to the Wizard. "You said mind control. But nobody is here. Are there spells powerful enough to reach someone out of sight?"

Skar nodded. "There is powerful magic that can control someone for hours, having them carry out the will of the caster. Could it be that Jenkins man?"

"I'm not sure," Jade said. "He's revealed himself to us twice before, why stay incognito now?"

Zok considered for a long moment, staring at the body, the tombs, the treasure lying out over the floor. "The most important question is . . . what was he looking for? What was worth destroying these coffins and killing High Priest Amon for?" His blue eyes flicked back up to the group. "Others could be involved. You all need to go back to the tavern. I don't want any of you in danger. I am going to go look into Jafr's room and see if I can learn anything. Then, I will tell the others that I found him down here dead."

"Do you need help?" Jade asked.

He shook his head. "I think it's best I do this alone."

They left the body behind, and Zok couldn't help but feel sick to his stomach as they exited the tombs and he was left alone. Not because of the gore, he had seen such things before. But the realization that something very sinister was at work here, pulling strings from the shadows. How certain could he be that what happened in the tombs wasn't witnessed? If Jafr's mind had been controlled, could that happen to any of them?

He crossed to one of the smaller buildings that housed rooms for other temple members. He knew who each belonged to. Easily enough he made his way to Jafr's door. It was locked. Zok glanced around, ensuring nobody was watching. Then he took out his dagger, jammed it between the door and frame, and broke the lock with a *snap*. The door swung silently open.

Zok stepped inside. It was a simple room. A bed sat

in the far corner, beside a desk crowded with parchments. There was a small kitchen and dining area that looked mostly bare. A first glance over didn't show anything suspicious. He headed to the desk and glanced through the parchments. Most of it seemed unimportant. There were notes on activities within the temple regarding services and schedules for a new squire. There was an event list for the Day of Sealing celebration, which was happening in two days. There was also a shopping list for the general store.

But then there was a letter. It was unsigned and written in curving handwriting. It read:

Jafr,

I will question Amon regarding the Lantern of Vicrum. You look in the tombs to see if it's been buried. If that doesn't work, we'll need to travel to Soleia.

Zok frowned as he read the letter over a few times. The Lantern of Vicrum? What was that? The name Vicrum was certainly familiar. A great Dwarf king who ruled over Soleia, which was once considered a golden city of immense wealth and influence. Vicrum had been instrumental in sealing away the dragons that had wreaked havoc on the world. This event was celebrated every year throughout Corventos as the Day of Sealing. But that was nearly sixteen hundred years ago, now. Vicrum was long dead, and Soleia was no more, a ruin in the desert far south.

Zok tucked the letter in his pack. He didn't understand what was going on. He didn't know who he could trust. That letter could have been written by someone else in the temple. The person who killed Priest Amon. This mystery he needed to solve on his own. Which meant there was only one choice.

He had to go to Soleia.

.

.

.

Sen

.

.

.

Sen always enjoyed a party. When major holidays came around, Somberdale celebrated with the charm of a small town. The atmosphere was relaxed, there was plenty of food, drink, and music. The Spring Festival on the first of Aujir was marked by flowers, colorful clothes, and the celebration of new life. The thirtieth of Copprum was Armistice Day, honoring the end of a three-decade civil war. Then there were the Fire Giant games in the summer, one of Sen's favorite competitions, autumn brought Haunting Day, and the Night of the Raven Mother followed to honor those who had passed, winter brought Viscera's Comet, and many other holidays and parties all in between.

But today was the twenty-first of Morívaec. The Day of Sealing. In remembrance of when the tyranny of dragons was brought to an end. Everyone knew the tale, even Sen who did not have much interest in the laws and traditions of Corventos.

From where he lounged on the beach, Sen could see the party before him. Children wore colorful masks of dragons, chasing each other around the legs of their parents. A band played on a wooden stage, singing the tales of Arcanist Viscera Dante. A food stand served small pastries that were supposed to look like the golden city of Soleia. But no one really quite knew what the city had looked like. It had mysteriously fallen to ruin during the civil war, the War for the World, as it was known. When Humans, Dwarves, and Elves were too preoccupied fighting each other in the north to notice events in the south. The people of Somberdale danced, cheered, chatted, and lounged about on the sand. Night had fallen, and blazing torches lined the beach as well as magical orbs of light that hung overhead. Out on the water, barges floated bearing loads of fireworks.

"Is this seat taken?"

Sen glanced up to see Jade smiling down at him, crinkling the red band tattoo that crossed her face. "I always have room for my Elven friends."

She sat, Foxy curling up beside her. "I haven't seen Zok since he told us about the Lantern of Vicrum."

"Neither have I. I think he's been busy with the funerals for High Priest Amon and Jafr."

Jade sighed, shaking her head. "This has been hard for him. He's worried he's going to find out there is corruption inside the temple, rather than an outside force at work here."

"What do you think it is?"

"Hard to tell. Perhaps Soleia will have more answers."

"I don't know what we're going to find there. It's just a ruin now."

Jade nodded. "I've never been to the Expanse. And I've never heard of a Lantern of Vicrum. But it's the best lead we have." She looked to him. "Is your ship ready?"

"My crew stored the last of the supplies today. We will be good for a sail down the coast. You and Zok have never sailed on my ship before, this should be fun."

An anxious expression passed over her face. "I'm not a big fan of the ocean. But it's faster than walking all that way."

Sen looked out over the beach. He saw the Wizard Skar admiring some masks. And Artemis with her wolf browsed the food stalls, her arms already full of various snacks and desserts. He asked, "What do you think of those two? They are coming with us, after all."

"It's good they are coming with us," Jade replied. "If Jenkins has a hand in this they should be involved as well. But as for what I think of them . . . they're too secretive."

"You think so?"

"Yes. Artemis will never give specifics on her life.

And much of what Skar says just doesn't make sense. I've never heard of Volcano Island. Not in all the long years I've lived."

"Neither have I, and I know all the islands," Sen stated.

They sat in silence for several minutes, watching the celebration. Then the Wild Elf asked, "How long of a journey will it be to the Expanse?"

"I was looking at the map this morning," he answered. "We will have to make port in Vonkai. It's the closest city. With fair winds and a smooth sea, it should take about a week."

Jade sighed. "Just great."

A few more torches were lit around the wooden stage as the music act departed. A Bard stepped up on stage, his clothes colorful and a lute in his hands. Children in various masks lingered in the shadows around the stage. Sen knew this performance well. It was the story of the Day of Sealing.

The Bard strummed a few times, bringing the crowd to a hush, before beginning. "It is said, over two thousand years ago, dragons ruled the land. And their dominion and power are what shaped the landscape." On cue children ascended to the stage, wearing dragon masks of different colors. "The white dragons with their breath of ice wreaked havoc in the north." A child with a white dragon mask roared. "The black dragons that breathed acid corrupted the landscapes, creating swamps and bogs." Another child in a black dragon mask bounded about, roaring and snarling. "There were blue dragons that breathed lightning, and green with their poison breath. But the most terrible and feared of all were the great red dragons that reigned fire from the sky."

In his peripheral vision Sen could see Jade's expression darken. It was curious, but just as soon as the look came it passed, enjoyment back on her face again.

As the children danced around the stage, the Bard continued. "It was considered the dragons of colorful scales were enemies of the people that lived in those days. But dragons with scales the colors of silver and gold could be reasoned with. But these passive dragons were quickly vanquished by the more violent, dominant breeds." Any children with masks of metallic colors dropped from the stage. And then some without masks came into the light. They were dressed in clothes made to mimic an ancient era. The Bard said, "To stop this terror, the people banded together to seal the dragons away. High Elf Arcanist Viscera Dante was the first to discover different planes of existence. She proposed the idea to her fellow mages to lock the dragons away in other planes. To set the trap, the Dwarves of the great under-mountain city De Behl Marr mined a great horde of gold and jewels. And with these riches they built the city of Soleia, the City of the Sun."

Sen watched with amusement as a small replica of what Soleia was supposed to have looked like was carried in a circle around the stage. Its buildings were gold and round.

A child with a fake beard walked to the center and the Bard stood over him, saying, "Dwarf Vicrum Grodstrum was named King over Soleia. The city gleamed like a pile of treasure in the desert sun. And the dragons were drawn to it." The children in the colorful dragon masks slowly approached the replica city. "As they came close to the city the armies of Humans, Elves, and Dwarves fought. Mages opened portals, warriors then pressing to send the dragons through them. The battle wore on, and though many dragons were sealed away, the armies of people were dwindling. It seemed they would ultimately lose this battle."

The children proceeded to play fight, the dragons roaring, and wooden swords and axes were raised high by those pretending to be ancient people. The little blonde girl that played the role of Viscera Dante waved her hands dramatically in the air, pretending to cast magic spells.

The Bard strummed his lute aggressively until he paused, continuing, "Thunderous footsteps were heard over the desert. From a dust storm came the Giants. The ground shook with their steps and their shadows were cast long over the sand." Children wearing heavy boots and fearsome Giant masks stepped up, making as much noise as they could. The

Bard said, "They turned the tide of battle, and the last of the dragons were either sealed or fled to be hunted down over the years. The Giants then returned to wherever they came from, never to be seen again."

Sen chuckled as the children finished their battle and the stage was cleared.

The Bard stepped up front, playing a few more notes on his lute. "That day was forever marked in history as the Day of Sealing. Such a momentous victory it was, that our calendar year begins then. And as such, this is the year 1560. And we celebrate 1,560 years without the oppression of dragons."

The audience cheered and clapped as the performance ended. Over the water, fireworks lit up the sky, flashing various colors and filling the air with *booms* and *pops*.

Sen turned to his Wild Elf friend. "Do you think I could have slayed a dragon?"

Her expression was pensive as she replied, "I'm not sure any one person can kill something with so much power."

"If a dragon were to descend on Somberdale right now, I'd like to see who would run and hide, and who would stay and fight."

A sly smile crossed her face as her green eyes glanced up at him. "Some might say those that run are the wiser."

"And I would say history is shaped by those who fight."

She laughed. "You are a very brave pirate, Sen. We are lucky to have you with us as we head to the Expanse."

"I'll never say no to adventure."

.

.

.

The sky was bright and clear again as the Scarlet Maiden left the docks of Somberdale. The plan was to travel straight down the western coastline and then make their way around the southwestern edge of Corventos, making port in

Vonkai. The ship was well-stocked for the journey. The food and supplies would be more than enough to last Sen, his crew, the four guests, and the two animals. They would need to resupply in Vonkai, however, for the return journey.

At the helm, Sen confidently directed his ship. The ocean was a sapphire blue around them, the waves gently rocking the hull. To his left he could make out the coast, even though they were quite a distance away. Cliffs, trees, mountain peaks, and beaches broke up the horizon line.

His gaze turned to the deck below. His crew was busy making certain the ship was in peak condition for such a journey. He could see his Bosun, a muscular female Half-Orc of green skin, shouting orders at her two assistants as they adjusted the rigging. Jade and Zok leaned against the railing, watching the coast pass by. Skar wandered about and appeared to get in everyone's way. And Artemis had climbed up to the crow's nest, the wind blowing her blonde braid out behind her.

"It is a good wind, Captain," his First Mate, Kailo, said as he stood beside him. "The gods of the sea and wind smile on us this morning."

Sen glanced over at the bald Human. "Let us hope so. We don't want to be forced to make port anywhere near the capital."

Rain, his Quartermaster and another Human herself stepped up. "Captain, the crew is in high spirits. They are glad to be back on the sea."

Sen smiled. "So am I."

The morning passed uneventfully. The air smelled of salt and wood, and the noises of conversations, feet on the deck, and sails rippling was a steady hum. Once Sen felt confident of their course and the waves, he passed over the helm to his Navigator. Then he headed down to the deck to see his friends. Each step over the wood was familiar, each imperfection well memorized. He knew this ship better than any other place or any other person. It was like the ship lived and breathed around him.

He had spent his formative years on this ship,

serving under Captain Willa Lance. She was a pirate to be feared, a threatening presence whenever her ship approached. But she was also a fiercely loyal captain, a good mentor, and would die for any member of crew. And so many on the seas took to calling her the Baroness. Sen had worked his way up through the ranks of her crew to become First Mate. Despite how much the Baroness loved this ship, when a far more powerful ship came along she became captain of it, instead. He remembered her telling him that there was no one else she would pass her ship to than him. And so he had become a captain.

It had been awhile since he'd seen the Baroness. He missed her friendship very much, but being a captain came with responsibilities. It was ironic, since in all other aspects of his life he avoided those. He had to ensure his crew was safe, that they were paid, and that they always had a good time. He had to watch over his ship and keep her repaired and sea-worthy. As much as he enjoyed partying in Somberdale, getting drunk in the taverns, and fighting for gold, the sea was where his heart was.

Sen approached Zok and Jade. The Paladin had his elbows resting atop the wooden railing, his shoulder-length brown hair blowing back from his face. Jade leaned with her back to the ocean, holding her fox in her arms and petting him lovingly. Sen knew the two of them were very attractive. Elven blood created a beautiful bone structure in their faces, a gracefulness to their bodies, and a brightness in their eyes. He'd seen the way others in Somberdale stared at them. Young men and women would blush and watch them from afar. But for their part, Zok and Jade did not seem interested. The Paladin would offer a smile in return at onlookers. The Druid would ignore them altogether. It didn't seem to come from haughtiness. Instead, it seemed Jade had too many things on her mind. Sen reasoned, though, at over four hundred years of age surely she had someone romantic in her life. At some point, she must have.

For himself, Sen was a young Dragonborn. His race lived a decade or two over one hundred years old. He liked the idea of finding a partner he could sail the seas with. Someone to go drinking with after a long day. There had been one such person in his life. A Human woman with scarlet hair that had sailed as a pirate, as well, before she tired of the life. She'd left to live in Vonkai, and part of him wondered if she was still there. He would need to check when he got into port. It would be nice to see her again. She would be proud that he was a captain now. He wondered what her reaction would be when he told her he'd named his ship after her.

"How are you liking the sea?" the Dragonborn asked, coming to a stop beside his two friends.

Zok smiled. "I've been on a fishing boat before with my father, but never a vessel this large. I am enjoying it."

Jade heaved a long sigh. "I don't like the ocean."

"If you are feeling sick, we have elixirs below deck," Sen suggested, seeing the slightly green look to her face.

"Thanks, Sen."

The large pirate hesitated. He wanted to check on his friend's wellbeing, but didn't know how to approach the subject. He rubbed one foot against the deck before venturing, "So, Zok . . . how have you been? After everything that has happened with your temple."

The Half-Elf was quiet a moment, staring out at the mountainous coastline. His white cloak rippled off his shoulders. "It's been a lot. I feel like I've barely had time to process my thoughts. I'm just reacting."

"It's your quick reactions that have given the leads you need," Jade stated. "Otherwise we may never have found out about the Lantern of Vicrum."

"And," Sen said slowly, "how do you feel about that Jafr guy? I know we've all killed before in self-defense. But that situation was . . . different. He was trying to get away. And he apologized right before. Are you . . . okay with all that?"

A sadness washed over Zok's face. "I wish it hadn't happened. It was all too fast. But there's no point in worrying over it now. Jafr is gone and all we can hope for are answers in Soleia."

Sen wasn't sure Zok *was* okay with it. A temple member had been killed by their hand. One they speculated had been under an enchantment. And the Paladin had lied about the circumstances. He worried about his friend.

A screech interrupted his thoughts. The three of them whipped around to see a seagull fall to the deck, an arrow pierced through it. Then Artemis came sliding down the rigging, her bow around the rope to prevent her hands from getting burned. She landed lightly, rolling to absorb the momentum. Her wolf trotted up, tongue hanging out.

"That thing pooped on me," Artemis said. "So now it can be dinner."

Sen let out a low whistle. "Nice shot. Is this your first time on the ocean, Artemis?"

The Half-Elf archer nodded. "It is. I love it!"

Jade asked, "Where did you get your wolf?"

Artemis kneeled down and hugged the large animal, his tail thumping happily against the deck. "I found him alone as a puppy. He's been with me for a few years now." She looked up. "Your fox is cute."

Jade smiled at that. "Thanks. I rescued him from a hunter's trap." Her gaze went up and down Wolfie. "Your wolf is much bigger than most. Is he a dire wolf?"

"I don't think so," the archer answered. "But I have noticed more power behind him than other wolves. Perhaps a mixed breed."

Zok asked, "Are you around other wolves often enough to notice?"

She shrugged. "I'm a Ranger. I'm in touch with the wilds and I've seen many animals. I can speak to them, you know. I know some spells."

Jade's brown eyebrows raised. "Those are Druid spells. Who taught you?"

"People I grew up with."

Sen held up a hand. "Wait, wait. You can *talk* to animals? This I have to see."

Artemis stood up, hands on her hips. "I will ask Wolfie a question. What should it be?"

Sen replied, "Ask him what he thinks of Zok."

The Half-Elf archer moved her hands in symbols of the spell, saying words in Elvish. Then she looked to Wolfie and spoke, but only the noises of snarls and growls emitted. The wolf responded in kind. She looked up at the others and said in Common, "He said Brother Zok smells like flowers."

The Paladin, who was frowning deeply through this process, replied, "Flowers? I think he smells the incense from the temple."

Wolfie made a few more noises and Artemis translated, "He also says he likes the fox."

"Aw," Jade replied. "I'm sure Foxy likes him, too." She sat her animal down and he went over to the large wolf, the two of them smelling one another before bouncing off to play.

.

.

.

Three days of sailing passed. The sea was calm and the winds steady. Sen couldn't have asked for better weather. The mountains fell away on the coast, and they passed the entrance to the river known as The Great Divide. It was a main route for trade to and from the capital. Luckily, the only ship they passed was far down the river and they were able to slip by unnoticed. His crew was on their best behavior for the guests, though one night of drunken fun resulted in a brawl between the cook's assistant and a deckhand. His four guests made themselves at home and helped out wherever they could. Jade spent most of her time below deck, unhappy with the way the ship rocked. He often saw Zok going through sparring movements with dagger and hammer. Skar was interested in exploring every inch of the ship, and Artemis was usually found in the crow's nest shooting down birds for food.

It was late evening on the fourth day, and Sen was in his quarters going over the map. A compass weighed down the paper on one end, a bottle of rum on the other. As his red scaled finger traced the coastline of the Korventine Empire he was pleased to see they were making good progress. They may even arrive a day earlier than planned.

His quarters were adorned with treasures he'd collected through his travels. Empty bottles from various ports sat on shelves. There was gold jewelry, shining gems, a chest of gold coins, statuettes made of ivory, goblets of silver, and other items that he kept just for their whimsy. His gaze moved up to his newest collection. The lanterns that had hung in the tomb where they'd fought Jafr. They glittered in the light, swaying with the ship. He had them hung all over the ceiling. It was the first thing he'd stolen that he was a bit ashamed of. He knew Zok would be very unhappy if he found out. Which is why he would *never* find out.

A knock came at his door and he heard Kailo's voice. "Captain! Rocks ahead."

Sen crossed the room in a few long strides, exiting with his first mate. "How much time do we have?"

"Twenty minutes, sir," Kailo replied as they hurried up onto the deck.

The sun had just hit the horizon, creating a golden shimmer on the water. Sen hurriedly went to the helm, taking the wheel in his large hands. He could see most of his crew on deck, awaiting orders. He also saw Zok, Jade, Artemis, and Skar watching. Up ahead there was a series of massive rock formations rising from the ocean. A few were columns that were ten feet wide and rose up over thirty feet high. But there was one that was much larger. It was big enough to be an island, and greenery grew on the top. A dark entrance looked out, large enough for his entire ship to sail into. A cave of some sort.

"Stay ready!" Sen shouted. "We're going around!"

He adjusted the direction of the Scarlet Maiden, moving to go the long way around the rocks. It was best not to risk going in between. He felt the ship respond and move under his instruction. The wind beat against his bare chest and the lowering sun warmed his scales. He expertly guided the ship, passing in front of the colossal cavern entrance. And as he did, a bird-like cry echoed from within, loud enough to make the whole crew flinch and turn at the noise.

"What was that, Captain?" Kailo gasped, his hands drifting down from where they'd covered his ears.

Sen frowned, staring at the darkness inside the cave. The scream sounded again, filled with pain, before it was abruptly cut short. A snarl reverberated out, along with the noise of bones breaking. His gaze drifted over to his friends. Surprise and interest were on their faces as they regarded the cavern.

Making up his mind, Sen shouted, "Lower the anchor and ready a boat!"

"Captain?" his Quartermaster Rain implored.

Sen descended to the deck, his footfalls making heavy thuds on the steps. "I'm going to check it out. There will be no beast on this sea that Captain Sen doesn't know about. Kailo and Rain, you are in command in my absence." He looked to the four non-sailors. "Come with me."

Two rowboats had to be prepared to carry the weight of two Dragonborn. The fox and wolf were left behind as the five of them descended to the ocean. Sen, Jade, and Artemis were in one boat, Zok and Skar in the other. The sun was halfway below the horizon by the time they rowed into the cavern. Darkness fell around them, but the noise of eating could be heard deeper within.

Sen dipped the oars into the water, his biceps tensing as he took them deeper. Once it became too dark Artemis lit a torch, the fire reflecting in their eyes. Sen could smell burnt meat in the air. He exchanged looks with the group, but they all kept quiet.

After a few more minutes they reached a rocky bank. Pulling the boats up, they went on foot down a tunnel. It was enormous, the ceiling soaring high above them. The tunnel turned sharply to the left, and the noise of eating became louder. As well as an intense heat that simmered in the air.

Sen paused at the corner and held up a hand. Signaling the others to wait. On the water, he was the Captain. And he wouldn't allow anyone to get hurt under his watch. He crept forward, keeping the rough wall at his back. As he left the torchlight behind, a new light source shone ahead. It was red and gold, and he followed it until he came to the entrance of a massive cavern. Stalactites hung from the ceiling, twisting downwards. And all around the room were piles and piles of gold. Coins were stacked in huge mounds, glimmering. Jewels of multiple colors sat by crowns, plates, necklaces, and brooches. Sen's yellow eyes widened as he took this all in, his breath caught in his throat.

Then his gaze drifted to the light source. A fire burned on the floor, and within could be seen bones and feathers from whatever creature had been slayed. And there, sitting just behind the flames, was a large gold dragon.

Its scales were the same color as the treasure about it. Wings were neatly folded at its back and its tail looped around a body as large as the Scarlet Maiden. A long neck held the head up high. And brown eyes gazed in amusement down at Sen.

"Well," the dragon said in his native language. "This is a surprise."

Sen swallowed his tight throat. He returned in Draconic, "My apologies, I did not realize this island belonged to anyone."

"Oh? Then why are you here?"

Another voice came from behind Sen, speaking in Draconic as well. "We heard noises. Screaming. And came to investigate."

The pirate turned to see Skar slowly moving forward. But he was alone, the others not making themselves visible. The Wizard came to stand by him. There was fear in his red eyes but his expression was carefully crafted to look calm.

A smile spread across the dragon's face. "Yes, that was my meal." His head moved closer. "You two look like dessert."

"Now, hold on," Skar said. "The tales say the dragons of gold and silver don't eat people."

The dragon chuckled. "Then the tales paint us a kinder color than we are. But, people are not my preference.

Still, I need something to top off my meal."

Sen held out his bottle of rum. "I have this."

The dragon regarded it. "That is very small for my mouth. But perhaps this will make it better." He shimmered and turned on the spot, his form shrinking down and down to their height. His body morphed and folded and became a Human. The Human was bald with golden brown skin. He wore loose silk pants and was bare-chested save for an orange vest. Jewelry of gold adorned his wrists, neck, and ears.

He held out his hand. "The drink?"

Sen passed it over. Under normal circumstances he would not share his personal stash of alcohol. But there were allowances to be made for a dragon.

After taking a long drink the dragon grinned at them. "You can tell your friends to enter. I can smell them. All Elven, I think?"

"Two Half-Elves and one full blood," Sen replied. He glanced over his shoulder and shouted in Common, "Go ahead and come inside."

Zok, Jade, and Artemis cautiously came forward. Sen could tell from their expressions they had an idea of what was going on, even if they couldn't understand Draconic and didn't see the gold dragon form.

"Hello," the dragon greeted in the language they could all understand. "I didn't expect so much company today. What are all of your names?"

"I am Captain Sen of the Scarlet Maiden. This is Skar, a Wizard. Brother Zok, Paladin of the Temple of the Holy Dragon. Jade the Druid. And Artemis the Ranger."

Amusement glittered in the dragon's eyes. "My name is Draxis. I am a gold dragon and this is my home."

Zok spoke, his tone cautious. "We are . . . surprised to see a dragon here."

"I am as surprised to see you here," Draxis responded. "Where are you tiny people heading?"

"Vonkai," Sen answered. "We're heading down the coast to make port."

A look passed over Draxis' face. Sen couldn't quite pin down the expression before it was gone, replaced with humor once more. "Ah, the desert. I haven't been there in a long time. Well, as you can imagine, I don't like wanderers coming into my home. I especially don't want to draw attention to myself or have more *unexpected* visitors arrive."

Sen swallowed his tight throat. Despite his bravado discussing dragons with Jade during the Day of Sealing celebration, actually being faced down with one was terrifying. The idea that this humanoid could grow again and burn them all in a second made him choose his words carefully. This was not a time for reckless action. He reminded himself again that on the sea, he was the Captain. And he was responsible for the group's safety. So, he answered in a calm tone, "We will not tell anyone about you. We understand that would put you and your treasure in danger, and we don't want that."

A low chuckle came from Draxis. "It would put someone in danger, certainly."

Sen took one step back. "We will take our leave now. You may keep the rum. If we can ever be of any assistance to you, please let us know."

Draxis considered for a moment. "There is something you can do for me. In exchange for leaving here peacefully."

Sen shared a glance with the others before asking, "And what would that be?"

"Pirates were in here not long ago, unfortunately when I wasn't home. They made off with quite a bit of gold. As much as they could carry, I'm sure. I intend to stay here for their inevitable return and enact my vengeance. But there is one treasure they stole I am eager to have back. If you happen upon it and return it to me, I will reward you greatly."

Sen's gaze went over all the piles of treasure around. His interest was piqued. "It would be my pleasure. What item is it that was stolen?"

"A compass made of gold. With no cardinal directions on it. If you find it, bring it back to me."

"I certainly will," the pirate replied.

Draxis waved his hand. "Now go. I am tired of speaking with all of you." When they hesitated, he turned and reverted back to dragon form, his wings splayed wide. That was enough to send them all back, walking quickly but without breaking into a full run.

The five of them went down the tunnel and back to their two rowboats. There was a moment's quiet hesitation as they all stood there. Sen could feel his heart pounding. He looked to the others. Zok and Artemis appeared relieved, Jade seemed deeply worried, and Skar gave him a nod in respect.

"How is that possible?" Zok said softly. "I thought all the dragons were gone. We should have asked how he was still around."

Sen shook his head. "I didn't want to anger him by bringing up a sore subject. Listen, don't tell my crew. I don't want any of them going back alone and getting killed. I will let them know when the time is right."

"Should we look for the compass and bring it back?" Artemis asked.

Sen smiled. "I think we should. It can't hurt to be on friendly terms with a dragon. Plus, I like rewards."

.

.

.

UNOLÉ

.
.
.

Unolé's search was not going well. She snuck around as many buildings as she could, eavesdropped on conversations, peeked into windows, and even paid off a few more residents of the Hells for information. But nothing led to the whereabouts of her sister. Her sleuthing gathered some information about slaves in the Hells. But there were a number of places they were taken. Either into dungeons to be tortured, into the Caverns of Carnage to be put to work, or immediately sold to a high-ranking devil for servitude. And none of those places Unolé could find, let alone get in.

As the day passed, her spirits dropped. She wasn't sure if night had fallen or not, there was no sun or moon in the s'.. But shops were closing up, and she was getting very tired. It was time to sleep until her meeting the next day.

"We could go back to that tavern," Unolé said softly to Teshuva, making her way down the alleys to avoid being seen as much as possible. "They may have a room to stay in."

"That sounds like a wise choice," the colorful coatl's voice entered her mind. He was still hidden in her dark hood. "We've done as much as we can for today."

"And not a damn thing to show for it."

"Patience, Unolé."

It was hard to be patient. Every day that passed could be the day she lost her sister forever. But she knew there was wisdom behind his words. Recklessness would not aid her here. She had to make sure she left no stone unturned and no avenue unexplored.

As she headed between buildings, making her way towards the tavern, a pig-like humanoid turned the corner. They both nearly ran into each other, jerking backwards with wide eyes. He surveyed her, gave an annoyed grunt, and then walked around her and off into the alley. Unolé turned to watch him go. She wasn't going to turn her back to anyone in this place. She noticed the pig man had a few whips on his belt and a sword strapped to his back, stained with old blood. But what caught her attention the most was a money pouch on his belt.

Her eyes shone. She'd lost a lot of gold coins already having to pay people off for information. It would be nice to get that money back. Plus extra. Unolé slowly followed the man, her steps not making a noise. The money pouch didn't look like it weighed too much. If she removed it quickly, he wouldn't notice.

Getting as close as she dared, Unolé whispered the words of a spell and lifted one hand. A spectral hand drifted out from her skin, floating forward to the money pouch. It fit its slender fingers around the knot and expertly untied it, the pouch coming free from the belt smoothly and silently.

Joy filled her heart as the spectral hand floated back, depositing the money in her grasp. Turning, she quickly scurried off around another corner. Pressing her back to the wall despite the heat radiating from it, Unolé put the pouch in her own pack, tucking it out of sight.

"You know some magic, I see," Teshuva's voice said, sounding thoroughly unamused.

"Just a bit," she replied. "A friend of mine in the Shadow Guild taught me."

"We should hurry before that creature notices he's been robbed."

"Sorry, couldn't resist."

Unolé followed his instruction, making her way back to the tavern without stopping. She used some of the stolen gold to get a room, and then went upstairs for the night. The room was small and cramped, windowless with only a lantern for light. She didn't even want to contemplate the smell. But it was safe, at least.

The Half-Fiend hopped up on the bed, pushing some strands of white hair from her eyes, and went to counting the coins in the pouch. Twenty-five gold and ten silver pieces. Not a bad haul.

Teshuva glided from her hood and settled down on the bed. He regarded her with accusatory eyes. "That was an unnecessary risk."

"It *was* necessary. If I'm going to keep paying others off for information I need coins to do so." At the disapproval coming from him, she added, "What? Does your god not like stealing?"

Teshuva sighed. "I am not judging. We will receive no mercy or help from anyone here in the Hells, and likely most other places we venture. Just be careful."

"I will."

She put up the coins and set her packs to the side. The bed was hard and the blanket stiff. She doubted she would sleep well. The thought that tomorrow she could have her sister back spun around in her mind. She knew better than to be hopeful. Hope just led to disappointments. But in a place as dark as this plane of existence, she had to have something to hold onto.

She didn't know what she expected the Hells to be like, but it certainly wasn't this. A society that feigned organization but was built on mistrust and secrets. She found the prevalence of slaves particularly disturbing. Slavery was illegal in the Korventine Empire. And although she'd never been outside of An'Ock, the stories and gossip she heard about the Eleste and the eastern lands called the Iron Gauntlet never mentioned slavery. Once, however, she overheard travelers from Eleste'si mention beings from the Deep Hollows kidnapping citizens for slavery. But she had no idea where the Deep Hollows were.

The creatures that lived here in the Hells were strange to look upon, but what had caught her attention most was their blatant cruelty. Still, she preferred that over cruelty hidden behind fake smiles. She would like to learn more about the Hells. Perhaps she could ask Teshuva for information. But that would be a chat for a later time. Right now, she had to focus on her sister.

And so, with her two daggers within reach, she fell asleep.

.

.

.

Unolé sat upon the red-tiled rooftop, gazing out over the capital city of An'Ock. Houses and buildings jumbled together in this district, the roads indistinguishable at a distance. The crescent moon cast silver light over the castle, high up past the Third Gate. Its towers rose black against the sky, its flags lifting slightly in the breeze. A gray castle with three towers on a field of white. The flag of the royal family.

"I thought I would find you up here."

She turned to see Fade ascending the roof, dark hair ruffled back from his face. His boots gave soft thuds as he closed the distance and sat beside her, crossing his legs. For a moment, they both gazed out over the city.

"I know it's late," she said. "I just needed some time to myself."

"Grandmother sent me looking for you," Fade replied. "You don't want to get on her bad side, Unolé."

"And what would she do if I did?"

Fade chuckled, shaking his head. The swirling tattoo-like patterns upon his skin barely showed in the darkness. "You are brazen. Keep in her good graces, at least for Unatchi's sake. There are not a lot of options out there for people that look like you. Or me, for that matter. The Shadow Guild is a good home. I know it's hard to see at first, but we all have each other's backs. Medric and Sasha have saved my life on more than one occasion. They would do the same for you."

"Unless the mission is more important?"

He sighed. "Fine. Be difficult. All I'm trying to say is the Guild can be your home, if you want it to be. It's better than the life you and your sister used to live."

Unolé reflected on all the years living on the streets, huddling in dark corners to sleep, and stealing from vendors for food. Now they had shelter. They had people that depended on them. They had access to clothes and food. But she worried about this life for Unatchi. The girl was so young to be part of a thieving Guild. She worried if they wanted to leave, they wouldn't be able to.

But what other options were there? This was better than living on the streets.

"I appreciate your words, Fade," she answered. "The Guild has been good to us. It's just been a big change. I worry about the way it impacts Unatchi most of all."

"She is a strong kid. She'll be okay."

A moment of comfortable silence passed between them. An'Ock was never fully quiet, even at night. Distant conversation could be heard, horses' hooves on stone, the wheels of carts, the sounds of animals. She could see light coming from The Proven Right, one of the districts inside the First Gate. That was the place to go for nightlife, with its rowdy bars, gambling, and fighting coliseum. She'd stolen quite a bit from there. The drunk patrons made for easy targets. Beyond that she could see the rising temple roofs of The Divine Path, the center of worship for the many gods of the city. And the final section of the First Gate, the Grand Bazaar, was quiet and dark. Its many shops closed for the night. Beyond this district, rising with the hill, she could make out the Sunrise Terrace. Where the wealthy lived. And higher beyond that, past the Third Gate, the castle grounds.

Fade said, "I wonder what it's like to live in that castle?"

Unolé regarded the imposing stone structure. "I'd like to think life is easier. But it probably isn't. Life is hard for everyone."

"I saw King Ulyssius Greycastle the other day. He was walking the streets just outside of the Sunrise Terrace with a big entourage. He was wearing so much gold! The thief in me was tempted, to be honest."

She laughed. "I would have liked to see you try."

"Have you been practicing the spells I taught you?"

She gestured in the air, whispering the memorized words. A spectral hand floated past her own and waved. Then *she let it drop and whispered another spell. A small flame, like that of a candle, flickered in her palm. It shone on Fade's bluish skin and green eyes. She knew his blood had a touch of another plane of existence, making his appearance exotic and foreign. For that, he was not always welcome in the city. Not unlike her, with her horns and tail. Some didn't seem to care about the way she looked. Others cursed her for it and called her a demon.*

Unolé let the spell fizzle out, darkness shrouding them again. "Thank you for teaching me. I'll get better at them."

"It's not like you're a Wizard. Study and practice aren't the answers, necessarily. You have innate magic from your fiendish bloodline. Kinda like me. Don't overthink it. Just remember the words and symbols, and feel *it. Magic is about emotion, above all else."*

"I can try. Thanks."

Another moment of silence stretched between them. Fade had been a quick friend once she joined the Shadow Guild. On nights like this, when her mind wandered to dark places and she felt very alone, his company was invaluable.

Fade stood and held out a hand. "C'mon, Unolé. It's time we go back inside."

She took it and they returned to the underbelly of the city.

. . .

Unolé was disoriented when she woke up. Her body ached, the surface she slept on was hard, and there was a terrible smell. At first she thought she was back on the streets with her little sister, sleeping in some alleyway. But as she opened her purple eyes, taking in the tiny and dirty tavern room, her predicament came back to her.

Moaning, she sat up and ran her fingers through her short hair. Teshuva uncurled himself from the foot of the bed, his deep voice saying, "Good morning. Or, whatever passes for morning here."

As she bent over to put on her black boots, she replied, "Do you sleep?"

"Not in the same way you do. But I still require physical rest and recovery from a long day."

"That's certainly what yesterday felt like." Unolé picked up her pack and pulled some food out. Hard rations she'd brought with her for the Shadow Guild's thieving contract. They were especially dry and sparse now, days later, but she preferred that over whatever food was served in the Hells. They probably ate slaves and prisoners. "Do you want any food?"

"I don't require food, although I usually like the taste. You keep it for yourself."

As she finished her breakfast and started putting on the rest of her dark leather clothes and red mask, Unolé said, "So our plan for today is to meet that red-skinned man, get information, pay him as little as possible, and then find my sister."

"We should prepare for the chance that your sister is not here."

Unolé let out a long sigh, dread gnawing at her insides. "I know. What will we do if she isn't?"

"Search another plane, and not give up hope."

The Half-Fiend picked up her two daggers, spun them in her hands, and then stuck them into her belt. She turned to the coatl. "I'll never stop searching. Let's go."

Teshuva hopped into her hood and Unolé exited the room. The stairs creaked under her steps as she made her way down to the first floor. The tavern was mostly empty, only the Succubus barkeep still working and a couple of skeletal patrons at one table. She picked a table that was against the wall with a good view across the room to sit and wait.

With her arms crossed, Unolé watched through the windows for the man she was supposed to meet. It seemed the activity of the city never dwindled. The streets were still busy with strange and malformed denizens going about their business. She saw a line of prisoners led on chains, naked with whip lashes over their bodies, and a carriage full of corpses rumbled by, drawn by black horses with manes of fire.

This wasn't a good place to be. Part of her hoped Unatchi wasn't here. She couldn't imagine the horrors her little sister would witness as a prisoner of the Hells.

Twenty minutes passed before the red-skinned man entered the tavern. His dark eyes trailed the room before spotting her, smiling to reveal his pointed teeth. Stepping up to her table he said, "I am ready to exchange information for coin. But let's do it somewhere more . . . private."

Unolé narrowed her eyes. "What is wrong with here?"

"This is sensitive information. If you want to rescue this little girl, then we should be careful who is watching and listening."

Her purple eyes held his gaze for several seconds before conceding. "Fine. Lead on."

They exited the tavern and returned to the city streets. The sky was a blood red, the buildings that lined the streets darkly colored and drab by comparison. Unolé heard many languages she didn't understand, some she did, all intermixed with laughs, screams, and sobbing. The Half-Fiend stayed focused. The plight of the people here was terrible, but there was nothing she could do about it. Only to remember never to wind up here as a prisoner herself.

They turned a corner and went up to a large rectangular building. The red-skinned man opened the door and they went inside. Unolé was greeted with a massive storage building. The ceiling soared high above her, and the walls were stacked with boxes and barrels. Perhaps once it was essential to a trade business, but now it had seen better days. The vast majority of the building was empty, the floor was dirty, and broken gaps in the walls and ceiling let in slants of red light.

"This is certainly private," Unolé stated, an edge to her voice. Her hands hovered by her daggers.

The man chuckled. "Indeed. I use it as a meeting

point often." From behind a stack of boxes stepped two other individuals. One was a purple-skinned woman with long dark hair and two horns that curved from her forehead back behind her head. The other was a skeletal creature, skin stretched tight across its bones, and leathery wings folded against its back. "No need to worry," the man said, "these are my business associates."

Unolé stopped ten feet away from them, unwilling to get too close. She put her gloved hands on her hips. "Alright. So what information can you offer me?"

The man stood with the others, regarding her with a heated gaze. "And how much coin are you willing to pay?"

"Whatever I think is reasonable."

"And you have the money with you?"

She hesitated, her gaze flicking across each of the three. Something didn't feel right. "Of course I do. Do you have information on the little girl?"

The man sighed, a small smile at his lips. "I contacted my network about new prisoners, slaves, or wanderers brought into the Hells within the last week or so. But no one matched the description you gave me. I feel confident in my sources. That girl is not here."

Unolé felt her spirits fall. Not here. A waste of time. She would have to start her search over again on another plane. "That is . . . unfortunate."

The man held out his hand expectantly. "Pay up."

"I think five gold is reasonable for what information you provided."

"I don't think so. Thirty gold."

Unolé gasped. "You are crazy if you think I'm paying that! You gave me nothing."

The man exchanged a look with his two associates. "I think we are going to take every coin you own. Plus those two daggers. And I think the horns of Half-Fiends sell for quite a bit these days, don't they?" The three of them laughed as they drew weapons. The man and woman both took out knives, the skeletal creature took out a black bow.

With a quick movement Unolé had a dagger in each

hand. "Don't try me."

The man and woman both rushed forward, blades out to stab. Unolé spun away and slashed out, catching the man across his side. The man then brought his knife around again, aiming for her face. But Unolé pulled backwards, the knife passing a few inches from her skin.

There was a rush of wind as the skeletal creature beat its wings, taking to the air. Unolé only had a moment to glance up at it when the purple-skinned woman lunged at her. The Half-Fiend parried but not fast enough. The tip of the knife cut a line of blood across her forehead. At the same time the red-skinned man came at her from the back. Unolé dropped and spun around, sweeping his legs out from underneath him. He fell with a heavy thud, the breath knocked from him.

Unolé barely had time to stand when the woman was on her, grappling her to the ground. The floor was hard and the impact reverberated through her spine. She had just a moment to see the knife coming for her face when she dropped both of her daggers and shot her hands up, grabbing her opponent's wrists. The knife's tip hovered just above her nose as the two fought for control. Her arms shook. The woman shifted her weight, bringing more of it directly above the knife. As the tip drew closer to her skin Unolé screamed out. And she felt a pulse of magic burst through her, hot and fiery. Flames erupted in the air between the two of them. The woman shouted and fell backwards, rolling to put out the fire on her clothes. Just as quickly as they came the flames vanished, leaving bits of ash flaking to the ground.

Unolé scooped up her daggers and jumped to her feet. The man and woman both stood as well, watching her warily. She was not as easy of a target as they had hoped. Unolé's gaze moved up to the skeletal creature. Finally, with an open shot, it notched an arrow.

Unolé tapped into the magic of her feather ring. Two black wings sprouted from her back, a few feathers drifting out into the air. With a great flap they propelled her backwards as the arrow impacted the floor with a *clang*, spinning off wildly. Soaring through the air with ease felt amazing, and her adrenaline surged with this power.

The man and woman both gasped, eyes wide in surprise. With a snarl the man then raced forward, knife flying in a series of quick slashes. Unolé blocked each one, the noise of metal on metal ringing around them. At last she got her opening and, with a quick stab, sunk her dagger into his shoulder. He cried out at the pain, stumbling backwards and holding his wound. The woman ran up to grab him and glared at Unolé. Then the two of them turned and ran off, leaving the building.

Unolé barely had time to react when she heard the bowstring snap. She pulled out of the way but the arrowhead still sliced her leg. Gritting her teeth at the sting, she flapped her wings and went up to meet the skeletal creature. It flew down, an impossibly wide mouth open in a silent scream.

They collided in mid-air, grappling for control of the other. The creature abandoned its bow and used claws instead, ripping through Unolé's clothes and into her flesh. She slashed out with her daggers, impacting each time and drawing blood, but her opponent was relentless. The world spun. She wasn't sure which way the floor was anymore as wings beat around them. Her stomach turned as she was pushed with enormous force, the creature trying to drive her back. Unolé blindly stabbed out, sinking a dagger so deep she felt blood coat her fingers.

Then she was shoved into the floor, her head cracking. The creature fell limp atop her, its blood soaking into her shirt. As she blinked her eyes, trying to bring world back into focus, a wave of dizziness swept through her.

"Are you all right?" Teshuva's voice sounded. She made out his vibrant form hovering above her. "Are you injured?"

Unolé let out a long moan, but her senses were coming back to her. Slowly pushing the skeletal body off, she sat up. "I'm . . . I'm okay, I think. Just dizzy." She looked over her body. Cuts ran across her skin, and now that the adrenaline faded the pain set in. "*Ouch.*"

The coatl looked her up and down. "The injuries don't look serious. But we should get out of here. More might show up."

The Half-Fiend touched some of her wounds, wincing at the sting. "That sounds good. Where do we go?"

"Back to the white world."

Unolé staggered to her feet, holding her wounded side. "Okay. Do I need to use the black feathers again?"

"Yes. But not here. Outside. Let us find a private location."

Teshuva returned again to her hood. Sheathing her two bloodied daggers, Unolé lurched back outside. She saw a few denizens of the Hells give her curious glances, but otherwise she was ignored as she made her way around the corner of the warehouse. She turned into the narrow street behind the building and found it to be decently secluded. Unolé pulled a black feather from her pack, holding it up.

"Okay," she said, "what do I need to do?"

Teshuva slithered from her hood, wrapping around the wrist that held the feather. "Concentrate on the white world. I will add my magic and my focus, and we should be able to return."

One eyebrow cocked. *"Should?"*

"Traveling between the planes isn't a perfect science. There are many ways in and out. There are forces at work, magic barriers, planar travelers passing through . . . one never knows what one might come across."

Unolé sighed. At this point, she would just be happy to get out of the Hells, regardless of where they ended up. "Alright, I am ready."

She focused her mind on the white world. The misty surroundings, the silver pools, the long bridge. As she held the image in her mind she felt a pulse of magic from Teshuva. And then they were both pulled away from the Hells, and back to the area between the planes.

.

.

.

RUUDA

.
.
.

Ruuda had grown up hearing stories of the Surface. It was hard to believe most of them. Especially because she was the youngest of twelve siblings and she inherently didn't trust anything they told her. A light in the sky so bright it lit the whole world? Ridiculous. Trees that covered the ground in thick clusters for miles? Unbelievable. Water that fell from the sky? Lies.

And yet, as she stood next to Taliesin on the city streets of Eleste'si, she realized all of it could be true. For she was seeing something her mind just couldn't wrap itself around. She couldn't comprehend it, and yet it was there. Soaring high, high above the buildings was the night sky. There was no rock wall or cavern that made a roof. It was just endless blue-black. It had no end and no beginning. Silvery light shone from it in the form of tiny points that glittered like a vein of platinum in the mines. And directly above was another source of light that was huge and round and bright. The stars and the moon, she realized. Though descriptions and drawings didn't do them justice.

The air was strange. It felt light and open. Scents that were unusual in the Deep Hollows were prominent here. Spices and florals and other sweet smells. The buildings were also a far cry from the simple, angular, stone structures of Balum Guar. These were crafted with beauty and intricacy in mind. Buildings of pastel colors were surrounded by gardens. And there, towering above it all, was the palace. It spiraled and rose above all around it, white and blue, like a great fountain.

It was breathtaking.

And it was too much. Ruuda immediately stepped back, hitting the outside wall of the tavern. Her gaze darted to Taliesin. He stood his ground, staring around at everything in wonder.

"It's incredible," he said softly. He lifted his hand, reaching up for the sky. "I can't tell where it starts." He turned to look at her. The hood of his black cloak cast most of his face in shadow, but two bright yellow eyes could be seen clearly. "What do you think?"

"I-I don't like it," she said, shrinking back. "We should return underground."

"Nonsense! We should make our way to that tavern we were told about. The Tranquil Grail."

"No."

"*Ruuda,*" his voice grew stern. "You are honor-bound to protect me until your debt is repaid. Now, let's go."

She reluctantly pushed off the tavern wall and followed him through the streets. They were cobblestone and remarkably clean, and their feet made no noise as they traversed. Taliesin kept their path to the shadows, following close to buildings and sticking to the narrower streets. Ruuda couldn't see anybody about, but she could hear conversations on other roads as they passed. They headed away from the palace, but as time wore on the city didn't show any signs of thinning. Where was the outer part of Eleste'si?

Taliesin seemed to think this, as well, for he slowed to a stop and said, "I have no idea if we're going the right way."

"Neither do I. We need a map of the city."

They both looked around for any signs that could aid them. But all they found was a wanted poster stuck to one closed shop. It showed an Elf with brown skin and hair, green eyes, and a red band tattoo across her face. Red and orange feathers were tucked behind one pointed ear.

"Elves looking for other Elves?" Ruuda questioned.

Taliesin shrugged one shoulder. "That one looks like a Wild Elf. At least, from the books I've read. They live in the mountains and the forests, supposedly. Unlike the High Elves

126

that own this city. The two groups don't get along."

"And I doubt either of them like you, *Dark Elf*."

"Or you."

"I'm okay with not being liked."

He looked up at the building next to them. "I need a better view of the city. Give me a boost."

"What am I, your servant?"

"Aren't you?"

Ruuda sighed and held out her palms. She wasn't going to answer that question. Taliesin stepped into her hands and she helped lift him onto the roof. He weighed nothing. Ruuda watched as he climbed on top of the building, a shadow against the night sky. From his pack he pulled out a journal and wrote some things down.

Then he crawled over to the edge and peered at her. "Do you want to look? I can pull you up."

"No. I do not want to climb up someplace I can't step down from."

"Suit yourself." He turned and slid off, landing soundlessly on the street. "Okay, I could make out the outer wall of the city. It's really far away. I actually think this place is bigger than Berenzia. But we're going in the right direction."

"Then lead on. I don't like being out here in the open."

More time passed as they wound their way through Eleste'si. Ruuda just couldn't get over how luxurious everything was. It seemed like a waste. In Balum Guar, things were designed for function. What was the point of spending extra time and resources on something that wouldn't be used? She recalled the blank stone hallways. The plain front of her home. The barren city streets whose only adornment were signs for directions.

This is something I have to get used to, she thought. *I can't go back there, anyway.*

She regarded the Dark Elf in front of her, his black cloak lined with white rippling with his movements. It was strange she would cross paths with someone who was also leaving the Deep Hollows. She did not believe in fate, but perhaps it was luck. They were stronger together. Who knew what dangers the Surface held? It was best to have someone watching her back. At least, for a little while.

They both heard the voices at the same time. Ruuda ducked quickly around a corner, Taliesin following suit. Two people approached down the street. As they drew closer, she could make out the words being said.

"The Queen is supposed to make her way down the main avenue tomorrow morning. I've got my patrol stationed along the eastern side. You know how the people get when they see her."

"I've never seen her in person. Is she as beautiful as they say?"

"Like a goddess made Elven."

"Incredible."

Ruuda noticed the guards were speaking Common. It was a language often spoken in the Deep Hollows, as well, along with Elvish, Dwarvish, and Gnomish. Common was taught in schools because it was considered useful to be able to read signposts on the Surface, or communicate with slaves that were captured. She had even heard of black market trade routes being established with some Surface-dwellers.

"You know Aust Mastralath is supposed to greet her on the street," one of the men commented.

"That rich man? I've heard of him."

"Rumor has it he wants to marry her."

"Ha! Don't we all."

The voices drew closer. Ruuda realized they would pass by. Hiding in the shadows looked too suspicious. They needed to try to blend in. Under the moonlight it was unlikely the color of she and Taliesin's skin and hair would be immediately noticeable. Maybe they could pass themselves off as citizens. But were there any Dwarves in this city? Or would seeing a Dwarf immediately bring suspicion? Making up her mind Ruuda unstrapped her barrel and crouched behind it, using the darkness to her advantage. And then promptly, to her horror, Taliesin sat on top of it and took out his journal, pretending to read.

Two guards passed by. They were clad in gleaming silver armor with details of leaves and flowers carved in. Longer blond hair hung at their shoulders, and their skin was a very pale. Ruuda stared at them from the gap between the barrel and the wall. She'd never seen High Elves that weren't slaves. She could tell they were taller and broader than Taliesin.

The guards hesitated, breaking off their conversation to look at Taliesin. He lifted his head just fractionally, giving a small wave. That seemed to satisfy them. They continued on their path, chatting once again about the Queen.

Ruuda stood up, sighing. "Get off my barrel!"

He rolled his eyes, sliding off and putting up the journal. "That was close. What do you think would have happened if they caught us?"

"These people live very pretty lives. Who knows how tough they'd be? In Balum Guar, intruders are killed."

Taliesin crossed his arms. "I'll have to take you to Berenzia one day. Our architecture is very beautiful and detailed. Our clothes are made from fine fabrics and our jewelry shines with gemstones. We live very 'pretty' lives, too. But intruders are made into slaves and, if they behave badly, they are sacrificed to our goddess. In some ways, this city reminds me of Berenzia. Except," his expression twisted into one of disgust, "*pastels?* Gods, those are awful colors."

Ruuda chuckled. "Agreed. Now let's get going."

It took them the rest of the night to reach the tavern. They had a few more close calls but were able to stay hidden. The city felt like a labyrinth, and Ruuda tried to memorize it as best she could. As the sky began to lighten, they finally found the Tranquil Grail. It was tucked away in a dark corner of the city, its walls slightly tilted and windows foggy.

Ruuda glanced up at the slowly brightening sky. "Wha . . . What's happening?"

Taliesin frowned. "I don't know. Is it daytime? I don't see the sun."

"Let's get inside, Taliesin. I don't like this."

He strode up to the door and knocked, stating the password, "Sanctuary."

The door opened and a rugged Dark Dwarf appraised them before gesturing for them to enter. Taliesin peered tentatively inside. Ruuda saw his shoulders relax as he stepped in all the way. She followed, and the door was shut behind her. They were faced with a tavern that had certainly seen better days. But the sight of people from the Deep Hollows was a relief. There were Dark Elves, Dwarves, and Gnomes mingling about. Curiously, she saw one man that appeared to be a High Elf but he had a blond beard. And the barkeep was an androgynous person with the coloring of a Wild Elf, who nodded to them as they entered. Multiple languages were spoken, some she could understand and others she could not.

"This is interesting," Taliesin stated.

"There's too many people. I don't like it."

He met her gaze. "Do you want to get a room? We can pass the day here and leave again at night."

"Alright."

"Uh . . . one room or two?"

Ruuda's gaze passed over the tavern. None of the clientele looked like they could be trusted. "One room. It's safer to stay together."

Taliesin paid and they went up a narrow staircase to an equally as narrow hallway. Finding their room number, they went inside and locked it behind them. Just for good measure, Ruuda pushed a chair up against the brass doorknob.

Ruuda had never stayed in a tavern before so she didn't know what to expect. But it wasn't too bad. The size of the room was decent, and two beds that looked clean and soft sat on either side. There was a writing desk with quill and parchment, a small closet, and a single window that looked over the city streets. It smelled of clean wood and freshly washed linens.

But it was the window that drew their attention. For through it, a great deal of light was coming. And it was getting brighter and brighter. Ruuda squinted. The light hurt. Taliesin pulled his hood back and approached the window, hand shielding his eyes and casting a shadow across his face. He gasped as he looked out and said, "Ruuda, you have to see this!"

The Dark Dwarf tentatively made her way over, holding up her own gloved hand against the light. Reaching the glass, she peered out. The cobblestone streets were coming alive with activity. High Elves with their blond hair dominated the population by far. But she did see a few with darker colors of hair. Shops opened, selling food and flowers and jewelry. The palace gleamed bright, and it was too much to look at. Her gaze was drawn to the sky. Gone was the blue-black of before. Now it was a soft, light blue. She'd never seen a shade like it. And things ran across the sky, puffy and white. Clouds? They were strange. And there, coming over the tops of the buildings, was the sun. Incredibly bright, it burned her green eyes as she looked.

Ruuda pulled away, blinking fiercely. "People live like this? It's awful!"

As Taliesin pulled away she saw his eyes were watering. "It's so hard to see." He grabbed the blue curtains on either side of the window and pulled them shut. The light coming through the cloth gave the room a soft, gentle illumination.

"The sun comes at the same time each day, right?" Ruuda asked.

"From what I've heard."

"That's terrible. Should we only travel at night?"

"Maybe . . . my sleep schedule is all messed up already." He rubbed his face. "I'm exhausted."

Ruuda felt the wear on her own body as well. Her muscles ached and her spine was stiff from the large barrel strapped to her back. "Let's get some sleep. Tomorrow we can leave this horrible city."

She unstrapped her barrel, ceremoniously setting it beside her bed. Her dual swords came next and she sat them atop her barrel. As she took off the rest of her packs and her thick boots, she glanced up at the Dark Elf to see he'd set just two small packs aside and had taken off his boots, cloak, and scale breastplate, revealing a loose black shirt underneath.

As they finished, cheering and applause could be heard from the window. Taliesin stepped over and pulled the curtain back, wincing at the sunlight. "It's . . . it's the queen."

She didn't want to look out into that brightness again, but curiosity got the better of Ruuda. She returned to the window, looking down at the street. A procession passed by. Soldiers in gleaming silver armor walked on either side of a white carriage. People had quickly filled the sidewalks, waving and smiling and making a huge fuss for the woman in the carriage. It was hard to tell details from this distance, especially in the daytime. But Ruuda could make out a High Elf woman with a silver crown that glittered with diamonds and sapphires. Her long blonde hair flowed over her shoulders. She wore a dress of blues and whites and held her chin high, waving delicately at the crowd.

"Good grief," Ruuda sighed.

"Agreed. The High Priestess of my city wouldn't parade around like this. And certainly not to applause."

"It's like a cult."

"Indeed."

As the carriage made its slow way through the city, a man stepped up from the side, flanked by a few armed Elves. His blond hair was pulled back into a low ponytail, and he wore clothes of silks and velvets. The carriage stopped for him as he produced a white rose, offering it to the queen. Through the glass Ruuda could make out shouts of "Aust!", "Queen Mirandril!" and "We love you!".

As the man, Aust, lifted the rose his sleeves fell back to reveal tattoos that looked like wrappings on his arms. Queen Mirandril took the flower, smiled, and her procession carried on and out of sight.

Taliesin pulled the curtains shut once again. "The Surface is strange."

Ruuda couldn't imagine her own people cheering out of joy like that. The only time that kind of racket went on was during death sport. She turned back to the bed and climbed onto it. It was much softer than anything she was used to. She shifted around uncomfortably, attempting to settle in. As she ended up on her back, staring at the wooden ceiling, she grasped her necklace. An iron disc with a hammer engraved on it. The symbol of the Forge King. The symbol of the god of her people. She recalled the spider symbol Taliesin wore around his neck. She could only assume that was his deity. She didn't know much about the religion of the Dark Elves. Turning her head to look at him, she saw he was curled into a ball under the blanket, turned away from the light of the window. Ruuda then looked to the door, ensuring it was locked and barricaded, before she allowed herself to relax and drift into an uncomfortable sleep.

.

.

.

The smell of food woke Ruuda. At first, she was confused. Was her family eating without her? Why wouldn't they wake her up? It was shameful to not be up early and contributing your day to work. Was it to make her look bad? To get her in trouble? If she overslept, it was another reason to gripe at her.

Ruuda blearily opened her green eyes, pushing the white blanket off of her. And then the tavern room came into focus, the softness of the bed under her strong body, and the Dark Elf that kicked the door shut behind him, carrying two plates of food.

"I brought breakfast up," he said. "I didn't want to wake you."

She sat, pushing her fiery hair back from her face. "Oh. Uh, thanks . . . I can pay you back for the food."

He shook his head. "Don't worry about it. I took plenty of money from my family when I left."

She took the plate he offered. "You stole your parents' money?"

Taliesin sat on his own bed, balancing the plate on his crossed legs. "It's my House's money . . . I think. It's fine.

They have a lot of it."

The Dark Dwarf looked down at her plate. Eggs, sizzling meat, and bread. It smelled delicious. As they both ate, she regarded Taliesin. He stared absently at the curtains. Long white hair was tied back into a ponytail, but strands too short fell on either side of his face. His pointed ears were long and narrow, very different from her small, rounded ones. The fading light created deep shadows under his eyes and cheekbones. For a moment it changed his appearance. It made him look wearier, like he was recovering from a long illness. Then he noticed her staring and smiled, the moment passing.

"Where did you learn to fight?" he asked.

"My family, more or less. It's an essential skill for all Dark Dwarves." She nodded to his spider necklace hanging against his chest. "Is that an amulet for your magic?"

He touched it with one hand, the other holding a fork. "Yes, it's a conduit for my spells. I'm a Cleric."

Her red eyebrows raised. She knew he'd cast healing magic on her, in the Deep Hollows, but many spellcasters knew basic healing spells. Clerics were much more powerful in that regard. Able to heal deeper wounds and cure toxins and diseases. "You're a healer? I didn't know the Dark Elves encouraged that kind of magic."

"They don't. I've never met anyone else that heals as prolifically as I do."

"Was it considered a . . . helpful thing?"

He shrugged. "I had my uses, I suppose. Others in my city were more interested in the fact that I was good with spells. Better than most my age. I wanted to use that to advance myself. To be a priest. But my family instead saw it as an opportunity to marry me off to another wealthy House. Or to be a consort to a powerful priestess. It didn't matter what I wanted, it was whatever increased our House's power."

"What is a consort?"

A look of confusion flickered over his face, followed by one of surprise at the cultural difference. "Oh . . . um . . . A consort is a man whose purpose is to serve as a woman's lover. Typically a priestess, but sometimes the Matriarchs of a House desire a consort. It can be for procreation, but usually it's just for sex. If a consort remains in the woman's favor he can stay with that House for many years. But, if the woman thinks he's betraying her, passing secrets along to another House, or even if she's unsatisfied with his sexual performance she can punish him. Flogging, sell him into slavery, or even death on the altar. But it doesn't always have to be so severe, of course. If he just talks back or is a smartass he'll get an Obedience Gag put on him."

"What in the Hells is an *Obedience Gag?*"

Again, he looked surprised at her bewilderment. "It's a gag that has a metal spider attached that goes inside your mouth. And the rest wraps over your mouth and your jaw to prevent you from speaking. They're individually locked with an arcane spell so only the woman who put it on can open it." One corner of his mouth tugged up in a sly smile. "My mother threatened me with it quite a bit. She never did it, though."

Ruuda was taken aback by such a system. "I take it you didn't get married off or sent to be a . . . consort?"

"Things . . . changed. And all of those options became closed to me." He paused, then asked, "What about you? Did you have a good relationship with your family?"

She stared hard at her nearly empty plate for a moment, pushing back at the pain those memories brought up. Then she answered, "No. No, I didn't." She looked back at him. "Well, we should get going. I want to make it out of this city before the sun."

They quickly prepared for travel once again, and headed downstairs. As Taliesin turned in the room key to the barkeep, he asked, "We are looking to get out of the city. Is sneaking past the gate an option?"

The Wild Elf replied, "That's not a good idea. It's heavily guarded and there aren't many openings. But there is one person who smuggles those that look like you two in and out of the city. She's a Dark Elf named Zayra. For the right coin, she'll get you out."

"Thanks for the information. Where can we find her?"

"Once you see the outer gate go left. There is a watchtower she stays by. It's not manned, but you'll have to be careful all the same," they replied.

"Understood." He flashed a grin. "Anything we should know about the world outside of this city?"

The barkeep chuckled. "Oh, Dark Elf. You two are not ready for it."

As they stepped out onto the shadowy streets, glancing about for soldiers or citizens, Ruuda said, "I know a little magic myself. Nothing like you. I'm better with my blades. But, if we really needed to, I can do illusion magic."

"Illusion magic?"

"I can change my appearance. Not much. Not enough to look like a High Elf. But I can change my skin color temporarily. I've heard there are Dwarves on the Surface with tan skin. Not gray like mine."

"Oh. That is good to know. I don' t know those types spells. But even if I did, I wouldn't disguise myself. I like the way I look. Why would I hide this?" He gestured proudly at himself.

A smile tugged at one corner of Ruuda's mouth. "We'll keep it in mind. Just in case."

"I think our best bet is finding this Zayra. Then we don't have to interact with any soldiers."

"I'm not a good liar. So I prefer Zayra, as well."

They wound their way through the streets of Eleste'si. They avoided any patrols or citizens that were out, clinging to shadows and narrow routes. It was another long journey, and they only communicated with looks and hand gestures to avoid making unnecessary sound.

At last the outer wall of the city came into view. It was thirty feet tall and made of solid, white stone. A few guards patrolled the top of it, but they were sparse. Heavy gates marked the way in and out of Eleste'si. Even at this time of night, soldiers stood about and checked with those passing through. There was a small line on either side. Ruuda and

Taliesin surveyed the scene for a few minutes, hiding around the corner of a building.

"I don't like it," Taliesin whispered. "We don't know what questions they'll ask."

"Then let's not risk it. Let's find Zayra," Ruuda replied.

"Agreed."

Staying within the first line of buildings, they turned left and made their way along the wall. Ruuda wondered what was on the other side. She didn't know a world without caverns and tunnels and underground rivers. Was it the same, just with more color? Would there be a place to hide when the sun came up again? Were the animals the same, or were they all new ones? These thoughts troubled her. But she was indebted to this Dark Elf, and so she had to follow him. Besides, there was nowhere else for her to go.

After another thirty minutes of sneaking along, they came to a watchtower. Its windows were dark and no patrols were in the area. Taliesin stepped out from behind the building, pulling his hood down once again and looking about. The moonlight shone on him. He said softly, "Zayra?"

Ruuda hung back, one hand on the hilt of her sword, as the moment of silence stretched out. Then a Dark Elf woman stepped out from the shadows, her arms crossed. Black clothes hugged a slender, yet athletic figure. She stood a few inches taller than Taliesin, and her shoulders were broader. Ruuda had noticed that the women of the Dark Elves were larger and more robust than the men. It was opposite of the Dark Dwarves, where men were the taller and stronger ones. It would be interesting to see which sex was larger here on the Surface.

Zayra's white hair was tied in a bun, and her gray skin had a few scars running across it. Red eyes looked them over before she said, "That's me. If you two want to get out of the city it's fifty gold coins."

Ruuda stepped up next to Taliesin as he pulled out the money, handing it to her. "Thank you."

Zayra took a moment to count it and then put it

away in a pouch. "What are your names?"

"I'm Taliesin Ostoroth. This is Ruuda Drybarrel."

The Dark Dwarf scowled. "I don't like just giving my name out."

Zayra said, "That's too bad. I need to know for my own records. Will you be returning to the city soon?"

The Cleric paused before answering, "No, it won't be soon."

Zayra snorted. "Well, good luck out there. You'll be killed within a week. There is a caravan of trade supplies leaving the city within the hour. I can smuggle you out in that. Follow me, and don't speak or make any noise." Her eyes narrowed at Ruuda. "I know that must be hard for you, Dark Dwarf, but try to stay quiet."

Ruuda gritted her teeth, but said nothing. She often wandered the Deep Hollows alone. And if that had taught her anything, it was how to be stealthy. She followed the two Dark Elves as they went further along the outer wall and to a grate that was built in. It stood only three feet high. Zayra took out some tools and pried it open, the bars giving with a soft creak. She immediately crawled inside. Taliesin followed and Ruuda after him. Despite being around four feet tall, stooping over was too difficult with a barrel on her back. So she crawled as well, cursing in her mind. The tunnel cut through the entirety of the outer wall. She surmised it must be for drainage purposes. The stone floor was wet and the tunnel narrow. The grimy water soaked into her pants and gloves. She didn't trust the handiwork of Surface dwellers. It felt as if the wall could collapse on them at any moment.

At last the end of the tunnel was reached. Zayra opened another grate and they went out, finally exiting Eleste'si. Ruuda looked about as she got to her feet, but there was nothing to see. They were in some kind of wooden stable. Covered wagons sat about, surrounded by crates, with large animals tied to them. The area smelled of dung. Zayra led them to the closest wagon and opened a few crates. She moved around the contents, compiling bags and food into a few and emptying out two others. Then she looked back at them. "Get inside."

"No," Ruuda said. "I'm not riding inside a crate."

The woman glared. "It's the only way out. If you aren't getting in, I'll leave you out here."

Taliesin sighed. He seemed unhappy, but responded, "It'll be fine. Let's get in the crates, Ruuda."

"What about my barrel? I'm not parting with it."

Zayra rolled her eyes. "Just put it in the wagon. They won't notice."

Ruuda reluctantly headed up to the wagon and unstrapped her barrel. She gently set it inside, ensuring it didn't look too conspicuous. Then she leaned over the crate she was supposed to ride in. It would be cramped. And it smelled terrible. Like old food. But she could deal with it.

As Ruuda put one leg in she glanced over at Taliesin. He struggled to sit down, pulling his knees against his chest. He said, "This is not going to work. It's too small."

Zayra growled and grabbed a fist full of his thick, white hair. His face twisted in pain as she pushed him down inside and then slammed the lid. Ruuda could hear it hit him as it closed. The Dark Dwarf stopped her movements, looking over at the woman. Zayra met her gaze. For a moment they held eyes. Ruuda wasn't sure what her own expression was, but the Dark Elf countered it with a look of challenge.

Ruuda said, "We didn't pay you to be an asshole."

"You paid me for results. Now get in, this wagon will be leaving soon."

Ruuda fixed her with one last heated look before sitting down in the crate. She was curled into an uncomfortable ball, but there was some wiggle room. Reaching up, Ruuda pulled the lid shut with a *thud* and darkness surrounded her.

.

.

.

ZOK

.

.

.

The port was a welcome sight after sailing for so long. Zok leaned against the railing of the ship, watching the city of Vonkai come into focus. It sizzled and shimmered in the sun, brilliant colors against the browns of the desert. The port was busy, and ships of many sizes came and went. The Paladin absently watched them. Even though there was still a long way to the ruins of Soleia, he couldn't get the city off of his mind. He had hoped that sailing would clear his head and make the right path easy to choose. But, if anything, it had made things more difficult. Now he wondered if he'd done the right thing in leaving without telling anyone else at the temple. Would it have been so bad to show the letter to Baelfire?

I didn't want to put anyone else's life at risk, he reminded himself. *Whoever Priest Jafr was working with knows someone is onto them.*

All of this was connected to the Lantern of Vicrum. Jafr had been looking for it. High Priest Amon had died for it. The third person involved may already be in Soleia. He could only hope they weren't too late to stop this. Before anyone else got hurt.

As Sen went through the process of docking the Scarlet Maiden, Zok looked over Vonkai. It was about the size of Somberdale, a beautiful city on the coast. But that was where the similarities ended. Instead of green trees and mountains, there was flat desert. The buildings were brightly colored shades of reds, blues, purples, yellows, and pinks. Vibrant cloths were strung up between buildings to shade the streets underneath. There was a large fish market, and to offset the smell many incense burners set about, giving off scents of spices and fruits. There was a variety of people here, much like Somberdale, although most had darker skin from the desert climate. They wore thin clothes of many colors with wide hats to protect their eyes from the scorching sun. A hot wind caressed his skin, and he could hear the sound of music played somewhere in the city.

Sen called up from the gangplank, "Let's move out! Kailo, Rain, you two are in charge while we're gone."

Zok headed down first, his armor shining. He'd spent the last day polishing it. He represented the Temple of the Holy Dragon when he wore it and wanted to make a good appearance. It was white with gold accents, and the eye of the Holy Dragon was emblazoned on his chest. Getting onto land, he turned to watch the others disembark. Jade's brown hair blew out behind her as she left the ship, the fox at her heels. Then came Artemis and Wolfie, and Skar with his dark blue robes shifting in the breeze.

"Do we need to ask for directions?" Zok questioned.

"I have a map," Jade replied, "but I drew it from information gathered during my travels. It might not be exact."

"How long a journey would it be to walk to Soleia?" Sen asked.

The Druid responded, "About a day and a half, if my map is correct."

"Let's get camels!" Artemis exclaimed, her face lighting up in excitement. "I've always wanted to ride a camel!"

The pirate captain chuckled. "Not a bad idea, little Half-Elf. Let's find us a tavern for some information."

They made their way further into the city. It was active and bustling, and everyone seemed to have smiles on their faces. Zok wished he could share in their light-heartedness. It felt like a shadow was over him. And he wouldn't be able to relax until he got answers.

It wasn't hard to find a prominent tavern. Facing the central road was one called The Clucking Chicken. Zok did not see any chickens around, unless he counted the one painted on the front door. They entered and the shade inside was a welcome relief. Already the heat caused the Paladin to sweat. It would be a miserable journey across the sand.

The tavern was painted purple inside, with more of those spicy scents burning. There were mostly Humans patrons, but Zok also spotted a Wild Elf, a Dwarf, and two Halflings. At the bar was a dark-skinned man with a yellow bandana tied around a bald head, gold earrings shining in the low light.

Sen approached the bar first, putting some coins down. "A bottle of rum, please. Does anyone else want a drink?"

Zok sighed, pushing forward. For his large Dragonborn friend, alcohol always came before anything else. "We're looking to travel to Soleia. Do you know the way?"

The barkeep grabbed the rum, answering, "It's easy to get there. Just head straight north for nearly two days, if you're walking. Some people are living in the ruins there, but you won't find much else."

Artemis leaned forward. "Where can we get camels?"

The man replied "Well, out back you can – is that a *wolf?!*"

Artemis patted Wolfie on the head. "Don't worry, he's tame. Out back where?"

The barkeep seemed disgruntled, but continued. "Behind this tavern there is a pen with camels. Tell the old man out there Filin sent you. That's me. But you better bring my camels back safely!"

"Of course," Zok responded. "Thank you."

They headed back into the heat, making their way around the building. At the back was a large fenced off area with fifteen camels roaming. There was no attempt to cover up any scent here, and the Paladin scrunched up his nose at the odors. "How many camels do we need?"

Sen shook his head. "I don't want to ride one. I can control my ship, I can't control an animal."

"How about three?" Jade suggested. "We can switch

out to rest our legs."

An old Human man stood up from the wooden stool he'd been sitting on as they approached. "'Ello! How can I help ya?"

Artemis bounded over to the fence. "Filin sent us to get some camels! We're heading to Soleia and back."

The man nodded. "Alright, alright. Which ones do ya want?"

The Ranger asked, "May I inspect them closer?"

"Be my guest."

Artemis vaulted over the fence with one arm, and her wolf sat down patiently to wait. The Half-Elf cast a quick spell and mingled with the camels, speaking in grunts. The camels returned conversation in kind.

At the old man's bewildered expression, Zok said, "She can speak to animals. Just let it happen. She'll be done soon."

Skar scratched his chin. "Do we really need an interview for this?"

"I think it's nice to have someone else in touch with nature here," Jade said.

Zok had never ridden a camel before but he considered himself fairly good with a horse. It would be nice to have these mounts to prevent exhaustion when crossing the desert. Despite the heat, he didn't want to take his armor off. He felt complete with it on. Like the Holy Dragon was wrapped around him in protection. It was different than the rest of the group. Jade and Skar wore no armor, and Sen didn't even have a shirt on. But Artemis wore leather armor of gray on her torso, forearms, and shins.

The Half-Elf Ranger headed back over to the fence, leading three camels with her. "These three are great! Their names are Dusty, Sandy, and His Majesty."

The old man seemed confused, but accepted the gold coins offered and provided saddles consisting of colorful blankets and rope. After getting the camels ready, they made their way through Vonkai and to the outskirts of the city. A wooden sign pointed in the direction of Soleia, although there was no road marked. Before them stretched the Expanse. Dry earth turned into sand dunes that rolled along the horizon. Overhead the sky was a solid blue, without a single cloud in the sky.

Artemis with her wolf, Jade with her fox, and Zok all mounted a camel and they began their journey. Jade stayed up front to navigate as they headed north. The desert environment fascinated Zok. Green and red plants with long thorns were scattered sparsely about. Large birds flew in lazy circles overhead, casting their shadows on the hard ground. He got occasional glimpses of animals. Lizards, insects, and some type of wild dog in the distance.

"Perhaps we will see that Jenkins fellow in Soleia," Skar commented. "The five of us together should have no trouble apprehending him."

"He's too smart to be vulnerable," Jade said. "If he is there, we should expect tricks."

"This might have nothing to do with him," Zok replied. "I can't think of why an old spellcaster would have interest in disrupting the Temple of the Holy Dragon. Of course, it would help if we knew what the Lantern of Vicrum is."

Artemis said, "Speaking of which, do we have a plan once we get to Soleia? Where would this Lantern be?"

The Paladin shook his head. "I do not know. Priest Jafr was looking in the tombs of Somberdale. So perhaps we should search any temples, catacombs, or mausoleums we come across. Filin said there are people living there, so we should be able to get some leads."

They traveled on in relative silence. The heat was oppressive and soon even Artemis' enthusiasm was replaced by weariness. Zok watched as the sun burned its way across the sky until the blue was replaced by oranges and reds. The temperature began to drop. As the sun dipped into the horizon, the group searched for a place to camp. However, the open sand dunes didn't offer any shelter. Not wanting to push on in the darkness and risk exhaustion the following day, they settled for a ridge with a good view around them.

Jade and Artemis set up a campfire and cooked some reptiles the archer killed. The Druid was able to find some safe fruits on the local plant life, as well. When the sun was gone the sky opened up into a spattering of stars. It had been a long time since Zok had camped in an area with such an open view of the sky. As the five of them appreciated the sight, Sen pointed out different constellations he used to navigate while sailing.

"That constellation represents the Tide Bringer," the pirate captain explained, lying on his back. "The Elves call her Ocea sometimes, I believe. And that line of stars there is called the Rift. Named after the planar travel of ancient times, of course. And this one is the Cow."

"I love cows!" Artemis exclaimed.

Skar gestured to an area of the sky. "My family used to tell me that constellation looks like a dragon."

"It is. It's called the Great Wyrm, very large in the sky and easy to see. I do love the stars."

"Do you have a favorite?" Jade asked.

Sen's voice took on a wistful tone. "After a long journey at sea, I always used the Tide Bringer to navigate back to Somberdale. I am not the most religious, certainly. But I've always trusted the Tide Bringer to guide me home."

A soft smile spread across Zok's face at that. He had his own images he associated with home. A coast, a boat, his father's voice.

And, at last, with full stomachs and tired bodies, they went to sleep.

.

.

.

Zok sat on one of the stone benches outside the temple, looking out over the beach. Somberdale was just waking up, and for now he could enjoy the sight of the ocean in silence. The waves rolled on and off the sand. Steady, strong. Even when they crashed against rocks they pushed on to reach their destination. Broken, but resilient. He wished life was like that. That people were like that. Himself most of all.

A shadow passed over him. He turned to see High Priest Amon smiling down. His robes were a pure white in the sunlight, trimmed with gold. His holy symbol, the eye of the Holy Dragon, hung around his neck.

"Brother Zok," Amon said in a gentle tone. "May I join you?"

"Of course, High Priest Amon."

He sat and smoothed out his robes, joining the younger man in looking out over the ocean. "It's a lovely morning. But, I tend to think every morning is lovely, in its own way. Priestess Liana teases that even if a storm is passing overhead, I will call the day beautiful."

Zok couldn't help but smile at that. "There is beauty in a storm, I suppose."

"Last night was your first here at the temple. Did you have everything you require? Was your room to your liking?"

"Everything was fine. Thank you for asking."

"If all was fine, then what troubles you?"

Zok gave a long sigh, his shoulders sinking. He felt the weight of his journey on him. "I just didn't think, when I first left Sunspire, that I would find myself on the opposite side of Corventos. It's been a long trip. It's changed me, I think."

"Mmm. All journeys do. Did you find what you were seeking?"

"I found the answers I was looking for. I learned who I was. But . . . "

When he drifted off into silence, Amon encouraged, "But?"

"I guess things just didn't turn out the way I thought they would."

"One of the surest ways to be disappointed is to have expectations, Brother Zok. Have hope, yes. But if you limit yourself to one outcome you may miss better ones along the way."

"I'll . . . keep that in mind, thank you."

A moment of quiet passed between them before High Priest Amon said, "I have hope you will be a great addition to our order. We will have a ceremony tomorrow to welcome you. To renew your oath with this Temple of the Holy Dragon." A smile played at his lips. "I trust you remember your oath?"

Watching the waves roll in, breaking along the rocks and sand, Zok said, "I devote my life to follow you, Holy Dragon. In your example I will be honest, and keep my word in all things. I will protect others as though their life is greater than mine."

Amon joined in, and they spoke in unison.
"I will show mercy to my foes, but punish those who do evil.
I will obey those with just authority.
I will answer for my actions and ask forgiveness for any wrong I have done.
And in all things I will be honorable.
May you guide my steps and my voice, so I may always serve you justly."

Amon reached over and placed his hand atop Zok's. The skin was leathery and wrinkled by age, but the touch was warm and gentle. Amon said, "When nothing else seems certain in your life, when times are at their darkest, say those words. And your strength will be renewed."

"Thank you, High Priest Amon."

.

.

.

A scream awoke Zok. He opened his eyes, immediately fumbling for his hammer and shield. It was still night, the desert lit in moonlight. In his first brief glance he saw the camels running off, Artemis trying to get control over them. Jade and Skar scrambled to their feet, and Wolfie barked at the ground.

Then he noticed what was wrong. The ground was moving. Sand shifted, a pile rose in the middle of their camp. The ground tilted and Zok felt himself rolling down the incline. Sand got in his clothes, his hair, his mouth. As he came to a stop he got to his hands and knees, and looked at what had emerged from beneath the dune.

Black and shiny in the moonlight, it stood four feet tall and ten feet long. Two pincers emerged, snapping at the air. A huge stinger hung over its head, the tip impossibly sharp. It was a massive scorpion.

Immediately a large pincer shot out and grabbed Jade, lifting her into the air. She cried out and fire erupted from her hands, but the grip didn't loosen. Sen jumped to his feet, reaching for his axe. But as he did the stinger shot out and sunk into his shoulder. He roared, staggered, and fell back.

Zok ran towards the scorpion, grabbing his hammer and shield as he went. An arrow whizzed past his head and impacted the beast's armor harmlessly, spinning off into the sand. Skar fired the burning orbs from his wand, but they did no damage.

Jade was lifted higher into the air. She fired down multiple bolts of flame but they didn't penetrate the armor. She cried out again as the pincer tightened. Zok rushed up, jumped into the air, and brought his hammer down on the joint connected to that limb. He heard a crunch and the pincer released Jade. The other one came at his face with a wide sweep. He took the blow with his shield but was sent tumbling back into the sand.

Getting his bearings again, Zok got to his feet, shield protectively in front of him. Artemis circled the monster, firing her arrows and looking for a weak spot. Wolfie and Foxy bit at the creature's legs, staying away from the snapping pincers and striking tail. He started forward but the stinger came arcing down at him. The Paladin jumped back as it impacted the ground, sand flying in the air.

He watched Jade shoot one more bolt of fire, then she dropped the flames. Her green eyes seemed to glow for a moment, a feral look crossing her face. Her body hunched, dropped, and then she transformed into a white tiger. With a snarl the tiger launched itself at the scorpion, claws slashing and teeth snapping.

Zok ran forward and swung his hammer at the beast's legs. It moved fast, scurrying around, pincers snapping and stinger striking as they pounded it with attacks. It began to get desperate, thrashing about. A pincer scooped Skar up and threw him down. The stinger struck at Artemis and she rolled out of the way. Jade as a tiger was thrown off its back, its legs attempting to stomp her.

And then the Wizard stood up, made a series of movements with his wand, and said in Draconic, "*Jīvæmav!*"

The scorpion was lifted off the ground, still flailing angrily but unable to reach them. With a grunt Skar said, "I can't hold it much longer!"

And then Sen leaped from the ground, axe glinting, and cut the scorpion's tail off with a spray of blood. Immediately the spell released and the creature dropped to the ground, sand bursting up from the impact. Sen was there in an instant, jumping onto its back. With a great chop he removed its head from its body.

There was a moment's pause as the five of them waited. But the body didn't move and nothing else came from beneath the sand. Zok sighed, lowering his weapon, when Sen staggered, coughed, and dropped to his knees. His red scaled hand grabbed the stinger wound.

Jade transformed back into her Wild Elf body. She gasped, "*Sen!*"

Zok raced up with the others as the pirate captain sat back, breathing heavily. It unnerved him to see someone as strong and powerful as Sen fall like that.

"I got stung," Sen grunted, removing his hand from the wound. The scales were bloody and some were turning black from the venom.

Jade dropped her pack to the sand, rummaging through it hurriedly. "I can fix this, just hold on. Hold on." She pulled out herbs and ointments and mixed them together. They smelled fresh like the forests around Somberdale.

Zok slowly went to his knees, putting his heavy shield and hammer down beside him. They watched in silence as Jade applied the ointment to the wound. Sen hissed, gritting sharp teeth against the pain. The muscles in his neck and chest bulged, but otherwise he held still. Blood stained the sand around the corpse of the scorpion, its vacant eyes staring at them.

As Jade worked, she murmured a healing spell. Her hands glowed with gentle green light, and she almost appeared to go into a trance as the minutes passed. After his adrenaline wore off Zok could feel the cold of the night. He shivered as he crouched in the sand. Foxy came to sit beside him, and the Paladin gratefully buried his fingers in the warm fur of the animal.

At last the Druid finished, and sat back with a weary sigh. "You will be fine. Just take it easy on that shoulder."

Sen examined the wrap of plants applied to the wound. "Thank you, Jade. It has stopped hurting."

"You scared me for a second there," Zok said, letting out his breath in relief.

The pirate chuckled. "You never need to worry about me. I am invincible!"

Artemis stood, looking around their now-ruined camp. "We still have half a night left. Do we keep sleeping here or find a new place?"

"I think we should stay here," Jade said, putting her herbalism supplies back in her pack. "That dead scorpion might help ward off other intruders."

As they gathered their belongings and rearranged their sleeping area, Zok said, "Jade, I've never seen you transform into an animal before. That was incredible."

She smiled. "Thank you. It's been awhile since I've done it. It can be a taxing transformation. But it is useful."

"Can you become a bird and scout the area?" Skar asked, smoothing out his bedroll.

"Hm," the Druid scratched her chin. "Birds are more difficult. It's been so long since I've transformed, I think I'll need to practice more before I can fly."

"I'd like to fly over the ocean as a bird," Sen said thoughtfully, lying back gently so as not to hurt his shoulder. "That is real freedom."

Skar also settled down on his bedroll and asked, "Where did you learn magic, Jade?"

"My mother was a Druid. Not a very powerful one, but she knew some spells. She saw the same talent in me and began training me as a child. But once I became an adult, she saw that I had more potential. It was decided I needed formal training from a stronger Druid. We found a man named Galen in the Firelit Forest. I spent many, many years with him and learned Druidic magic."

Zok crossed his arms under his head and he lied back, staring up at the starry sky. Jade had mentioned a Master Galen a couple times in the past. "Are you still in contact with him? Galen?"

"I am not. He passed away from old age nearly two hundred years ago." There was a pause and she said, "Where did you learn magic, Skar? You said it wasn't at the Citadel."

"No, it was . . . well . . ." Confusion crept into his voice. "You know, I don't really remember. I must have been young. I'm sure I had a teacher, as well."

Artemis chuckled. "You must have a terrible memory. Are you sure you're a Wizard? Don't they have to study a lot, or something?"

Skar's tone was offended as he said, "I can do more magic than you, Ranger."

"Not everyone needs magic," Sen said. "I can beat things into submission with my fists."

Conversation died down as they all settled into sleep once again. Zok reflected on the power of a Druid to be able to transform and fly away. He wondered if he had that power, how would he use it? His feet had taken him far. He didn't necessarily have a desire to fly. There was no wanderlust. But the ability to get to different places more quickly would be nice. His father in Sunspire was so very far, far away. He missed him. He knew his path would lead him back there one day. All Paladins had to take on a quest. One that sent them to the various temples of the Holy Dragon across Corventos with the purpose of doing good. He had been to all but two. De Behl Marr and Sunspire. When he had finished doing good in Somberdale, he would journey to the southeast of Corventos. He would journey back home.

With thoughts of home and the future in his head, he drifted off to sleep.

The next morning brought an early start to traveling. They ate while walking, the sun casting their shadows alongside them. Sen seemed to feel better but still was careful with the wound in his shoulder. It was another three hours of walking before they could make out shapes ahead. The colors blended in with the desert, but the forms were hard and angular. Buildings.

The group picked up their pace, encouraged by the sight of their destination. As they drew nearer details could be made out. Zok wasn't sure what to expect. He knew the old stories of Soleia, the City of the Sun. He knew of its wealth and beauty, and then its mysterious disappearance. Would all the beautiful buildings still be there, just abandoned? Or would there be nothing but a couple of huts and vagabonds?

The answer was somewhere in between. What lied before them was a ruin. Golden buildings stuck out of the sand at different angles, dirty and damaged from hundreds of years of disuse. None were more than two stories tall. There were no city streets, no market, no town square. It was all just sand dunes. There were some people about, living in tents that flapped in the hot wind.

"Wow," Jade said as they approached. "There's not much left."

They rode the camels into the city, searching for any clue as to where to go next. From one of the tents stepped a Dwarf. His skin was dark brown from the sun, and his red beard was braided tightly. He gave them a half-hearted wave with a dirty hand. "Greetings. What brings you to Soleia?"

Zok dismounted his camel. "We are searching for any old tombs or temples here that run underground."

The Dwarf's eyes flicked over his attire. "Are you with the two women that just came in?"

The Paladin frowned. "Two women? What did they look like?"

"Human with dark hair and one of those creepy Half-Fiend types. They were wearing clothes like yours."

Priestess Liana and Whitney. Zok's mind spun. What would they be doing here? "Yes . . . we are. Where did they go?"

The Dwarf pointed to a sandstone tower a mile off. "They went inside there only two hours ago."

"Thank you." Leading his camel, Zok quickly walked towards the tower, trusting the others were following. Why were two priestesses from his temple here? Were they involved in Amon's death? Or, like him, were they following clues that led them to the Lantern of Vicrum?

The sand made his steps heavy but the Paladin barely noticed. His gaze was fixed on the tower, standing up against a background of blue sky.

"What is wrong?" Jade asked, her voice cutting through the cobwebs of his thoughts.

"It's Priestess Liana and Priestess Whitney," he replied, not looking back. "They are the ones in that tower. I need to get there before they leave."

The ruined buildings of Soleia rose and fell around them as they reached the tower. Tying the camels off, Zok tried the splintered wooden door to find it was ajar. With him at the front, they went inside.

The first room was covered in sand about a foot deep. Bright sunlight came from a broken window. But otherwise the area was bare. The group trudged through and to a winding staircase that ran along the wall. Zok cautiously led the way up, trying to make as little noise as he could in full armor. The tower was strangely silent. If the two priestesses were still here, what were they doing?

The second floor was a circular room with mirrors lining it. A few were smashed, and Zok looked at his own broken reflection, dirty and sunburned from travel through the desert. In the center was the body of a dead lizard-like creature, hefty and long. A basilisk, the Paladin knew.

"It's recently dead," Artemis whispered, crouching by it. "Your friends must have done this. It makes sense why the mirrors are smashed."

"It does?" Skar asked, creeping closer.

The Ranger gestured to the items in question. "A basilisk's gaze can turn people to stone. I doubt it being in this tower is a coincidence. There must be something here worth guarding."

"Then let's keep going up," Zok answered softly.

They ascended the stairs again, their footsteps gentle. Another window allowed a view over the Expanse as they passed. All rolling dunes and clear sky. As they neared the next landing Zok prepared himself for whatever lay beyond. Would there be another fight? He didn't want what happened to Priest Jafr to happen to the others. Whatever he could do to avoid death, he would.

.

.

.

SKAR

.

.

.

This set of stairs was much longer than the rest. They left the windows behind and the tower darkened around them. Skar lit his wand and their paced slowed, careful not to trip. He hoped there would be treasure in this place. He wasn't the type to be interested in gold or jewels. He liked to collect unusual things. Rarities. Oddities. Bones. Things he could study from an arcane perspective. Like his two-headed worm. Traveling with this group of people had proven profitable from that standpoint. Already he had a small bottle of sand from Somberdale's beach and a finger bone from the tombs underneath Brother Zok's temple. He needed to keep that treasure a secret so as not to upset the Paladin.

Those Elf-folk were an interesting group. He respected Jade's magical prowess. As a spellcaster himself, he knew the craft wasn't easy. Artemis Wolfsbane was a bundle of energy, sometimes he found her exhausting to be around. And Brother Zok was the opposite, very serious constantly. He was glad for the other Dragonborn, Sen. If not for his personality, at least for someone he didn't have to look down to talk to. He actually had to look up to meet Sen's gaze. The red Dragonborn was huge.

They went up the stairs for ten more minutes before reaching the top. They were faced with a long, rectangular room. The floor extended ten feet out before dropping into a massive hole that took up the entire room. On the opposite side was another open threshold, showing a new corridor beyond. The hole was thirty feet across and descended down into darkness. There were no windows, and the light from Skar's wand didn't penetrate the bottom of the pit. He wasn't sure how high they'd climbed to this next level. But if they were to fall, it certainly would be a serious injury.

"Well," Artemis sighed, "this is interesting."

Skar lifted his light higher as they surveyed the area.

Jade pointed to the ceiling. "There are numbers in Elvish."

Everyone looked up. The ceiling was made up of square tiles. And each tile had an Elvish number on it. Skar couldn't read them, but Brother Zok appeared emboldened by this discovery. The Paladin went over to the edge, looked back and forth from the numbers to the hole a few times, and then stepped out.

And he stepped onto something solid. He appeared suspended in the air, but as he bent his knees to test, there was clearly something solid under him.

"An invisible bridge?" Skar suggested.

Zok studied the ceiling some more before taking one step forward and another to the left. He said, "You just follow the numbers."

"What do they say?" Sen asked skeptically.

Jade translated, "There is just a bunch of random numbers all over. But right here there is a one. Then a two, three, four, and a five over there. And so on. It's revealing a path. Sen, I'll take you with me. Artemis, take Skar."

Skar was hesitant, but Artemis was a patient leader as she showed him exactly where to step. It was a strange sensation, not seeing any floor but feeling one. The Ranger and the Druid both had their animals carried on their backs, and neither canine appeared very happy with the experience.

It was a long, slow cross as they carefully made their way over the gap. A few times Skar felt the edges of the path. His Dragonborn feet were large, after all. But he carefully shuffled along and tried to stay completely focused. Artemis held tightly onto his hand and pointed out each step.

"Careful, follow me closely," she stated, her head constantly moving back and forth from the ceiling tiles to their feet.

Skar tried not to focus too much on the darkness below him. The drop into nothing. But it was hard when he had to stare at Artemis' boots. He gathered his courage and continued to follow. There was no turning back, after all.

At last they all reached the opposite side. Breathing a sigh of relief, they pressed on down another stone corridor. They came to a fork in the hall. The ceiling rose high above them. But the wall they were faced with only extended fifteen feet high before ending.

"Which direction?" Brother Zok asked.

"I've always liked left," Sen suggested, and led the way around the corner.

They walked on for another twenty feet before the path wound right and then broke off into two new directions. There was hesitation as they all took in the paths, the walls that stopped at fifteen feet high, the plainness of their surroundings.

"We're in a maze," Jade stated.

"I love mazes!" Artemis exclaimed.

Sen frowned. "How is that possible? This tower didn't look large enough for a maze."

"Perhaps it's not very big?" Brother Zok suggested. "Or . . . there's some kind of magic at work here. Illusion based or transmutation. If the Lantern of Vicrum is here, there have obviously been things put in place to protect it. There's no telling what else we might find."

The pirate captain shuddered. "Why can't things just be as they are? I don't like this trickery and manipulation."

Brother Zok hopped a couple times, attempting to look over the walls, armor clanking with his movements. He turned to the bronze Dragonborn. "Skar, could you levitate me like you did that scorpion? Maybe I can find a fast way through."

"That is cheating!" Artemis gasped.

The Paladin gave her an exasperated look. "Maybe, but I think it's best we get through this quickly so we don't lose Liana and Whitney."

Skar gave his wand a twirl, preparing for the spell. "How much do you weigh?"

Brother Zok frowned. "Not as much as that

scorpion."

Skar cast the spell, focusing his efforts on the Half-Elf. His brow furrowed in concentration as he lifted Brother Zok high enough so that his chest was even with the maze walls. He watched as the Paladin glanced around, then froze. Blue eyes popped wide and he gasped. "Drop me!"

The Wizard looked at him in irritation. "What? I just cast the spell! I'm not going to-"

"*Drop me!*"

Skar did, releasing the spell in an instant. Brother Zok fell to the ground just as a spear flew through the air right where he'd been. It clattered against the opposite wall and fell to the floor.

"What the hell was that?" Sen asked, pulling out his axe.

"A minotaur," Brother Zok gasped. "It saw me."

Artemis notched an arrow to her bow, a dark smile spreading over her face. "Finally! I was beginning to think we wouldn't get to fight."

The group moved quickly through the maze, trying to choose directions they thought led them to the exit. There was no point in attempting to move quietly, the minotaur knew they were there. But would they run into it or avoid it entirely?

Everything looked the same to Skar, despite his sharp and educated mind. Brother Zok led, choosing directions quickly, and it all blurred together. They panted from exertion as they jogged through the maze. The fox and wolf followed up at the back of the group, tongues lolling out. Skar felt the ache in his calf muscles, the soreness of his feet.

Just when he was certain they'd been running through the maze for a half hour and surely must be close to the end, there was a great roar from around the corner and the minotaur sprang into the view. The Wizard caught a glimpse of brown fur, armored legs, and a large axe in its hands before it swung at the person at the front of the group: Brother Zok.

The Paladin brought up his shield and the impact

echoed down the corridor. He was sent sprawling back, caught by Sen. The red Dragonborn drew his own axe, leaping at the enemy with a battle cry. The two weapons clashed. The minotaur was just as large as Sen, its biceps bulging as it put all its strength into each attack.

The rest of the party reacted at once. Artemis held her arrow taut and waited for an opening. Jade bent down and transformed into a white tiger again, clawing and snapping at the minotaur's legs. Zok attempted to get around Sen to help out, but the hall was too narrow and the fighters too large.

Skar raised his wand and fired off the burning orbs. They swirled past Sen and curved, striking their target accurately. The minotaur barely flinched, pushing hard on the attack and driving the pirate captain backwards. As Sen was sent stumbling Artemis got her opening, burying an arrow in the minotaur's shoulder. It growled but didn't slow down, aiming an overhead strike for Brother Zok. The Paladin spun out of the way, and the axe smashed the ground where he was.

Jade as a tiger leaped onto the opponent's back, claws drawing blood. The minotaur reached back, grabbed hold of her, and threw her fifteen feet away. As she landed with a whimper, Foxy ran over to ensure she was okay.

Skar concentrated on another spell and let loose a burst of ice from his wand. It streaked through the air, narrowly missing Sen, and struck the minotaur's arm. Ice began to coat the fur, but it just grunted and broke it apart with its free hand, burning eyes now turning towards the Wizard.

The pirate captain went on the attack again, shouting as he used his recovering shoulder to slam the minotaur with attacks. Another one of Artemis's arrows cut through the air, sinking into their opponent's thigh. Brother Zok backed up Sen, taking strikes with his hammer whenever he had an opening.

The minotaur roared out, its axe striking harder as it pushed forward once again, throwing the two off-balance.

And as it raised its weapon high for a mortal strike, Artemis let loose a third arrow that sunk into its throat.

The minotaur staggered, blood soaking down its chest. It attempted a lazy swing at Sen before it fell backwards, dead.

"Nice work," Jade said as she returned to her Wild Elf form.

Brother Zok rolled the shoulder that supported his shield, wincing. "That thing hit *very* hard. I'm going to be feeling that blow for a few days."

Artemis bounded over to the minotaur's body, looking it over. "Maybe it has some gold coins on it."

"Why would it have gold?" Skar asked, curious.

The Ranger shrugged. "If adventurers come through here, I'm sure it takes what it can off them. That's what I would do if I had my own maze to prowl in. Oh, look!" she held up a brown leather bag that was tied off with rope. "I bet there's some good stuff in here." She immediately opened it and glanced in. "Hm, looks empty."

Jade frowned, pushing strands of dark brown hair from her sweaty forehead. "The minotaur was carrying around an empty bag?"

Skar watched as Artemis reached into the bag, feeling around. Her arm went deeper, and deeper, and deeper. Despite the bag only being ten inches long, her arm kept sinking well past that depth. Finally, she was up to her shoulder, staring at the bag in wonder. The others' expression mirrored hers, eyes wide.

"An enchanted bag," Skar said, his interest piqued. "That's incredible! I wonder what is in it?"

"I can't feel anything," Artemis said.

"For enchantments like this," Skar explained, "only whoever put an item in the bag would know how to get it out. Or, I've also heard turning enchanted bags inside out does the trick."

Brother Zok held up his hands. "Let's not do that just yet. There's no telling what could fall out. We'll do it in a safe environment."

"Tymus could look at it," Sen suggested, strapping his large axe again to his back.

"That is a good idea," Jade agreed. "We need to check in with him again, anyway, about the translation of that red tome."

Artemis stood and made a wide, sweeping gesture over the body of the minotaur. "Shall we save some to eat later?"

That was met with a gasp from Brother Zok and Skar, and a scrunched nose from Sen and Jade.

"What?" the Half-Elf archer asked. "I'm sure it's delicious! We could cook the meat under the desert stars."

Brother Zok rolled his blue eyes, pushing ahead into the maze. "Let's go. I want to get out of here before anyone else makes a ridiculous suggestion."

Artemis crossed her arms, following with Wolfie on her heels. "If you get hungry later and we can't find meat, don't complain to me, city-boy."

Skar chuckled in amusement as he followed behind the group, but not before taking some fur from the minotaur and putting it in his pack. It was only a couple more minutes before they reached the end of the maze. The Wizard wasn't sure if it was from skill or luck, but he was happy to see a large room open up before them. It was dark, the light on his wand casting the stone in an eerie glow. It smelled old, like the chamber hadn't been disturbed in a long while. But the most interesting thing about the area was a portal at the far end. Standing upon an altar, it glowed dark blue and pulsed with magic. It was ten feet in diameter, and it lit the area a few feet around it in bluish light.

And there, staring at it with deep frowns, were Priestess Liana and Priestess Whitney.

Brother Zok immediately reacted, holding up his hammer. "Priestesses!"

"Brother Zok," Liana said as she and the Half-Fiend turned. "This is a surprise."

The Paladin's voice was venomous as he spoke. "Is it? All of us are here for the same reason."

"Yes, the Lantern of Vicrum," Liana gestured to the portal. "Hidden away inside this tower."

"And you killed Priest Amon for it."

A smile played at Whitney's mouth. "We did what we had to do. The old man knew the location but wouldn't give it."

As Skar listened to their argument, his body tense in preparation for a fight, he heard a voice enter his mind. It was genderless, coming across as a hiss. It said, *You belong to me now, Wizard.*

Skar felt his body tighten, and suddenly he had no more control. His head slowly turned to the person closest to him. Artemis.

Zok snapped, "Why do you need the Lantern? What could *possibly* be worth all of this?"

Skar watched the scene unfold, but felt disconnected. His arm lifted his wand towards the Ranger. He resisted, but was powerless to stop it. A laugh sounded in his mind.

Liana chuckled. "You've come all this way and you still don't know what it does. It's power, Brother Zok. Power that I, and the rest of my people, need."

Skar brought the wand even with Artemis' head, and began to cast a spell.

"Look out!" Zok shouted. At the same time Artemis spun and disarmed the Wizard with a quick hand movement.

A burst of light came from Liana as she cast a spell. The beam shot forward and hit the Paladin. He didn't get his shield up in time and was sent tumbling back, smoke coming off of his skin. Jade's hand shot out into the air and a vine ripped itself free from the ground. With a flick of her wrist the vine had wrapped itself around Liana's ankle and yanked her to the ground, the priestess' head hitting with a *crack.*

Whitney raced towards the Druid with two knives drawn but Sen jumped in between, knocking her strike wide. He followed that up with a swift punch to the side of her head. The Half-Friend crumpled to the ground.

And just as quickly as the violence had started it

stopped, leaving the room in silence once again.

Zok picked himself up, wincing at his blistered neck. "Skar, are you all right?"

The Wizard blinked in confusion, rubbing his forehead. Whatever connection had been between himself and the thing that controlled him was now gone. His body was his own again. "Yes, I . . . it was like I lost control of my body for a moment. A voice in my head told me to turn on you. I am very sorry, Artemis. I could have hurt you."

The Half-Elven Ranger laughed. "You couldn't have hurt me, Skar. But thanks, anyway."

Liana moaned, slowly sitting up and holding her head, an equally as confused expression on her face. "What just happened?"

Zok sighed in relief. "You two were controlled through magic. But you are okay now."

"I think I have been for a while," Liana stated.

"Do you know who did this?" Jade asked.

The Human priestess shook her head. "I don't. I just remember his voice, giving me orders I couldn't disobey. He really wanted the Lantern."

Brother Zok looked to the portal. "Why don't you two go rest? We'll go through here and see what we find."

It was agreed to and Liana and Whitney went downstairs, both nursing their wounds and preparing some healing to prevent any concussions.

The five of them turned to the portal. It shimmered and throbbed as if alive, shedding dim light on their faces.

"I don't know about this," Sen said. "We don't know if it's safe to pass through."

Brother Zok let out his breath slowly, steeling his nerves. "I agree. But we've come this far. I can't go back without finding the truth. You don't have to follow me."

"I will come," Jade said. "We support each other."

"I'm not afraid," Artemis chimed, twirling an arrow in her hand.

"I will come as well," Skar said.

Sen sighed, hanging his head. "Well, I don't want to

be left behind. Let's go, dammit."

They cautiously proceeded forward, stepping onto the dais. Brother Zok approached first and reached his hand out. It passed through the portal, and he hesitated before pulling it back out. He hadn't been harmed. Drawing himself up, he stepped forward and through, vanishing from sight.

Jade and Artemis followed immediately afterwards. Skar glanced to Sen, but the pirate gestured for him to go first. The Wizard went through, felt a slight tingling sensation in his body, and then was faced with a square stone room. It was plain and featureless, save for a creature made of shadow at the far end. The body was humanoid, but the edges were blurred and the face was blank. The being was manacled to the stone wall behind it.

"This is strange," Brother Zok said softly.

As Sen came through the portal as well, axe clutched tightly in his hands, the group slowly went forward.

And then the shadow humanoid spoke. No mouth moved, but a deep voice emanated from it all the same. "You are not who I was expecting."

"Were you expecting Liana and Whitney?" Brother Zok asked, taking one more step forward as the rest of the group stopped.

The shadow replied, "Are those their names? It's not important for me to learn. But I felt my connection snap." His head swiveled towards Skar. "It was fun prying in your mind for a moment, Wizard."

"You're the one responsible for the mind control?" Jade asked, an angry edge to her voice.

"Not just mind control, but *possession*. I took over the body of that Human priestess, and through her magic I controlled and influenced the minds of the others. You all are so vulnerable, so defenseless. It is too easy."

Sen snorted, switching his axe to one hand. "Those are tough words coming from someone who is chained to a wall."

"How did you end up here?" Brother Zok demanded. "Who are you?"

The shadow cocked its head to the side. "And why should I answer your questions?"

The Paladin responded, "Because you are responsible for the deaths of High Priest Amon and Priest Jafr. You have been judged and justice will be brought to you. You are not leaving this room alive. What do you have to lose by answering me?"

With a laugh the being said, "Brave Paladin. But your threats are hollow. My name is Fenvell. I was once a prisoner inside what is now known as the Lantern of Vicrum. I switched my bondage for another. Vicrum Grodstrum. I trapped him inside, but . . . didn't quite get my freedom. I have been seeking a way out of this imprisonment. As the power of my people has grown, so has mine. By infiltrating the minds of others, I was going to use the power of the Lantern to gain my freedom."

"Vicrum Grodstrum?" Jade shook her head. "The Dwarf king of Soleia? Are you trying to convince us he's not dead, but actually *trapped* inside the Lantern?"

"Believe what you will," Fenvell said. "But tell me, Elf, what do you think brought about the ruin of Soleia? It is not destroyed. I *buried* it."

Artemis spoke up. "How would the Lantern get you your freedom? Is Vicrum magical, or something?"

"Vicrum is trapped with a Wish curse. He cannot be released unless he fulfills the wishes of the one that has the Lantern. I was going to tap into this power to free myself. But it matters not. The summer solstice is approaching. My probes into the minds of your people have proven how powerless you are. We cannot be stopped."

"Who is *we*?" Brother Zok demanded, his voice on the edge of shouting. "You better start talking, or I won't be merciful. Why would you invade the minds of *my* people? What made you think they would know about a Lantern in the desert?"

Fenvell turned his head towards the Paladin. "Why would you think those are the only minds I invaded? I have been searching for a long time. My people are known as the

Foresight. And we are coming for the king of An'Ock."

"I've had enough of this!" Sen strode forward, spinning his axe in his large hand. "Go ahead and come! We are not afraid of you, and you all will die." With that he swung his axe hard and fast, and chopped Fenvell's head off. It rolled down to the ground, and then it and his body vanished.

The tension melted in the room, muscles relaxing and held breaths let out.

"That was crazy," Skar said. "Was he telling the truth?"

Artemis put her bow and arrow away. "I don't see any reason why he would lie. But . . . where is the Lantern, then?"

As soon as the words left her mouth a new portal swirled into being, right on the spot Fenvell had been. It pulsed with the same magical energy.

A look of determination crossed Brother Zok's face, and without waiting for the others he bounded through. After a moment of hesitation and exchanging of glances, the rest of them followed.

.

.

.

ARTEMIS

.

.

.

The group found themselves back outside. They stood atop the tower, overlooking the Expanse. Artemis blinked her blue eyes rapidly, adjusting to the change of light. As she looked out over the ruin of the city, now aware that it was simply buried, she could see the layout more clearly. It was designed in a wide circle, the buildings clustered closer together in the center. What she initially had thought were ramshackle huts were actually the tops of buildings that must have been large at one point. She could almost imagine this place as it had been. Perhaps they could fix what had been broken.

And there, sitting on the roof, was a wooden chest. It was secured with a lock, but as Artemis crouched down to examine it the lock snapped as a burst of shadow scattered from it. There was a moment of hesitation, and then the Ranger opened the chest. Inside was lined with golden velvet. And sitting in the center was a lantern. It was made of solid gold, and jewels encrusted its corners. Despite not being lit, it glowed warmly from the inside.

"The Lantern of Vicrum," Skar breathed. "We have passed the barriers. The prize is ours."

Artemis looked up to Brother Zok. "We are here because your people were killed over this thing. It's only fair you handle it."

The Paladin nodded to her and gently picked it up. He looked it over for a moment, the sunlight glinting off of it and reflecting in his eyes. "How do we release Vicrum?"

Skar leaned closer, studying the item. "There are faint arcane symbols carved on it. A sealing spell. I should be able to unlock it."

"Go ahead," Brother Zok encouraged, handing the Lantern to the bronze-scaled Dragonborn.

Skar sat it down and muttered a spell, waving his hand over the item. Instantly the light from within grew stronger. The glow increased as Skar finished his incantation. They all took a step back, shielding their eyes from the brightness.

And then the light dimmed and formed into a Dwarf. Braids and precious stones weaved through his black hair. Tan of skin and dark of eyes, he wore blue clothes of fine craft. His body was slightly transparent, and they could see the desert through him.

His voice was kind and deep as he spoke. "I am finally free." He regarded his translucent hands. "I see. Not quite free yet." He turned to look at the group. "Have you destroyed Fenvell?"

"We have," Brother Zok stated. "Is it true you are King Vicrum Grodstrum?"

"I am." His gaze swept out over the buried Soleia. "I feared this would happen in my absence. How long has it been?"

"A thousand years?" Jade guessed. "Perhaps more?"

Artemis knew Dwarves could live over eight hundred years. Halflings and Gnomes also had lives that lasted centuries. It seemed strange that, despite having Half-Elven blood, people like her did not have a greatly extended lifespan. While full-blooded Elves could live to one thousand years, Half-Elves only lived a couple decades over one hundred. She did not know how old King Vicrum was on the Day of Sealing, but that was 1,560 years ago, now.

Vicrum let out a sad sigh, seeming to give himself a moment to grieve for his home and lost time. Then his eyes sharpened. "So tell me, why have you sought the Lantern?"

Brother Zok spoke. "Fenvell possessed members of the temple I am a Paladin of. He was trying to find a way to get to your Lantern to use the magic to free himself. I followed the clues in an attempt to bring justice for the murder of two priests. Fenvell is gone, and so justice has been served." He paused, then asked, "What exactly *was* Fenvell?"

"I wish I knew," the Dwarf king answered. "All I know is that he is from another plane of existence. One called the Gloomdwell. But his origin and true nature are a mystery to me. Once I am free, I will look into his past and see what I can learn. Then the world will be better prepared for future threats like his."

Jade spoke. "Fenvell said the Foresight would come during the summer solstice for the king of An'Ock. That is nearly a year away. The more we can prepare before that day, the better."

Vicrum stroked his dark beard pensively. "Interesting. We have ample time to rally a defense. The king should be warned, though."

"We will warn him," Brother Zok replied. "We are heading back north soon."

"That is good. Now, please free me. Unless there is something you wish?" His tone carried an edge.

The group exchanged glances. Artemis said, "It seems unfair Soleia could just be buried like this because of Fenvell's actions. Is there a way to return the city to its former glory?"

Vicrum deadpanned, "With a wish."

Brother Zok regarded the group with a sly smile. "We better get some shovels, then."

Vicrum sighed. "What would you want to use this magic for, if not for the return of Soleia and my freedom?"

The Paladin replied in a more serious tone, "We are facing a threat aside from the Foresight and what Fenvell wrought. There is a powerful spellcaster that has been using us. To what end, we don't know. But we find ourselves outmatched. If we could increase our power, then we could stop him next time we cross paths."

The rest of the group glanced at Brother Zok in surprise.

"A spellcaster, you say? Fighting someone who can manipulate reality around them is daunting, I agree," Vicrum

169

thought for a moment as his eyes took in Brother Zok's armor. "I, too, am a follower of the Holy Dragon."

Zok's eyebrows rose. "I serve the temple in Somberdale. Our High Priest was murdered for your Lantern."

Vicrum nodded. "I can help you, to an extent. Name one thing you want a piece. One way you want to be stronger. If it's within my power, I will make it so."

There was a moment of silence while everyone considered. Artemis was very confident in her ability to fight. She was a seasoned warrior and didn't need help defending herself. And yet, when faced with Jenkins she hadn't been able to hurt him. She had been powerless against his orders. If there was a way to improve, perhaps it was to be more magical? Maybe that wasn't it. She didn't rely on magic during combat, and what little spells she knew were to influence nature. Perhaps she needed a way to move around a battlefield faster. She was an archer. She had her daggers for close combat, but that was not where her power was at. If she had a way to quickly distance herself from opponents, it would make her deadlier. Perhaps even enough to stop Jenkins next time she saw him.

And so Artemis spoke up first. "I'd like the ability to teleport. I know this can be accomplished with spells, but that magic is beyond me to learn."

Vicrum nodded. "I can grant you this power."

Sen said, "I don't wear armor, it slows me down. But if I could make my scales tougher to withstand more blows, I could defend my friends better."

The Dwarf nodded once again. "I can do that."

Skar gestured to his large form. "I am not quiet or stealthy. My magic can take me far but not that far. I would like to be able to go intangible to sneak through walls and doors."

Vicrum considered for a moment. "I can make it so you temporarily pass through the border plane. This will be dangerous, but if you want I can give you this magic."

"Thank you," the Wizard replied.

Brother Zok stated, "I'd like to be faster. Run faster,

fight faster, dodge faster. All of it."

"Mmm . . . that is a dangerous thing you are requesting, as well. But if you are okay with the risks, I will fulfill it to the best of my abilities."

"I understand the risks and am willing to take them."

"Very well." The Dwarf King looked to the Druid. "And you?"

Jade considered for a long moment. When her green eyes looked to Vicrum, there was a passion and determination in them. Artemis knew whatever decision she'd come to had been carefully weighed. This was personal. Jade said, "I want to be unharmed by fire."

Vicrum regarded her for a moment before answering, "This I can do." Then he began to speak a spell, making symbols with his hands. His eyes closed. Artemis could feel the magic affect her. This was no simple spell that was happening. Usually with a couple words and gestures a spell could be completed. But this was taking time. Minutes dragged on, but Vicrum never broke his concentration. Artemis could tell the others were feeling the effects as well. Sen shivered, Skar flinched, Jade squeezed her hands into fists, and Brother Zok began twitching.

Artemis could feel something disrupt inside of her. It was slightly painful, but nothing she couldn't handle. But then . . . something *hurt*. She felt a stab in her chest and she doubled over. She was surprised to see the others react the same way at the same time. And then, for just a split second, she saw their shadows tear themselves from the ground and lift into the air. But then she blinked and everything was normal again. Their shadows were at their feet where they belonged, and the pain was gone.

And then the changes began.

Sen's scales rippled. He glanced down at his bare torso and flexed. A sheen went over his scales and they all became metal, shining like silver in the sun. He flexed again and they returned to their normal red. The pirate lifted his head to the sky and laughed in triumph.

Skar closed his eyes in concentration and then his

body became opaque, the desert visible through it. He released his concentration and returned to his fully physical form, smiling.

Jade winced as smoke drifted off her hands. She gritted her teeth in pain as the skin on her hands blackened, working its way up onto her forearms in a pattern very much like fire. For a moment she cried out, and then the smoke drifted away, the pain seemingly gone. She stared in shock at her now black hands, like they had been plunged into the ashes of a campfire.

Brother Zok turned on his heel and ran down into the tower. It was only a few seconds before Artemis spotted him racing across the desert, much faster than any living thing could travel. He then turned in a wide circle and ran back up the tower and to the roof again, his brown hair blown back from his face and eyes sparkling with adrenaline.

Artemis turned and looked at a point on the ground. She concentrated, picturing herself there. And all at once she felt her body rip itself free from the ties that bound it, and she reappeared at the spot she was staring at. She felt a little disoriented and dizzy, but it was nothing she couldn't shake off. The Ranger looked back up at the group, silhouetted against the sun, and teleported back to the top of the tower.

They all shared a look of excitement.

Finishing his spell, Vicrum's shoulders slumped with exertion. "Well, there you go. I hope you are pleased."

"Extremely," Brother Zok stated. "Thank you. And now we wish for Soleia to be returned to its former glory."

Vicrum strode forward to the edge of the tower, and began a new spell. There was a fire in his voice, a determination in his words as he cast. The ground shook, and Artemis watched the people that had been living in the city ruins start to run away from the epicenter of the shockwaves. The sands rolled, like a massive creature had awakened underneath. The tower they were on shook, and the Ranger crouched down to keep her balance better, one arm thrown over Wolfie.

And then everything shifted. Artemis couldn't tell if

the buildings were getting taller, the sand was sinking lower, or both at the same time. But suddenly the architecture of Soleia was revealed, coming out of its slumber like a great desert beast. Golden spires and rounded rooftops rose above the dunes. Windows of stained glass revealed themselves, statues of Dwarves, Humans, and Elves, rounded temples, graceful towers, and long rectangular buildings lined with columns. It was beautiful. Artemis had never seen a place like it before. It was a far cry from the functionality of the architecture in the Southern Kingdoms. This was made to look like a pile of treasure in the desert.

The whole process took about fifteen minutes, and the five of them watched in awe. Artemis was vaguely aware that the people who had been living in the ruins now stood cheering, amazed at the return of the city. Finally, with a few more rumbles and sand cascading from rooftops like waterfalls, the whole process was completed. Soleia, the City of the Sun, in ruin since the War for the World, was now returned.

"It's beautiful," Skar breathed, pushing his dark blue hood back so he could see it more clearly. "I can see now why dragons were drawn to it."

"Yes," Vicrum said, a tired smile at his face. "It was always a sight to behold."

Brother Zok looked to the Dwarf king. "You should be aware, on our journey down the coast we ran into a gold dragon named Draxis. He didn't seem overly aggressive, but I don't know if this city will draw him out."

Vicrum's dark eyes went wide. "Draxis is still alive? I've known Draxis since he was a tiny wyrmling. He used to live in this city. We were very close. I will have to contact him, and tell him to come home."

The group exchanged bewildered glances. Artemis said, "You know Draxis? He asked us to fetch a gold compass for him. He said pirates had stolen it."

"Ah, yes, I remember his compass. I'm sure he would like it back, it can be used to find enchanted items. If you do find it, come here to Soleia. You can find myself and Draxis here." His gaze swept over them. "Is there anything else you would request of me?"

"No," Brother Zok stated. "We wish for you to be free of your curse."

Vicrum's shoulders relaxed in relief. There was a swirl of magical energy around him and the Lantern. And then the Lantern cracked, and his body became solid. A weight was behind him, and they could no longer see through him to the desert beyond.

"Thank you," Vicrum said. "You have done a great deed here today. Who are you?"

"I am Brother Zok of the Temple of the Holy Dragon. This is Captain Sen of the Scarlet Maiden, Skar the Wizard, Jade the Druid, and Artemis the Ranger . . . and Foxy and Wolfie."

"Are you an adventuring group?"

"We are," Artemis answered in excitement. "We stop threats and kick ass! Monsters and villains don't see us coming. We're like phantoms, the five of us."

A wide smile spread over Brother Zok's face. "When people ask what happened here to restore Soleia, you can tell them it was through the help of the Phantom Five."

Vicrum smiled in acknowledgement. "I will do that. Thank you, Phantom Five. Now please, come into my city to celebrate. You will always be honored guests."

.

.

.

Soleia was reborn in celebration that night. Food was gathered and hunted, and a large feast was had under the starlight in the city center. The people that had been living in the ruins danced and sang and played instruments. It was the most fun Artemis had in a long time. It was nice to be here, where no one knew the name Wolfsbane, and she could be free to be herself.

She lounged on one of the inactive fountains, staring at the party. Wolfie sat at her feet, his tail wagging as he responded to the atmosphere about him. Torches had been lit, casting the square in a honey glow. The Half-Elf sipped on some wine. Those that had been living in the ruins of Soleia didn't have a great deal of food and drink to offer, and none of it tasted very good. But she knew that would all change soon. The lives of those people would never be the same again. It was a nice feeling. She liked helping people.

Her gaze drifted across the crowd and she saw Vicrum embracing a dark-skinned man with a bare chest. It took her a moment before she realized the man was Draxis.

It certainly didn't take him long to arrive, she mused.

The two spoke for a moment before Draxis' brown eyes took in the party. They fell on her and he gave a roguish smile, heading over.

"Is this seat taken, tiny archer?" he asked with a raised eyebrow.

Artemis patted the area next to her. "Be my guest. It's not every day I get to chat with a dragon. But I suppose your golden-scaled form won't be joining us tonight."

He sat beside her. "No, I think I will be keeping that a secret for as long as I can. Have you found my compass, yet?"

She chuckled. "We found your old friend Vicrum, shouldn't that be good enough?"

"I did not know he was still alive. It warms my heart to see him again."

Artemis smiled. "We'll still look for your compass. I know you got Sen's attention when you mentioned a *reward.*"

"Ah, a man with an eye for gold. I think we can get along."

"When we return with your compass shall we come here? Or back to your little island cave?"

"You can find me here. I will help my good friend get Soleia back to the power it once was. I know you don't live a very long time, Half-Elf, but what you and your friends have done here will have a ripple effect. The world has been changed."

Jade stepped up, Foxy at her heels. She gave Draxis a wry grin. "I *do* live a long time. And I am eager to see what this city is like in another six hundred years."

Draxis chuckled. "Is this where a Wild Elf like yourself will retire? The desert?"

"Perhaps. It has a good view of the stars, after all."

His eyes glanced over her attire. "You are a Druid, I presume."

"I am."

"Why don't you stay now? We could use someone with your abilities to coax the land around into life again. Soleia used to be an oasis in the desert. A true beauty unsurpassed in any other city."

Jade inclined her head. "I appreciate the offer. Unfortunately, there are things I have to see to, first. But perhaps I can come here afterwards to help."

Draxis stood and placed a hand on Jade's shoulder. "Then I look forward to a long friendship. If you'll excuse me, ladies, I'm going to find some wine." With that he vanished into the crowd.

Jade sat down where he'd been. "Are you enjoying the party?"

"I always do," Artemis answered.

"You did not have to come all this way to help. Thank you for all you've done."

"Did you think I wouldn't care about Brother Zok's problems?"

"Well," Jade shrugged, "it isn't your fight, after all."

Artemis' gaze grew distant as she stared at the celebration. "Nothing is anybody's fight, if you think about it. Yes, members of Brother Zok's temple were killed. But that was their own issue, not his. But he still got involved. It could have been for a sense of duty or vengeance. But, knowing he's a Paladin, I think it's because he has honor. And empathy."

"Mm. Empathy can be hard to find in people."

"That's certainly been my experience, as well."

Jade studied her face, her green eyes narrowing. "Where are you from, Artemis? What have you experienced that turned you into such a deadly warrior, but someone who still cares about others?"

Artemis abruptly stood. "It's just who I am. It's getting late. I'm going to go check on the camels. Goodnight, Jade." And she left the conversation behind, as well as the memories that line of talk brought up.

Artemis ensured the camels were well-fed and comfortable. Sandy, Dusty, and His Majesty hadn't been happy with the way the ground had moved when Soleia was unearthed. The group fell asleep inside one of the buildings, happy to be out of the elements. They slept soundly that night, and for the first time in a long time, Artemis did not dream of a bloody battlefield.

The next morning they said their farewells to King Vicrum and Draxis and began their trek across the desert. The group amused themselves by practicing with their new abilities. Brother Zok would dash around, stirring up sand and dust. After a long day of travel they made camp once again, but didn't have any more disturbances in the night. Sen's wounded shoulder was healing rapidly, and Jade changed out the ointment for him. The exposure to the intense sun had darkened their skin. Jade's usually tan tone was now a deep bronze. Artemis and Zok both had fair skin. While they still tanned, there was some burning across their faces.

The next morning they only had to travel a couple hours before they reached Vonkai. Artemis reluctantly parted with the camels, returning them again to the Clucking Chicken tavern. They spent some time in the market resupplying for the sail back. Artemis couldn't resist buying some treats – pastries and candies and chocolates. It was too bad they didn't get to try minotaur meat, but perhaps another time.

At last, in the early afternoon, they boarded the Scarlet Maiden once again and left the port of Vonkai. The day was bright and sunny, and a warm wind caught their sails. Artemis went up to the crow's nest once again to watch the coast go by. But this time she was able to simply teleport to the top. She observed Sen take the helm, giving orders to his crew. Jade vanished below deck, Brother Zok helped maintain the ship, and Skar watched the waves.

Artemis reflected that things had certainly been interesting since she'd wound up in Somberdale. She liked this group. The five of them worked well together. She had never been the type to overlook a wrong that could be corrected, to stand up for the weak, and to stop those that hurt others. She was glad to be of help in stopping the evil that infiltrated Brother Zok's temple. It was sad two people had to die before the truth was uncovered. She was glad Priestess Liana and Whitney were still alive. The two had elected to stay behind in Soleia for a time, helping the city get up and running again. Artemis thought that was admirable.

They passed around the southwestern corner of Corventos, and Artemis watched the desert coastline pass by. She reflected that in a year the whole landscape of the Expanse would be different. Trade routes would connect to Soleia again, and the desert would have more population. As the day wore on the desert turned into the peaks of the Black Reach Mountains. They were far from the coast now, but Artemis' keen Half-Elven eyes could make out the jagged lines against the sunset sky.

She noticed that the course they were taking pulled further from the coast than last time. She was curious where Sen was directing the ship until she saw their destination up ahead. A small island with white sand beaches and covered in palm trees, perhaps just five miles across. And there, somehow, floating above it was a series of tiny landmasses. They went up in a spiral, like a broken tower, high into the air. Some were small, just the size of boulders. Others were a mile or so wide. Some were just rock and others were covered in grass. From somewhere high above a waterfall tricked down, dropping into a pool on the lowest island.

"Drop the anchor!" Sen shouted. "We're staying under the floating islands tonight!"

Artemis looked to a spot on the deck and teleported down, frightening a deckhand. She bounded across the wood and up to the helm. "Captain Sen! Those are incredible, what are they?"

The large Dragonborn grinned down at her. "We just refer to them as the floating islands. I don't know what kind of magic keeps them up but I thought I would entertain you all with some sight-seeing on our way home."

Jade strode up, fascination on her face as she took in the islands. "I have heard of this place. There was a rift in the planes here, long ago, and it caused this. Supposedly these floating pieces of land came from a plane that is only sky, where everything hovers."

Artemis could tell Sen didn't like that story as much as he preferred "some kind of magic keeps them up". As the ship was secured for an overnight stay, the sun dropped below the horizon completely and plunged them into darkness only lit by a crescent moon. Brother Zok and Skar stared at the display in wonder as rowboats were prepared. The five of them left the Scarlet Maiden as well as a few members of the crew. The rest remained on board to watch the ship overnight. They dipped oars into black water and crossed over to the island. Artemis craned her neck to stare up as they approached. She couldn't see the top of the tower of islands in the dark; it was difficult to tell how high up it went. Maybe in the morning she would teleport to a few and check them out. For a moment, she thought she saw a large shape, high above, eclipse the moonlight. But just as quickly it was gone, and she couldn't be sure if she'd seen something flying or it was a palm leaf blowing in the wind.

They came onto the beach, dragged up the boats, and made a campfire. The fresh air and ocean wind felt good in Artemis' blonde hair. As they sat in a circle around the fire, eating and reclining in the soft grass and sand, they lapsed into easy conversation.

"We did a good thing for Soleia," Jade said, her fox asleep in her lap. "But there is still the Foresight to consider. Do we go to An'Ock after this to warn the king?"

"I don't think I could sail the Scarlet Maiden up to the capital city," Sen said. "It's too dangerous if they recognize the ship as a pirate vessel. I could take us to another port and we could make our way on foot. I could even take us back to Somberdale, but that is a longer journey to walk."

"I know the Firelit Forest well," Jade stated. "If we return to Somberdale I could take us down that path. There are other Druids that live there I am friends with. They could offer us shelter, if we needed it. Or, we could cross through the mountains and open land to get to An'Ock. That route would be faster, but we would be more exposed to dangers."

"I've never been to the capital," Skar commented. "It should be fun!"

The Druid turned to the Paladin. "How are you feeling about everything, Zok? Do you need to go back to the temple and explain what all has happened?"

The Half-Elf rubbed his face with a long sigh. "I do. I need to tell them the truth of what I discovered. Perhaps going back to Somberdale is best. We can journey to An'Ock from there. That also gives us a chance to have Tymus look at the bottomless bag we found."

"It's settled, then," Sen said. "We return to Somberdale, take care of some business, and then go to the capital to . . . speak to the king."

Artemis waved her hand dismissively. "We'll figure it out! I can be very persuasive."

Sen chuckled. "The five of us have been having such fun together already, let the adventure continue!"

Jade smiled slyly at the pirate. "An'Ock is far from the ocean, Sen. Can you handle it?"

"Surely there must be some way to entertain myself in one of the largest cities in Corventos."

They laughed and chatted about what the capital would be like and the best route by land to take there. Conversation then quieted down and they put out the campfire and went to sleep, the sound of the waves a soothing background noise.

·

·

·

It was the shouting that awoke Artemis first. Her

blue eyes snapped open and she reached for her bow, taking in a commotion of dark silhouettes against the stars. And then two strong hands grabbed her wrists, twisting her arms behind her back. She cried out, kicking in the darkness. Her feet made contact and she heard a groan of pain, but the hands that held her didn't loosen. She just had a second to take in the scene – four figures wrestled Sen to the ground, someone had Skar's wand, Brother Zok's face was pushed into the dirt, and Jade fought and kicked and threw fire as she was tackled – before a bag enveloped her.

It went over her entire body, and Artemis turned and twisted in it, trying to get to her dagger so she could free herself. There was a sharp blow to her head and her muscles relaxed. Stars danced before her eyes. The sounds were muffled now. She could hear Wolfie and Foxy growling and then whimpering. She heard Jade shout, "No! *No!*" There were more cries of pain. A clanging of armor that must have been Brother Zok.

The Ranger felt ropes bound around the sack, preventing her from moving. As her foggy head cleared she concentrated and attempted to teleport out of the sack. But of course, nothing happened. She could not see her destination and so she was unable to free herself.

The shouting quieted down, and Artemis felt herself dragged by her feet. As the bag went over rocks she was sure they were bruising her back. Who had ambushed them? And why hadn't the crew on board the Scarlet Maiden seen people approaching? They were on an island. Surely whoever had found them must have come by ship. She considered that perhaps their assailants came from the floating islands. There couldn't be a good ecosystem there for people to live, but perhaps they were hiding in wait for easy prey. If that was the case, they were mistaken. Artemis was anything but easy prey. And if she found even one fur on Wolfie's head out of place, people were going to die.

She was dragged for an extended period of time before she was lifted. The world spun, the blood rushed to her head, and then she was thrown over someone's shoulder and carried. She squirmed, but a rough punch to her side stopped her movements.

Artemis was only carried for a few minutes before she heard footsteps on wood. The deck of a ship? There were muffled voices and laughter. The world flipped again and she was sat on her knees. Commotion sounded around her. She flexed against the ropes that wrapped around her legs, her ankles, her arms, but they did not give. The smell of burlap filled her nose, and for a moment she panicked as she had trouble breathing. Then the bag was grabbed roughly and she heard a ripping noise. The top was cut open and pushed down to her shoulders, letting her head free.

Artemis blinked in the torchlight, taking in the deck of a ship. But it was not the Scarlet Maiden. This ship was much larger, and its open sails snapped in the wind. A glance to either side revealed the rest of the Phantom Five and some of Sen's crew in the same predicament. Skar seemed woozy, a line of blood trailing down his face. Sand and grass were in Jade's hair from her struggle, and Brother Zok had a bloody nose. Her gaze turned to Sen who looked around in confusion, his sharp teeth bared. There were two unopened, wriggling sacks that she knew contained a fox and a wolf.

Measured footsteps descended from the helm and onto the main deck. Artemis saw brown leather boots, then dark clothes and a coat that had been worn by wind and water. Her gaze moved up to see the face of a Human woman surrounded by auburn hair. An amused smile played at red lips, and her dark eyes were shadowed by a wide-brimmed hat.

"Well, well," she said in a silky tone, "what have we found? Another group of pirates following us? Did you intend to take the treasure we came for? I want answers, or I'll start-" She stopped abruptly as her gaze fell on the red Dragonborn. "*Sen*?!"

Sen blinked in surprise. "Captain Lance?"

The woman threw her head back and laughed. "Untie them! It looks like we've stumbled upon an old friend."

182

Sen

.

.

.

Sen laughed heartily as the ropes binding him were cut free. Shrugging off the sack – which had barely fit over him – he stood and embraced his former captain. "If it isn't the Baroness! It is so good to see you!"

She hugged him tightly in return. "Sen! I knew the wild winds would blow you my way again. Sorry about roughing up your crew here."

He waved his hand dismissively. "They are a tough lot. They can take it." Out of his peripheral vision, he saw Zok, Jade, Skar, and Artemis scowl as they were untied. "What are you doing here? You mentioned treasure."

Captain Willa Lance laughed. "That I did. Come morning we are sending a party out to search these floating islands for something extra special I've been tracking." She called over her shoulder, "Bring some rum up! We've got special guests."

Sen turned to the members of his crew that had been captured with them. "Go tell Rain and Kailo that the five of us will be spending the night aboard the ship of my old captain and most of tomorrow. Enjoy yourselves!"

"Yes, Captain!" The small group ran off.

The Baroness smiled as she sat heavily down on a barrel, popping open a bottle of rum that was handed to her. "Look at you giving orders. How has sailing your own ship been? Have you been taking care of her?"

"She is my heart," Sen said, sitting across from her on a crate. "But what about your new ship here? Has she proved as effective as you thought? What do you call her?"

The four others slowly sat down on various crates, boxes, and barrels. Zok wiped the blood from his nose, glowering at Captain Lance. Jade and Artemis comforted their animals. And Skar glanced about the ship in curiosity.

"She's called the God's Hand," the Baroness replied. "She's been a good ship. Without her, exploring these floating islands wouldn't be possible."

Sen nodded. "What exactly is it you are searching for here?"

She leaned forward, resting one elbow on her knee and an excited smile springing to her face. "It's called the Horn of Swords. The stories say when someone who is worthy blows it, it summons a group of warriors to fight for you."

Zok scoffed, "It summons warriors? Like real people, or illusions, or . . .?"

The Baroness shrugged one shoulder. "There is only one way to find out, Sir Shiny Armor."

"Why would you need warriors? Do you not have enough crew?" Skar asked.

Captain Lance reclined back, taking another long drink. "What I need is to be able to call forth extra blades in moments of trouble. To keep my own crew safe, and to surprise my enemies. The stories say there is a temple atop these floating islands. And inside is the Horn."

"You're going to climb up all these islands?" Zok asked incredulously.

"I have ways of getting up. Best not to spoil the surprise. If you stick around tomorrow, you will see." She winked.

Sen raised his bottle in the air. "I will definitely be joining. Anyone else coming along?"

"Yes, absolutely!" Artemis agreed.

"It sounds like good fun," Skar answered.

Jade smiled. "You went underground to fight goblins for my friend, I will return the favor for you here."

Zok gave a heavy sigh. "I *am* curious now, to be honest. Why not? We'll all join in tomorrow to find this temple."

"Here's to adventure!" Sen said, before taking a big

swig of his rum.

They were given guest rooms to sleep in for the night. The others had to share, but Sen got a private cabin with a window. As he lay in bed, his mind turned over their trip. He was glad they had found answers in the desert. But he was disappointed the answers didn't lead to Jenkins. The old man was still a mystery. And the fact that he could show up anytime made the pirate captain nervous. Magic was a frightening thing, at times.

Sailing again had made him realize how long he'd stayed in one place. Over a hundred days without being gone from Somberdale for more than a night. Why had he stayed for so long? Was it his friendship with Zok and Jade? Or had he gotten lazy? Gold had been easy to come by in and around the port. He no longer had to journey far out on the ocean and hunt down trade ships. Perhaps it was because he missed sailing with *her*. Miriam. His scarlet maiden. He'd always hoped she would be his First Mate. But she had left before the ship had become his. She had grown tired of a life of pirating. She had wanted to settle down, to not put her life at risk every day. When she left, she had been bound for Vonkai.

When his friends had been otherwise occupied with shopping in Vonkai, Sen had gone to the barkeep Filin to inquire about Miriam. To Sen's disappointment, Filin had said the name and description were familiar but the young woman no longer lived in Vonkai. He had been hopeful she'd moved to Soleia and they would find her among the ruins. But she wasn't there, either.

If he told her he was sailing less, that he was settling down as well, could they be together again?

Sen mused that hadn't been the only dissatisfaction Vonkai had brought. After returning from Soleia, his crew confessed they'd spent a night drinking in the city and had left the ship unattended. They'd been robbed. Not too much had been taken, the thieves apparently were in and out within minutes. But he had lost the entire collection of lanterns he'd stolen from the tombs under Somberdale. He wasn't sure if he was relieved or angry he'd lost those. But they would remain a secret. He knew Zok would not be pleased with the entire situation.

Sen's thoughts drifted to what lay ahead. A short adventure with the Baroness, then a week's sail back to Somberdale. Get Tymus to check out the bottomless bag. Maybe they would find out what happened to that Wizard, Rowland, from the goblin tunnels. And then a journey on foot to An'Ock, the capital of the Korventine Empire. He'd never been so far inland before. But he did enjoy exploring. Finding out what trouble he could get into in a city so large would be fun. Perhaps he could compete in something larger than bar brawls for gold.

Sen reflected that he was glad to go adventuring with Zok and Jade. If the crew of the Scarlet Maiden were like his extended family, then Zok and Jade were his siblings. He would lay down his life for them, and he knew they would do the same for him. The three of them balanced each other nicely. Where Sen skirted the line of morality, Zok kept to an oath of honor. Where Sen focused on the small issues of each day, Jade saw the bigger picture of the world around them and time on a grander scale. If Artemis and Skar decided to stick around for awhile it would be interesting to see how the five of them all played off of each other.

With thoughts in his head of his friends, of Captain Lance, and of Miriam, Sen fell into an easy sleep.

.

.

.

The next morning was bright and windy. As Sen stood on the deck of the God's Hand, tightening the black bandana around his head, the waves splashed against the hull. Most of the Baroness' crew were above deck. His friends all stood to the side, staring in wonder at the floating islands now that the sun shone on them. The masses of land spiraled into the sky, and very far above he could see one chunk that was much larger than all the rest. A true floating *island*.

The Baroness came up from below the deck. And with her was another woman, shorter and slighter. Her clothes were not as flashy as the captain's, instead they were simple whites and browns. Straggly, dark blonde hair fell from underneath a three-pointed hat.

"This is my First Mate," the Baroness said, gesturing to the woman beside her. "Everyone calls her Lady Quickhands. She'll be leading the expedition to the temple."

Zok grinned, pushing his shoulder-length brown hair back from his face. "Quickhands? How did you earn that title?"

The woman drew a dagger from her belt and twirled it deftly between her fingers. The morning sun sparked off of it. "Would you like to find out?"

The Paladin drew out his own dagger. "I certainly would."

There were amused chuckles as the crew and the Phantom Five drew back, giving the two of them room to fight. Sen crossed his muscular arms as he leaned back against the side of the deck. He knew Zok sparred often with members of his temple. It would be interesting to see how his skills held up against a pirate.

Zok and Lady Quickhands circled each other for a moment, their blades out. The First Mate had a lazy look of confidence on her angular face. The Paladin's brow was furrowed in concentration. The ship swayed and creaked under them.

And then Zok lunged forward, his dagger out to stab. With a lightning-fast move Quickhands deflected it, sending him stumbling to the side. He spun on the balls of his feet, striking out in a horizontal slash. She parried once again, sending his attack wide. The Paladin regained his footing and came at her with a series of strikes. Sen knew his friend was good. His actions were precise and fast. But Quickhands was better. She waited until the last moment each time to block, making it difficult to predict her moves. They danced back and forth on the deck, the noise of their weapons ringing out into the air.

And then Quickhands went on the offensive. With a quick step forward, she closed the gap between them, and her dagger slashed and stabbed at the Paladin. His eyes widened as he parried and dodged, and he staggered backwards in an attempt to regain his footing.

Amused smiles crossed the faces of the rest of the Phantom Five as they watched this exchange. The Baroness gave a low chuckle, her arms crossed.

With a few more fast strikes Quickhands disarmed Zok. His dagger spun off to the side, embedding itself in the wood of the deck. She brought the blade up to his throat and said, "Do you feel I've earned my name?"

A smile of admission crossed Zok's face. "I do. Perhaps you can teach me sometime."

"Hm. Perhaps."

The Baroness clapped. "Good show! Let's get moving now. Everyone to your posts! We're taking the God's Hand up."

Sen clapped his friend on the shoulder as Zok came to join them. "Not bad! Don't be too embarrassed; pirates are a hardy lot."

"I am not embarrassed," the Paladin answered, sheathing his weapon. "It is good practice. Quickhands proved she was better with a dagger."

Artemis' voice was hushed as she said, "Something is wrong with Quickhands. Wolfie doesn't like her."

Jade nodded. "I noticed Foxy is uncomfortable as well."

Sen glanced down at the two animals. He was not an expert on canines, but they did seem to be wary of Quickhands. They watched her with heads bowed and tails still. "I'm sure the Baroness wouldn't have a First Mate that couldn't be trusted."

"Let's just keep an eye on her," Jade suggested. "Did you know her from your previous time under Captain Lance?"

"No," Sen responded. "She must be my replacement. I'll talk to her. Maybe-" He broke off as he noticed the sails spark with enchantment. "Oh, it's time! Hang on, friends. You are in for a special surprise."

They grabbed hold of the railings and rope around

them, confusion etched on their faces. Sen was excited to see their reactions. The God's Hand had been taken from another pirate by the Baroness. It was rare for Captains to trade their ships. Such a strong bond was formed. But the God's Hand was enchanted, and powerful magic weaved through every part of the ship. The Baroness reluctantly parted with the ship that was now Sen's, and took this one as her own. This was not the first time he'd experienced its magic. But it had been awhile and he was eager to see its power displayed once again.

The Baroness confidently took the helm, a wide smile splayed across her face. She barked a few more orders, and then spoke the words to activate the enchantment.

The ship lifted from the water. A gasp sounded from Skar and Foxy leaped into Jade's arms as the God's Hand rose into the air. The wood creaked as the wind hit it more fiercely, the rigging swaying. The Baroness laughed at their reactions as she guided her ship higher and higher.

"It flies?" Zok gasped.

Sen grinned. "Yes. Yes, it does."

The ship made its way up into the floating islands. The Phantom Five watched in amazement as they passed small rocks the size of their fists and massive chunks of land as large as the ship. Water sprinkled over the deck as they passed close by the waterfall. Up and up they climbed. Sen stole a glance over the side and saw the island they'd camped on had grown small indeed. His stomach clenched up and he pulled back. It was best not to look straight down. Instead he craned his head up and saw they were making for the largest chunk of land in the sky. It was as large as the island they'd spent the night on, if not larger. As they drew closer they came under its shadow.

Sen didn't know much about other planes of existence. And that was how he preferred it. The idea of it was quite frightening, even for a swashbuckling, heavy drinking, bar fighting barbarian such as himself. He was shocked that these floating islands came out of a rift. Planes influencing each other in such a way was scary. He still remembered the spooky stories his friends would tell him around campfires during his childhood. Planes of demons, devils, massive spiderwebs, and fey creatures that could control your mind. Supposedly there were other planes that were peaceful. But interplanar travel was illegal. The knowledge was not taught or practiced in schools. It was for fear of repeating the past, of course. Letting dragons lose on the world again after planar magic had been used to lock them away. He knew Arcanist Viscera Dante and her group of Clairvoyant Arcane did extensive investigation into other planes even after the dragons were gone. But Viscera and the rest had gone into one plane and never returned. Supposedly there had been a sole survivor, half-mad, who had kept a journal full of the terrors they'd found. Those stories had been enough to keep a young Sen awake at night.

Now that he knew what caused these floating islands, he felt nervous around them. But, there was treasure to be found! If he kept his mind focused on that, then he could push through everything else.

They drew up even with the largest island and found a jungle. Dense trees and thick brush covered it. The green was vivid against a background of blue sky. The land rose up in the distance to a massive hill, its summit hidden in cloud.

"Incredible," Jade breathed.

The God's Hand moved to hover over the edge of the island. The Baroness came down to Sen. "Are you and your friends still interested?"

"Certainly," Sen answered. "Do you have an idea where the ruined temple is?"

She pointed. "It's on the hill. But Quickhands has a new trick that will ensure the Horn is found. She'll be leading the expedition."

"And you?"

The Baroness patted the wood of the railing. "I will remain with my ship to keep her safe while you're gone."

Zok frowned. "Keep her safe? From what?"

Captain Lance gave him a piercing look, then forced a smile as she answered, "You never know what dangers lurk up here in uncharted territory. I will be ensuring the safety of my ship. I trust Lady Quickhands to accomplish this task."

Sen found it odd the Baroness wasn't joining them. He remembered her as one always on the front lines of danger. But, he could see the wisdom in her words. What if a roc lived on these islands? Or a phoenix that could set the whole ship ablaze?

A rope was tossed over the side and Quickhands led the climb down. Sen was next, his biceps bulging as he slowly lowered his massive body down to land. The grass was soft beneath his boots, but the wind was strong. His purple pants snapped against his legs. He watched as Jade, Zok, Artemis, and Skar descended, carrying the fox and the wolf. He knew Artemis could just teleport down, but there was an unspoken understanding between them all. It was best to be careful how they displayed these new-found powers. He knew there were great spellcasters in the world who could do incredible things. But it wouldn't take long for someone to notice this wasn't a spell that was being cast.

As they all stepped onto the floating island the rope was pulled back up. Lady Quickhands reached into her pack and took out a compass. She flicked it open and stared at it in silence for a few moments. It immediately caught Sen's eye because it was made of gold, shining brightly in the morning sunlight. But a closer inspection revealed there were no cardinal directions on it. Just a black needle that slid about before settling in the direction of the hill.

The Phantom Five all came to the realization at once, exchanging wide-eyed glances. This was Draxis' compass. The Baroness' desire to keep her ship safe took on new meaning, now. She feared the dragon was coming for it.

"It's this way," Quickhands said. "Try and keep up. I don't care about leaving stragglers behind."

She led the group into the thick of the jungle. As they delved into the trees, it was as if the autumn months didn't touch these floating islands. The colors were still bright and vivid, flowers blossomed, and fruit hung from some branches. Sen did not recognize the food, and thought it was best not to try it. Artemis reached up for one but Zok quickly intervened, shaking his head. The smell of the ocean was still strong up here, and the salt comforted Sen. It made him feel like he wasn't actually so high in the air.

Quickhands deftly made her way through the dense foliage, ducking and weaving. Jade and Artemis had no trouble keeping up, their animals eager and excited by all the new sights and smells. Zok's armor hampered more dexterous movement, but the leaves and thorns struck harmlessly on him. It was more difficult for Sen and Skar. Both Dragonborn struggled with their bulky forms in such an enclosed space, getting small cuts and scratches on their scales.

It was a long thirty minute trek across the island. The ground steadily inclined, and Sen could feel the burning in his calves and they went higher and higher. The clouds were close overhead, shrouding the top of the hill and the tallest of the trees. Sen noticed the animals were not comfortable getting near Quickhands. It was curious. And it made him wary. If there was something dangerous about her, he intended to protect Captain Lance.

At last they broke into a clearing. The jungle parted to reveal a rocky area and a long stone path that led up into the hillside. The front of the hill was a sheer cliff, and in it was carved a structure. Time and winds had worn the fine details away, but columns and arches could still be distinguished. The clouds clung to it, giving an aura of mystery and ancientness.

But that was not what caught everyone's attention, drawing eight pairs of eyes to the center of the clearing. There was a flash of movement, a rush of powerful wind that pulled at their clothes and scattered their hair. Sen's eyes watered and he squinted to make out the two large forms. One appeared like a whirlwind, a twister, all made up of air. The other was solid and *huge*. Standing nearly twenty feet tall, it had a humanoid appearance. But that was all Sen could make out before the whirlwind lashed out and the other creature was sent flying back over the hill. Out of sight and far, far away.

The whirlwind then turned, and two tendrils that functioned as arms reached out towards them. There was a face in the midst of all the mess of dirt, cloud, and smoke that made up its form. Gaping eyes and a mouth that was twisted into a snarl.

"What is this?" Brother Zok shouted, holding his shield protectively in front of him.

"An elemental," Jade yelled back, her brown hair blowing around her tan face. "It must have come from the other plane along with these islands."

"Is it dangerous?" Sen asked, hefting his axe in both hands.

As if in answer to his question, the elemental struck out. A burst of wind hit them all, sending them flying back into the rocks and trees. Sen managed to keep his footing as he slid back, bending his knees and crouching low. He glanced to each side and saw his friends get back up, groaning. Quickhands was limp on the ground.

With a roar, he ran towards the air elemental. Artemis' arrow shot past his head but the strong winds threw it off-course. It flashed backwards and sliced across Skar's arm. The Wizard cried out and staggered, holding the wound. As he drew closer and closer to the creature Sen struggled to keep his speed. The wind pushed against him, threatening to throw him off-course. When he came within range he swung his weapon at the creature, its form rising high above him. As his axe made contact it went through his opponent, but he did feel something solid. There was pressure he cut through, and the elemental shouted at the wound. It's shout sounded like wind howling through a cavern entrance.

Jade was then at his side, her hands lit with fire that she hurled at the creature. The bolts blasted its side and it lashed out at her with one arm. The Druid rolled out of the way, turning and continuing to pelt the elemental with flames.

Sen spun around and attacked again, hitting the enemy. It turned at an incredible speed and struck him. The impact reverberated through his ribs and he was sent into the air. He saw a flash of clouds above him and he tensed his muscles, preparing for impact. His scales flashed, and metal coated them. A loud clang sounded as he hit the rocks. The breath was momentarily forced from him, but the pain was lessened from his newfound powers.

Sen blinked and sat up, clearing his head. Artemis raced over to the fallen Quickhands and checked her over for wounds. Skar cradled his injured arm and fired off magic from his wand. It pelted the wind elemental with explosions, and it reeled back with a howl.

Zok glanced back at the unconscious Quickhands and then turned on his heel, facing down the creature. He returned his shield to his back and bent his knees, every muscles in his Half-Elven body tensing. And then he shot off. Running at an incredible speed, he crossed the distance to the elemental within a second. And then he began to run in circles around it, going the opposite direction of its vortex. The Paladin raced so fast he was a gold and white blur. His armor made the most awful noise at his speed, but the effect was immediate. The creature wailed and thrashed, its body starting to lose its form.

Jade slowly backed up, covering her face against all the debris that flew through the air. But Skar moved closer, shooting bolts of magic in rapid-fire, the sleeve of his robe stained with blood.

Sen stood and walked a few feet closer. But the noise was deafening and the suction from the wind made it difficult to breathe. Jade stepped next to him, grabbing onto him for support as the gale threatened to knock her over.

The wind elemental screamed, and then its form exploded. Sen and the Druid staggered back, and Artemis flinched, leaning over Quickhands to protect her. Zok and Skar were thrown high into the air, and they crashed into the trees. And finally, the wind subsided to a gentle breeze, and the creature was gone.

Sen let out his breath in relief, and his scales reverted to red again.

Quickhands moaned and sat up. She brought a hand to her head as she asked, "What happened? I got knocked out for a moment."

Artemis helped her up, answering, "Some kind of wind monster. We all got blown back. Brother Zok and Skar are somewhere around here."

"They might need healing," Jade said. "We should find them quickly."

Sen followed the Wild Elf as she stepped back into the jungle. He asked, "Was there something else there with the elemental-thing? I could have sworn I saw it fighting some large creature."

She nodded. "I saw something, too. But it was gone before I could see details. Who knows what kind of creatures live up here?"

As they walked deeper they found Skar first. He was unconscious, a lump swelling on his head. Jade quickly cast a healing spell, her hands glowing with a gentle light.

"Is he badly hurt?" Sen asked.

"Nothing major," she answered. "I can heal most of his injuries. He'll need rest, though."

The wound across Skar's arm closed up, leaving behind a bloodied sleeve. The Wizard slowly opened his eyes."Ouch." He grit his teeth. "I am all right. Thank you for your assistance."

Sen helped the other Dragonborn stand, and then looked about for the Paladin. "Zok? *Zok?*"

A long groan answered him. As Skar turned to limp back to the clearing, the Druid and the pirate captain followed the sound to find their Half-Elf friend hanging over a branch fifteen feet above them.

Zok blearily blinked as his eyes focused. "Oh hey. That hurt. But I think I'm okay."

Sen chuckled. "I can't reach you up there, friend. But I'll catch you if you drop."

"Your speed was impressive," Jade stated as she crossed her arms. "How do you feel after that?"

"Hungry." The Paladin took a moment to angle

himself before rolling off the branch. Sen caught him gracelessly, but he still managed to prevent Zok from crashing to the ground. As he was deposited safely to his feet, Zok said, "Thank you. Did we kill the elemental?"

"Killed or dispersed," Jade replied. "It shouldn't trouble us again."

"You know a lot about this kind of stuff," Sen commented as the three made their way back towards the clearing.

She chuckled. "I *have* been around for four hundred years. And I had a very good teacher in my Master Galen. You could learn, Sen. I have book I can recommend."

The pirate scrunched his snout. "I prefer hands-on learning."

They came back into the clearing to find the others waiting. Quickhands was frantically searching through the bushes and rocks, a string of profanity spewing from her mouth.

"What's wrong?" Sen asked.

Without looking at him she answered, "I can't find that *damn* compass! It must have been knocked from my hands when that wind hit me."

Sen glanced around, and he saw a devious grin spread over Artemis' face. As he made eye contact with her, she winked.

"Well," the red Dragonborn sighed, "we could spend hours here and never find it. But I think the Baroness wants us back quickly. So let's get going."

Quickhands turned around and glared at him. "That compass was important you big, red imbecile."

"Oh?" Sen challenged. "Why is that? Did you steal it from someone special?"

A moment of tense silence stretched out as the two glared at one another. Then Lady Quickhands got back to her feet. "The Horn is more important. Let's go inside these ruins and fetch it."

They crossed the clearing now littered with branches, leaves, and other debris from the fight. The steps leading to the ruins were cracked and crumbled, and they treaded carefully as they made their way up to the entrance. There was no door, just an open square threshold. As they stepped inside they were faced with an enormous square room. Columns made of stone supported the ceiling, but many were crumbled and laid in ruined chunks about a cracked and dirty floor. Sen had never been inside a temple before, so he couldn't be sure what this place of worship had once been for. But now it was bare, save for a stone pedestal in the center that stood four feet high. And sitting ceremoniously atop it was the Horn of Swords. It had a long and graceful curve with an off-white color.

"At last," Lady Quickhands smiled, hurrying over to it. "The Horn."

Sen quickly stepped in front of her. She stopped abruptly and fixed him with glower as he said, "Hold on. I can bring it back to Captain Lance myself."

"This is *my* expedition," she snapped. "I will be the one to bring it back."

"And why should it matter?"

"Why does it matter *to you?* I am her First Mate. This is part of my job."

Sen crossed his arms. "And how did you meet her, exactly? How long have you been working with her?"

"Why these questions?"

"Because there is something off about you and I don't like it."

Quickhands made to move past him but he blocked her. Her expression darkened as she glared up at him. "Don't test me, Dragonborn. I don't care how big you are, you do not want to cross me." As they held heated looks for a moment, she finally answered, "I've only worked with the Baroness for a month. But she hired me for my skills, and that should be good enough for you."

"It will be good enough," Sen stated, 'if I can bring the Horn of Swords back."

Quickhands stepped up closer to him, reaching for her daggers. "Step aside, or I'll-"

Their argument broke off at the noise of a single, deep note of music blasting through the air and reverberating around the ruins. The two pirates flinched, and spun around to see Skar standing at the pedestal. The Wizard lowered the Horn from his lips and said, "Enough. I can carry the Horn back. There is no need to fight."

"Damn it all, you Dragonborn are a *stupid* lot!" Quickhands shouted. "You can't just *blow* the Horn. Not unless you're-"

Suddenly, in a swirl of magical energy, a horde of warriors solidified into existence around them. There was a pregnant pause as the Phantom Five and Quickhands stared in silent shock. The warriors appeared to be Humans with stoic faces, covered in hide armor. Great weapons of swords, axes, and spears were in their hands. They all turned as one to Skar, and he gaped at them.

A prolonged moment of silence, where nobody moved, was broken as the warriors drew their weapons and charged at the Wizard, battle cries sounding into the air. Quickhands then jumped in front of him and wrestled the Horn from his hands. She brought it to her mouth and blew as the fighters drew within five feet. As she did, her form shook. The guise of a hardy Human pirate shimmered, cracked, and then faded. Revealed underneath was a hunched humanoid form of green skin and stringy black hair. Crooked and stained teeth came from a hideous face. Black eyes bulged and watered.

The warriors slid to a stop, lowered their weapons, and waited.

"You may leave," Quickhands commanded them. "We don't need you right now."

As one, the warriors nodded. And then they vanished.

The Phantom Five gawked at the form of Quickhands, their hands hovering above their weapons.

"What are you?" Zok demanded.

Her gaze swiveled over them all before she answered, "I am what is commonly referred to as a hag. I don't want to fight you."

"Does the Baroness know this?" Sen demanded.

"Of course she does," Quickhands answered. "That's why she hired me. After witnessing the power her magic ship gives her, she's been hunting for more magical items. My knowledge of the arcane is indispensable to her."

"That knowledge didn't stop those warriors from attacking Skar," Zok said. "Why did that happen?"

The pirate scoffed. "Didn't you pay attention? The Baroness clearly stated only someone who is worthy can blow the Horn. Is your bronze Dragonborn friend here a fighter?"

"I am a Wizard," Skar answered.

Quickhands shook her head. "A spellcaster. The creator of this Horn only respected warriors of steel. So those it summons will only answer to similar fighters."

"So, they would have killed him," Artemis stated, dropping her hands to her side. "You saved Skar's life, it seems."

"That I did. Can we trust each other now?"

Sen felt the eyes of his friends on him. They were waiting for him to make a decision since it was his old captain. He considered for a moment, then nodded. "If the Baroness trusts a hag like yourself, then I trust her. In repayment for you protecting our friend, you may take the Horn of Swords back."

As they left the ruined temple, Quickhands recast a spell to resume the illusion of a Human. Sen did not know much about hags, just that they were deformed, fiendish creatures that lived in the wilds. They were supposedly not friendly. And, truthfully, Sen wouldn't call Quickhands friendly at all. But he respected the Baroness' decision to employ a hag for her arcane knowledge. He would not cross his former captain.

And so, in silence, they walked back to the God's Hand.

.

.

.

JADE

.

.

.

No one mentioned the incident in the ruins to Captain Willa Lance as they returned to the ship. She was pleased to have the Horn of Swords, and she and Sen celebrated with a round of rum. Jade wasn't sure what she thought about Lady Quickhands' secret. She knew hags to be deeply rooted in nature and that they lived off the land. That was something she could identify with. But she also knew them to be tricksters and prone to violence, not above killing those that wandered onto their land. Their obsession with the occult and the darker side of magic did not sit well with her. If she was to offer advice to the Baroness, it would be to be wary of Quickhands desiring the more powerful magical items for herself. But this wasn't Jade's situation to get involved in. And so she remained silent.

The God's Hand returned them to the island they had camped on. Parting on friendly terms with Captain Lance, they boarded the Scarlet Maiden. Sen took the ship out to sea once again, and it was decided they would return to Soleia to give Draxis his compass before venturing north to Somberdale.

As afternoon turned to evening Jade went below deck to her room she shared with Artemis. It was small and functional, consisting of two hammocks for beds and two crates for belongings. The Half-Elf Ranger was still above deck, spending her time in the crow's nest.

Jade did not like the ocean. She grew up in a nomadic tribe that wandered the Korventine Empire and Eleste Highlands and Lowlands. She had spent much of her childhood landlocked. But her grandparents governed a city in the south of Eleste called Oceala. A beautiful gem sitting on the coast. Her family visited it often as she was growing up. She recalled days playing with her brother, Heron, in the shallows of the Bay of Nailo. But that was before she'd realized what could live in the water. Before she understood the great depths of the ocean could hold monstrosities larger than castles. Her grandparents had laughed at her fears and assured her the bay had always been safe. But experiences as children tended to stick with people, and Jade had never quite outgrown her fear of the ocean.

She did miss Oceala, however. It always felt like it existed in another world. Away from the troubles of the rest of Corventos.

Her mind drifted to all that had transpired the last few weeks. It was certainly not the trouble she thought she'd find when she decided to stay in Somberdale. But perhaps it would lead to the answers she sought. Despite her friendship with Therond, Zok, and Sen, the deeper reason she agreed to help them was in hopes of finding answers to her vision. A vision she started having a couple years ago. When she'd brought it up to her parents they had simply laughed and told her not to be scared of nightmares. But Jade felt this was something more. It had been a couple months since the vision had returned, however. It was both comforting and worrisome. She didn't like to experience the fear it brought. But at the same time, she needed to keep the details clear so she could search for clues in the waking world.

But so far no solid information had been found. Delving into the goblin tunnels, clashing with Jenkins, the murder that led them to Soleia, and these floating islands had not provided any answers. Unless it was all connected somehow?

Jade sighed, lying back in the hammock and pushing her hair from her face.

Now I'm just desperate for theories, she thought.

There was one new bit of information, however. There was still a dragon left in the world. Draxis the gold dragon, friend to an ancient Dwarven king. He must have truly stayed well hidden to have remained alive and undetected for so long. Did that mean there were other dragons in the world, or was he the only one left? She realized she should have asked him about her vision. Perhaps when they returned the compass to him, he could provide answers.

Foxy happily leaped up and curled on top of her. Jade pet him absently while her other hand grasped the red stone necklace she always wore. The last gift of Master Galen. She reflected that he would know what to do. He always seemed to have the answers. She could still see him as clear as if it had been yesterday, as opposed to nearly two hundred years. A wizened Half-Fiend of mud-colored skin and great horns like a bull's. Always dressed in clothes made from the forest where his home was. He was the most powerful Druid she knew, his magic with the earth so deep and powerful it had extended his life well beyond the eighty years his kind typically lived. She missed his wisdom. Her mind settled into memories of training in the Firelit Forest with him until she fell asleep. A world of browns and greens, where she was one with the wilds and they moved at her command.

.

.

.

Fire.

It was the first thing she could see. Its intensity forced her to squint her green eyes. Heat sizzled against her skin and caused her to sweat. Jade spun around, searching for a way out. She was in a city. Rounded buildings topped hills that sloped down to a curving coastline.

Oceala.

Jade panicked. If there was ever a city she could call home, it was Oceala. And now it was being destroyed. Finding her bearings amidst the cobblestone streets, she raced towards the manor where her grandparents lived. She had to rescue them. Vaguely, at the back of her mind, a thought nudged her that she needed to be afraid of fire no longer. It could not harm her. But that seemed ridiculous, now. It was everywhere, and the heat was nearly unbearable.

Jade glanced around for Foxy but could not find him. She cried out, calling for him, but he did not come. She hoped he was safe. She would not leave Oceala without her family, which included her fox.

The manor appeared up ahead, wreathed in fire. A scream escaped her throat as she ran up to it, crying out for her grandparents. And then she saw the figures racing from it. Her brother. Her grandfather. Her grandmother. They were burning, their skin blistered and mouths opened in silent wails of agony.

A burst of violent wind hit Jade, flinging her from her feet. She fell into smoke and ash, losing sight of her loved ones. She turned to the source of the wind, pushing up onto her hands and knees.

Rising from the darkness and the fire was a great red dragon. Its wingspan filled the sky, its eyes burned as pools lava. A long neck arched down to a horned head that stared at her.

Jade held up her hand, preparing to cast a spell; a feeble attempt, but the only thing she could think to do. The magic did not come, however, as fear took hold when the red dragon opened its mouth wide and a torrent of fire engulfed her.

.

.

.

Jade woke up with a start, breathing hard. Foxy blinked awake, regarding her with irritation. She could still feel the heat on her skin, and sweat trickled down the sides of her face.

"Are you okay?" Artemis' voice sounded in the dark, a slurred, tired tone from the other hammock.

"I am," Jade replied. "Just a nightmare."

"I get those, too, sometimes. The cost of a life of adventuring, I guess."

For a moment Jade considered telling her. Maybe Artemis would take this vision seriously. Maybe she would understand why, ever since the first vision two years ago, she'd dedicated her life to preventing its fulfillment. But as she opened her mouth, Skar suddenly appeared, using his powers of intangibility to walk through the wood of the door.

"Sorry to wake you, ladies," Skar stated.

"Oh my *gods, Skar!*" Artemis exclaimed. "You can't just walk into people's rooms!"

"Oh, uh, sorry, right. It's just . . . There's a situation on deck. You should come up immediately."

They quickly put on their boots and Artemis grabbed her bow and quiver. Their steps thudded on the wooden stairs as they ran up and out into the chilly night air.

All of the crew were on deck, their eyes wide and faces pale. Zok stood at the helm with Sen, his brow furrowed in concern. As he caught sight of the others he raced over to them and said, "There are things in the fog, look!"

Jade glanced about the ship. What she initially thought was just the darkness of the night she now realized was dense fog. It blocked out the moon and stars, and clung tightly to the edges of the ship. A glance up to the crow's nest showed it to be nearly invisible due to the thick, gray fog. Her Elven eyes looked deeper, probing the mists for movement. At first, there was nothing. And then she saw them.

Shapes drifted about the ship, vaguely humanoid. Mere shadows in the fog. They floated alongside and hovered about the sails. A glance over the side of the ship revealed more shapes below them, perhaps even in the water.

"What is going on?" Jade asked. "Where are we?"

From the helm Sen said, "We should be closing in on Vonkai. But this fog just enveloped us. It formed in a matter of minutes."

"Shouldn't we stop if we can't see where we're going?" Artemis asked.

"I . . ." Sen hesitated. "I don't know. I don't know what is going on."

One of the deckhands, shaking with fear, said, "Captain, there are *things* in this fog!"

Another member of the crew, trying to show

courage despite shaking hands, countered, "It's just the moonlight playin' tricks on our eyes! There's nothin' here."

Zok walked purposefully over to the edge of the ship. "I'm going for a closer look. Throw down a rope ladder."

As one of the deckhands complied, Zok climbed over the side. Jade and Artemis went to the edge and looked down, watching him. He moved carefully, the ladder swaying with his movements. Wind blew his dark brown hair back from his face. He stopped halfway down and looked about.

And that's when the shapes moved closer. Their details now distinguishable, they appeared as macabre specters. People in various stages of decay, some full skeletons. Rotted clothing hung in tatters against their bodies that faded into nothing at the legs. Screams sounded from members of the crew, and they cowered.

Jade whipped around to see what Sen would command, but the Dragonborn was frozen with shock and fright on his face. The specters drifted onto the deck, mouths hanging wide. One came within two feet of Skar. It was different than the others. Instead of decaying, it appeared as a healthy female with smooth, dark hair. A wide grin revealed pointed incisors. She spoke in a velvet voice. "I look forward to meeting you."

All at once, the specters vanished. Gasps sounded about the Scarlet Maiden. Jade turned quickly back around to see Zok staring up at her in confusion.

First Mate Kailo shouted, "Captain, orders?"

But Sen was still unresponsive, his eyes two full moons.

Then Artemis bounded up towards the Dragonborn, saying, "Captain Sen, I think we should stop the ship!"

Sen blinked, and awareness came back to his face. "Yes-uh-drop anchor! Ease the sails!"

The ship gradually slowed, and then stopped abruptly as the anchor caught something. The ship shook and Jade stumbled.

Zok climbed back onto the deck and he said to the Druid, "What stopped us? We can't be that close to land."

Jade turned to the closest member of the crew she could see, Rain the Quarter Master. "Is there a reef here?"

"No," Rain replied, panic on her face. "I don't know what we've hit."

Silence stretched out over the Scarlet Maiden. Nobody moved. The rigging swayed in the cold wind, and the noise of water against the hull was a steady drumbeat. And then slowly, the fog cleared. It rolled back from the ship like a wave from the shore. And what it revealed caused gasps and shouts of fear to sound from the crew.

They were no longer on the ocean. Instead, they found themselves in a large pond. The land rose up on the banks and then flattened into a thick, dark forest. A layer of clouds covered the night sky.

Jade took the scenery in with a sweeping glance about. This was not a place she recognized. And even if it was, there was no reason for them to be here. How could the ship have possibly ended up in a landlocked pond from sailing along the coast of Corventos?

The Druid turned to look up at her friend, Sen. The fearless, drunken, massive Dragonborn that got into bar fights for fun. And she had never seen him so confused, so lost, or so scared in all the time she'd known him.

.

.

.

PART III

UNOLÉ

.
.
.

The white world felt peaceful and safe after her venture into the Hells. Unolé was glad for the quiet, for the escape from the heat. But there was a numbness in her chest at the failure of the mission. Her sister, Unatchi, had not been found. And there were no clues to guide her to her next destination.

She glanced around, hunched slightly over at the pain her wounds caused. The white world had changed. It still held the barren trees, the bridge, the silver river, and the strange fog that cast everything in the same color and made distance difficult to discern. But before there had been small pools of water to serve as portals into the planes. Now, there were small stone structures, like mausoleums, that dotted the landscape.

"It's changed," she said.

"Ah, yes, it does that," Teshuva mused, sitting on her shoulder. "Always in a state of shifting and altering. Do not fear, though. Those stone buildings are the new portals to the planes."

"That's interesting. Do you think we can pause a moment so I can clean off my wounds?"

"Of course. The water in the river is pure and clean. You can use it."

Unolé headed over, wincing as the rough cloth and leather of her clothes rubbed against the cuts. She stopped at the edge of the river, considered, then said, "Teshuva, turn around. I'm going to take off some of my clothes so I can better disinfect and patch myself up. And wash that awful Hells grime off my clothes."

The coatl complied, flying off to wrap around a

nearby tree branch. He turned his back to her. "Don't be so glum. I know you feel we wasted our time, but hope is not lost yet."

Unolé stripped off her boots, black pants, red corset, and black jacket. Still in her undergarments, she pulled a blanket from her pack and wrapped it around herself for modesty. Then she proceeded to dip her clothes in and out of the river. The water was indeed clear and refreshing. "Thank you for saying that. But this plane-hopping thing is going to get really old, really fast if all the places are like the Hells."

"Not all planes are so inhospitable," the coatl said, folding his colorful wings against his back. "Your Material plane is not, after all."

Tossing her clothes over a branch to dry, Unolé set to work washing off the cuts and scratches that littered her muscular body. "And what are the others like?"

"Hm. I am no expert. But there are planes of primal elements. Such as one that is only a great ocean, and another that is endless sky. There is one referred to as the Wilds, where fey creatures such as pixies and dryads and ancient Elves live. There is another called the Gloomdwell, a terrible plane of undeath where demons live in a great abyss known as the Chasm. And there is, of course, the plane that is home to the gods. But it is impossible to reach. The gods themselves erected a gate to prevent any travel to or from. There is the Hells that we just visited. And I'm sure many more that have yet to be discovered."

"And the native people of the Hells are the devils?"

"Yes. A varied race, known for their cruelty."

Satisfied that her injuries were cleaned off, Unolé rummaged in her pack for some bandages. It wouldn't be enough to cover all her cuts, but she could take care of the deeper ones. Rolling out the tan cloth, she wrapped it around any wounds she could and asked, "How do people from my plane end up there? I saw so many as prisoners. But there were also some walking around freely."

"Some, perhaps, accidentally passed through a portal. Devils like to attempt to open rifts into other planes.

Sometimes they are successful. From there, they can capture people for slaves or other terrible purposes. Or they can tempt the weak minded with promises of power in exchange for their soul. The society of the Hells is built upon power and favors and mistrust. And those that can't keep up with stronger devils will try to exert their influence on other planes. The people you saw walking freely were attempting to take advantage of this system. Gambling with their own souls and lives in hopes of bargaining some favor from the devils. Likely to enact revenge on someone, or gain wealth, or other things. Mostly Humans, I'm sure. They are a shortsighted and greedy group."

"Interesting." Unolé nodded. "Is someone in charge in the Hells?"

"The god they worship. He is called the Hoofed King, or the Chained One. They follow his desires like a cult."

"You know so much. Who are you exactly, Teshuva?"

He chuckled. "That is a much bigger question than you realize. And the answer is not a simple or short one. I promise I will tell you everything. And all about the goddess I serve, the Silver Dancer. But for now, we should find your sister."

Finished, Unolé checked over her many bandages and felt the scratches on her face. The bleeding had stopped. Beyond those and many bruises, she wasn't seriously injured. For that she was thankful. As she sat on the edge of the river, wrapped in a blanket, waiting for her clothes to dry, she asked, "Does your . . . Silver Dancer go by other titles?"

"The Maiden of the Moon is one."

"And who calls her that?"

There was a pause. "Truthfully, I have never met anyone else that worships her. But I know others must, for I have seen her temple." He must have taken her silence as disbelief, for he quickly added, "I know the way it sounds. But the Silver Dancer has always been with me. And she can be with you, too."

"I . . . will give it some thought. That's all I can promise."

Their conversation quieted down as she waited for her clothes to dry and rested her tired body. When at last it was time she said, "Alright. I'm going to get dressed again."

Teshuva kept his back turned as she pulled her black and red clothes from the tree branches. The material was stiff, but clean and dry. She got dressed and returned the red mask over her eyes. Then she rolled up her blanket and stuffed it back into her small pack.

"Okay," she said. "Where to next?"

The coatl uncurled and glanced around. "Hard to say. I haven't seen entrances to the planes look like this before. We could go up to each and I can see if I get a feel for where they lead. Then make our best guess."

"Or," Unolé countered, "we just pick one and go through."

"Oh?" He glided over and wrapped around her upper arm. "That is a risk. There is no telling what we could leap into."

She shrugged. "If it's too dangerous, we will leave. Let's just hop in, look for that dark, winged beast, ask if anyone has seen my sister. Simple."

"Then let us go."

Unolé smiled. It was nice not to travel alone. She walked along the silver river to the nearest structure. It was small and square, with a latticework door. Pushing it open, she stepped inside. It was clean and featureless, save for a shimmering portal on the opposite wall, and a singular red rose on the floor.

"A rose," she stated, staring at it in confusion.

Teshuva shifted on her arm. "Perhaps left by another traveler as a message? It is best to leave it alone, I think."

"Alright, then. Shall we?" She reached a hand towards the portal.

"I am with you."

And so she stepped through.

.

.

.

RUUDA

.
.

It was hard to tell how long she'd been inside the crate. Hours? A full day? All she knew was that she was thirsty, she was hungry, and she was in a lot of pain. She could wiggle around some, but it had been so long now nothing would bring relief to her screaming muscles and joints. The endless rattling of the carriage was gnawing at her sanity, as well. She had to get out. She no longer cared about walking around on the Surface and the risks it brought. She had to get out *now*.

She whispered, "Taliesin?"

There was a long pause before he answered, and his voice carried an edge of exhaustion. " . . . Yes?"

"I don't like this. I want out."

" . . . I agree. Let's leave this carriage."

"We'll have to move fast to avoid being caught. Are you ready?"

There was a long, tired exhale of breath before he replied, "I can't move. I need your help to get out of the crate."

A smile tugged at one corner of her mouth. "*You* need *my* help?"

With a tone of irritation he said, "You can gloat later! Just get me out . . . Please."

She blinked in surprise at that last word. If she could barely move inside the crate, she knew it must be worse for him. Obviously the journey had dulled his sass. She assumed it wouldn't take long to return once they got out.

Ruuda pushed against the lid of the crate and slowly opened it. Biting her lip against the pain, she gently stood up. Her body struggled to obey her commands, muscles

212

stretching after so long in confinement. A quick look around showed the back of the carriage had only boxes and her barrel. No people were inside. A canvas flap gave her a quick view of grass, but that was all she could see.

Carefully, she stepped out and crouched next to the crate she knew Taliesin was in. The ride was rickety and bouncy, and she had to continually adjust her balance on the balls of her feet. She opened the lid and softly set it aside, then looked in. The Dark Elf was curled into a tight ball, his knees against his chest. Yellow eyes flicked up to her and he offered a strained smile.

Ruuda reached down and wrapped her hands under his arms. Her muscles tensed as she gently lifted him. He gritted his teeth and squeezed his eyes shut as he stood, immediately supporting his own weight once he was free to move. Climbing out, he adjusted his pack and then knelt by the exit, looking at her expectantly.

Ruuda turned and grabbed her barrel. Then she gave a nod and they both hopped out. The change in momentum threw her off balance, and she stumbled a few steps before dropping to her knees. She sat her barrel to the side and then took in the world around her. Her first real view of the Surface.

It was all rolling hills of green. Trees dotted the landscape, their leaves green, red, orange, and yellow. The sky was covered in gray clouds, obscuring the sun, which she was grateful for. But everything was so massive and so open. And for a moment, it overwhelmed her. She felt like she would fall into the sky, or tumble across the hills with nothing to stop her.

She dropped her hands to the ground, her breathing hard and labored. She started to feel dizzy.

"Oh, gods," Taliesin moaned as he dropped next to her. "It's so huge . . . I'm feeling sick."

"Yeah . . . me, too." Ruuda rolled onto her back and closed her green eyes. It was too much. She needed a moment to adjust. She heard Taliesin do the same beside her, panting.

She was afraid to look up at that sky. So big, so far away. She missed the narrow tunnels and caverns of the Deep Hollows. But she was a five day journey from home by now. She had to be brave and face this world. Other people lived here, after all. It must not be so bad.

Ruuda slowly opened her eyes. Clouds stared back at her. Immediately her gut clenched and a wave of dizziness washed through her. She grabbed hold of the grass, but it broke off in her fists. Blindly she reached over to the Dark Elf beside her and felt his black cloak beneath her fingers. She tightened her grip on it. He was the only solid thing in this huge, empty space around her.

Minutes passed as they both lied there. Eventually the nausea left Ruuda and she became accustomed to her surroundings. The feeling that she would just slip away into the sky stopped, and gravity reasserted itself.

Ruuda sat up, pushing her long, wild hair back from her face. "Alright. Where do we go from here?"

Taliesin sat as well, sighing. He glanced around, then pointed into the distance. "That looks like a river."

She followed his finger and did see a wavy line of blue cutting through the hills. "I agree. It's very big. Much bigger than the rivers underground."

"Let's follow that. That way we won't get lost and end up going in circles."

"Sounds like a plan."

The Cleric stood and offered his hand to help her up. She took it and was surprised at how strong and sturdy he was as he pulled her to her feet.

She strapped her barrel to her back once again. She noticed Taliesin pause to search through the grass. "What are you looking for?"

"Spiders, of course. That's why we're out here, after all."

"Oh, right." She had forgotten he was researching the supposed disappearance of spiders. She'd been so focused on just surviving each day. "You're sure they're all gone?"

"Absolutely. The question is: are they gone all over the world, where did they go, and why?"

"Those are three questions," she pointed out. "But alright. I'll help you do this research."

The Dark Elf pulled out a leather journal from his pack. "How about you record our travels? Make notes about where we go, what we do, and any clues we find."

She took it and turned it over in her hands before frowning up at him. "You want me to do the research recording? Why not you?"

"So I can focus on the bigger picture, obviously. Lead the expedition."

"Obviously." She tucked it away in her own pack. "Lead on, then. Let's get to this river."

He flashed a white smile and started to walk. Ruuda followed as they made their way across the hills. This wasn't her first time seeing grass. There was some in Eleste'si and variations in the Deep Hollows. But she had never seen so much before. It was very soft. Everything smelled and felt different. She didn't like the change, but she had to admit the smells were pleasant.

After an hour of walking they came to the river. It was very wide, and the water churned and splashed down it. They turned and followed its course. She saw the wisdom in using it as a landmark for travel. She knew the Dark Elf intended to return home after he finished his research. By following the river, he could simply turn around and follow it back. But she didn't know what she would do. Could she go back to Balum Guar? Did she even want to? For now, she had a purpose in traveling with Taliesin and aiding him. Repaying her debt to him. But once that was done, then what? What would she do with her time?

Get revenge.

Ah, yes. Revenge for the life that was robbed of her. The reason she left the Deep Hollows in the first place. It wasn't the first time the thought had crossed her mind. She had no idea how to achieve it, though. Perhaps here, out on the Surface, she would learn things to help her. At the very least, she'd get more combat experience. She had trained with other Dark Dwarves plenty, and had fought the various beasts and monsters that roamed the caverns. But that was the extent of her experience. She would be sure to take advantage of this opportunity to learn more and refine her skills with her two swords.

The day passed uneventfully as they walked alongside the river. They snacked on the move, but eventually the need for a full meal and rest took over. Ruuda found a place close to the riverbank that was secluded by a grove of trees. She immediately set up a campsite. Taliesin watched her with a look of curiosity, leaning one shoulder against a tree.

"Have you never camped before?" Ruuda asked, checking the ground over for sharp rocks or thorny plants.

"No. I've always slept in my bed."

"I guess I'm the expert here, then. Can you at least get a fire going?"

"Yes, I can do *that,*" he responded, getting to his knees. "I've been educated."

"Educated? What do they teach in your Dark Elf schools?"

As he worked, he said, "My parents ensured I got sent to only the finest schools. I was taught a bit of everything. History, religion, mathematics, arts. There was combat training, arcane and spell instruction. And, of course, survival skills."

"Fascinating. I got a general education, as well. But then the focus turns to what your family's trade is. And that becomes your specialty."

"And your family . . . brews beer, you said?"

"Yes. We do."

Once she finished setting up the campsite, Ruuda opened her barrel and took out a pan to cook food in. She noticed Taliesin regard her barrel with one raised eyebrow, but he didn't say anything. They cooked some of the vegetables they'd packed along. It was a familiar smell of home, and Ruuda found comfort in it. As they ate a dinner of the vegetables and some of the meat they'd bought at the tavern, they both reclined against the trunks of opposite trees. Smoke drifted lazily in the air from the ashes of the fire.

"This Surface is a strange place," Ruuda remarked. "The trees here are so big."

"Yes, and there's so many of them!" Taliesin nodded. "How do people move around up here when there are so many trees in the way?"

"And it's so open, too! How do you sneak about when there is so little to hide behind?"

"Right?! And like today, there is no sun because of all those strange cloud things. But will they be there tomorrow? How do people know what to expect? And it's really windy up here, too. It's annoying."

"I agree. I don't like it." Ruuda had to constantly push red and orange strands of hair from her face all day long. The wind continuously touched her skin, and she had noticed Taliesin occasionally messing with his own white hair in irritation.

A sideways grin spread across his face as he settled deeper against the tree. "Well, no spiders today and no clues. I guess that means we push on tomorrow."

"Aye. Another day of traveling awaits."

Before they went to sleep Ruuda filled out a page in the journal with their activities of the day, what the landscape had been like, and what they'd seen. She even decided to include a sketch of their campsite. Then she took her bedroll from the barrel and spread it at the roots of a tree. This was the most secluded spot she'd been able to find, and it would do for a good rest. She wasn't sure what precautions needed to be taken for animals. So, she slept with her swords right next to her, just in case.

As the world grew dark and the smell of the fire faded, the two fell asleep to the steady sound of the river.

.

.

.

Ruuda hated being in this room. If she could have

erased it from the house so she wouldn't have to spend another day in it, she would have. She didn't know if spells that powerful existed. And even if they did, she only knew basic magic. Perhaps she could pay a spellcaster one day to make this room crumble in on itself and destroy the entire family business. Of course, if she was going to go that far, she might as well ask for a spell to fix her actual problem. Which wasn't the room, or her family, or even the beer brewing business they ran.

The problem was her.

Ruuda stared angrily down at the large bucket, stirring the beer within. It was an automatic process now. She'd done it for so long she didn't even need to think about the movements. Her forearms and biceps were hard and strong from the daily physical labor. She glanced up at her family. All busy at work. All completely focused on their own tasks.

The room was long and rectangular, made of stone with a few wooden tables and cabinets. It was the largest room in the house, the only one capable of holding all fourteen members of her family easily. Her parents sat in the corner, going over business contracts with furrowed brows. Two of her brothers evaluated their handmade glass bottles for imperfections. Two of her sisters were assembling barrels. She knew others of her siblings were currently out checking on the hops, fermenting the yeast, and delivering barrels full of beer to happy customers. For everyone was always pleased with their product. They had been for all the many generations the Drybarrels had been brewing. That was how they got their name, after all. Because clients would drink the beer so fast the barrels would be dry.

At least, that was the story her parents had always told her. It used to inspire her and make her proud. All Dark Dwarves yearned for purpose. Their work was their life. Laziness, frivolities, and hobbies were punished. The only thing that mattered was production.

The scrape of a wooden chair drew Ruuda from her thoughts. She looked to where her father was getting up. He was a broad and bulky Dark Dwarf with slate-colored skin and a thick auburn beard that was braided. He went over to her siblings, looking over their progress with a stoic expression.

Ruuda swallowed against her tight throat. He was making his daily rounds to check on his children's work. It was the worst part of her day. Because he would go to each of her eleven siblings and approve their product. And then he would come to her. And the result would be different.

She glanced out the window near her workstation. She could see the plain stone streets of Balum Guar. Dark Dwarves crossed her vision continuously, all going about their daily business. She wondered if her life would have been different if she was born into another family. One of miners or traders or blacksmiths. Would she have gotten the Blessing then?

Her gaze was drawn back to her father as he opened the cabinet where the beers finished their fermentation. He took the oldest one and opened the bottle. Smelled it. Then took a drink.

And he immediately spat it out. His face darkened as he turned to Ruuda and crossed the distance to stand in front of her. "Ruuda. You have failed again. It's another bad batch."

She met his eyes. His were a dull green, barely any color to them. Unlike hers, which were a bright, brilliant green. Her siblings would make fun of her for them, saying they made her stand out instead of blend in. The point was to be a cog in the great machine of Balum Guar. Which she failed out on multiple accounts.

"I'm sorry, Father," she answered softly. What else could she say?

"We're losing money on you, girl," he snapped. "If you don't learn how to brew properly, we'll end up losing the business."

"I . . . I know."

"Your brother can brew, why can't you?"

All she could do was stare at him.

He sighed. "Dammit, Ruuda. Get your head out of your ass and work like you're part of the Drybarrels. Go back *to your room today. Your brother can pick up your slack."*

"But-"

"Go."

Face burning, Ruuda turned and left the room.

.

.

.

A bright light woke Ruuda up. Her face scrunched in displeasure as she rolled onto her side. She slowly opened her eyes to see the sun was in the sky again. Turning the whole world into bright lights and colors. It was awful.

She looked to Taliesin. He was sleeping on his stomach with his blanket pulled up over his head; the only thing visible was his hair.

Ruuda sat up, rolling her shoulders out. "Taliesin . . . Taliesin, wake up."

"Hm?" He pulled the blanket off his face and immediately winced. "Ugh, it's bright. The sun has returned."

"Aye, it has."

The Dark Elf sat, pushing the blanket off him. He glanced around and then frowned, his fingers trailing over the grass. "Ruuda . . . The grass is wet."

"What?"

"It's wet! Feel."

She touched the green plants and found little droplets of moisture covered them. "That's strange. I wonder why."

"Maybe it's how the Surface plants get water? It just . . . appears each morning?"

"That makes sense," Ruuda agreed. "I doubt someone comes and waters all the grass, after all."

"Good point. Did you sleep well?"

She frowned at him. It was an odd question to ask. Did it matter? Her day didn't change whether or not she slept well. Perhaps it was an Elvish thing. She wasn't aware of all the cultural differences, after all. Perhaps that was a standard morning greeting, or perhaps Dark Elves took sleep seriously.

So she decided to answer, "It was alright. Uh . . .

What about you?"

He shrugged casually. "Not too bad, all things considered."

After a quick breakfast they packed away their things and traveled once again. Ruuda didn't like waking up with the memory of her family and her failures. It just rubbed salt in the wound. She cleared it from her mind to keep her focus on survival. The sun made it hard to keep a careful eye on their surroundings. Especially with the way its light sparkled off the river. It was very irritating. But she did her best to be wary of any dangers.

As they walked they saw various strange animals. Small winged creatures that flew in the sky, furry things that scurried along the ground or up into trees. But nothing that seemed immediately dangerous. The river's flow slowed over time, becoming more gentle and less noisy. The hills around them were clear of other travelers, and it was a strange sensation to feel like the only two people in the wide, open world.

The day went slowly on, and Ruuda noticed that the sun moved across the sky throughout the hours. She and Taliesin discussed it, and came to the conclusion it must help track when night would arrive. It would be easier now to plan when to search for a campsite, since they could see how close the light was to the horizon.

Ruuda made sure to keep notes in the journal as they walked. And Taliesin would stop on occasion to check darker areas for spiders. But none turned up. And now, Ruuda was getting curious. Perhaps he was right, and they really were missing.

The day wore on and the sun edged closer to the horizon line. And so they searched for a spot to spend this night in. They found a riverbank that dipped below a small ridge with a few trees, offering protection from view. It was a nice area. The river fell over the ridge in a waterfall ten feet high, and boulders lined the shore.

"This is really beautiful," Taliesin said, standing on one large rock and watching the waterfall. "I kind of like how the light reflects off of it. It's like crystals."

Ruuda sat aside her barrel and came up to join him. "I can see that." She glanced down at the river, calmer and shallower in this area. "The water is very clear. We could boil it to replenish our supply."

"That is a good idea. It does look very clean. I haven't had a bath in so long."

She gave him a look. "Don't start undressing and swimming around and leave me alone to defend the campsite."

He rolled his eyes. "Fine. I'll just wade in with my clothes and rinse everything off at once. You should, too. You stink."

She self-consciously reached up and felt her hair. It was a bit dirty. "Alright. But quickly. Going in the river makes us vulnerable."

Taliesin waved his hand dismissively, sitting down to pull off his boots. "You worry too much."

He sat his boots and socks to the side, and Ruuda noticed his feet were badly blistered. He dangled his feet over the boulder and dipped them into the river. Breathing a long sigh, he leaned his head back and closed his eyes.

"That feels nice," he murmured.

Ruuda took off her own shoes and sat her swords on top of them. Her feet weren't as bad as his, but there was some swelling and tenderness. Despite often wandering the Deep Hollows after her family would get mad about her beer, she still wasn't used to this much hard, continuous travel. She removed her belt and pack and then waded into the river. It was cold, and she flinched at the change of temperature. Wading up to her hips, she then took handfuls of the water and washed out her hair.

"Does everyone in your family have hair that colorful?"

She turned to see the Dark Elf's yellow eyes open again, regarding her as he swished his feet around in the water.

"No," she answered. "I dye it."

He tilted his head to the side, and she watched his gaze move over each shade in her hair and beard. The red, orange, gray, and then white. " . . . Which colors are dyed?"

She smiled. "That's my secret."

He chuckled and stood, unstrapping the scale mail on his torso and forearms. He untied the white sash from his hips and revealed a gray belt underneath. Angular designs were carved into it, as well as one bearded face.

Ruuda frowned. "That is a Dwarvish belt. Where did you get it?"

As he took it off, he answered, "It's been with my House for many years. A present from some Dark Dwarves after a successful trade negotiation with our business. I took it with me when I left because it's enchanted. It's supposed to make me hardier against wounds and sickness. It also enables me to speak Dwarvish."

Her eyebrows raised in disbelief. "The enchantment on that thing is powerful enough to make you speak another language?"

"*Sabhabaan. Kayf bo halakum*?"

"That is impressive. I have an enchanted item, too. My sword."

He glanced to where both her weapons sat. "What does it do?"

"Next time we have to defend ourselves I'll show you."

Taliesin sat the belt aside and then slid into the river. He immediately splashed around, washing off his face and his hair. "Ah, finally! I've been living like a peasant."

As she curled her toes into the sand at the bottom of the river, enjoying the way it felt, she asked, "Is your family wealthy?"

"Yes. I come from a very powerful House."

"What's the difference between your family and your House?"

He sank lower in the river, getting up to his neck and running fingers through his hair. "Well, my family is my parents, my sister, and me. My mother, Sariel Ostoroth, is the

Matriarch of the House and is in charge of everything. My father, Lucan, assists her in anything she needs. My sister, Andraste, is older than me by twenty years and is the perfect child who can do no wrong. That is my family. My House has a larger scope and includes the trade business we run, the slaves we own, and lesser Houses that work for us in order to be under our protection." He waded out of the river, his black shirt clinging to his slender form. "What about you? How big is your family?"

She laughed and followed him to the shore. "I have eleven brothers and sisters. I am not going to name them all for you. We have a few slaves, as well, to help with the brewery business."

"Eleven! Where do you fall in that line?"

"I am the youngest."

He laughed at that, thoroughly amused. "That must be a crowded home. I think-" He broke off, gaze drawn up to the sky. "Oh, wow, look at that!"

Ruuda did and saw the sky had gone from blue to filled with color. Dark blue, purple, and shades of red. "What is happening?"

"Let's look!" Taliesin bounded over to the ridge and pulled himself up. "Whoa, Ruuda, come see!"

She hesitated, and then complied, clambering up the earth to kneel next to him. The sun was sinking into the horizon, and the sky around it was the color of fire. It bled into darker shades the further away it went, finally ending in black. "It's . . . It's beautiful."

"I think so, too. I've never seen so many colors in one place in all my life."

Ruuda hadn't, either. The Deep Hollows was often a lightless place, and the torches and lanterns placed in cities did not provide an abundance of light. Everyone that lived there had excellent darkvision. There was no need to have much color in things when the dark hid it. This display of the sky was unlike anything she'd ever seen before. It was somewhat frightening, but another part of her found it very nice to look at. The only thing in this Surface world she liked so far.

They watched the sun vanish, and the colors fade from the sky. Then they ate their dinner around a campfire and fell asleep once again. After another tiring day Ruuda found herself in a deep sleep, dreaming of endless green hills and an ever-changing sky.

The next morning more clouds rolled in. They were darker and heavier than the ones before. As the two of them ate breakfast in silence, stretching out their sore legs and preparing for another day, they heard voices from the other side of the ridge.

The two met wide eyes and then dropped, pulling as close to the earth as possible. Ruuda reached out and grabbed the hilt of one of her swords, getting ready in case they were attacked. As the voices drew nearer, they could make out words.

"How much longer to Vesper?"

"It's still awhile. We can get faster horses in the town. It's a further journey south to Oceala."

"And you're sure it's a good place to retire?"

"Positive! I told you I've been when I was a child."

"That was eight hundred years ago! It's probably a tourist trap now."

"You wanted to go to the coast. Well, there is no place better. If you'd like, when we reach Vesper we can ask for advice on the city."

"Yeah, that sounds good."

The voices faded as the travelers passed by without going near the ridge. Taliesin and Ruuda stayed completely still and quiet until the voices could no longer be heard, and then for twenty minutes after that. Just to be sure they weren't seen.

Ruuda relaxed, sitting up. "That was close. What were they talking about? What's a tourist trap?"

"I don't know. What's a coast?"

She shook her head. "No idea. But it sounds like this Vesper place might be on our route."

"That's good, we can search for clues about the

spiders there."

The Dark Dwarf frowned. "Are you sure it's safe for us in a town?"

Getting to his feet, he shrugged. "Maybe? It can't hurt to try. We could sneak around. Maybe people won't care how we look."

"Sure. You hiding from those travelers was a sign of confidence in our ability to interact with Surface dwellers."

He gave a sheepish smile. "I was caught by surprise. I panicked."

They packed up and walked again. Ruuda was quite sore now, but she pushed past the aches. Her body would adapt. The temperature was cooler this day, and a steady windy blew leaves from the trees. She decided she liked the sky this dark and cloudy. It was easy on her eyes.

Hours passed and after a brief stop for lunch they pressed on. The clouds got darker, and the landscape around them became strewn with boulders and trees. It made traveling slower as they wound their way around the obstacles and navigated the ups and downs of the terrain.

Suddenly Taliesin stopped, glancing around. "I felt water."

Ruuda slowed to stand next to him, the top of her head even with his ribs. She frowned. "Water?"

"Yes. Water just . . . hit my face."

"But where-" She paused as she felt droplets hit her hair. "I feel it, too! Where is it coming from?"

They both turned around, searching for the source. There was a steady hum and then water fell all around, soaking into the grass and splashing off the river. They looked up in unison and saw that it was falling from the sky.

"I don't like it!" Ruuda exclaimed, backing up and under the cover of a thick tree.

Taliesin joined her. "I don't understand . . . Is this rain?"

"Rain? Wha-Oh, wait, I've heard about this. But why is it raining? What caused it?"

He shook his head. "I don't know."

Ruuda reached back and placed one hand on the trunk of the tree as they watched the rain fall. It was steady now, and it obscured the distant landscape.

After several minutes of watching, Taliesin reached out one hand and held it past the tree they were taking shelter under. He wore dark gloves, but his fingers were exposed and rain landed on his deep gray skin and rolled off the curve of his fingers.

A smile brightened his face and he laughed. "It feels fun!"

The Dark Elf stepped out from under the branches and out into the rain. He flinched as the rain hit him all at once, and then he grinned and spread out his arms. "Ruuda, come out! You have to try it!"

"No. I don't want to."

"It's not bad, it feels good."

She shook her head once. "I don't like getting wet."

"Suit yourself." He spun around and laughed, his boots splashing in puddles.

Despite the fright she felt at this weather phenomena, as she watched Taliesin's joy she couldn't help but smile. After a couple of minutes she was almost tempted to step out as well, but then it was as if the clouds opened up and the rain hammered down. Taliesin hunched over, gasping in surprise but still grinning. The tree could no longer protect Ruuda and she began to get soaked.

"I think we should find shelter," he called to her over the hiss of the rain.

She jogged away from the tree and they both hurried across the terrain, each step making a splash. The water was cold and wet as it ran under Ruuda's clothes and pounded against her barrel. The two of them raced around the large boulders and eventually found a cave set inside a small hill. Hurrying inside, at last they were free of the rain.

Taliesin was laughing as he sank down to the dry ground, leaning back against the cave wall. "That was fun!"

Ruuda chuckled, sitting opposite of him. "I am glad you enjoyed that, I certainly did not! My beard is all soaked, now." She reached back and unstrapped her barrel, setting it to the side. "I guess we can stay here until morning."

He nodded. "I agree. Some extra rest will be nice."

The Dark Dwarf looked out of the cave entrance. A sheet of rain barricaded it and blurred the world beyond, turning it into a haze of greens and grays. It had a nice smell to it. Not like anything she'd smelled in the Deep Hollows before. It was a fresh, clean scent.

Her gaze turned to Taliesin. He watched the rain as well, a small smile still lingering on his lips. Strands of white hair stuck to his forehead and the sides of his face as beads of water ran down his skin. His black and white clothes hung heavily, and the droplets shone on the metal of the spider medallion he wore around his neck. Ruuda had to admit, even though he was a Dark Elf, he was quite handsome.

"Taliesin," she said softly, "why did you leave the Deep Hollows?"

Still watching the rain, he answered, "I told you. I'm researching the disappearance of spiders."

"Yes, but *why?*"

He bit his bottom lip and was silent a moment. Then he replied, "I want to be a priest for the Silk Weaver. Our goddess. Religion governs every aspect of Berenzia, and everything that is done is for the Silk Weaver's approval. But, she only allows women to obtain priestesshood. They are her chosen, not men. And spiders are her symbol. Supposedly, she is like a spider herself. I thought that if I could find out what was happening to the spiders, then I would be allowed to become the first priest."

Ruuda raised an eyebrow. "And leaving the Deep Hollows was your first plan of action to be a priest? That seems extreme."

He turned his head to look at her. "No, no I've tried for years. I talked to my parents, I talked to the priestesses. I tried to convince everyone I could that I was worthy of this. I even confronted the High Priestess regarding it. She is the one who rules over all of Berenzia. I got in big trouble over that. Really pissed her off. Seeing no other options . . ." His gaze moved back to the rain. "I left."

Ruuda understood that feeling. Of being backed into a corner, not knowing where else to turn, and so deciding to run.

A moment of silence stretched out before he asked, "Why did you leave the Deep Hollows, Ruuda? I know it wasn't just because of me. You were running away when I found you."

She sighed and answered, "I wasn't running away. I was kicked out by my family."

The Dark Elf looked at her with sympathy. "Why?"

"I disappointed them one too many times. I couldn't be who I was supposed to be. I couldn't fulfill my assigned role. So I was told to leave."

"That's awful. I'm sorry."

" . . . Thank you."

They sat in silence for a few minutes, watching the waterfall that ran off the front of the cave. The sound of it was soothing. Ruuda took a moment to squeeze out her thick hair. Drops of water ran from her neck and down her back and flat stomach. They were cold against her skin, but after a week of hard travel, it did feel nice on her tired muscles.

"I used to have a pet, once," she said. He looked at her expectantly when she hesitated. She wasn't sure why she was telling this story. Perhaps because she was feeling vulnerable, and it would feel good to get it off her chest. "You remember those things you found attacking me? They are called quags. They are dangerous, but once I found a baby. It was a runt, wounded, and had been abandoned by its parents. I secretly took it in."

"Secretly?" he asked.

"Yes, we weren't allowed to have pets. Attachment of that kind is . . . Well, it's considered a weakness. So I had to hide her. I tried to care for her and bring her back to health. But after a year . . . she died." She reached into her barrel and pulled out a locket. She flicked it open and held it out to him. "There is a drawing of me and her inside. I called her Baby Q."

Taliesin crawled the few feet between them and then sat on his knees, taking the locket. His eyes scanned it for a long moment, studying each detail. Then his gaze moved to her. There was pain in it. She had noticed he was easy to read. Every emotion was written clearly on his face. It hurt her to see the pain in his eyes. Because it was a reflection of what that memory brought up.

For a moment they held eyes. And he reached up a hand towards her, moving for a gesture of comfort. But then he hesitated, and dropped it back to his side.

"I'm really sorry, Ruuda," he said. "That must be a difficult loss."

As he handed the locket back to her she replied, "It is. Thank you, again. For listening. I've never told anyone about that."

He returned back to his seat against the cave wall and offered a smile. "Thank you for listening to my problems."

"In Balum Guar, both sexes are equal," Ruuda said. "Our god, the Forge King, doesn't choose."

"It's not my place to argue against the Silk Weaver's decisions."

Ruuda frowned heavily at that. The statement was automatic, distant, emotionless. She could easily tell it was a mantra he had heard over and over in his life. "But you still want to be a priest?"

He nodded. "I want to prove I am as powerful as the priestesses. And that I can serve the Silk Weaver faithfully as her Cleric."

That system didn't sit well with Ruuda, but who was she to judge another religion? So she answered, "I hope you get what you're after, Taliesin."

He smiled. "Thanks."

They watched the rain for awhile longer and then prepared a dinner of bread, hard cheese, and dried meat. As they both settled back to eat, Ruuda pulled out her cup and a large bottle of beer from her barrel. She poured her drink, and noticed Taliesin raise his eyebrows as he watched.

"What?" she inquired.

"Is that your family's beer?"

"Well, yes but no. It's my beer I brewed." She paused, studying the way he looked at the bottle with curiosity. "Do you want to try it?"

"I prefer wine, but sure. I'll give it a try."

As she poured a cup for him her nerves tensed. This was the last batch she had brewed before leaving home. She had tasted it herself and thought it seemed pretty good, but her father had always disagreed with her sense of taste. A third party opinion would be interesting. She'd never had that kind of feedback before.

She passed the cup to him and he tilted his head back and took a drink. And then he immediately spat it out.

"Gods! Ruuda, what *is* that?" he asked, his face scrunched in displeasure.

She pursed her lips. "It's my *beer.*"

"It's awful! And your family does this as a business? You Dark Dwarves have terrible taste."

She rolled her eyes and drank out of her own cup without hesitation. Who could trust the opinion of someone who preferred wine, anyway?

As the light darkened outside, signaling night, they spread out their bedrolls to sleep. Ruuda kept her barrel to one side and Taliesin to the other for protection. Swords within arm's reach, she fell asleep with dreams of a baby quag, incessant rain, and spiders in the shadows.

Her sleep was deep, her worn body thankful for the extra hours to rest. But in the middle of the night she was awoken by a flash of light and a loud boom, as if a great drum in the sky had been pounded.

Ruuda jerked awake with a gasp, green eyes flying wide. She look to the side to see Taliesin also sitting up, his blanket falling off his shoulders.

"What was that?" he asked.

Ruuda stared at the cave entrance. It was still raining, and it was completely dark outside. Her darkvision helped her see some of the land, but nothing looked out of the ordinary. "I . . . don't know. Was there an explosion? I saw a flash of light."

They waited, muscles tense, when another flash of light lit up the hills for a brief moment. They both jolted, swearing. And then another loud boom sounded, shaking the world.

Ruuda scrambled backwards, dragging her swords with her. The cave was only twenty feet deep, but she pushed herself against the furthest rock wall to stay as far away from the outside as possible. It was colder now; even the stone chilled her through her clothes.

Taliesin also backed up, but more slowly, taking the rest of their belongings with him, including her barrel. He sat against the far wall as well and said, "It must be something with the weather. It's really scary."

She nodded rapidly. "It is. I don't like it."

They both jumped at another flash and boom. Ruuda's heart pounded in her chest, her hands shaky. Neither of them moved as the display dragged on. But as the lights and noises became more distant and further in between, sleep once again claimed them.

.

.

.

Ruuda's green eyes tiredly blinked awake. She felt groggy, as if she'd slept for too long. But there was also a deep peace throughout her body. The extra rest had been sorely needed. She stared at the cave wall and was confused. The last thing she remembered was sitting against the back of the cave, her blanket wrapped around her against the chill the strange weather had brought in.

But now she was lying down, bedroll wrapped tightly around her. Something very warm was against her, warding off the cold. She craned her neck around to see Taliesin's back was against hers, the Dark Elf still sleeping heavily. Ruuda mused that if this had been any other situation, she would have instantly distanced herself. But the warmth was necessary for survival. Plus, after opening up to each other last night, she felt closer to him. There was a trust. If they were going to live through this venture on the Surface, they had to be a team.

Ruuda rested her head again and closed her eyes. For once, she was going to allow herself to sleep in without worry. She deserved that much.

Another hour passed as the Dark Dwarf drifted in and out of sleep. Eventually, she felt Taliesin stir beside her, and then his warmth was gone as he rolled onto his stomach and stretched with a satisfied moan.

"Good morning," Ruuda greeted, rolling onto her back. "Uh . . . How did you sleep?"

He regarded her with half-lidded yellow eyes. "Very good, I feel refreshed. What about you?"

"Same. I'm ready to tackle another day." She sat up. "The rain has stopped."

"Oh, good." The Cleric slowly pushed himself up and tightened his ponytail. "The rain was nice but what followed was not. I hope that doesn't happen again."

After taking their time with breakfast and packing once more, the two stepped back out into the world. It was still cloudy, but not as dark and heavy as the day before. They found the water level of the river higher and the current stronger. The ground was muddy and soggy to walk on, and it didn't take long before their boots were stained.

As the morning wore on Ruuda found her throat scratchy. She had to cough and clear it often. It wasn't until Taliesin started sneezing that she realized some type of allergy must be affecting them. It was unpleasant, but she could only hope their bodies adapted soon.

The morning passed and after a quick break for lunch they continued on. It was quiet and peaceful. Ruuda was so caught in her thoughts of brewing beer that it took her a moment to notice Taliesin had slowed to a stop.

She turned around and saw him staring at a boulder. "What is it?"

"I feel . . . something," he said tentatively. "There's magic around here."

Her brow furrowed. "Magic? What kind?"

His expression darkened. "Necromancy."

She followed as he slowly approached the boulder, looking around. Then he located a wide hole in the ground, like an open maw of dirt and roots.

"Down there," he said. "Let's check it out."

"No."

"It'll be alright," he assured. "The magic feels . . . old. Whatever happened here was awhile ago. But it will be fun to see what this necromancer was up to."

He climbed down, vanishing from sight. She hesitated before following, using the roots and rocks to support her weight. A strong smell of mud and earth hit her, and it almost reminded her of the Deep Hollows. It was still too fresh of a scent, though. The darkness was a welcome relief to her eyes as she found herself in an open cavern nearly thirty feet in length. Taliesin stood in the center of it, surveying a floor that was covered in bones.

Ruuda flinched, unease gnawing at her insides. "Taliesin, I don't like it . . . Those could be undead."

He crouched down, his cloak draping across the muddy ground as he touched one of the skulls. "Maybe. They seem inactive, though."

"Don't touch it!"

He gave a short laugh. "Back at home, one of the few ways I was allowed to make myself useful was by protecting our graveyards against necromantic magic. I've touched many bones in my years. It doesn't bother me."

Ruuda's gaze swiveled about the area. She didn't see anything else in there. No tombs, no items, no belongings left behind. "It's so empty in here. Were these bodies buried here?"

He shook his head and picked up the skull, surveying it. "Unlikely. Perhaps this was a holding area for the necromancer to prepare before attacking somewhere nearby. Only that attack never happened. I wonder-" He broke off and instantly dropped the skull as the jaw attempted to snap shut around his fingers.

The Dark Elf jumped to his feet as all the bones in the area shook and twitched, drawing themselves together.

"What is happening?" Ruuda exclaimed, unsheathing both of her swords.

He quickly backed up next to her. "You were right. I activated the magic. That was a stupid idea."

"Do we run?"

"Of course not." He raised his hands up in front of him, and a glow of dark magic surrounded them. "We finish them off and put them out of their misery." As the skeletons assembled themselves into bodies, standing up on the wet dirt, words in a harsh language Ruuda did not understand tumbled from Taliesin's mouth. "*Isikhali toda darada etta zhoarir.*"

Then he drew a symbol in the air and a spectral whip appeared before him. He moved his hands as if wielding it, giving it a crack, before it whizzed through the air and struck at the undead. The first hit sent the skeleton from its feet. Then it lashed around its neck and snapped the bone.

Ruuda spun her swords in her hands before charging forward with a battle cry. As she neared the first undead she raised up her enchanted sword and said, "*Liquor.*"

Flames erupted over the blade, shining off the metal and her eyes. She carved through the first opponent, then spun around to the next. Chop. Slash. Stab. Taliesin's whip made a wide sweep of the room, it's crack echoing around her. At first it was too easy. The swords moved as an extension of herself, and she felled the enemies around her. She stole one glance back at the Dark Elf, his hands weaving through the air as he controlled the spectral weapon.

And then the fight began to turn. More and more undead crawled their way out of the ground, and Ruuda began to get overwhelmed. A bony hand struck out and raked across her bicep, cutting through her brown tunic and drawing blood. She backed up and pointed her index finger at the ground, then clenched her hand into a fist, a burst of magic pulsing through her. The ground she had pointed at burst with rocky spikes, cutting off the legs of the skeletons that were rushing through and sending them to the ground.

As another slash from an enemy cut a line across her forehead Ruuda slowly made her way towards Taliesin, parrying and dodging as blow after blow rained down on her. Still controlling the whip with one hand, Taliesin pointed to the undead nearest Ruuda and the noise of a deep gong rang through the air, causing the creature's head to explode. Shards of bone pelted her.

The clattering of bones and screeching of the undead became a cacophony, and the Dark Dwarf staggered next to the Cleric, her swords spinning through the air as she defended herself. "There are too many! We need to get out of here!"

He growled as a skeleton got close enough to cut his arm, and then his whip yanked the enemy backwards and tore it apart. "I agree! Let's run." He dropped the spell for the whip and the weapon vanished. He turned to run but one of the undead grabbed a hold of his cloak, yanking him down to the mud.

Ruuda leaped over the Dark Elf and slashed through the creature, cutting off its arms. It launched itself forward, biting into her shoulder with sharp teeth. She cried out and kicked it off as another tackled her. She landed with a splash, tasting earth and blood in her mouth.

Taliesin rolled onto his back as the creatures swarmed him. The cave lit with silvery light as magic burst forth from his hands, incinerating the undead it touched. But they kept coming and coming, a wave of bones and screams. He shouted in pain as blows rained down on him and sharp fingers tore at his skin and clothes, scraping across scale armor.

Ruuda swung her weapons around desperately from her position on the ground, her fiery sword no longer scaring the skeletons away. They were all over her, grabbing at her limbs and attempting to pull her body apart. With a frustrated cry she swung both swords as hard and fast as she could, and momentarily she cleared the area around her. Ruuda rolled to her knees and looked across at Taliesin. He was drowning in bones, firing magic as fast as he could.

Ruuda sprang to her feet and ran to him, using her momentum to slash through all the undead on top of him. She was immediately pummeled again, staggering against the relentless attacks.

Now free, Taliesin stood up, and the yellow of his eyes seemed to glow, as if lit with their own internal sun. He made wide, sweeping gestures in the air with his hands, dark magic following his fingertips in smoky lines. He snapped out a spell, and then the spider medallion burst with dark light. A force of energy rippled out from it with alarming speed. And as it hit each undead it vaporized them into a shower of bone shards. It slammed across the entire cave, and within a second it leveled all of the creatures to dust.

There was a pause as Ruuda stared at the Cleric, his hands still outstretched in the air. And then his eyes rolled back and he fell. She raced over and caught him, and he regained his footing.

"Thank you," he said hoarsely, the glow in his eyes now gone and his medallion back to normal. "Let's get out of this cave."

They two of them climbed out and made their way over to the riverbank. They sat in a grove of trees, trying to stay out of sight. Ruuda watched as the Dark Elf leaned wearily back against a trunk, catching his breath. Both of them were splattered with mud.

"Well," Ruuda sighed, "Let me first say I am glad we got out of that alive. And that I pointed out it was a bad idea. But, what was that *spell* you did? It was amazing!"

He gave her a weak grin. "Thank you. It's not an easy spell. I taught it to myself. It destroys the weaker varieties of undead."

"I think you should have led with that magic."

"It saps my energy! I could barely run right now if we had to."

"Fair enough."

He cocked his head to the side. "Ruuda . . . Liquor?"

She smiled. "Did you like my fire sword?"

"I did very much."

"I chose that word to be its activation."

Taliesin chuckled. "I figured."

They sat in comfortable silence for a moment, patching up their wounds. After he had recovered the Dark Elf used healing spells to finish off their efforts, and Ruuda reflected that traveling with a Cleric certainly was nice.

As they prepared to travel once again, Taliesin said, "You were incredible with your blades. I've been trained in how to fight, but I doubt I could ever do anything as amazing as that."

"Oh . . . Uh, thank you." Ruuda was taken aback by that. Because despite her also knowing magic, her spells felt very simple compared to what he could do.

.
.
.

SKAR

Silence held over the deck of the Scarlet Maiden for several minutes. The crew stared at the landscape around them in disbelief, and Sen stood frozen at the helm. Dark, rain-drenched mountains ringed a land of dense trees and fog. Heavy clouds hung overhead, reflecting in the pond and turning it shades of gray. There was no entrance or exit. They had sailed through the fog, and somehow ended up stuck.

Jade pulled herself together first, a calm expression taking over her face. She strode to the side of the ship, saying, "We need to go investigate where we are. Lower a rowboat."

The crew hesitated, and then Brother Zok was at her side, repeating, "She said lower a rowboat. We're not going to find answers on this ship."

Artemis followed, the usual smile gone from her face.

Skar said, "The five of us should go. We are capable of handling anything that is out there. Let's go, Sen!"

As they prepared the rowboat, setting Foxy and Wolfie inside, they glanced back to see Sen had not moved. His red eyes were wide, his fists clenched around the wheel of the ship.

"Sen," Brother Zok said, "Are you coming with us?"

"I . . ." The large red Dragonborn hesitated, panic in his eyes. "I should stay with my ship."

The Paladin frowned. "But we need you."

"I . . . can't . . ."

Jade put her hand on Brother Zok's shoulder. "Let's not pressure him. The four of us can handle this."

They all got into the rowboat and were slowly

lowered to the pond. They gently touched the water, sending dark ripples spreading out. Then the Paladin took the oars and rowed them in the direction of the shore.

"What is wrong with Sen?" Skar asked, keeping his voice low.

"He's afraid," Jade responded.

Artemis rolled her blue eyes. "Everyone is *afraid*. That isn't going to get us out of this mess."

"I think planar travel scares him," the Druid replied.

Brother Zok frowned. "You think we ended up on a different plane?"

"I don't see another alternative. If we can find out where we are and how the rift happened, then we can get back."

They reached the shore and dragged the boat up and onto the dirt. A thick smell of pine lingered in the air. The fox and wolf smelled all around, but not with their usual happy dispositions. They appeared wary of the world around them.

Skar turned, surveying the forest, and then his gaze landed on a little girl standing at the tree line. He gasped, startled, causing the others to whirl around. The girl was Human, with stringy dark hair and a dirty dress.

Brother Zok's brow furrowed as he looked at the child. He took a few steps forward. "We mean you no harm. We were traveling and got lost."

The girl's eyes stayed fixed on Wolfie as she responded, "Do you need help? I can lead you to my village."

"How far is it?" Brother Zok asked.

"Just a twenty minute walk." Still she stared at the wolf, huddling in on herself in fright.

The Paladin glanced back at the animal. "Does the wolf scare you? He is friendly. He won't hurt you."

"Well, let's not make promises," Artemis added.

The girl said, "I've seen others like him. Big like that. They attack the villages."

Jade turned to Artemis. "We don't want any trouble. Maybe we should leave our animals here. There is food for them in the forest, I'm sure."

The Ranger gave a long sigh, but conceded, "You're right." She dropped to one knee and cast her spell of animal speech. She proceeded to explain to Wolfie and Foxy what was happening. Both animals licked her face, and then trotted along the shore of the pond, sniffing at each thing they passed.

Artemis stood up and addressed the child. "The animals will stay here. Take us to your home."

As they walked into the forest, following a dirt road, Brother Zok asked, "What is your name?"

"Lily," the girl replied. She gave a shy smile. "Your armor is very shiny. We don't have many shiny things here."

"And where is here?" he inquired.

"What do you mean?"

"Are we still in the Korventine Empire?"

The girl looked at him curiously. "I've never heard of an empire before. This kingdom is called Glenpeleg."

"Kingdom? Who is the ruler?"

A frightened look passed over her face. "It's bad luck to talk about her. It will draw her attention. My village can tell you more. Just follow me."

They walked the rest of the way in silence, weaving through the trees. Skar took it all in with curiosity. He had always thought traveling to another plane would be interesting. A great arcane study. But such travel was illegal, and so he had never attempted it. He hoped there would be no consequences for this planar venture. They hadn't meant to go through a rift, after all. But at least he could do some research here and report it to . . . Report it to . . .

His thoughts came to a dead end. Report it to whom? A name had been just there, in the shadows of his thoughts. But once he focused it was no more. Perhaps he was thinking about the person who taught him magic. That would be . . . That would be . . .

A feeling of anxiety passed through him. Why couldn't he remember how he learned magic?

His line of thought was gratefully interrupted as they came to a wide clearing in the trees. A village sat before them. A wall made of tree trunks tied together surrounded it. Above it they could see thatched roofs. The girl led them to a gate, and as they approached they could see this outer wall had deep scratch marks all over it, and the ground was torn up with heavy paw prints.

Two Human guards wearing old, shoddy armor raised equally as worn spears at their approach. "Hold up! Who are you lot?"

The girl said, "I found them by the pond. They said they are lost. They don't know where they are."

One of the guards shook his head. "We don't like outsiders here."

"We don't want any trouble," Jade said. "We're just looking for information."

"Like who your ruler is, how we ended up here, and how we can leave," Artemis stated dryly.

The guards exchanged glances. One answered, "We don't like that kind of talk. It can get people killed. But if you want to risk it, you need to talk to the nomads." He pointed with his spear further along the road. "They have a camp a few miles north."

"Thank you," Brother Zok said. "Could this village be a safe place to rest for the night if we need it? We truly don't want any trouble. Just answers."

The guard sighed loudly. "I suppose. But we won't let you in if you come after nightfall."

"Why not?" Skar asked.

When the guards just frowned, the little girl replied, "That's when the monsters come out."

The group looked at each other warily. The Paladin then said, "Thank you all for your help, then. We will take our leave."

They turned to the direction the guard pointed and headed down the dirt road as the girl returned to her village. The forest enveloped them once again, the shadows thick. There was hardly any noise outside of their own footfalls and the clanking of Brother Zok's armor.

"What in the Hells is going on here?" Artemis asked.

"Everyone is acting spooked."

"Something has them afraid to give out information," Jade supplied. "And I'm sure it's more than large wolves and nighttime monsters."

"Will your animals be safe?" Skar asked, concerned for the wolf and fox.

Artemis answered, "Since that town built a large wall around it for protection, somehow I figure these so-called 'monsters' aren't after other animals. They're after the people."

"Perhaps we can help them," Brother Zok said, ducking underneath a low branch.

"Maybe," Jade replied. "But we do have other priorities."

The flat road wound its way further through the pines until eventually it sloped up into a hill where the trees were sparser. There they saw a small encampment. Colorful tents sat about, and a few fires had meat cooking over them. A large group of people mingled in the area. Their clothes were colorful, but dirty and worn from travel. As the group approached, several of the campers looked about in fascination.

"Hello," the Paladin greeted, stepping forward and taking charge. "My name is Brother Zok. We are travelers who got lost on our journey. We're seeking answers and were directed here."

There were a few chuckles as the campers regarded them with amused smiles. Then one Human man with an eye patch said, "Ah, another round of lost wanderers. Encarna will want to talk to you. Follow me."

They followed further into the encampment, and Artemis' hands hovered above her daggers. Skar was confused about the change of reception. The guards had been unwelcoming. But these nomads appeared friendly. They were led to a large red tent and the man whispered some brief words to someone inside before they were let in. The Human held the entrance for them before shutting them inside.

A lantern lit the area in a warm glow. Strings of beads hung from the roof, and the floor was covered in rugs of various patterns and designs. Incense burned scents of citrus. And sitting at the back on a pile of pillows, smoking a pipe, was a dark-skinned woman with wild black hair. She wore clothes made for hard travel, and a large scimitar sat across her lap. She gave them a red smile as they sat down.

"Hello," she said. "My name is Encarna. I was told you don't know how you ended up here."

"We do not," Skar answered. "We were just sailing on the ocean and came into a fog bank. There were ghosts and things inside the fog. And once it cleared, we were here."

"Interesting," she stated. "You are not the first this has happened to. I am glad you found your way to me."

"You can help us?" Brother Zok asked.

Jade seemed less accepting of the situation. "Are you the person we *should* talk to?"

Encarna chuckled. "Fair question. Yes, I am. Because I, like you, ended up here on accident. In fact, many of us nomads did. Various rifts and portals in other planes swallowed us up and deposited us here."

"Are you from the Material plane?" Jade asked.

Encarna shook her head, her gold hoop earrings swaying. "Oh, no. I came from the Gloomdwell. Just a couple years ago. Not entirely on accident. I was chasing rumor of a woman named Corentin. And those rumors led me to the rift. Unfortunately, I haven't been able to return." She glanced them over, taking in their weapons. "You may be the help I'm looking for. Are you all fighters?"

"I am a Paladin of the Holy Dragon," Brother Zok answered. "We are all fighters or spellcasters."

"We need to get home," Jade interjected. "We have important matters waiting for us."

Encarna only grinned. "I think you'll change your mind once you hear the story."

"Enlighten us," Artemis said dryly.

As food and drink were brought in, Encarna reclined easily back on her pillows. Smoke drifted lazily from her pipe as she began. "I hunt monsters for a living. Especially undead. Which is a profitable business in the Gloomdwell. As I was researching a new target, I came upon the name of a woman. Corentin. A strong spellcaster who wanted to live forever. She was part of a proud and noble family. And they were greedy. As her parents grew older, they became desperate to stave off death. And so they turned to the only solution they knew." Her smile widened. "They became vampires."

The group exchanged surprised looks, the lantern light glowing in their large eyes.

Encarna continued. "Corentin and her siblings became vampires, as well. But the flesh of animals alone did not sate them. They hunted people hungrily. And so they made many enemies. In-fighting in the family began. Struggles for power, for decisions, for land they wanted to claim. Corentin already thought herself stronger than the rest of her family. And so she wanted to get rid of them. She hired a mercenary to kill her parents and siblings. The mercenary knew this was no small task, and so he crafted himself a blade made of sunlight. With it, he was able to kill Corentin's family. But Corentin saw the obvious threat, and murdered the mercenary, stealing the sword so it couldn't be used against her."

Skar pondered over this. He could guess where this all was leading, and it made him uncomfortable.

"Knowing what had happened, people feared Corentin even more," Encarna said, the smoke from her pipe curling into the air. "So she hid herself away. Utilizing deep planar magic, she manipulated rifts to create a demi-plane for herself. She lured people in to rule over and eat at her leisure. Eventually she wound up leaving most travelers alone, preferring to use their fear and subjugation as a way to entertain herself. Because, as the rumors I found say, she has been alive nearly a thousand years. And so," she raised an eyebrow, "I followed her here. To this kingdom of hers she has named Glenpeleg. I was hoping to merely gather information, learn if this was a task I *could do*, and then return to the Gloomdwell to find the highest bidder for the vampire's head. Alas, I am trapped."

There was a collective release of breath in the tent as the four of them considered her story.

At last Brother Zok asked, "Do you know for certain this Corentin is here?"

"Oh yes," she said. "I have seen her. We even fought once. I barely escaped with some nasty scars. I could show them to you." She winked suggestively at the Paladin, whose eyebrows sprung up on his forehead.

"All these people here," Artemis said, "are the offspring of wanderers that ended up trapped in this demi-plane?"

Encarna reluctantly withdrew her gaze from Brother Zok. "Yes. She keeps everyone in a state of fear through use of the feral dire wolves that roam the woods as well as swarms of crows. And, of course, vampire spawn she's created."

"Shouldn't the solution be simple?" Skar asked. "The blade of sunlight can be used against her."

Encarna nodded. "Clever Dragonborn. That is my thought as well. I've been attempting to track its whereabouts. For awhile Corentin kept it inside her castle with her. But it's been moved around in the years to prevent it from being found. Ironically, Corentin had a weapon made she herself cannot destroy. I've found two leads. Perhaps while I research one, you could look into the other?"

"I don't know," Jade sighed. "We really have pressing issues on the Material plane. Would stopping this vampire allow us to return home?"

"I'm certain of it," Encarna stated. "Her magic holds this demi-plane together. If she was dead, then the rifts would open and people could exit. If they chose, of course. Keep in mind the people in Glenpeleg have known no other life than darkness and fear. Isn't that worth fighting for?" Her dark gaze moved to Brother Zok.

"It is," the Paladin answered. "If people are living under oppression we need to help them."

Artemis leaned back on one hand. "I'm all for

stopping tyrants, but why haven't these people attempted to kill Corentin themselves in all this time?"

"From what they tell me, they have," Encarna answered. "But once a rebellion gets a steady following Corentin comes with her monsters and wipes them out."

"I empathize with these people," Skar said. "But there is a lot to consider."

Jade let out her breath in a long sigh, leaning back. "Thank you for the information, Encarna. And your faith in us. We will need to discuss this amongst ourselves."

Encarna gave a single nod. "I understand. It's getting dark. You should find a safe place for the night. The nomads and I go to fortified caves. You are welcome to come."

There was a quick exchange of looks before Brother Zok said, "Thank you. But I believe we will take a room at the inn in the village we passed. We will need to discuss further with other comrades before making a decision. Can we find you here?"

She nodded. "We will be here for another few days. I am venturing on my own to search an old tower for this Sunsword. If you choose to help, go to the ruined keep known as Sunil-Cathal. That is my other place of interest. I'm sure we will cross paths again."

.

.

.

ARTEMIS

.
.
.

Leaving the camp behind, the four of them headed back into the forest. They were quiet as they walked, each lost in their own thoughts. Artemis liked to help others, but this was different than accompanying Brother Zok on his quest to Soleia. There was much to think about, and she appreciated the silence to mull over the details.

They reached the village again, and the guards glanced them over with distrusting looks.

"Hello again," Brother Zok greeted, but his voice was wearier this time. Weighed down by decision. "We would like to stay at a tavern for tonight."

The guards exchanged looks, then opened the wooden gates. One said, "Don't cause any trouble."

"Never," Artemis replied sardonically as they entered.

The village looked as if all the color had washed from it. Muddy roads were nearly indistinguishable from the rest of the ground. Thin trees sprouted at intervals, and dry bushes clung to life. The houses and buildings were made of wood that cracked and slumped. A perpetual scent of hay and dung and earth stained the air. It was a small town. More than a couple hundred people, at most, had to live there.

The residents themselves were hunched and sullen. All Human, their clothes were drab colors that hung off thin bodies. The oppression of Corentin was vividly apparent. Still, some semblance of everyday life could be seen. There were food stalls were people shopped, the owners offering small smiles to the patrons. A group of children played with a ball in the open street. One man struggled to get a stubborn donkey to leave the stables.

Artemis reflected that, even in a place as dangerous and gloomy as this, people still tried to lead normal lives.

Jade pointed to a building a block away. "That looks like a tavern."

They crossed over to it, passing the shops of a butcher and a carpenter. The tavern, called the Cheery Inn, looked to be on its last legs. The front porch awning slouched, and all the windows were dirty. Inside was mostly empty. A few tables were occupied by groups drinking and sharing hushed conversations. The barkeep, a Human male with a large gray mustache, cleaned dishes. All eyes turned to them in surprise as they entered.

It appeared they would have difficulty keeping a low profile here.

Brother Zok confidently crossed the tavern and went up to the bar. "Hello. We are new here, travelers that have come across your village. We are seeking two rooms for the night, and some dinner as well."

" . . . Right," the man slowly looked them up and down. "We do have availability. Beef stew is on the menu tonight. In total, that will be fifteen gold."

The four of them split the cost, laying their coins out on the splintered bar. The Paladin said, "Thank you kindly."

They moved to a table by a window, diluted light streaming in. Sitting down on rickety chairs, the group exchanged contemplative glances.

"I think we should-" Brother Zok started, but Jade cut him off with a hand in the air.

"Not here," she said. "We can talk in the privacy of our rooms."

The Half-Elf Paladin sat back with a mild look of irritation, but accepted the suggestion.

"Should we get Sen?" Skar asked.

"Let's not bother him until we know exactly what our plan is," Artemis answered. "It might take quite a bit of convincing to get him off the ship, after all."

"We should at least let him know we are staying here for the night," Jade said. "I can transform into a fast animal and head back to the ship before bed."

"Why don't we stay on the ship overnight instead?" Skar inquired.

Brother Zok leaned forward. "We need to experience how these people live. Get a feel for the land."

Artemis snapped, "You could ask all of us first before making that decision."

The Paladin glowered at her. "Then go back to the ship. I want to see how these people are suffering."

"Alright," Jade interjected. "Let's all calm down. The situation is stressful as it is."

They remained silent until the barkeep brought over their food. Swirls of lazy smoke drifted from bowls of stew. It was good, if not a bit bland, and lifted their spirits from the simple food they had on the ship each night. When the barkeep returned a second time to fill their cups, Brother Zok asked, "Since we are new here, can you tell us a bit about the woman who rules this land? Corentin?"

Immediately the man's eyes shifted from side to side. "Careful, stranger. Talk like that will get you killed." He quickly hurried back behind the bar.

Finishing the food, they went upstairs to one of the rooms. It was small and basic, with two beds and a singular window that looked out over the town.

"I think we should stay and assist these people," Brother Zok stated, moving to the center of the room, the words tumbling forth from pent-up emotion. "They need our help! They live under tyranny. If we can do something about it, then we should."

Jade leaned against the wall with her arms crossed. "I sympathize with them too, Zok, but we have other problems to deal with. We have to warn the king of An'Ock about Fenvell and the Foresight."

"That is not until the summer solstice," the Paladin protested. "That is nearly a year away."

"A lot can happen in a year," Jade said. "And there is the matter of Jenkins to consider."

"He could be here for all we know!" Brother Zok

stated. "I feel the Holy Dragon led me here for a reason."

Artemis watched as Jade opened her mouth to retort, but then closed it and looked away. It seemed as if the Druid had something more to contribute, another point to bring up, but thought better of it.

"We have another problem," Skar commented, sitting on one of the beds. "We don't know a way out of here. Like Encarna, we could be stuck here for years if we do nothing."

Artemis put her hands on her hips and regarded the Wizard. "Are you up for waging war against a *vampire?* Not to mention his minions? This isn't a Minotaur in a maze, after all. And may I point out, if we had saved that minotaur for food, we would have extra rations in a situation such as this."

Brother Zok rolled his eyes. "We were not going to *eat* the Minotaur!"

"Maybe we should sleep on this," Jade offered. "It's been a long day. Clearer heads in the morning should help."

"That is a good idea," Skar acquiesced. "I am quite tired."

The Paladin deflated, his eyes downcast. "Alright. We'll talk again in the morning. You two have a good night."

Artemis watched Jade and Brother Zok touch each other's arms as they passed, and the two males left the room. Despite their disagreement, it was clear they still respected each other's opinion greatly. The Ranger took off her boots and hard traveling gear, setting her daggers, bow, and quiver aside. She hopped up into the bed, saying, "I want to check on Wolfie first thing in the morning. Make sure he's alright."

Jade nodded. "I agree. It might be safer for them to stay on the Scarlet Maiden while we figure this out. Speaking of which, I think I'll run out quickly and tell Sen where we are staying."

Artemis frowned. "Even with the warning about the woods at night?"

"I'll transform into an animal. It will be fine."

Artemis stared up at the ceiling, her arms behind her head. "Have you ever fought a vampire before, Jade?"

251

The Druid chuckled. "I have not had the pleasure, no. I'm sure if we had to, though, we would be alright. I've seen the way you fight, Artemis. You are a force of nature on the battlefield."

A smile tugged at the corners of her mouth. "Thank you."

A knock sounded at the door.

Artemis sat partway up, staring across at her friend. Jade looked puzzled. The Ranger climbed out of bed and went to the door. Artemis opened it halfway, revealing a tall, pale woman on the other side. Black hair was pushed back from her face, and she wore fine clothes of wine red and deep black.

"Hello," she said, dark eyes taking in both women. "I hope I haven't come by too late in the evening."

"Actually, you have," Artemis stated. "What do you want?"

"To talk to you for a moment. It's a matter of great importance. May I come in?"

The Ranger glanced back at her friend. Jade was standing tall, her chin raised, seeming unthreatened. She gave a small nod.

"Sure," Artemis said, stepping aside. "Who are you?"

The woman entered, and the warm glow of the lantern cast deep shadows under her sharp cheekbones. "My name is Corentin. I am the ruler of this kingdom of Glenpeleg. It's been so long since anyone new has stumbled through my rifts. I just had to see for myself who it was."

Artemis' body momentarily froze, taken aback by this brazen encounter. She stole a quick glance at Jade who also seemed shocked.

"Is that all you came here for?" Jade asked, quickly regaining her composure, her expression dark.

"That was my only intention," Corentin answered. "May I have your names?"

"It doesn't matter," Artemis snapped, walking over to stand beside the Wild Elf. "We won't be here much longer. We intend to leave, and you can keep ruling this place as you see fit. We don't want trouble." She wasn't sure if that statement would hold true come morning, but she wanted to see how this vampire would react to her words.

Corentin tilted her head to the side. "I'm afraid that is not possible. No one leaves Glenpeleg."

"You created the rifts, but you can't control them?" Jade asked in a disbelieving tone.

"It doesn't matter if I can, I will not," the vampire answered. She slowly walked across the room, examining their packs and weapons. "I haven't had new toys in awhile. You really can't leave until we get to play." A smile spread across her face, revealing pointed incisors. "Besides, I think I have something worth your while." She gestured towards the window.

At that moment, Brother Zok and Skar burst into the room, weapons out.

"Who are you?" the Paladin demanded. His armor was off, but he held his hammer at the ready.

Artemis responded, "This is Corentin. She's come to threaten us."

"Oh," Corentin said, "I haven't even begun to threaten yet. Go ahead, look out the window."

The closest were Artemis and Jade, and they tentatively went up to look onto the town below. A small group of people stood on the ground, glaring up at the window with mad grins on their faces. Their skin was deathly pale, their hair stringy. It was clear they were vampire spawn. And in chains they held Foxy and Wolfie.

Artemis felt her throat clench up, a wave of dizziness washing through her.

Jade exclaimed, "She has our animals!"

Chaos erupted outside. A murder of crows sped by the window, and the howls and barks of canines sounded in a cacophony. Frightened screams of townspeople could be heard. With a loud bang one vampire spawn launched itself at the window. It perched on the outside and grinned maniacally at them.

Brother Zok said, "Leave this town alone! We are not

afraid to face you."

"You should be, Paladin," the vampire replied. "I'll see you all soon." She spun on the spot, melting into shadow, and then she vanished.

The noises outside ceased just as quickly. And as Artemis looked back out the window for her wolf, the streets were empty. Hot tears, unbidden, ran from her eyes. And then she turned and bolted out the door. She heard the others call her name, but she didn't stop. Bounding down the stairs she sped across the tavern room. The Ranger barely processed that a large group of people were cowering inside, staring in fear out the windows.

Artemis flung open the front door and ran barefoot out onto the street. Lanterns fought in vain against the shadows, insects buzzing around their glass. A flurry of wings sounded overhead. The crows leaving the town.

"Artemis, wait!" Jade shouted as her friends ran from the tavern in their pajamas.

But she didn't listen. She made for the gate to the town. The guards looked startled at her approach, holding up placating hands.

"Open the gate!" Artemis demanded, not breaking her run.

"Wait, ma'am!" one of the guards said. "You can't go outside the walls!"

The Ranger slid to a stop, her breath coming out heavy. *Open the damn gate now!*

"Ma'am, there are wolves out there!" the guard exclaimed. "No one is allowed out!"

Jade's hand closed around her arm. "Artemis, it's too late. We won't catch them."

The Half-Elf whirled on her. "You may not care about your fox, but I *do* care about my wolf!"

A pained expression crossed the Druid's face. "Corentin will not get away with what she's done."

"She made a direct threat against us," Skar breathed, standing just behind the Druid. "What do we do?"

"We stop her," Jade answered. "There is no other

choice now."

Brother Zok nodded. "We'll get your animals back, I promise. Tomorrow, we go to Sunil-Cathal."

.

.

.

The next morning they got dressed once again and packed their belongings. Jade had chosen not to venture out to the Scarlet Maiden, instead remaining with Artemis through the difficult night. They went downstairs and asked the barkeep for directions.

He gave them a curious look. "Take the road east for about three to four hours. It's a straight path, you can't miss it."

"Thank you," Brother Zok stated. He hesitated, then asked, "What happened last night, with the vampire spawn and the wolves . . . does that happen often?"

The man grimaced. "It's usually accompanied by the vampires taking prisoners to the castle. But as far as I've heard, no one has gone missing. Not sure what that was all about."

"Can you tell us how it usually happens?" Jade asked. "The details?"

He looked uncomfortable, but answered, "We'll hear the crows first. They attack those still outside, the guards especially. They distract them so the wolves can attempt to break down the gate or climb over it. They succeed sometimes. They hunt down people in the streets or drag them out of their homes. People try to flee inside this tavern. Strength in numbers, you know. My husband and I live in this tavern and have tried to fortify it as best we can. But usually the vampire spawn don't come."

"That is terrible!" Skar gasped.

The barkeep just averted his eyes.

"Thank you," Brother Zok said. "Please, stay safe today."

After a quick breakfast, they set out and through the forest path. The weather had not changed, still feeling as if it was on the verge of a rainstorm.

As they walked, Skar asked, "Are we sure we shouldn't have gone back for Sen this morning? We may need his help."

"Let's first check out this ruin," Brother Zok replied. "No need to waste our time and his if it turns out to be empty. If we find this Sunsword, then we can see if our friend is brave enough to fight alongside us."

Artemis' mood was sour. Her wolf, who she'd had since he was a pup, had been taken. What kind of monster threatened an animal? She felt murder in her heart, that familiar bloodlust. It had been some years now since it had burned in her veins. She would channel it, and use it to kill Corentin. *Nobody* took Wolfie from her.

After a couple of hours walking through the trees, they came upon Sunil-Cathal. Perhaps it had once been a great stone fortress, guarding the crossroads. But now the wilds had overtaken it. Most of it was caved in, but some three-story walls still towered amongst the branches and pine needles. Large pieces of stone littered the ground, having sunk in over time. The front door was rotted wood, still mostly held together but ajar.

"Let's see what we can find," the Paladin said, leading the way to the door.

Artemis regarded him, the ends of his white cloak now stained with mud. He certainly seemed to step into a leadership role since their arrival. It bothered her a bit that this was his assumption. Then again, she preferred not to lead. Or follow, for that matter. She'd never worked as part of a team before. It was strange, but the companionship was appreciated. Still, she couldn't help but wonder if she was on her own perhaps she could sneak into Corentin's home easier and assassinate her.

They entered the ruins and were faced with an open chamber with halls branching off. Brown pine needles lay scattered over the floor, causing their steps to crunch.

"Do we know what we're looking for?" Skar asked, glancing over the walls.

Jade replied, "The sword itself might be too much to hope for. But perhaps another clue to its location."

Artemis walked along the edge of the room, searching for hidden compartments within the walls. She ran her fingers along the rough surface. If she had wanted to store a powerful weapon in this ruin, where would she have placed it? Perhaps in a chamber below ground?

Just as she turned to search for stairs, a female voice called from overhead, "Are you looking for this?"

The group turned as one to see a figure standing on a broken stone balcony. She wore clothes of black, red, and gray, with a red mask covering part of her face. Brown horns curved on either side of a head full of short white hair. Her skin had a yellow tone to it, and her purple eyes were almond shaped. A tail flicked as she shifted her weight to one leg. Strangely, a colorful winged serpent was wrapped around her bicep. And in that hand she held a rolled up piece of parchment. Artemis had heard of this race of people but had never seen one before. A Half-Fiend. Someone with bloodline that was connected to the Hells. A product of Human and devil.

"Hello," Brother Zok greeted. "We are peaceful travelers. Just searching these ruins for a relic."

"I overheard you talking about a sword," the woman stated. "I've been searching these ruins as well. Perhaps we can help one another?"

"You are also searching for the Sunsword?" Skar asked. The others shot him a warning glance.

The woman hooked a whip around a column on the balcony and hopped down to their level. As she walked up she said, "No, I'm searching for a little girl that looks like me. Have any of you seen her?"

"I'm afraid we've just got here," Jade said. "We came in through a rift less than a day ago."

The Half-Fiend seemed disappointed. "Right. Well, I was looking through here for her and found this parchment left in a chest. It mentions a sword." She held it out and Brother Zok took it.

"Just sitting in a chest?" Artemis asked, disbelieving.

"It was locked, but I am very good at picking locks."

"And that was all that was in the chest?"

The Half-Fiend narrowed her eyes. "Of course."

Artemis was certain she wasn't telling the truth. But she supposed whatever other belongings or gold coins were in that chest were of no concern to them. They only wanted the Sunsword.

Brother Zok unrolled the parchment and read aloud. "I discovered the blade of the sun here five years ago while making these ruins my home. It was buried deep, but the forest had uncovered it. I guarded it in hopes that a new rebellion would form, and this weapon could be used against Corentin. Alas, a magical seal is placed on the hilt. The blade will not come forth from it. Our best mages have researched it and discovered a missing gemstone on the hilt. Separated from the sword to prevent it from being activated. One of our scouts got inside the castle and believes the gemstone is in there. I will continue to guard the blade until that time. If you find this parchment, know that I have been killed fighting for what is right. For freedom. If the sword has not been moved, it lies beneath this ruin. Keep fighting. Tyranny will not prevail when hearts are brave."

They all exchanged glances. Jade asked the Half-Fiend, "Could you take us to where you found this?"

"Sure. Follow me."

She led the way to a narrow corridor that ran for thirty feet before descending into stairs. They headed down and found a small room at the bottom. A chest with a broken lock sat to the side, along with a dirty cot and some old blankets.

"Thank you," Brother Zok said. "What is your name?"

"I'm Unolé. This is my coatl Teshuva."

A deep voice sounded in Artemis' mind. "Hello."

They all gasped, staring at the colorful creature.

"Remarkable," Jade said. "Are you fey?"

"I am not," Teshuva answered. "My origin is

complicated. Perhaps another time."

"We are pleased to meet both of you," the Paladin said. "I am Brother Zok of the Temple of the Holy Dragon. This is Jade, Artemis, and Skar."

Unolé offered a small wave. "You said you all just arrived? Was it through the white world?"

"No, we sailed into some fog and went between planes," Artemis replied. "What is a white world?"

"An inter-planar location," Unolé responded. "I've been using it as a go-between to try to track down the little girl. My sister. She's been taken and I'm not sure where to."

"I am very sorry to hear that," Brother Zok said. "We will help you find her, if we can."

Unolé appeared taken aback by the offer. "Oh . . . That is kind, thank you."

They thoroughly searched the room, and it wasn't long before they located a latch on the floor underneath the cot. Opening it revealed a small space that contained only a black hilt. It's make was spectacular, with graceful curves to protect the wielder's hand. But there was no blade. And in the center of the hilt was an empty space the size of a gemstone.

Brother Zok reached for the hilt, but a magical barrier prevented his hand from passing through. He frowned. "I guess we need the gem, then."

"But it's inside the castle," Skar said. "Are we supposed to sneak inside, get the gem, and then come back here for the sword?"

"If it was easy, it would have already been done," Jade commented.

"Then let's do this," Artemis said, crossing her arms over her chest. "If someone else could sneak into the castle, then so can we."

"We need Sen," Brother Zok stated, standing up, his armor clanking with his movements. "Let's go back and get him, then set out for the castle." He turned to Unolé. "Would you like to accompany us? Perhaps your sister has been taken as a prisoner to this castle."

The Half-Fiend grimaced. "That could be. I'm a little confused at what is going on. I arrived here just an hour or so ago."

"We will fill you in," Jade said. "Let's head back to the Scarlet Maiden."

.

.

.

UNOLÉ

.
.
.

As they exited the castle and headed onto the dirt road, Unolé wasn't sure how she felt about traveling with this group. They seemed friendly enough, but she knew through her years as a homeless orphan, at the Shadow Guild, and even from her brief time in the Hells that many times kindness was a façade. A manipulation. Still, perhaps she should take advantage of their knowledge of this land. If they could lead her to where Unatchi was, then a partnership would be worth it.

They were a strange looking group. The bronze Dragonborn dressed in heavy blue robes kept looking about absentmindedly. The blonde Half-Elf with the bow had a dangerous look about her, like a tiger on the prowl. The Wild Elf seemed to come straight out of nature, adorned with feathers and beads and the colors of the wilderness. She couldn't tell if the red band across her face was a tattoo or paint. And the Half-Elf dressed all in white and gold was a curious sight. So bright in this dark land. The ones with Elven blood were attractive, she knew, but she'd never put much stock into looks. Hers had always been a bane, after all. She was surprised none of them mentioned her fiendish appearance. She must not be the first Half-Fiend they'd come across.

As they traveled, Jade stopped the group and pointed to the tree line. "I see a tower. Perhaps from the top we can see where Corentin's castle is."

"Maybe that's Encarna's tower," Artemis said. "She did say she was investigating one today."

"Good," Zok nodded. "It will be nice to talk with her."

261

Unolé frowned as they wound through the trees towards the structure. "Who is Encarna?"

"A woman we met yesterday that also got trapped on this plane," Jade replied. "She's been here a couple years and is trying to organize a resistance effort. She is the one that told us about the Sunsword."

They came to a small clearing and saw the tower rose several stories above them. It wasn't in much better shape than the ruined fortress. There was a wooden door, but it was unlocked. Stepping inside, they saw a cracked staircase spiraling upwards. Zok led the way up, and their footsteps echoed softly. They passed narrow windows that allowed views of the pine forests. Reaching the very top, they came upon a wide, circular room ringed with windows. Obviously it functioned as a watchtower of sorts. And in that room Unolé saw a dark-skinned woman lounging against one of the windows.

"Well, hello again," she said, her dark eyes immediately darting to Zok. "I didn't expect to see you so soon. Have you been to Sunil-Cathal yet?"

"Hello, Encarna. We just came from there," Zok answered. "And we found information concerning the Sunsword."

The woman's face brightened at that. "You did? What did you find out?"

"It is located there," Artemis responded. "But unable to be accessed without a gemstone hidden inside Corentin's castle. You weren't the first to go looking for it. We found a note from someone who had hoped to start a rebellion with it. The place looked longed deserted so all participants must have been killed off some time ago."

"But the sword was there?" Encarna pressed.

"Yes, the sword was there."

"Excellent!" She paced excitedly. "We'll need to mount a stealth mission into the castle to get the gemstone. We'll need secret ways to transport it back to reunite it with the Sunsword. Then, stage an attack against the castle."

The Ranger crossed her arms. "Wouldn't it be easier

for a small group to handle all this? A full force is too noticeable."

"Smaller groups have not stood a chance against Corentin in the past," Encarna replied.

"Where is this castle?" Unolé asked.

The woman pointed out one of the windows. "You can see it from here."

The group made their way over and peered out. An ocean of pine trees rippled out underneath them. Gray mountains cracked the horizon line to their left. And to the right, up on a rise of land, was a castle. It was made of dark stone with sharp towers that stabbed the clouds.

"And who exactly lives there?" Unolé asked, confused.

"A vampire named Corentin," Encarna answered. "She's been ruling this kingdom as a tyrant for nearly a thousand years. I am part of a movement to kill her and free these people."

The Half-Fiend glanced at the group she had just met. "You all have only been here a day and already you want to fight a *vampire?*"

"Not necessarily," Skar replied. "We are trapped here from planar magic created by Corentin. We are hopeful her defeat will allow us to return home."

Unolé was curious if her black feathers and Teshuva could simply create a portal. Or was this vampire's magic too strong? She decided to keep this information to herself. If her sister was a prisoner here, help getting into the castle would be beneficial. She didn't want them to leave before she got the answers she came for.

Encarna asked, "Will you all join me in striking the castle?"

"We will," Brother Zok replied. "But first we are going to get the other member of our party. He is a strong fighter and we will need his help, I am certain."

"Alright," Encarna said. "Any information can be exchanged at our nomad camp. I look forward to working with you all. Especially you, handsome."

The Paladin's face turned pink at the compliment.

"Let's go," Jade said, amusement in her tone.

They exited the tower, and it was decided before going to get Sen they would stop in the village to get a map and resupply. Unolé took in the landscape with curiosity as they walked. She had grown up in An'Ock, and the stone walls of the city had been a constant sight. Once she'd joined the Shadow Guild, she'd spent most of her time beneath the city in their underground home. Occasionally she would go into the farmlands that ringed the area, and the furthest she'd ever been had been across the Great Divide river for a contract. But this? These thick forests and mountainous terrain were new to her. It was a relief from the oppressive heat of the Hells. But so far she couldn't tell if this plane was worse or better.

As they neared the walls of the village, Unolé said, "I'm going to cast an illusion spell on myself. I don't want any trouble from those that don't like Half-Fiends."

"I understand," Zok nodded.

"My Druid mentor was a Half-Fiend," Jade commented. "I remember him facing so much discrimination he chose to live in the Firelit Forest away from people."

Unolé had seen the Firelit Forest in the distance, only a day and a half walk from An'Ock's outer wall. "I understand that desire. People can be annoying." She spoke the spell and drew the symbols in the air the way Fade had taught her. Her form shimmered, and then her tail and horns vanished, and her hair took on a bright blonde color. But those were the only things about her appearance she changed. She knew purple eyes were unusual for a Human, but not entirely unheard of. This would pass for a temporary disguise.

As they approached the familiar gate the guards gave them looks of exasperation but let them in. Unolé took in a shabby town with muddy streets and buildings barely standing up. The group seemed to know the way, and she followed them to a tavern. It was dark inside, the windows stained.

Zok stepped up to the bar, drawing the attention of the barkeep. "Hello again. We're wanting to know where we can purchase a map of Glenpeleg."

The barkeep replied, "You'll need to go to the general store, just two shops down the street from here. By the way, did your friend find you?"

The Paladin blinked. "I'm sorry?"

"Your friend. Big, red Dragonborn. He was here late this morning looking for you. I remember him distinctly 'cause I told him to put on a shirt and his response was that he hadn't worn a shirt in over ten years. Odd fellow."

"Sen was here?" Jade gasped. "Do you know where he went?"

"Well, he got quite drunk and left with someone. Don't know who, they stayed in a dark cloak the whole time."

Jade frowned. "Strange. Thank you for the information."

The group stepped away and huddled together. Unolé wasn't going to join but noticed a small opening left in the circle for her. She tentatively stepped up.

"Maybe it was one of his crew that came and got him," Skar suggested.

"Let's do a quick sweep of the town, then go to his ship," Zok said. "He can't have gotten far."

"Um, who is this?" Unolé asked.

"Our friend the pirate captain," Artemis replied with a wink. "Huge red Dragonborn with a black bandana tied around his head. Trust me, you will *not* be able to miss him. Often seen carrying a bottle of rum."

Unolé nodded her understanding. "Let's go find him, then."

They left the tavern and made their way through the streets of the town. Teshuva went in her hood to hide, not wanting his colorful appearance to draw attention. Despite moving silently and not bothering anyone, stares followed their every step. Unolé knew they stood out amongst the drab clothes of the people that lived here.

The group split up to do a thorough sweep of the

town. Unolé wandered between shops, avoiding the thin groups of people that crossed her path. Not seeing anyone big or red in the immediate vicinity, she quickly ducked into a narrow alley between two wooden buildings.

"Teshuva," she said, "what do you think of the situation?"

The coatl wound down to her forearm and met her gaze. "Hm. I've never been here before. It certainly seems an unpleasant place. I do think there is merit in exploring the castle for your sister."

"I agree. But should we do it with these people or alone?"

"Help is hard to come by, Unolé. I think we should reap the benefits of any kind souls that we meet."

She glanced back out to the street, but didn't see anyone from the group. "They are a . . . colorful lot. They don't blend in, that's for certain."

Teshuva chuckled. "I daresay not. But neither do we. I believe the Silver Dancer guided our journey so we would cross paths with these adventurers."

Unolé frowned. "Are you sure? It could just be a coincidence."

"I do not believe there are coincidences with who comes in and out of your life."

She couldn't help but smile at that. Such a nice sentiment, to believe that everyone around her could impact her life in some way. That those she had met in her past, like the Grandmother and Fade, had changed her. Or that there were some she hadn't yet met whose purpose was intertwined with hers. It made her almost feel guilty for not telling her new allies about the other items in the chest at Sunil-Cathal. The gold coins. And the sword. A sword with a skull on its hilt and a black blade. She preferred daggers, truthfully. They were stealthier weapons. But the sword had just been so fascinating to look upon that she had to have it. Teshuva had warned her against taking it, saying he'd sensed dark magic coming from it. But she'd sensed no such thing. He could be a superstitious coatl at times.

As Teshuva slithered into her hood, Unolé stepped back out to search longer for the Dragonborn. But she could not find him. She met up with the others and they concluded that Sen was not there. After heading back onto the road Unolé dropped her illusion spell. The path wound for about twenty minutes through the pines and stopped at a dreary pond. Unolé was shocked to find, floating in the center, a large ship. On the back were the words *Scarlet Maiden.*

"Jade and I can go back in the rowboat," Zok suggested. "We'll return shortly."

As they departed, Unolé glanced at the two she was left with. Artemis and Skar.

"So, where are you from?" Artemis asked conversationally.

"An'Ock," the Half-Fiend answered. "Yourselves?"

"The south," Artemis replied.

"I am from Volcano Island," Skar said proudly. "Would you like to see my two-headed worm?"

Unolé blinked. "Excuse me?"

The Half-Elf rolled her blue eyes. "You can't just whip your worm out in front of everyone, Skar. It's creepy."

The Dragonborn huffed and dug into a pocket of his robes. He then pulled out a small wooden box and opened it with flourish. "Behold!"

Unolé leaned forward and saw there was, indeed, a worm with two heads. "That's weird. Where did you get it?"

"I . . . You know, I do not remember."

Artemis reached in and poked at it. "It's so—*ouch*! It bit me!" She pulled her finger back.

"Oh, so sorry!" Skar said, putting the worm away. "I did not know it could bite."

"Are you some kind of Wizard?" Unolé asked, taking in the oddity of his appearance.

"Why yes I am! And what skills do you bring?"

Unolé patted the daggers at her belt. "I've been trained to be a Rogue. A specialist in unseen attacks, stealth, and getting into difficult places."

"You steal things?" Artemis asked, raising one

eyebrow.

"I do contracts. Whatever they ask me to do is not my business."

Unolé could tell her dodging of the truth amused the young Half-Elf, but she didn't push the topic further.

Soon Zok and Jade returned with worried faces. The Paladin said, "Sen hasn't come back. And no one was sent to retrieve him. Whoever was in the cloak was not one of his crew."

"What do we do, then?" Skar asked.

Jade took a long breath before replying, "We should go check with Encarna and her camp. Maybe they know what could have happened to him. It's not a far walk from here."

Unolé could sense the growing panic in the group around her. In a way, she knew how they were feeling. That cold sense of dread that someone they cared for, even loved, was hurt. The feeling had been with her constantly since her sister was taken.

"That is a good idea," Zok said, his lips pressed into a thin line. "Let's not waste anymore time."

It was with new determination they set back off into the forest. Unolé followed at the back, keeping a lookout for danger. She knew she wasn't the best at spotting animal tracks or other perils in nature. But the Shadow Guild had honed her skills in searching for traps, hidden compartments, locks, and things that had been covered up. If there were man-made hazards here, she felt confident she could spot them.

Their journey, however, went uninterrupted and they reached the clearing of Encarna's camp. Unolé cast the illusion spell upon herself as they entered. The camp hummed with activity, the people putting belongings into packs and quickly writing notes on pieces of parchment. A few looked up at their approach, but otherwise the nomads seemed too preoccupied with their own business to pay them any mind.

"Excuse me," Brother Zok said, approaching one individual. "We are looking for Encarna. Has she returned?"

The nomad nodded. "Just did an hour ago. She's over there."

The group headed in the direction given, and found the woman giving orders to two men.

"Both of you take the west road," Encarna said, hands on her hips. "But be back here before nightfall, if you can. I don't want anyone traveling these roads in the dark. We are so close now; we can't afford to lose anymore fighters."

"Yes, ma'am," both answered.

Encarna turned at the group's approach. "Ah! Twice in one day! I must be lucky. What brings you here again?"

"We ran into some trouble," Zok sighed. "Our friend has gone missing."

Immediately the smile dropped from Encarna's face. "Oh . . . I am so sorry to hear that."

"We do not wish to jump to conclusions," Skar quickly said. "We know he was spotted in the nearby village not long ago, and left with someone in a cloak. But we have not been able to locate him."

"Has something like this happened before?" Jade asked.

Encarna frowned. She glanced at the two men she had been speaking to. "Go ahead. I'll see you both soon." As they nodded and left, she said, "When Corentin captures people it's not so subtle. At least, not that I have heard of."

Skar brightened at that. "He could be all right, then!"

"Maybe he wandered off drunk with a new friend," Artemis suggested.

"I don't like it," Jade said. "It's dangerous here; he doesn't know what is going on like we do."

"Let us hope for the best," Encarna stated. "But in this land, hope doesn't go far. If your friend has been taken by Corentin, our best bet is to get the Sunsword and take the castle." She made a sweeping gesture across the encampment. "I have sent my fastest to other villages to spread the word. Weapons should be prepared, armor gathered, and anyone able and willing to fight the vampire should be ready. In a few days, I believe we can strike."

This talk made Unolé uncomfortable. She worked better alone. But, she would follow whatever path she must to rescue her sister.

"That is good to hear," Zok said.

"Can I count on your help?" Encarna asked.

"Of course."

She smiled. "Good. We could use your help to lead the people. Will you stick around?"

Jade stepped forward. "We are going to look for our friend some more. But we'll be in touch."

Encarna appeared disappointed, but inclined her head. "Good luck."

They stepped away from the camp and back into the woods. After walking for awhile in silence, Artemis stated, "I don't want to wait around for Encarna and other half-trained fighters to aid us. They have my wolf captive. I'm not putting his life in danger by relying on others. I think we go to the castle on our own, get the gem, and then get the Sunsword. The four of us are strong fighters. And much less noticeable than a larger force."

"I have to agree," the Wild Elf said. "This is an issue of stealth, not force."

Unolé raised her hand. "I am good with that. I can pick locks and hide in the shadows. I won't be a burden, I'll be an asset."

Zok inclined his head. "It's decided then. Let's pick up a map and then make our way to the castle."

Unolé found the general store to be small but quaint. It had only basic items, nothing deadly like she was used to from the Shadow Guild. The owner was friendly and eager for business, however. Perusing shelves full of dusty bottles, worn leather harnesses for beasts of burden, frayed rope, and other simple wares they purchased a map, rope, and bandages. They map was crude but functional, and it assisted in their navigating as they returned to the road once again.

Glenpeleg was mostly forest and mountains, with

winding roads connecting tiny towns. The sky grew darker, but they decided to push on and not waste time finding a village to sleep in. Unolé didn't mind camping in unsafe conditions. She was used to that from growing up homeless. She often had to protect her sister as they hid in the Common Grounds, the impoverished part of the city.

Once it became too dark to safely travel, they made camp on the side of the road. A simple dinner was prepared without lighting a campfire. The five of them set against the trunks of trees, their weapons nearby. Conversation helped relax their active minds after such a long day.

"Where did you and Teshuva meet?" Jade asked, chewing on a piece of bread.

Unolé blinked in surprise at the personal question. "Oh, um . . . it's a bit complicated. We met in this . . . white world. This place between the planes. He's been helping me travel between them to find my sister."

Artemis frowned. "Why did your sister end up in another plane?"

"I saw this creature take her. A black beast with wings. Like a bird, but it had four legs. I'd never seen anything like it. Teshuva thinks it's an interplanar being."

"Is your sister somebody important?" Zok inquired.

Unolé shook her head. "No. We're not of any importance. I don't understand why she was taken. I'm afraid she is dead."

"That is awful!" Skar gasped. "I am terribly sorry!"

The Half-Fiend was taken aback by the sympathy in the Dragonborn's voice. "Thank you." She wanted to change the subject. "I don't know much about all of you. Artemis and Skar told me where they are from, what about you two?"

Zok squared his shoulders proudly. "I am a Paladin of the Temple of the Holy Dragon. I'm currently living in Somberdale, but I am from Sunspire."

Unolé wasn't overly familiar with geography, but she did know those two cities were very far away. She wondered what took him on such a journey, but decided not to ask. That seemed personal.

"I'm also currently living in Somberdale," Jade supplied. "But I grew up as a nomad that traveled the Korventine Empire and the Eleste Lowlands."

"What brought you all together?" Unolé asked curiously.

The four of them exchanged short laughs before Artemis answered, "Unlikely circumstances. A spellcaster we call Jenkins has taken a particular interest in all of us. We don't know why, but we have been adventuring together to try and find answers. We call ourselves the Phantom Five."

"Interesting," the Rogue said. "I've never heard of such a person."

"He is a mystery to us as well," Zok said. "But I'm certain we'll find answers."

Their conversation went on for awhile longer before the light left the forest altogether. They spread out their bedrolls on the ground and lay down to sleep.

Unolé stared up at the canopy of trees that obscured the sky. Clouds still hung low, and the lack of moonlight made the world very dark. Her darkvision only aided her in the immediate vicinity. She knew Elves had keener eyes and hoped the Druid would know of any danger that approached.

Minutes passed as her body relaxed. She felt Teshuva curl against her side and it was a comfort. He was her one constant through all of this chaos. Her thoughts drifted to her sister. If Unatchi had ended up here, it was possible this vampire took her captive. It was a frightening thought. But even more frightening was the idea that she could pass through another plane without finding her sister.

As these worries tumbled around inside of her, she noticed a new light in the forest. An ethereal glow that grew stronger and stronger. She frowned, and then sat up to find the source. As she did, she came face to face with a hovering specter. A ghostly entity that wore drifting rags for clothes. The head of a skull had wild white hair flying out from it. There was a moment's pause. Then she opened her mouth to shout, and the specter's hand shot into her chest.

A shout did escape her mouth then, but one of pain

as it felt like a sword of ice stabbed through her. Immediately the others sat up. A second specter crept from behind a tree near Zok, and its hand went into his back and out through his chest. He cried out, his entire body going rigid before the hand yanked back out.

Unolé's purple eyes swiveled back to the ghost in front of her, and it hissed and withdrew its hand. She felt breath back in her again and she slumped to the ground. The world was out of focus. Each muscle felt weak. She was vaguely aware of spells being fired, lighting up the forest in flashes of color.

"Unolé!" Teshuva's voice pierced her clouded mind. "You must fight! Gather your strength!"

One hand fumbled for a dagger at her belt. Her grip closed around the hilt as the eerie light of the specter loomed closer to her again. She slashed out and felt the blade tear through something not quite fully there. Another blink and her vision cleared, the pain easing from her chest as warmth returned.

A streak of magic flew past her head and impacted the specter, sending it reeling back. She drew her other dagger and struck in a long sideways slash. It cut through the creature, but she knew it only did minimal damage. Her simple daggers were not made to fight ghosts.

Another bolt of magic and the specter dispersed in front of her. She whirled around for the second and saw Zok strike it once with his hammer before Jade sent a ball of fire shooting from her hands. It slammed a hole through the specter, dispersing this one as well.

The forest went dark once again. And their panting seemed too loud in the shadows.

"How unpleasant," Skar stated, putting away his wand.

"Is everyone all right?" Jade asked, the flames dwindling out on her hands.

Unolé watched the fire magic and noticed the Druid had blackened hands that faded on her forearms. She was curious if this was another symbol like the red band across her face. "I believe I'm okay. It stunned me but the pain is gone now."

"Me, too," Zok answered. "I will be fine."

"I guess there are indeed monsters in this forest," Artemis sighed, spinning an arrow in her hand before returning it to her quiver. "We'll need to take watches throughout the night. I don't mind the first."

Just as the last words left her mouth a cacophony of howls and barks and growls sounded from the east, followed by screams. They all jumped and turned as one towards the source, eyes popping wide.

"The wolves are attacking people!" Zok gasped, and leaped to his feet. He took off running into the trees, and Unolé thought he moved impossibly fast.

The others hurried after him, and Unolé took up the rear. The darkness of the forest was deep and foreboding, but the sound of battle ahead helped them keep direction. Unolé thought she could see other shapes in her peripheral vision. Specters floating between the trunks, shadows with a life of their own, crows lining branches that looked like skeletal fingers.

As the noises of screams and growls got louder, Unolé took out her new sword with the black blade. This would be an excellent opportunity to try it out. Ahead of her, Zok already had his hammer and shield at the ready, and Artemis reached back for an arrow.

They broke into a clearing and found another village before them, about the same size as the last. Another wooden fence stood around it, but the gate was broken in. The five of them raced over the ruin and took in a town full of rampaging wolves. These wolves were larger than normal, with thick black fur and eyes that burned like coals. They tore through the streets and broke through doors and windows, dragging shrieking people out. Crows sped by overhead, dive-bombing guards that tried to fight back.

"Oh my gods!" Unolé exclaimed, horrified at the carnage.

Artemis loosed an arrow that shot clean through the

head of one wolf that dragged a little boy by his leg. The animal went down, and the child's father raced over to free him. As another wolf made for a fleeing couple Jade twisted her hand in the air and a vine sprang from the mud and locked around the animal's hind legs, pulling it backwards. Zok and Skar jumped into the fray, trying to drive the wolves away.

Unolé spun her sword in her hand and ran for the nearest animal that bit at a guard's legs. With a cry she swung the blade down hard and fast, sinking it into the beast's back. And then a dark voice spoke inside her mind.

Yeeeessssss. It's been so long since I've had blood.

"Teshuva?" she asked incredulously.

The wolf turned on her, biting at her shin. She quickly jumped back, swinging the sword out in an attempt to get the beast to back off. The blade made contact, slicing a line of blood across its shoulder.

Again, the voice spoke. *Good. More. More!*

"Teshuva, what are you saying?" Unolé demanded, backing up from the wolf's lunges.

The coatl's voice entered her mind. "I have not said anything, Unolé. Is something wrong?"

Not having time to ponder this further, she focused on the battle, striking down the wolf as it got too close to her torso. A crow swooped down, talons aimed for her face. She ducked and the crow scratched harmlessly off of her horns. Another crow followed behind, and its talons struck along her cheekbone. Grunting from the pain, she spun around and sliced into the crow, killing it.

Unolé brought a hand up to her face to feel the wound, but strangely she could not feel the broken skin. She brought her fingers away to see there was still blood, but no wound. Frowning, the Rogue grasped the sword with both hands once again and charged into battle.

Artemis stood atop a roof and shot her arrows from above, possessing a full view of the town. Skar and Jade utilized magic to pepper the wolves' feet and drive them back out of the gate. Zok ran around the town, still seeming so, so fast, and helped people caught in the animals' jaws.

Within a few minutes, the town was cleared.

Catching her breath, Unolé jogged up to the others. She quickly cast her illusion spell once again, not wanting any trouble. "Did any of you hear someone speaking?"

"What?" Jade frowned.

The Rogue paused, then said, "Nevermind. I think we got them all."

A village guard hurried up to them, his helmet off and armor scratched up. "Thank you! That was very kind of you to help. We didn't expect them to break down the gate so quickly."

Zok put up his hammer and shield, giving a nod. "You are welcome. We are always happy to help."

A few guards ran past to the gate, attempting to quickly repair it. As the others went to help, Unolé trailed behind, looking at the blade in her hands.

Where had that voice come from? A deeper part of her was certain it was the sword. Dark magic was in it, just like Teshuva had warned. But if that was the case, did that mean it had also healed her wound?

These were things to ponder later. Unolé sheathed the blade and jogged the rest of the way to the gate. She helped prop up the heavy trunks as they were lashed together once again. Jade and Skar used their magic to help secure the bindings.

As they finished, a guard said, "Please, stay at the tavern tonight. You should not be traveling after dark."

Artemis offered a sheepish smile. "It appears we got overconfident. I think a room would be nice."

Jade rubbed her face in a tired gesture. "I agree. We need a solid rest if we are going to travel further tomorrow." She paused, then glanced at the guards. "Have you seen a large, red-scaled Dragonborn by chance?" When they shook their heads, she sighed. "I didn't think so. Thanks, anyway."

They received more thank you's as they passed through the town towards the tavern. It appeared no one was seriously injured. They had arrived in time. Entering the tavern, they saw one of Encarna's nomads binding up a scratch along his shin. When he saw them he offered a small wave.

"Hello," Zok said, stepping up to him. "Are you all right?"

The man gave a dismissive gesture. "Oh, I'm fine. Nothing that won't heal. What are you doing here? Rallying the villagers to fight?"

"We're just passing through," Jade stated. "We heard the wolves and came to help."

"Good thing you did," he replied. "It was a large attack tonight. Those wolves may have made off with ten people if they hadn't been stopped."

Zok growled in frustration. "This is horrible! People should not live in fear like this!"

The nomad inclined his head. "Let's hope we don't much longer."

They attempted to pay for rooms but the tavern owner allowed them to have two for free due to their help in battle. Unolé was flattered by the gratitude. She'd never been rewarded before for an action. In the Shadow Guild, it was expected for a contract to be completed perfectly. There was no reward for success, but there was punishment for failure.

And that thought troubled her. She had not returned to the Shadow Guild after failing in her last contract, after all. Would the Grandmother think she and Unatchi had been killed? Would a search party be sent for them? Or would it just be another casualty of a dangerous enterprise?

She did miss Fade. He, certainly, would be worried about her. If she did go back to An'Ock with these new allies, the Phantom Five, she would need to talk to the Grandmother. If she explained the situation, surely she would understand. She didn't want to be banished from the Guild. But right now, the only thing that mattered was finding Unatchi. She knew Fade understood that, and hopefully he could help smooth things over.

With thoughts of home turning through her head,

Unolé accompanied Jade and Artemis into one of the rooms. There were only two beds on the opposite walls.

"I can sleep on the floor," Jade quickly volunteered. "A bed is not my preference, anyway."

Artemis hopped into one of the beds. "Well, I also like to camp but I won't say no to a soft mattress tonight!" She patted it. "Well, mostly soft."

Unolé sat down with a long sigh. It had been an interesting day. "Thank you. I'm sorry your friend is missing. Maybe we'll run into him tomorrow."

The Druid's green eyes dropped to study the wooden floor. "Sen is strong. He likes to think himself invincible. But there is magic and power in the world – in all these planes – that goes beyond physical strength. And I don't think he's ever had to face it before."

"I understand that. I didn't know what to do when I saw that flying creature take my sister. I'd never encountered a situation I couldn't sneak my way out of. It is frightening."

Artemis lay down on her back, gazing up at the ceiling. "It's been my experience that enemies who face you head on in straight physical combat are either stupid or weak. If Sen is hurt, whoever is responsible is manipulative and cunning."

"Your magic is really strong, Jade," Unolé said. "I know a bit myself, but nothing like that. I was taught by a friend and am still learning."

"You were taught?" the Druid's voice was questioning. "I thought Half-Fiend's have an innate use of magic?"

She shrugged. "I suppose so. My friend told me my fiendish blood allows me to use emotion to produce magic. But I also have words and gestures I have memorized. Is it like that for you?"

"Somewhat," Jade responded. "Magic is different for everyone. For people like Wizards, they learn through years of study. They must recite exact words and make exact gestures to cast a spell. That's why they are protective of their spellbooks. But I am a Druid. While movement with my hands and speaking words in my native Elvish tongue helps focus the magic, I get it from my connection with nature. I *feel* it. People like Paladins or Clerics are similar. It's about emotion and a connection with their deity more than an exact science."

Unolé found this all very fascinating. "And how do you get more powerful in magic?"

"For Wizards, it's through more and more study. For Druids it's through deeper meditation and time in nature. Zok has mentioned praying and dedicating himself to the Holy Dragon can bring him more power. It is unique for everyone, I suppose."

"Interesting. Thank you, Jade. I really don't know much, but I want to learn more."

The Wild Elf smiled. "I have many years of knowledge I never mind sharing."

They three of them settled in for the night, and Unolé found her dreams filled with fiery magic, large wolves, and a black winged beast.

.

.

.

ARTEMIS

.
.
.

Artemis was tired. Not physically. She'd been through worse situations. She'd slept less and struggled more. But this was an emotional weariness. It was so much to process in such a short amount of time. And yet, stopping to rest was not an option. She needed her wolf, Jade needed her fox, and they needed to get home.

It was a long morning of walking. The sky remained overcast and gloomy. After Brother Zok got them lost once, the Ranger took the map and led the way. She was an excellent navigator, and could easily find the best routes on their trek towards the castle. She was itching for battle. She wanted to get her hands on Corentin and show her that she was not someone to be crossed.

At last, as the afternoon hit, there was a break in the forest. Only a few miles across, they found themselves on some sort of farm. Rows of corn sat to the side, and scarecrows peeked out. A creek ran the length of the clearing, turning most of the land into a swampy mess. There was a pen full of goats made from rickety wooden stakes. And beyond that was a simple hut. On the opposite side of the clearing was a barn. The area smelled of mud and earth and goat fur.

"Fascinating," Artemis said.

"Which way from here?" Zok asked, peeking over to look at her map.

The Ranger pulled it away from him in irritation. "I'm leading. Straight across this farm is the fastest route. Just follow me."

As she strode forward Skar asked, "Is it okay for us to cross this person's land?"

"Farmers *love* me!" Artemis assured. "There is nothing to worry about."

They crossed to the creek. The Ranger strode into it, confident its depth and current wouldn't be an issue. She got halfway through with the water up to her knees when there was a loud *squelch* and she felt both of her shoes come off. Bare toes stuck into the cold mud and she stumbled.

Artemis looked up to see Brother Zok use his speed to leap across and Jade transform into a deer that leaped gracefully over the water. Unolé bounded over, splashing herself, and Skar waited until the Half-Fiend wasn't looking before going intangible as he walked through.

The group turned to look at her.

"What's wrong?" Jade asked.

"My shoes came off," Artemis growled, reaching down with one hand to feel for them. "They got stuck in a patch of thick mud."

Brother Zok laughed. "Mighty Ranger of the wilds, I see."

Artemis grabbed a hold of one boot and pulled as hard as she could, but it wouldn't come out. She huffed, then collected herself and strode out of the creek barefoot. "I'll just ask this nice farmer if they have extra shoes."

"I don't know," Unolé mused, "What if they work for Corentin?"

The Ranger tightened her braid. "Then I'll ask the goats for information first." Pleased at a confused look from the Rogue, Artemis crouched down next to the goat pen and cast her spell. Then she said to the animals, "Hello. Is the person that owns this hut here?"

This drew the attention of a few goats. One wandered closer and answered, "No, the person is out."

"Damn. Well, are there shoes inside the hut?"

"You are asking too many questions."

"I need shoes! I don't have hooves like you."

The goat eyed the grass on the opposite side of the fence. "Get me some of that grass and I'll answer you."

Artemis looked incredulously at it. "You *have* grass!"

"The kind out there is better!"

She sighed, pulling out a handful from the ground. "You drive a hard bargain. Here." She stuck her hand through the fence and offered the grass.

The goat ate it, taking its time before responding, "There may be shoes in there."

Artemis pursed her lips. Then she stood up and faced the group.

"What did you learn?" Skar asked, red eyes peering out from under his hood.

She drew herself up before answering, "There may be shoes inside."

Suddenly, a thunderous boom split the air, and there was a brief flash of light before a fireball slammed into the ground at their feet. The impact threw Artemis into the air, and her stomach turned before she hit hard on her back. The skin on her arms burned, but she pushed the pain from her mind. She rolled back to her feet , drawing her bow and an arrow at the same time.

The ground where the fireball had hit was scorched and barren, and the Ranger was glad to see the goats were far enough away to avoid the fire. Brother Zok, Skar, and Unolé slowly picked themselves up, their clothes singed. Only Jade still stood, arms over her head protectively, but unharmed.

A whoosh of wind tugged at Artemis' clothes and a figure sped by. She twisted around to follow it with the point of her arrow, and saw a gray-haired woman dressed in rags riding a broom. Flames flickered from her hand and went out as she made to turn back around.

Brother Zok pulled out his shield and hammer. "Should we try talking to her? We don't have to fight."

Unolé spun a dagger in each hand. "I think if she wanted to talk she wouldn't have attacked us."

As the woman flew towards them, hand lighting up once again, Artemis released her arrow. To the Half-Elf's surprise, the woman sharply turned and avoided being shot through the chest. But the arrow impacted her broom and sent her spinning, the second fireball impacting in the creek.

Snarling, the woman muttered the words of a spell, and pointed a withered finger towards the corn fields. Artemis turned to see the scarecrows climb down from their perches, vanishing into the crop.

"Watch out!" the Ranger called, notching another arrow. "We've got scarecrows coming."

Skar loosed an icy blast from his wand as the woman swung by overhead. She dodged and then unleashed five pointed blasts of magic that separated and came at each of them. Skar got hit on the leg, crying out. Brother Zok attempted to block with his shield but the magic went straight through and cut a slice into his upper arm. Jade got hit as well, interrupting the spell she had been casting. Unolé deftly rolled out of the way, avoiding the attack.

Artemis saw one head straight for her face and she spun on the balls of her feet. It attempted to turn with her but not fast enough, just catching the side of her faded blue tunic. She then aimed and in a split second fired another arrow.

With a shout the woman sent a small burst of fire forth, burning the arrow up in midair. Then she pointed a finger at Unolé and snarled out a spell. The Half-Fiend hunched, shrank, and became an orange cat. The cat yelped and ran up a nearby tree.

The scarecrows burst forth from the corp, two coming after Artemis. Another launched at Brother Zok, pummeling the Paladin with blows that sent him reeling back.

With a growl Jade spun her hands in the air and cracks of electricity followed her movements. Then she shot one hand forward and a bolt of lighting erupted from it and struck the old woman. She screeched and dropped a few feet in the air, her bones lit up through her skin. Then she regained her composure, smoke drifting from her form. She flew in a great circle around the group and sent another fireball down.

Artemis dove away from the impact, the boom ringing in her pointed ears. She spat out grass and mud from her mouth. Looking up, she saw the two scarecrows were on fire but still coming after her. She rolled out of the way of one kick, and blocked a punch with her bow. On the defense, Artemis stumbled backwards to put more distance between herself and her attackers. And then both of them froze as ice struck from behind, completely encasing them. Not wasting a second, the archer spun into two kicks that shattered the frozen scarecrows. Their bodies fell apart, and she saw Skar on the other side, the last of the ice spell leaving his wand.

Brother Zok backed up behind his shield, the fiery scarecrow pounding on it. When he at last got an opening he charged forward in a series of hard swings that took off both of his opponent's arms and at last the head. The scarecrow crumbled to the ground.

Artemis notched another arrow and aimed up at the gray-haired woman. They locked eyes and the woman's voice spoke in her head. *"These people are your enemies. Kill them all."*

She blinked and realized the old woman was right. These people weren't her friends. She didn't have friends. They needed to die.

Her arrow swiveled and shot at Brother Zok. He cried out and brought his shield up just in time, stumbling back from the impact. She then turned to Skar and fired another one. The Wizard's eyes popped wide and he shot off a quick spell that deflected the attack.

"What are you doing?!" the Paladin exclaimed.

Growling, Artemis put away her bow and drew both daggers from her belt. She charged Skar first, the closest opponent. In her peripheral vision she saw Jade and the gray haired woman locked in a battle of magic. She would deal with the Druid later.

Artemis sprung on Skar in a series of quick strikes. Her daggers flashed and spun, and the bronze Dragonborn dodged and deflected as best he could before he cried out in pain. Blood stained her daggers.

And then Brother Zok was on her. She twirled away from the Wizard to give her more room to fight the Paladin.

The hammer swung down at her head but she nimbly dodged and gave a quick stab. It impacted his breastplate, creating a long scratch across the symbol of the Holy Dragon. He attempted to bash her with the shield but she stepped back quickly, out of range.

Artemis dropped to the ground and spun around, sweeping his legs out from underneath him. She lifted both daggers up to stab down at his throat when a blast of magic caught her in the side.

Thrown to the ground, the Ranger looked to find her attacker was a wounded Skar, barely able to stand as one hand clutched his bleeding side and the other held his wand up. She slowly stood, knowing he had nowhere to run. Sheathing both her daggers, Artemis drew out her bow and grabbed an arrow. Skar stared at her, his face twisted in fright.

Then the earth erupted underneath her, shaping into a hand that closed swiftly around her middle and pinned her arms to her sides. She struggled and shouted out, every muscle in her body tensing against the hard rock. But it didn't give.

Looking over her shoulder Artemis saw Jade concentrating on the earth spell, a remorseful expression on her face.

Brother Zok shakily stood and lifted the handle of his hammer. "I'm sorry."

He struck her in the head and her world went black.

.

.

.

Artemis slowly opened her blue eyes, her entire body aching. She saw a barn roof overhead, and could smell hay and manure.

"She's awake!" It was Skar's voice.

Artemis groaned and gently sat up. Beside her knelt Jade and Brother Zok, both of their hands lit with healing magic that was concentrated on her. Behind them she saw Skar and Unolé, a Half-Fiend once again, watching. Relief washed over their faces simultaneously.

"How do you feel?" Brother Zok asked, dropping his spell.

Artemis held her head. "Well, I have a terrible headache. But otherwise, I could be worse." She looked over them all. Cuts, bruises, and burn marks covered their bodies. She knew if it hadn't been for the Druid's healing prowess, they would be much worse off. It was too bad one of the them wasn't trained as a Cleric.

"I checked in the hut for shoes," Unolé said, her arms crossed as she leaned casually against the wall. "There were none, I'm afraid."

"What happened to that old woman?" Artemis asked.

"I killed her," Jade answered. "The spell on Unolé and yourself broke then." She glanced outside. "It's evening now. I think we should stay here to rest and recover for the night. Our wounds need more tending."

Artemis scooted back to lean against a hay stack. The smell reminded her of home, and it was comforting. "Sorry for beating you two up." She looked at both Skar and Brother Zok. "That woman's magic was too strong for me to fight."

The Paladin offered a soft smile. "Don't worry about it."

"She was some kind of witch," Skar said. "We looked into her hut and it had strange items throughout it. Witch's brew items and a cauldron. Very disturbing."

"How long have I been out?"

"A few hours," the Wizard supplied. "We were worried about you."

Artemis grinned. These people were not so bad, after all. "Thank you."

They settled down in the barn, binding up their injuries and resting their tired bodies. The sky slowly darkened outside, and they watched the clouds roll by as a cold wind blew in. The stalks of corn swayed, and the smell of burnt grass from the fireball lingered.

Just before darkness descended entirely they heard the noise of carriage wheels against the muddy ground. Exchanging worried looks, the five of them hid inside the barn. Artemis crouched behind a hay stack and peered over the top.

A black carriage with a hooded driver rolled up and came to a stop a few yards from the barn. The door opened, and a large red Dragonborn stepped out. Then the door closed behind him and the carriage pulled away.

They all exchanged shocked glances, but no one moved or spoke. Sen just stood where the carriage had left him, looking about as if confused.

"We should go out to him," Skar whispered.

"It could be a trap," Brother Zok muttered. "Why was he left here, exactly where we are?"

Sen glanced up at the sky, sniffed, and adjusted his bandana. But still he did not walk towards the barn.

"Something is wrong." Jade shook her head, crouched behind a crate. "I don't like this."

"We can't just leave him out there, though," Brother Zok sighed. "What if he needs help?"

The group hesitated for several more seconds, turning over the options in their heads.

At last Artemis whispered, "Let's get him. But cautiously."

Skar immediately stood up. "Sen!"

Sen turned to the Wizard, his eyes lighting up. "Skar! It is good to see you."

Artemis frowned, and glanced across the barn at Jade. The Druid gave her a confused and worried look. No one else moved.

"We've been worried about you," Skar said, stepping forward to the barn entrance. "We didn't know where you've been. Are you hurt?"

"No, not at all," Sen responded. "I've been looking for all of you as well."

The pirate walked up to the Wizard and the two embraced, the wind pulling at Skar's dark blue robes and

Sen's purple pants.

Brother Zok then stood. His tone was friendly but cautious as he asked, "What happened? We were told you came to the town to find us but left with someone."

As Jade emerged as well, Artemis decided she would join. She came up from behind the hay. But she was wary. If she had been influenced by mind control, perhaps Sen was, too.

"Oh, yes, I got robbed," Sen stated sheepishly, and a smile crept across his face. "I got too drunk at the tavern and a man led me outside and took all my gold and things."

"But not your axe," Artemis said, seeing the large weapon still on his back. That seemed odd.

"Too heavy for him, I suppose," the pirate captain reasoned.

"So, where have you been?" Brother Zok asked. "Why were you in that carriage?"

"I, uh, just got a ride to find you all," Sen answered.

Jade frowned. "A ride from whom?"

"Just . . . someone I met."

There was a prolonged pause. Something did not feel right. Artemis' nerves tingled, and she noticed no one in the barn was relaxed. Even Unolé, standing in the far corner, had her hands close to her daggers. Sen's gaze swept over each of them, and his fingers twitched. Whether it was nerves or something else, Artemis could not tell.

Brother Zok took a step closer to the red Dragonborn. "Are you being forced to do anything against your will?"

"No," Sen replied quickly, shaking his head. "Why are you asking that?"

"I was just put under a charm spell," Artemis replied dryly. "We're worried the same has happened to you. We couldn't find you. Not even your crew knew where you went."

"Sen," Jade pressed, compassion coming through in her voice. "You have to tell us where you have been the last two days."

There was a prolonged pause where no one moved, no one breathed. And then the pirate made for the door. "I have to go."

Artemis slid over and blocked the entrance. She had to crane her neck up to meet his gaze, but she did so with a resolute stare. "We're not done talking."

Sen's expression darkened. He pulled out his axe. "Move aside."

Rising to the challenge, the Ranger pulled out her bow and an arrow. "Don't do this, Sen."

Tension filled the barn as the two held eyes. No one moved or said a word.

Brother Zok then put his hand on Sen's enormous arm. "Friend, we just want to-"

Sen swung his axe back, the blunt of the blade slamming into the Paladin and sending him to the ground. Artemis loosed her arrow but the axe flashed back in front of him, the arrow bouncing off and flying out of the barn.

Sen then took a wide swing at Jade. The Druid rolled out of the way, and the axe impacted the floor where she'd been. Brother Zok jumped up from behind and wrapped his arms around the pirate's thick neck.

"Sen, *stop*!" the Paladin shouted.

The Dragonborn slammed backwards into the barn wall, forcing Brother Zok to let go. Unolé came up with her daggers but Sen grabbed her forearm and lifted her from the ground. He tossed her to the side, and she collided with the hay.

"Stop!" Skar shouted, and he shot his hand forward at Sen's chest. He went intangible, and the hand passed through the broad pirate. Skar opened his mouth to make a threat, but then his eyes went wide and jaw fell slack. In his moment of hesitation, Sen was able to leap away.

"He's not real!" the Wizard exclaimed. "He is a shell!"

Brother Zok frowned, and his blue eyes flicked back and forth between the two Dragonborn. And then he darted past Sen's defenses and swung his hammer as hard and fast as he could. It slammed into Sen's chest, and cracks spread out from the blow. The Dragonborn's body wavered, and then fell apart like pieces of pottery. There was nothing on the inside.

There was a moment of suspended silence as they all stared at the wreckage, panting.

"Who did this?" Jade breathed, fire and fury laced through her shocked tone.

"Does somebody have your friend?" Unolé asked.

"I am going to find out," Brother Zok stated, a look of determination on his face.

He sat down on the barn floor, his muddied white cloak pooling around him. He rested both hands on his knees and sat up straight, taking on a meditative pose. His blue eyes drifted shut, and he remained still. Mud and dried blood covered his face and body, and his longer brown hair was dirty with sweat. But serenity shone through, and for a moment he looked every bit the noble, holy warrior he strove to be.

There was a flash of yellow light, and a sword appeared hovering over his lap. The blade was broken, snapped off halfway. His brow bent in concentration, and then furrowed in a look of distress. A few seconds passed and then he gasped, his eyes blinking open again. The sword before him faded.

"I scryed on Sen," Brother Zok breathed, panic in his eyes. "It's not good."

"What did you see?" Skar asked, leaning forward along with the others.

The Paladin met their eyes. "I saw him in Corentin's castle. In a prison cell. He's been tortured." His expression turned serious, resolute. "We have to save him."

The noise of carriage wheels cut through their mounting panic. They all turned as one to see the black carriage come back into view. The hooded driver turned to them, and they saw the face of Corentin.

"Hello," she said. "Why don't you all take a ride to my castle? We have a lot to talk about."

290

Sen

.
.
.

Pain.

That was all that existed now. Pain unlike Sen had ever experienced. He was barely aware of the cell around him, of the manacles binding his wrists and ankles. They were a backdrop as he drifted in and out of consciousness.

The only thing that anchored him to reality was thinking of his friends. He wished he had left the Scarlet Maiden with them. But nothing had made sense. The ocean, his ship, the one place he was in control had been taken from him. He hadn't known what to do. He'd panicked.

And then there was the tavern. He'd gotten too drunk. Boasted too much. And drew the attention of someone. It wasn't until he was led away and attacked he realized this was not a normal person. Their strength was incredible, their speed inhuman. Their incisor teeth had been pointed. He'd been overpowered, bound, and thrown into a carriage.

Sen recalled a long ride. Out the window he could only see forest. And then a castle that towered up to the heavy clouds. Corridors. Rooms. Stairs. And then a chamber filled with frightening instruments of torture.

A whip had been taken to his back. A blade used against his scales. A fist beat him, belonging to a smiling woman with smooth, dark hair. And then a tongue had licked the blood from his body, a horrifying violation. He'd been so afraid those teeth would sink into him. Turn him into one of *them*.

But they hadn't. He had been tossed in a dungeon cell, and had been left alone since.

Sen worried about his friends. The Phantom Five, as

they had taken to calling themselves. A team. Would they end up like him? Had they already, and they were in another part of the dungeon? The idea that Zok and Jade were locked up here as well, tortured, made him feel sick.

Another, clearer part of his mind reasoned that he was the bait. His friends were being lured in. And then the vampires would make a meal out of all of them.

A desperate moan escaped him. He longed for the sound and smell of the ocean again. The creaking of the ship under his boots. But now, that life seemed so far away. There was only pain. And only death.

.

.

.

TALIESIN

.
.
.

Crack!

The legs of the chair broke off as Taliesin slammed it against his bedroom door for what felt like the hundredth time. His arms hurt, and he panted, glaring at the black wood that separated him from the rest of his house. From the rest of the world.

His yellow eyes glanced over his progress. The door and dark walls around it were dented, scratched, and cracked from weeks of effort attempting to break out. He glanced behind him at the single window of his room. It, too, had the same damage around it. But neither broke under his attacks. There was only one explanation. His mother had magically sealed them to prevent him from escaping.

Taliesin let the chair slip from his limp fingers, catching his breath. Sweat seeped into his clothes. A fine tunic and pants of expensive material, black with white embellishments of spiderwebs. A common fashion in Berenzia. It mirrored what his large bedroom looked like. All dark with silver and white accents. Images representing the Silk Weaver were scattered throughout. An enormous four poster bed had a metal spider hung above the headboard. Unconsciously, he reached for the spider medallion he always wore around his slender neck, his holy symbol, the conduit for his spells. But his mother's spells were too powerful for him to overcome.

Anger brought new fire into his veins. He stepped up to the door and pounded his fists on it, shouting, "You can't keep me in here! I am not your prisoner!" He banged and banged, demanding someone listen to him.

And at last, for the first time in months, his door opened.

His sister quickly stepped in, shutting the door behind her, an annoyed expression on her dark and narrow face. "Taliesin! You must calm down. The whole house can hear you."

He flung his arms out. "Good! That is the intention! *Where is Mom?"*

Andraste sighed, crossing her arms. Her long white hair was pulled up in a bun, and earrings made of platinum dangled against her neck. "I do not speak for her. I come of my own accord. Can we talk?"

Taliesin felt his fire go out. Unclenching fists he hadn't been aware he was gripping, he motioned to the bed. They both sat on the edge, feet hanging over the side. His sister was not much taller than him, considered short for a female, and a fine dress wrapped her petite frame.

Taliesin glanced it over and stated, "You're going to the temple, I see."

"Every opportunity I get, if I'm to have a chance to become a priestess one day."

He glanced away and snapped bitterly, "You are lucky, then."

Andraste sighed. "Baby brother, you need to stop this foolish pursuit! Men cannot *become priests. It's not the Silk Weaver's decree. But you can serve her in other ways. You can serve our House in other ways."*

Taliesin looked towards his desk, intricately carved, like so many other pieces of furniture in the three-story home. A sign of House Ostoroth's wealth and status. Parchments were scattered about, the edges curling inward. A fine quill sat in a pot of ink. Numerous books were stacked on the corners. Fictional stories, histories, spells, religion. He loved to read and learn. And sitting above on a shelf was a small altar to the Silk Weaver, the goddess of Berenzia. The altar used to bring him hope and happiness. Not anymore. Not after what happened in the temple seven months ago.

He turned back to his sister. "How can I serve our House if I'm locked in my room?"

"By remembering your place," a voice said from his

door.

Both turned to see the matriarch of House Ostoroth, Sariel, standing there. Long white hair draped over her shoulders, and she, too, wore a fine dress with a plunging neckline. She inclined her head at Andraste. "Leave us."

His sister glanced at him once before exiting the room. Sariel then closed the door and crossed the room to stand over Taliesin. Her red eyes looked him over in detail. All the members of his family had red eyes. Most of the Dark Elves of Berenzia did. Other colors such as gray, black, or yellow were uncommon. He'd been told his great grandmother had had yellow eyes, the trait skipping two generations before coming to him.

"You look healthier," Sariel said simply.

"I am," Taliesin replied. "I taught myself a restorative spell two months ago and cured the disease. I'm not sick anymore."

"No lingering effects?" Her tone was stoic.

He thought of the scar over his heart, shaped like a spiderweb. He had assumed once he was cured it would fade. But it hadn't. However, he replied, "No, I'm completely healed." Then, firmer, "I healed myself."

"Your magic is impressive, Taliesin. I wish you would devote those skills to damaging spells instead of healing spells."

He had nothing to say to that, just fixed her with a stare.

Sariel sighed and said, "I will need to consider the matter further before letting you out of this room. Your actions shamed our House. Fortunately, I was able to smooth things over with no damage to Andraste's aspirations of priestesshood."

The words stung. "And what about my aspirations?"

"I assume the High Priestess made her thoughts on that quite clear."

"I don't accept it."

Sariel growled in aggravation, a finger coming up to point at his chest. "You are fortunate she did not kill you,

Taliesin!"

His own voice raised in response. "Then why didn't she?"

"Mercy is not the way of the Silk Weaver. You are old enough to know that. Suffering, pain, and punishment is her way. And aside from that, we are a powerful House. We hold respect and influence in Berenzia. The High Priestess did not pass up an opportunity to make an example of us. Of you. To show what happens when Dark Elves overstep their status."

Taliesin stood then, anger and hurt throbbing in his chest. "Maybe she should have just killed me, then! That would be preferable then having to watch life go by without me through my window!"

Sariel's blood-colored eyes narrowed. "You may have only been born a son, but you are still my child. I do not wish to listen to your screams as you are bound to the altar and slowly killed over days or weeks."

He held her gaze, remaining silent.

"If you can remember your status as a male, and behave like you are part of House Ostoroth, then I will permit your freedom. For now, we go to the temple to worship. I'll return to this room next week to see if that attitude has finally left you."

Without another word, she left his room and shut the door behind her.

Taliesin stood there for a few minutes, and the passion and emotion slowly faded from him. He deflated and headed over to the window. A chair that was still intact was beside it. He sat down and rested his forehead against the glass, looking out over the city.

Berenzia was lit with lanterns of green-blue light that sat on the street corners and over doors. But otherwise the city was dark. He could see it all perfectly, his Dark Elven eyes adapted to such light conditions. Buildings rose and fell around the colossal cavern that Berenzia made its home. Huge stalactites hung from the ceiling, vanishing up into shadow. The ground slowly rose to its zenith in the center of the city, where the massive Temple of the Silk Weaver stood.

Built from onyx with a statue of an enormous spider perched at its top.

Dark Elves could be seen moving about the city streets. Slaves in manacles – Human, Half-Elf, High Elf, and a few other races – walked obediently along behind their female masters. A cart rolled past belonging to three Dark Dwarves, their merchandise hidden behind strong crates. A group of children played in an alley, battling each other with wooden weapons. Atop one manor there was some kind of gathering. Dark Elves lounged on blankets in various forms of undress, not an uncommon sight. Sexuality and pleasures of the flesh had a variety of purposes under the Silk Weaver. As a display of beauty, of confidence, as part of dark rituals, and as a weapon of power and punishment. Taliesin could see multiple silhouettes in a window taking off their clothes. One male figure was apparently taking too long, or was too reluctant, and was backhanded across his face.

Taliesin averted his eyes, a knot forming in his throat. Perhaps his mother was right, after all. It didn't matter what he accomplished with his magic. As a man, he would only ever be a second class citizen. Worth only what skills he could bring to battle or to bed. His greatest value was in his physical attractiveness. He was only ninety-eight years old, though. The edge of adulthood. What path his future would take had not been decided. But as far as his mother was concerned she would be the one making the decision. And it would not be what he wanted, but what benefitted the family.

He saw his family exit the house. His father, mother, and sister were flanked by a few soldiers and a few slaves. The soldiers were there mostly for show. Assassinations in the form of poison, curses, or blades happened more often than not. In this heavily status-driven society, there was constant battle for power. But no one would strike in the open. If the attacker could get away with a kill, then that was a quality valued by the Silk Weaver. If they were caught, then obviously they were weak. Punishment was death on the altar or enslavement.

Taliesin watched his family wind through the streets of Berenzia towards the temple. He had been to the rituals at the temple a few times before and did not like them. The females took charge there, and he was not allowed to participate. But he would have preferred that to another day trapped in this bedroom. He hated the four walls that surrounded him.

But, like so much else in his life, it appeared he was powerless to change his situation. That had never stopped him before, though. He always fought for what he wanted. Despite what his mother commanded, he would not submit.

.

.

.

"Taliesin." A gentle hand touched his forearm.

Blinking, he stirred from his memories. He turned his head to see Ruuda glancing at him curiously, green eyes searching his face.

"I asked if you're ready to go," she said.

Her Dwarvish accent made him smile, as it often did. A welcome relief to the hurt those memories brought up. "I am. We will make it through this with charm and stealth."

She raised one eyebrow. "You can bring the charm. I'll bring the stealth."

Taliesin stood, clipping his pack to his belt, and turned to look out over the ridge they had been resting on. The land opened up below them, the shadows darkening as the sun dipped below the horizon. Gone were the rolling hills, boulders, and clusters of trees from before. Now the river wound its way through flatlands. And there, a few miles in the distance, was a great guard tower. Two large stone pillars rose on either side of a metal gate. One side of the tower connected with the river, and the other side was open land. It made the possibility of sneaking past unlikely. Even from this distance, he could see the area was heavily patrolled. A lined formed at the gate, travelers waiting to pass through as they were checked.

He and Ruuda had come upon this a couple hours

before. Eavesdropping on some people informed that this was a check point for those going to and from Vesper. Apparently the town was only a few days further down the river. There was no particularly strong reason Taliesin wanted to go to Vesper. But it would be a good opportunity to resupply, bathe, and sleep in a bed again. And perhaps a good place for knowledge on where the spiders had vanished to. But to get there, they had to go past the tower.

They had laid in the grass along the ridge for some time, observing the situation. Unless they sacrificed days from their travel time, there was no way to go safely around. Even worse was the possibility that they would get lost and never find the river again. A discussion led to the decision that they would wait until nightfall and attempt to pass through like every other traveler.

The wind blew red strands of Ruuda's thick hair in front of her face and she tucked it behind her ears. "I've never talked to anyone from the Surface before. What do we say?"

He shrugged, fiddling with his spider medallion. "I guess we listen to everyone else and try to copy what they say. Keep our hoods up and hope our features aren't noticed."

She frowned. "I don't have a hood."

He glanced down at her barrel. "You're not carrying a cloak around in that thing?"

"No."

"What *do* you have in there?"

A grin lit up her face. "That's my secret. Maybe one day I'll show you."

Taliesin chuckled, turning his sights again on the guard tower. Ruuda's company was an easy comfort now. Something to guard against the daily struggles for survival. The wind blew his dark cloak back from his shoulders, but he barely noticed the weather now. He was used to its ever-changing nature. A few days ago his legs had stopped hurting. His body adapted to the new demands placed upon it. He recalled that when he'd been sick with the disease for five months he'd lost so much of his physicality. He'd worked hard to rebuild his muscles, his stamina, and fill out his face. At the worst of the sickness he hadn't even recognized himself in a mirror.

But the days spent sweating through sleep, shaking with cold and hot flashes, and vomiting up his food were behind him. With unsteady hands and a weak voice he'd cast the restoration spell he had spent a week learning. And his health returned. Now he found himself traveling the Surface with nothing but his magic, his wits, and a Dark Dwarf. Life was fascinating.

"What do we do if they are hostile to us?" Ruuda asked.

"Run," he replied.

"Right. Good plan."

They started down the ridge, heading into the plains below. Grass slapped at their shins and the sun vanished, dropping the world into night. Taliesin looked up. The moon lit up a sky full of stars. He liked the night sky. It was easy on his eyes, and beautiful to behold.

They cautiously approached the guard towers, and Taliesin pulled his hood up to better hide his face. They came to the back of the line and stopped, giving each other uneasy glances. Ahead of them were ten other groups of travelers. One had a carriage pulled by a horse. It was the second horse they'd seen on their venture, and they found the animals to be quite intimidating. He could make out mostly High Elves and Wild Elves, with a few Humans and Half-Elves in the mix. There was one very large being that seemed to be part lizard, with a body covered in scales.

Ruuda shifted nervously beside him as they waited. She pulled strands of hair in front of her face to help hide her identity. As the line got smaller and smaller, Taliesin could see a couple of guards in Eleste'si armor doing the questioning. His keen ears made out what was asked in Common.

"What is your name?"

"Where are you from?"

"Where are you going?"

"What is your business?"

He quickly thought of answers to provide as they neared the gate. The towers seemed quite tall from this close, and figures of patrolling guards eclipsed the stars as they walked back and forth. The carriage pulled up to the gate, shimmered, and then illusion magic on it dropped and extra cargo was revealed. Taliesin's eyebrows shot up as an argument ensued, the guards now searching the extra crates. There was dispelling magic present here. He hadn't expected something so advanced. It was curious.

After several more minutes of questions the carriage was allowed to proceed. There was one more person before Ruuda and Taliesin. The two exchanged nervous glances. Her eyes were bright in the dark due to her excellent darkvision. She could see even further than he could.

At last it was their turn. Taliesin stepped up, Ruuda right next to him. He held his face forward, confident the shadow of his hood would help hide him. Perhaps he was overreacting, anyway. How bad could things really go?

The guard, a young High Elf, looked up from his parchment to Taliesin. "What are you-*oh dear gods*! What happened to your face?"

Taliesin blinked in surprise. A bolt of anger shot through him at the remark, realizing the guard was referring to the dark gray color of his skin. His thoughts spun, not expecting this question, trying to come up with an answer that wouldn't arouse suspicion. "You know . . . journeying through the wilderness. We are quite dirty."

"Oh." The guard seemed satisfied. "What are your names?"

"Taliesin Ostoroth and Ruuda Drybarrel."

"Right. And where are you going?"

"Vesper."

The guarded nodded. "What is your business there?"

Taliesin gestured to Ruuda. "You see this barrel? We trade in beer, and we are going to Vesper to fill it up."

Ruuda kept her head hung as the guard's eyes flicked up and down the very large barrel strapped to her back.

The guard asked. "Where are you from?"

This was an easy lie. "Eleste'si."

"Trading in beer from Eleste'si, I see. Can I see your papers?"

The Dark Elf froze. "Papers?"

"Yes. The papers for the merchandise you're trading."

Taliesin began to panic. "Well . . . you see . . . we lost our papers on our travels. We were attacked by big dogs. You know . . ." He fumbled for the Surface term. " . . . Wolves! Wolves. We ran into the river to get away and lost the papers in there."

The guard stared at him for a long moment, gaze searching his face. Taliesin stayed very still, offering what he hoped was a sincere smile. He could feel tension radiating off of Ruuda.

At last the guard nodded. "Stay here for just a moment." He turned to head towards one of the towers.

Taliesin knew this was not good. He needed to push things along quickly. "Do we need to pay some gold to get past the gate? I have plenty on me."

The young High Elf frowned. "Are you trying to bribe me?"

"Uh . . . no, of course not!"

A woman's voice sounded from the side. "What is going on here?"

Taliesin looked to who was approaching. A High Elf with her blonde hair tied back in a ponytail, two shorter strands falling on either side of her face. She wore a curious robe of light pink that had blue arcane symbols all over it. A similarly blue sash was tied around her waist.

The guard immediately stopped, giving the woman his full attention. "Jasita, I was just asking them-"

She held up her hand and he stopped talking. Calculating eyes studied Taliesin's face, and then Ruuda's.

"We're just trying to pass through," the Cleric stated, trying to keep his voice as calm and placating as possible. It was the opposite of the way he felt.

The High Elf, Jasita, gave a nod. "Of course. But first, let's chat in the tower. Follow me." She turned and headed to one of the tall structures.

Taliesin looked to the gate. It was still open, the carriage slowly passing through. He knew if they didn't act now, they would lose the opportunity. He cast his hand out and spoke a spell, and a sphere of darkness erupted in the vicinity. The guard shouted in surprise as he was blinded. Taliesin reached down and grabbed Ruuda's hand, pulling her behind him as he ran out of the darkness and towards the carriage.

Jasita shouted orders as they reached the carriage. He let go of Ruuda's hand and dove inside the back, colliding into a crate. Assuming she was just behind him, he fired a silvery bolt of magic through the front of the carriage and at the horses' hooves. The entire structure jerked as the animals ran, panicked noises coming from them. Curses flew from the mouths of the drivers.

Taliesin turned to Ruuda but found her hanging onto the back edge of the carriage. Her gripped slipped and she fell, slamming hard into the earth. He gasped and jumped from the back. The impact made him stumble, but he quickly regained his footing and pulled Ruuda up again.

They ran. A glance behind showed their pursuers were four armed guards and three pink-robed individuals. The ones in the pink floated into the air and flew after them, faces impassive.

Taliesin couldn't help the shout of panic that came from him. He fired a stun spell towards them but with a wave of their hand one of the flying people cancelled the magic. Ruuda whispered a spell and her speed increased, pulling in front of the Dark Elf but keeping a firm grip on his hand. Their pursuers kept up.

He cast a new spell and the spectral whip appeared behind him. He gestured with his hand and it attacked one of the flyers. Not bothering to watch if it hit, he continued to race as fast as he could move his legs. The land was flat and dark all around them. There was nowhere to hide.

Suddenly Ruuda stopped moving and he was sent tumbling to the ground, their hands wrenched apart. Rolling to his knees he saw she was completely frozen in a running position. The flying individuals were fast approaching, and one had their hand out to concentrate on the spell that immobilized Ruuda.

Taliesin jumped to his feet and turned to keep running. But then he stopped. No, he would not leave her. They left the Deep Hollows together, and no matter what obstacles arose they would face them side by side. Taking a deep breath, he reluctantly turned and knelt in front of Ruuda, making himself a shield. He raised both his hands up as the three in pink robes landed next to them, the four guards jogging the rest of the way.

Jasita stared down, a scowl on her face. "Did you really think you could run from mages of the Citadel?"

That name meant nothing to him. His heart pounded in his chest. "We didn't do anything! We haven't hurt anybody!"

Jasita replied, "Your spectral whip just did."

He stared up at her. In his peripheral vision Ruuda was still frozen. The moonlight shone off the guards' armor and the blades in their hands.

Taliesin pulled the coin pouch from his belt and tossed it a few feet in front of him. A last ditch effort for their freedom. "You can take the gold. Just let us pass."

The High Elf woman stared down at the pouch for a moment, and he hoped that he'd finally done the right thing. But instead she said, "Take the Dark Elf and Dark Dwarf to the tower."

The guards grabbed Taliesin's arms and yanked him from the ground, their grip painfully tight. Another gripped his jaw, forcing his face upwards, and stuffed a cloth into his mouth. A preventative measure to keep him from casting spells. He gagged on it, the texture rough and taste disgusting against his tongue. He turned his head to watch Ruuda as the holding spell on her was at last lifted. But her fire was gone, and she gave him a desperate look when the guards pinned her arms down, as well.

Under a blanket of stars on the Surface, so very far from their home, Ruuda and Taliesin were dragged off to the towers.

.

.

.

JADE

.
.
.

The five of them sat crammed into the carriage. Unolé, Artemis, and Skar on one side with Jade and Zok on the other. The windows showed the passing pine trees, the forests dark in the night. The noises of crows and canines sounded from the shadows on and off.

"How have you been enjoying Glenpeleg?" Corentin asked from the driver's seat.

Every muscle in Jade's body was on edge. She was furious at the capture of her fox, of her dear friend Sen, and of the magical clay golem sent to taunt them. They were the actions of an evil person. It reminded her of another such cruel person from her past. A warlock who gloried sacrificing people that spread his evil along the Amakiir River and marched with his undead northwest through the Firelit Forest to the town of Skyview beyond. She and her Circle of Druids had stopped him. But at great cost. She wished to do what she had done then. Tap into her elemental magic and kill Corentin.

But she couldn't yet. Not without knowing where to find Sen and the animals. She had to play Corentin's game a bit longer.

Artemis was the one who answered. "Oh, aside from the general gloom and pervasive oppression of the people, sure, it's a nice place."

The vampire chuckled. "Perhaps I will be merciful and turn you into a vampire spawn. Then you can see that fear is the only way to ensure continuous power."

Zok scoffed. "It's a pity to see a soul that was once Human fall so far into depravity."

"I know your kind, holy man." Corentin's tone held a

sneer. "You take an oath but nothing holds you to it except your own belief that what you are doing is right. And beliefs so easily change."

Zok looked away at that, glaring out of the window.

"What exactly is going to happen once we get to the castle?" Jade spat.

"I'll be waiting for you," the vampire replied. "So for fun let's see what happens first, shall we? Do you find your Dragonborn friend, your animals, or do I find you?"

They all frowned at that, confused at her meaning. But then her visage shimmered and vanished. An illusion. A powerful projection spell. The horses continued to pull the carriage, knowing their destination still.

"She didn't mention my sister," Unolé said with disappointment. "Does that mean she's not here?"

"Or she doesn't realize you two are connected," Skar offered.

"Maybe," Unolé sighed, her shoulders drooping. "But I haven't seen any other Half-Fiends here."

"Brother Zok," Artemis said, crossing her arms, "what was with that broken sword?"

He shifted uncomfortably. "It's a . . . family relic. Enchanted with the scrying spell. I didn't know for certain it would work, or that it would even come to me. I just prayed to the Holy Dragon."

Jade reflected that she used to be able to scry as well. But she lost her magic after the battle with the warlock. She was stronger every day, though. She would need her power back if she was to defend Oceala against her visions of the red dragon.

"Speaking of strange magic," Unolé began dryly, "What is going on with you all? I saw Skar reach through the Sen golem, and a fireball not damage Jade at all. And Zok can move really fast. Is this some really powerful magic?"

They all exchanged looks. Their abilities were still so new, still being discovered, it felt strange to discuss them openly with someone else. But Jade could see no harm in telling the Rogue. She was putting her life on the line to assist them, after all.

"They are a form of magic," the Druid replied. "A permanent bodily enchantment, if you will. We got them from a very powerful person in thanks for freeing him from a curse. I am invulnerable to fire. Skar can go intangible. Artemis teleports. And Zok is fast."

Unolé cocked an eyebrow. "That's interesting. I guess it's a good thing you are my allies, then."

"If we are going to survive this, we have to act as one," Zok stated. "What is our plan once we reach the castle?"

"The gemstone is important," Jade said. "But more important is Sen and our animals. We find them and get them out. Hopefully our search still takes us to the gemstone."

"Get the Sunsword, and go back and kill Corentin," Artemis continued. "Then get the hell out of this plane and back home."

"Do you think we need Encarna's help? And the warriors she is amassing?" Skar asked.

"After we get the gemstone we can attack the castle again with their aid," Zok replied. "Overwhelm the vampire and free these poor people."

They slipped into a silence after that, preparing themselves mentally for the challenge ahead. Jade would have felt more confident if they were simply going in to get the gem or confront Corentin. But the prisoners made things more difficult. If they began to win, would Sen and the animals be killed? And if they did succeed and left to get the Sunsword, how much longer could they afford to stay here in Glenpeleg? The summer solstice and the Foresight were not what concerned Jade. They had a year to deal with that. But the threat of the red dragon loomed over her constantly. She had no idea when this cataclysm would come to pass. And she needed to be on the Material plane to defend her home.

Time passed until the forest dropped away around them and they came to an open patch of land. A long stone bridge spanned over a great chasm in the earth. And on the other side, fully protected and separated, was the castle. It rose high and dark over them, and crows circled its spear-like towers. The air seemed colder. Jade wondered if it was her own Druidic magic sensitive to the presence of undead. The castle reeked of it. Corentin's power held strong here.

They crossed the bridge and the carriage pulled to a stop before a set of great wooden doors. The five of them exited, glancing once at the castle before heading inside. The doors were unlocked, and on the other side was a grand foyer. A spiral staircase wound up to another set of large doors, and two corridors branched off on either side. It was completely silent, and they were completely alone.

"Where did you see Sen in your scrying spell?" Jade whispered.

"Beneath the castle," he answered. "Let's find a way down."

He turned and went to the corridor on the left, the group following behind. Artemis notched an arrow on her bow, holding the weapon at her side, still barefoot. Unolé kept a dagger in each hand, moving soundlessly. The hall was narrow and plain. After fifty feet they passed an open door that looked into a long dining room. A balcony overlooked it from the second story. They saw an armored man standing on the balcony, a large sword in his hands. Once he saw them he turned and walked slowly away, vanishing from sight. They hesitated, but then pressed on. They were here to rescue their friends, they didn't have time to pursue someone who wasn't an immediate threat.

The group passed a lounging room that had blood stains on the furniture. The hall forked a few times and directions were simply selected by what looked to head towards the center of the castle and hopefully a way down. Once they heard a laugh sound around a corner, but upon investigating there was no one there.

Jade thought it was curious they hadn't been attacked by anything yet. She was grateful. They were not at their strongest, still recovering from the fight with the witch. But with each corner they turned and each door they passed, she grew tense with the expectation of an ambush. The silence and stillness of the castle was pregnant with threat.

They passed a broom closet, checking through for any secret doors. Then they crossed through a casual dining room. There was the thunder of footsteps from the story above them. All five flinched, heads snapping up to look towards the ceiling. But the sound was instantly gone.

Exiting that room, they entered a large kitchen that was heavily bloodstained. Noses crinkled at the smell, and eyes warily took in an assortment of knives that were scattered over the countertops. The kitchen was long and narrow, and at the far end there was a brief movement. The man in the heavy silver armor walked past, not even glancing in their direction. They crept forward and peered out the far end, but he was already out of sight.

They continued to make their way down the halls. There were no decorations here, no glamour or tapestries or statues. It was all plain and functional. As if to purposefully make navigating the castle difficult. After what felt like an hour of searching, the came to a door that was locked.

"I can take care of this," Unolé whispered, crouching down next to the door. She drew a set of lock picks and went to work, purple eyes narrowed and fingers moving deftly. It only took her a few seconds to unlock the door, and she pushed it open.

They were faced with a small library. Book-crammed shelves lined every wall, and a round table sat in the center. The room was covered in dust and cobwebs. There was no window or any other light source, so Skar lit the end of his wand and held it up for everyone as they filed inside.

"What is worth hiding in here?" Artemis wondered aloud and walked slowly along the bookshelves.

Skar spoke a spell and made a few gestures in the air with his wand. He then passed the wand over the room, eyes narrowed, before stopping at one shelf. "There is a strong magical essence right here. Something is heavily enchanted."

Jade grabbed a handful of books from the area Skar pointed at, setting them on the table. There was nothing on the wall behind, but as the books moved Skar's wand followed with his spell of magic detection. She opened the books as the others gathered closer, the wand's light making their faces pale. The first few books she thumbed through had nothing of interest. But when she went to open another she found it was magically sealed.

"Locked?" Unolé asked. "Can I help out?"

The Druid held the book up, examining it. "No physical lock, I'm afraid. A spell has been cast on this. I may be able to dispel it. Maybe."

Jade sat the book back down and held a palm over it. There was such a disconnect from nature in this land. Everything felt like it was dying. She closed her eyes to concentrate, recalling the teachings of Master Galen. Of connecting with nature as she wandered the lands. Of battling all that was unnatural and impure.

And then the magic came. It flowed from her center, down her arm, and to her blackened fingers. Her hand glowed green as she murmured the dispelling words. She felt the tether on the book tense, fight back, and then break. And the front cover popped open.

Immediately a blast of magic exploded from it, black with necrotic energy. Jade only had a moment to cast her hand in a second dispel magic spell. She was able to cut off the brunt of the energy, but enough got through to slam them all back into the walls and create cuts along exposed flesh.

Just as suddenly as it came, it was gone. The group stared at the open book, breathing hard.

"Is everyone alright?" Zok asked.

"Yes," Artemis sighed. "Good reaction, Jade."

The Druid let out her breath slowly, calming her nerves. "I should have checked further before opening it. I'm glad no one is seriously hurt." She approached the table once again to look at the find.

It was not a book after all. Merely a case designed to blend in with the library. And sitting inside was a white gemstone. An opal.

There was a collective intake of breath as they

stared at their discovery. Artemis quickly went to the door of the library and shut it, standing with her back to it and her bow at the ready.

"We found it," Skar breathed.

Zok held out the bottomless bag they'd taken from the Minotaur. "Let's put it in there. It will be safer."

Jade picked up the gem and dropped it gently inside. "One problem down. Let's go find Sen and the animals and get out of here."

A look passed over Zok's face. Thoughts raced past his eyes and he pressed his lips together. She could tell he was about to speak, and gave him the few seconds he needed to arrange his ideas. Then he said, "I could go get the Sunsword."

"What?" Artemis asked, frowning.

"I'm fast," he explained. "I could leave this castle, run to Sunil-Cathal, and get the Sunsword. You stay here and rescue the others. When I return, we can all face Corentin together."

"That's crazy!" Unolé gasped. "We were just talking about needing an army to take this castle."

"But we are already inside!" Zok pressed, eagerness now on his face. "We don't need an army, we were *invited in!* Corentin does not expect this. She thinks we are only here to get the prisoners and leave. It's an opportunity to surprise her."

Jade could see the logic in this. And she liked the idea of a faster route to get back home. But still, she didn't like splitting up. They were all stronger together.

Zok apparently could see the indecision in her eyes. He leaned closer to her. "You know I'm right, Jade. Let's take care of two things at once, then stop this vampire as a team. As the Phantom Five."

The Druid met his gaze, considered a moment more, and then nodded. "I agree. But hurry, Zok. This castle is too quiet."

He reached up and put a hand on her arm, then glanced at each of them. "I trust you all to save Sen. And your animals. I will be back with the Sunsword before you are in danger."

Jade gave his hand a squeeze. "Go."

Artemis opened the door for him, giving a nod of respect, and he left the room.

A moment of silence passed as they waited, half expecting to hear the sounds of battle as something tried to stop Zok from leaving. But there was only silence.

"Is this a game?" Unolé asked, her arms crossed. "I thought we were going to be hunted down in this castle."

Artemis shook her head, relaxing her grip on her bow. "Corentin and whatever else is in here are prolonging a fight. They want us to be scared."

"That just means the situation will be more dangerous when we run into them," Jade said. "We'll be tired from traversing through the castle. And they'll be well rested."

"Hmph," the Half-Elf Ranger scowled, "then they underestimate us. Let's get going." She turned and opened the door, heading out into the corridor once again.

More time passed as they searched the castle. Jade pushed any worries about Zok from her mind. She trusted him to do his job, as he trusted them. As they rounded yet another corner, they came to a short hall that ended in a wooden door. Another lock was latched over it. And standing there was Encarna.

All of them jumped, startled at each other's presence.

"Encarna?" Jade whispered. "What are you doing here?"

Her mouth was open in surprise. "Me? What are all of *you* doing here?"

Artemis replied, "We came to rescue our friend and animals, of course."

"I thought you were waiting to go in with an organized force?" Encarna frowned.

Artemis shrugged. "We wanted to take matters into our own hands."

The dark-skinned woman relaxed. "I understand that. I decided to go in on my own to search for the gemstone. But still no luck. I didn't want to risk anyone's lives if I didn't have to. I wanted to give it one more shot."

"Well," Skar said, "then you should be happy to know we-"

Artemis quickly covered the Dragonborn's mouth, giving him a warning look. But Encarna seemed to understand, and a smile leaped to her face. She said, "Well, what is the plan now?"

"We came here for a rescue," Jade answered.

Encarna gestured to the wooden door she stood beside. "It's locked. I can try to-"

"I've got it," Unolé interrupted, going to work once again.

As they waited, there was the noise of movement behind them, and soft laughter. They whirled around, but the hall was empty. Jade strode over to the corner, peering around either side. She looked back to her friends. "They're gone."

"We're being watched," Skar groaned. "It's a trap."

"Of course it is," Artemis muttered. "That doesn't mean we can't outsmart them."

Unolé pushed the wooden door open, saying, "All done."

They were faced with a narrow stone staircase that wound down into darkness. Getting their weapons at the ready and Skar producing a light once again, they headed down. They were quieter without Zok's heavy armor, but still their soft steps sounded too loud in the tight passage. Unolé led, her tail flicking behind her to keep her balance and help her move without a sound. Skar was just behind, keeping the light raised. Then Jade, Artemis, and Encarna followed at the back.

They descended ten feet, twenty, thirty, and then forty feet before they came to the end. Another wooden door with a lock. Unolé struggled with this one for a few minutes, breaking two lock picks before she was able to open it. They stepped through to the other side.

It was staggering to come from the narrow corridors of the castle to such a huge, open room. It was so large that heavy columns sat at intervals to support the weight of the stone above it. It was not completely dark here. Lit torches were attached to each column, and the shadows they cast spiderwebbed across a floor splattered with old blood. At the far side of the room there were dungeon cells. But at this distance, even with her darkvision, Jade couldn't see what lay inside.

Without speaking, she pointed out the prison cells to the others. They nodded and crept into the space. All ears were alert, all eyes wide, all muscles tense as they prepared for danger. But nothing moved or made a noise. The four stayed in the shadows as much as possible, moving from one column to another. It was cold here, the torches doing little to stave off the chill. Jade wasn't certain she even breathed as they crossed one half of the room and came upon the cells.

Two cells were empty. But inside a third was Wolfie and Foxy, curled asleep against each other. And inside the last was Sen, chained up, beaten and bloody, and unconscious. Her heart broke at the sight, and she felt the fury rolling off Artemis and Skar next to her.

Unolé pulled out her lock picks once again, and crouched down next to Sen's cell. But as she reached up for the lock a smooth voice behind them said, "Oh no, let's not do that."

Jade just had a moment to turn and see Corentin standing there, sharp teeth bared, before the vampire attacked.

.

.

.

ƵOK

.
.
.

Trees flashed past the Paladin as he raced down the winding dirt road towards Sunil-Cathal. His legs moved in a blur underneath him, but it was almost effortless. He had so much stamina, he felt as if he could run for hours. He was certainly not silent, his armor rattled with every movement. But stealth was not what he was going for here. He had to be as fast as possible. He hadn't really let himself loose since first trying this newfound power in the desert. But if there was any time to test his limits, it was now.

Zok ran along the road, not knowing how much time had passed. He was thankful for the clear path. This kind of speed would not have been possible if he was running through the forest. Too many obstacles to trip over or run into. Despite moving faster, his visual capabilities did not change. If he wasn't careful, he could run into something before even noticing it was there.

At last, he saw the ruined fortress ahead. Zok slowed down, sweat running down the sides of his face. But as he jogged towards the front doors he heard a flurry of wings behind him. Whipping around, he saw a murder of crows descend. Instantly knocked from his feet, there was a terrible clanking as beaks and talons pounded against his armor. He felt scratches against his exposed skin, and black feathers blinded his vision before the crows pulled off into the sky.

Zok immediately rolled to his feet, looking up. The birds circled around for another attack. He didn't have time for this. He needed the Sunsword. Pulling out his shield for cover, the Half-Elf ran to the door. Once inside, he was still exposed. The roof was caved in, and the crows took the opportunity to dive him once again as he ran for the hallway.

Zok crouched down under his shield, the impact of the birds shaking his arm and hammering at his joints. He gritted his teeth, waiting for the attack to pass. Once it did, he sprinted again for the corridor. Darting inside the cover of the hall, he bounded down the stairs to the room Unolé had shown them.

There was the cot again, and he fell to his knees and pulled out the bottomless bag. He'd never used such an item before but he understood the basics of the enchantment. Concentrating on the opal, he reached in and felt his fingers close around the gem. His gaze then turned to the hilt lying before him. Holding the opal out, he pushed it it downwards. There was momentary resistance from the magical barrier, but then it dissolved and he was able to push the gemstone into the slot on the hilt.

Zok grasped the hilt and held it up, but no blade appeared. He frowned, turning it over in his hands. Frustration built up inside. He wasn't a spellcaster like Jade or Skar. He wasn't attuned to the arcane world. The magic he knew was very basic. He wondered if he had made a mistake coming here. Perhaps one of them should have. They would know how to activate a magical sword.

And then he recalled Master Amon's words, said to him so long ago when he first came to Somberdale. When it felt as if the weight of the world was upon him.

When nothing else seems certain in your life, when times are at their darkest, say those words. And your strength will be renewed.

Pushing the panic from his mind and heart, he laid the hilt across his lap, closed his eyes, and spoke his oath.

"I devote my life to follow you, Holy Dragon. In your example I will be honest, and keep my word in all things. I will protect others as though their life is greater than mine. I will show mercy to my foes, but punish those who do evil."

He felt energy pulse from the hilt. He pushed on.

"I will obey those with just authority. I will answer for my actions and ask forgiveness for any wrong I have done. And in all things I will be honorable."

The sword seemed to call to him. He grabbed the hilt and held it up before him, answering the call with the last of his oath.

"May you guide my steps and my voice, so I may always serve you justly."

The magic then connected with him. And a shaft of pure sunlight shot up from the hilt as if it was the blade. The light brightened the room around him, and the sword itself was almost too brilliant to look at.

A smile crossed his face. And then he stood and ran back up the stairs, down the corridor, and out into the open ruin once again. The crows were waiting for him, and they descended on him the moment he emerged. But shield in one hand and Sunsword in the other, he sprang on the attack. With a few wide slashes of sunlight, the birds were dead or dispersed, fleeing into the sky.

Zok turned his sights on the direction of the castle. And he ran.

.

.

.

UNOLÉ

.

.

.

The attack happened all at once. From a sheath at her side Corentin produced a large sword and swiped at them all with one wide swing. They scattered, Unolé diving to the side and rolling behind one stone column. But from the shadows, snarling, ran two male, bare-chested vampire spawn. One raced straight at Unolé, claws outstretched.

The Half-Fiend dropped as the claws raked where her head had been, creating long scratches in the stone. She stood and swiped out with both of her daggers, but the vampire spawn was too fast, dancing away from the blows. She hurried backwards, trying to put more distance between herself and her opponent so she could assess the predicament.

The battle with Corentin raged to the side. She attacked with power and fury, impossibly fast. Artemis scrambled for cover, firing arrow after arrow that the vampire swatted from the air. Skar shot forth an icy blast of magic that their opponent shrugged off. Jade spun on the balls of her feet and flung her hand at Corentin, a bolt of lightning shooting from her fingertips and lighting up the room in one blinding second. It impacted the vampire and she stumbled back. It had hurt her. But she stood upright again, smiling.

The second vampire spawn tackled Skar, latching onto his back and scratching at him. He cried out, firing bursts of magic that his enemy dodged.

Unolé brought her daggers up protectively as the vampire spawn launched forward, teeth bared. She parried the blows, going in for a quick stab. The monster spun out of the way, slashing backwards at her. The claws caught her arm, leaving behind five lines of blood. Unolé turned into a kick that hit his side, but she might as well have kicked stone.

Jade's fists lit with fire and she hurled them at Corentin. The vampire dodged both and raced towards her, going into a series of quick slashes with her sword. Fear crossed Jade's face as she avoided each blow until the last one caught her side. The Druid shouted at the pain, stumbling backwards.

Artemis slid in between them, a dagger in each hand, opting for melee combat against the vampire. Their blades clashed, the sounds echoing in the large room.

Skar kicked back at the vampire spawn on him, struggling to get him off as he tore at his bronze scales. And then a sword erupted through the monster's chest, causing him to scream as he was thrown to the side. Encarna stood, a scimitar in her hand, and she gave a nod to Skar before going after the vampire spawn once again, the creature still not dead.

Teshuva's voice sounded in the Half-Fiend's mind, "Unolé, we are in trouble! These foes are powerful."

"We've got this!" she replied, as much to herself as it was to him.

Unolé concentrated on the magic of the feather ring on her finger and the wings sprang from her back. She propelled herself backwards, getting more distance from the snarling vampire spawn. She flew up into the air, surveying the battle. Artemis and Corentin clashed, the torchlight shining off their blades. Skar and Encarna battled the vampire spawn that would not go down, both of them covered in scratches. Jade raced to help Artemis but the second spawn, seeing he could not reach Unolé, went after the Druid instead. Jade made a gesture in the air and a vine ripped itself free from the stone, striking at the monster.

Unolé put her daggers away and drew out the black-bladed sword with a skull on its hilt. The deep, scratchy voice said inside her mind, *"Yes. Kill them all!"*

Assessing the biggest threat, Unolé dove down to Corentin. Her blade sliced through the air with incredible speed. But at the last second the vampire spun around, deflecting the blow. The impact rattled up Unolé's arms and she was sent spinning away, colliding into one of the columns. Dropping to her feet, the Rogue ran towards the vampire. Corentin's sword moved so fast she battled both Artemis and Unolé at the same time, growling. The Half-Fiend's movements could barely keep up, acting purely on instinct. She felt the vampire's blade get small slices and stabs against her on attacks she didn't parry fast enough. At her side Artemis struggled, the wounds from their fight with the witch opening up again.

And then one of the vampire spawn tackled Unolé from the side, slamming her into the stone. Her head swam and she frantically kicked out. The creature laughed and dove closer, the kicks not strong enough. But then a green vine wrapped around the creature's middle and threw him out of the way. Jade ran up and shoved both of her palms forward. Lightning cracked from them and arced the distance to Corentin. It slammed into the vampire and threw her from her feet. She slid across the ground and smacked into a column, smoke rising from her body. But as Artemis pounced on her, seeing an opportunity, she jumped back to her feet and blocked the blow, face now contorted in rage.

Unolé slowly got to her feet, pain wracking her body. She looked to the Druid who slumped back against a column. The lightning spell had clearly exhausted her, and blood stained her side.

"What do we do?" the Half-Fiend asked, breathing hard.

Jade shook her head. "If we leave, Sen will be killed."

Not giving them another moment to converse, the vampire spawn ripped free of the vine and launched himself at them. Jade spun and sent out bolts of fire from her hands, battling once again. Unolé turned to see Artemis struggling to keep up with Corentin. The Half-Fiend hefted her sword and began racing the distance to the two fighters. Corentin's sword flashed through the air and sliced deep into Artemis' thigh. The Ranger cried out at the pain, dropping to her knees. The vampire's face split in a smile as she raised the sword to chop off her head.

And then the room erupted in a blaze of sunlight. A white and gold streak crossed the room within a second and blocked Corentin's blow. The vampire recoiled at the light, hissing, but didn't have a moment to recover. A sword made from the sun struck over and over at Corentin, and she was forced to back up to parry each blow. Unolé's eyes adjusted to the light, and she saw Zok there, the white of his cloak and armor seeming to glow, his face determined.

To the side Skar pummeled one of the vampire spawn with multiple blasts of magic, forcing him to the ground. And then Encarna swung her sword down with a cry, removing the creature's head. Satisfied, they turned to the other spawn that battled Jade.

Knowing the spawn wouldn't last long against the three of them, Unolé ran towards Artemis. The Half-Elf Ranger struggled to her feet, groaning at the pain from her injuries. Unolé helped her the rest of the way. "Are you alright?"

"I will be when we kill this shithead," Artemis spat through clenched teeth.

They both turned and made for Zok and Corentin. The two were locked in an intense battle, swords spinning around their bodies. The vampire was on the defense, her dark eyes panicked now.

Corentin backed up towards the far wall of the room and Unolé saw she was making for a door. But the vampire didn't stop to open it, instead casting one hand backwards and unleashing a thunderous force that splintered the door apart. She then turned the spell on Zok and the Paladin was shoved backwards, keeping his footing but sliding along the stone. Corentin turned and ran out of the door. Zok righted himself, and then pursued.

Unolé was the first to race outside, closely followed by Jade, Skar, and a limping Artemis. Encarna stayed back, keeping them safe from behind. They stood on a wide chunk of land that overlooked the chasm that surrounded the castle. The sky was dark and angry overhead, pushing down on the structure. A cold wind stung her numerous wounds as Unolé slowed to a stop, regarding the situation before her.

Corentin stood at the very edge, panting and hunched. Like a cornered animal. Zok slowly approached, the Sunsword held tightly in one hand.

"Are you going to kill me now, Paladin?" the vampire spat. "Hardly the divine thing to do."

Zok's expression darkened. "You imprison and murder people. Do not look to me for mercy. Justice has caught up to you this day."

Unolé's heart pounded in her chest as she stood in a line with the others, the sword down at her side. Whatever the vampire tried, she was ready.

Corentin's dark eyes swept over them all, then settled back on the brightly lit Paladin. The light from the Sunsword was hurting the vampire, and she growled in frustration. Then, she made her move. She shot forward with her blade out, attempting to streak past Zok and kill the group behind him. Unolé tensed as she saw the bloodlust in the vampire's eyes. A flash of light. And then Corentin's head toppled from her shoulders, dropping to the ground with a wet thud. The body teetered, and then crumbled as well.

Zok lowered the Sunsword from his fast strike, letting out his breath in relief.

"Stab her in the heart," Encarna spoke, stepping out next to the others. "Just to be certain."

"Wait!" Artemis interjected.

Zok paused with the Sunsword in midair, looking back at her expectantly. The rest of them watched as the Ranger limped forward and over to the body. She was dirty, wounded, and bleeding, but she held her chin high as she surveyed the vampire.

Artemis bent down and pulled off the tall black boots from the body. "Payback for what I lost in this awful place."

Zok smiled, then spun the Sunsword once before plunging it into Corentin's chest. The body collapsed into ash.

And then there was a thunderous crack and the ground shook, making the group stumble. The castle swayed above them, an awful noise of stone grinding on stone.

"Her magic has ended," Encarna said. "The castle is coming down. Let's get out of here."

.

.

.

SKAR

.
.
.

The group rushed back inside the huge room, running for the dungeon cells to free their companions. The castle rumbled continuously, the columns shaking in a frightening way. As they ran the length of the space, cracks formed in the ceiling and stones started to pummel them from above. They hurt as they hit Skar's already tired and wounded body. He didn't know where the energy came from to keep going, but the only other alternative was death.

They sprinted up to the prison, and Unolé slid down on her knees, already pulling the lock picks from her pouch. Her hands shook but she worked quickly. Blood dripped on the floor from all of their wounds. The Half-Fiend got both cells open.

"Put Sen on my back," Jade said. She bent down and then transformed into a large brown warhorse. Possibly the only animal strong enough to carry Sen.

The group picked up the Dragonborn's heavy body and slung him over her back, the chains of his manacles clanking. Foxy and Wolfie bounded from their cell and jumped onto her back as well, staying low. Jade turned and galloped through the room, heading for the stairs. Encarna raced after her.

"See you outside," Artemis stated, and teleported away.

Skar, Zok, and Unolé all shared a glance before turning in unison in the direction of the stairs. The castle was coming down around them. The only thing left was to run. Skar could tell Zok was exhausted, his legs shaking where he stood. He had worn himself out on the run to and from Sunil-Cathal.

Just as they began to move, an armored figure dashed from the side and slammed into Zok. The Paladin shouted out as he crashed into the ground, dazed. Skar spun around to find the figure they saw earlier from the dining room balcony. A tall man in full silver armor with a big axe. A helmet hid his face.

Unolé struck out with her sword, grimacing at the obvious pain each movement caused. Skar cast a line of ice from his wand, and it impacted the man's shoulder. A hiss sounded from the helmet and his movement slowed as he battled the Rogue.

Skar turned to Zok. The Half-Elf blinked, a low groan escaping from him. The Wizard moved to help him up when he felt a blow on the back of his head. He dropped to the ground, and for a moment the world blacked. He opened his eyes again, a wave of nausea passing through. He saw the armored man turning away from the blow he'd just dealt, Unolé attacking ferociously. Pieces of the ceiling came down around them. With a crash one landed close to Zok's head, almost crushing him.

And then there was a flash, and Artemis appeared in the air, arrow pulled back on her bow. Her eyes darted to the armored man and she released the arrow. It went straight through his head, dropping him where he stood.

"*Let's go!*" Artemis pressed, yanking Skar to his feet while Unolé helped Zok up.

The four of them ran up the stairs, the world slowly clearing for the Dragonborn. The steps cracked and swayed under them, causing them to stumble into the walls and each other. They reached the corridor and dashed down each hall they came to. Artemis seemed to know the way, leading them with shouts of direction.

Skar's legs burned, his head hurt, and each breath was painful. But he pushed and pushed. Unolé had her arm around Zok, helping him as his eyes took in the scene dazedly. Artemis nimbly maneuvered around fallen debris, and at last she pointed to the front doors ahead, thrown wide open.

They ran out of Corentin's castle, the carriage long

gone now, and onto the bridge that spanned the chasm. On the far side was Jade still as a horse, Encarna standing beside her.

"*Hurry! Hurry!*" Encarna screamed, frantically gesturing.

The bridge cracked underneath them, and it rolled with the force of the quaking as they hurried across. Skar stayed completely focused on his friends waiting for him, the noise of the castle collapsing was thunder in the background.

And, finally, they made it to the other side.

Zok dropped next to Jade, Unolé doing the same beside him. Artemis and Skar turned around to watch what was happening. Corentin's castle dropped on its foundations, sending up a cloud of dust and smoke. With a few more violent shakes and rumbles, the whole thing was over.

.

.

.

JADE

.

.

.

It was the first time Jade had seen sunlight in days, and it came through the cloth of the tent to turn the area a honey yellow. She rested on a blanket, and glanced around to see the rest of her companions doing the same. Bandages wrapped around their wounds, and they were bruised and dirty but alive.

After the castle had collapsed, Encarna had located Corentin's carriage. It was a tight fit but they all went in the back. The ride was a blur, Jade recalled murmuring healing spells to keep her friends from bleeding out as they traveled. Encarna took them back to her camp of nomads. They received some medical treatment and were offered a tent to rest in. All of them went into one tent except for Sen. He was given his own for further care.

Foxy stirred at her side, his fluffy tail rising into the air. Jade gently sat up, her side heavily bandaged from Corentin's sword. She winced at the ache. It would take awhile to heal fully, even with her own magical capabilities.

Moving softly so as not to disturb her friends, Jade left the tent with her fox. The nomads of the camp were preparing a meal; the smell of cooking meat wafted through the air. Encarna noticed her and walked over.

"Good morning, Jade," the dark-haired woman greeted. "How are you feeling?"

"Better," the Druid nodded. "I don't remember much after the battle, how long has it been?"

Encarna chuckled. "Nearly a day. Your group sustained many injuries. We took care of you as best we know how, but you should take it easy for awhile."

"And Sen?"

She sighed, biting her red lip. "We've done what we can but he won't wake up. He needs a Cleric. And there are none here in Glenpeleg."

Jade inclined her head, her shoulders drooping. "Thank you for what you've done. There are Clerics in our home town. If we can get back there, we can get him taken care of. Do you have any news about rifts out of this plane opening?"

"I sent some scouts out a few hours ago. They should be back soon."

"Will they be rifts that take us back to the Material plane, or another one?"

"I'm not expert, but the rifts should appear roughly where people came in and should go back to the plane of origin. So one should be near your ship to your home plane."

"That's a relief."

A smile brightened Encarna's face. "You've done a great service to these people. Know that you have saved many lives."

"I will admit I was caught up in my own worries when we arrived and wasn't eager to assist. But people should be free to live as they want. Tyrants and those who oppress others need to be stopped." She hesitated, then added, "It's been awhile since I've focused on issues other than my own. It feels good."

Encarna patted the Druid on the shoulder. "It sounds like you ask too much of yourself, Elf. But I appreciate the help. Your group going in without an army at your back stopped many casualties."

Zok's voice sounded from behind, "That is what we do. We help others." He walked up next to the Wild Elf. "But I'm afraid we can't stay any longer. Others need us back home." He paused, then asked, "Are you going back to your home, Encarna?"

"I'm heading back to the Gloomdwell soon. I need to ensure everyone in this land knows of their freedom first. I'll miss your face, Zok." She winked.

"It's unfortunate we didn't have longer to know each

other," Zok answered. "Perhaps our paths will cross again."

"I should be so lucky."

Reddening a bit, the Paladin asked, "What about the Sunsword? I still have it, and must admit I feel a connection to it. Unless the people of this land request otherwise . . .?" He drifted off, but his expression said the rest for him. He wanted the sword.

Encarna chuckled. "The only person who could lay claim to that sword was Corentin. You keep it. It suits you."

He gave a small bow. "Thank you."

"I am sorry you all cannot stay longer to reap the gratitude of the people," Encarna said. "When they ask who is responsible for stopping Corentin, what should I tell them?"

Jade and Zok exchanged glances. Then the Paladin answered, "Tell them the Phantom Five did."

Artemis, Skar, and Unolé soon woke up and joined the others outside. As the meal was finished they sat around the campfire with Encarna and a few other nomads, consuming a meal of cooked goat, warm bread, and spiced carrots. Towards the end of their meal the scouts returned, saying a few rifts had opened up in the land, and one was on the pond where Sen's ship was trapped. Invigorated by this news, they quickly finished their meal and packed.

The carriage was used to transport Sen's large body gently through the forest. They stopped at the village to purchase a few more supplies and were happy to see a change had come over the people. Children were staring in wonder at the sky, and the guards at the town gate seemed curious that no monster attacks had come overnight. The Phantom Five did not linger to tell what had happened, though. They wanted to get home soon and trusted Encarna to spread the news.

They took the road back through the forest and to the pond. Two rowboats were sent out. They bid farewell to Encarna one last time before returning to the Scarlet Maiden.

Jade stepped onto the deck, breathing a sigh of relief. The crew brightened at their return, but their faces fell when they saw Sen's unconscious form.

"What happened?" Kailo gasped.

"He was captured and gravely wounded," Zok answered. "We'll need to take him to my temple as soon as we get back to Somberdale. Who is in charge while he is gone?"

"I am the First Mate," Kailo replied. "Rain is the Quartermaster. We will ensure we get home quickly." He pointed out the shimmering rift over the pond, like a long cloud of mist. "The crew are saying that is a portal to our home plane."

"It is," Zok responded. "Let's leave as soon as the ship is ready."

As Kailo and Rain both shouted orders, Unolé wandered up to Jade, Teshuva curled around her arm. "Thank you for allowing me to come," she said.

"Of course," Jade replied. "I know you've been traveling the planes alone searching for your sister, but you are free to come with us. We can help."

A small smile played at Unolé's lips. "Getting passage through this portal with you is appreciated. I will think some more about what to do next."

"I understand. Let me know if you need anything during our journey."

One of the deckhands called, "Lady Jade, they say you are a healer."

The Druid turned to see a group of deckhands carrying Sen on a large slab of wood. She gave them a sad look. "I can try again, but I think we've reached the limits of my capabilities for Sen. Let's go below deck and see if another spell will help." She didn't have much faith in it, but if it helped the crew's morale she didn't mind utilizing her energy to heal some of the minor wounds on the pirate captain.

Artemis and Skar joined to help maneuver Sen below deck. They descended the wooden stairs and went to Sen's personal quarters. As he was lowered into his hammock, Jade noticed a long wooden box sitting to the side. Almost coffin like.

She frowned and pointed to it. "What is that?"

A deckhand replied, "Not long after Sen left the ship he returned with the box. Told us to put it in his quarters and not mess with it."

Jade froze at that. "Have you opened it?"

"No, we trust our captain's orders."

Jade glanced over at Artemis. The Ranger shared her wary look. The Druid then said, "Go back to your duties above deck. We will take care of the captain."

"Thank you, Lady Jade." The deckhands hurried back up the stairs.

The Wild Elf approached the coffin-like box. She passed her hand over it and spoke the words for a detect magic spell. "It's magically sealed shut."

"I can take a look inside," Skar offered. "I'll go intangible so I won't be hurt."

"Still be careful," Artemis warned, one hand hovering over her daggers. Wolfie and Foxy roamed the room, sniffing at the variety of items inside Sen's quarters.

Skar bent down and his form became slightly opaque as he pushed his head and shoulders through the wood of the box.

"What do you see?" Artemis asked when he paused for too long.

"Waiting for my eyes to adjust to the dark," the Dragonborn called back.

The archer sighed dramatically, placing her hands on her hips. She looked to Jade. "How long do you think he can hold this intangibility up before his head gets stuck?"

As the words left her mouth Skar's from flickered, and then his robes dropped off, revealing bare bronze scales underneath. Skar gasped and attempted to pull free from the box, but he was stuck.

Jade and Artemis yelped, hands flying over their eyes. "*Skar!*"

"I'm stuck!" the Wizard cried, struggling. "Hold on! Hold on! I-ugh-I'm out!"

Jade peered through her fingers to see the

Dragonborn sitting on the ground, his robes pulled back on.

Artemis laughed. "Well, that's the first time I've seen a naked Dragonborn."

Skar appeared flustered. "I thought I could hold my intangibility longer!"

The Ranger winked. "Just be grateful you didn't get your head cut off. Did you see anything inside?"

Skar considered for a moment before answering, "I think there was a body. It was hard to see."

Jade glanced up and down the box. Perhaps a coffin, then? If the Sen golem was responsible for it, why would Corentin want it brought onboard the ship? The Druid drew symbols in the air before her, focusing her energies, and cast a spell to dispel the magic. The lock opened. Bracing herself, Jade slowly opened the lid.

Inside was a male body with deathly pale skin. His mouth hung slightly open to reveal pointed incisors. A vampire spawn.

Jade gasped. She turned to Artemis. "Get Zok."

The Ranger teleported away. Instantly there was a thunder of footsteps down the stairs and the Paladin appeared, closely followed by Artemis.

"What's wrong?" he asked.

Jade pointed to the coffin. "A vampire spawn was smuggled on board. We need to kill it before it wakes up."

The Paladin reacted instantly. He pulled the Sunsword from his belt and lit up the blade, casting the room in brilliant light. He spun it once in his hands before plunging it into the chest of the creature. It twitched and then faded into ash.

Zok looked up at them. "How did that get here?"

"The golem Sen brought it here," Jade snapped in anger. "No doubt to attack the crew if we escaped. Or to spread vampirism onto the Material plane."

"I'm glad Corentin is dead," Artemis said. "But at least I got some nice boots out of this!" She held one leg out showily. The black boots came up to her knees, and she had them bound tightly with leather cord to ensure they fit her properly.

Jade laughed at that. She understood keeping a prize from a victory. The orange and red feathers she always kept tucked behind one ear were a testament to her first battle as a Druid. A mission Master Galen sent her on to utilize Druidic magic in taking down a group of harpies in the Black Reach Mountains.

"Let's go home," Zok said. "I'm done with vampires."

They returned to the deck above with the coffin and tossed it into the pond, happy to be rid of it. The Scarlet Maiden made a wide turn and angled itself at the rift. The sun glimmered off of the pond's surface, and a pleasant wind filled the sails. It was a good day to return home, Jade reflected.

The ship sailed forward, and all the crew watched in anticipation as they approached the rift. Everyone held their breath as they passed through. There was a strange sensation, like they went underwater. And then it cleared as they exited to the other side.

They found themselves on the ocean once again. But it was night. The world was black around them, the waves accented silver by moonlight. The crew immediately talked in excitement, and Kailo and Rain took out a star chart to find their position.

Jade went over to lean on the railing at the edge of the deck, the wind blowing her brown hair back from her face. Her companions did the same on either side of her.

"It's good to be back," Zok sighed. "I need to return to the temple, tell them everything about Master Amon and Priest Jafr. And Priestesses Whitney and Liana. I didn't expect to be gone for so long, they are probably all worried about me."

"And we need to travel to An'Ock," Skar said. "To warn the king about Fenvell and the Foresight. That will be quite the journey!"

Jade raised one eyebrow at the Wizard. "Does that mean you are sticking around?"

"Definitely!" Skar nodded.

"I am, too," Artemis said. "We can be an adventuring group! The Phantom Five. Everyone will know our name! Plus, I really want to see what's hidden inside this bottomless bag. You said there is someone in Somberdale who can find out?"

"There is a gnome Wizard named Tymus," Zok answered. "He's been trained at the Citadel. I think he's our best bet. I, too, would like to know what is inside."

Jade leaned forward to see the Half-Fiend Rogue. "What about you, Unolé? Are you going to stick around?"

She smiled, strands of white hair blowing over her red mask. "Thank you for the offer. If we are going to be an adventuring group, then perhaps that will lead to answers about my sister. An'Ock is my home, as well. I can help you all navigate the city."

"Thank you," Zok said. "We will help reunite you with your sister."

Unolé's expression saddened, but she kept the smile on her face.

"Let's not forget about that Jenkins man," Jade stated. "I still want to know who he is and what he wanted from all of us."

Before they could discuss further Rain sprinted up, her eyes wide. "Sorry to interrupt, but we've determined our location!"

"Are we still in route to Vonkai?" Artemis asked. She glanced at the rest of the Phantom Five. "We've still got a compass to return to Draxis, after all."

Rain shook her head. "We are nowhere near Vonkai, I'm afraid. We are only a few hours out from the coast of Somberdale."

They all blinked in surprise. Somberdale. What a strange occurrence to be transported so far. It appeared the compass would have to wait, but Jade was glad at the news. Now they could get Sen the medical help he needed quickly.

The group stayed on deck as lights appeared on the shoreline far ahead. The ship was busy with activity, all of the crew happy to be home. Soon the fire of the lighthouse could be seen, and Jade gazed at it in relief. The flame flickered in the blackness of the night. And then suddenly it expanded and swirled into a storm of fire that surrounded Jade. She gasped, recoiling. Her friends were gone. The ship was gone. A wild look around revealed she was in Oceala.

Another vision.

Jade took in the burning buildings, the screams of people fleeing. The heat caused her to break out in a sweat. Just like every time she had this vision, she turned and ran for the manor where her grandparents lived. Smoke turned the sky gray, and she could hear a thunderous roar. The red dragon, but she didn't see it yet.

The manor loomed up ahead, a dark silhouette against the fire. It was crumbling. Just like each time she had this vision, her grandparents stumbled out as did her brother, wailing.

But then something changed. Running through the flames she saw Zok, but his hair was short and his beard was gone. It took her a moment to even realize it was him. And then there was Artemis, a new bow in her hands, one of ivory and gold. She turned and fired at something in the air, teeth clenched. Skar raced past, his wand casting rapid spells. Unolé descended from above, black wings out, daggers in each hand.

And then the red dragon landed in front of her, seeming to fill up the world. It breathed a line of fire. Jade closed her eyes . . . and then the vision was gone. The ship and the dark ocean returned around her. The wind felt too cold now, and she shivered.

Her vision had changed. It was the first time in two years she'd seen something different. That could only mean the event was still going to happen. Oceala would still be attacked. But her friends would be there, too. How soon would this be? A small part of her mind pointed out that all of her friends were there *except* Sen. But no, she wouldn't dwell on that. He would live.

"Are you alright?" Zok asked.

She turned to the Half-Elf beside her. They were

336

coming into port at Somberdale, the beach and little buildings visible. Now was not the time to burden him with this knowledge.

So she replied, "Yes. Everything is fine."

.

.

.

End of Book 1

The People of Corventos

Amon – Human High Priest of the Holy Dragon, lived in Somberdale, deceased

Andraste Ostoroth – Dark Elf of Berenzia in the Deep Hollows, sister to Taliesin

Artemis Wolfsbane – Half-Elf Ranger, member of the Phantom Five, from the south

Aust Mastralath – High Elf of Eleste'si

Baelfire – Human Cleric of the Holy Dragon, living in Somberdale

Captain Willa 'Baroness' Lance – Human pirate, captain of the ship the God's Hand

Corentin – *of Glenpeleg*, vampire tyrant, deceased

Draxis – Gold dragon, originally from Soleia

Encarna – *of the Gloomdwell*, Human monster hunter

Fade – planar-touched race, of An'Ock, member of the Shadow Guild

Fenvell – shadow being from the Gloomdwell, deceased

Filin – Human barkeep of Vonkai, keeper of camels

Galen – Half-Fiend Druidic teacher to Jade, lived in the Firelit Forest, deceased

"Grandmother" – leader of the Shadow Guild, currently residing in An'Ock

Greycastles – royal family of An'Ock, Human

Herond Moontide – Wild Elf, brother to Jade

Jade Moontide / Galanodel – Wild Elf Druid, from a nomadic tribe, currently living in Somberdale, member of the Phantom Five

Jafr – Human priest of the Holy Dragon, lived in Somberdale, deceased

Jasita – High Elf mage of the Citadel, posted at the guard gates near Vesper

Jem – Human assistant to Tymus, living in Somberdale

Kilo – Human First Mate to Sen

Lady Quickhands –Hag, First Mate to Captain Willa Lance

Liana – Human priestess of the Holy Dragon, lived in Somberdale, last location was Soleia

Lucan Ostoroth – Dark Elf of Berenzia in the Deep Hollows, father to Taliesin

Medric – member of the Shadow Guild

Mirandril – High Elf, ruling Queen of Eleste'si

Miriam – former lover of Sen, last known location was Vonkai

Old Man Jenkins – Human spellcaster

Phil – Human squire for the Holy Dragon, living in Somberdale

Rain – Human Quartermaster for Sen

Rowland – Human Wizard of the Citadel, last seen in the tunnels of the Doorway Mountains

Ruuda Drybarrel – Dark Dwarf of Balum Guar in the Deep Hollows, last location was the guard gates near Vesper

Sariel Ostoroth – Dark Elf of Berenzia in Deep Hollows, mother to Taliesin and Matriarch of House Ostoroth

Sasha – member of the Shadow Guild

Sen – Dragonborn Captain of the Scarlet Maiden, from Somberdale, member of the Phantom Five, currently unconscious following torture and imprisonment

Skar – Dragonborn Wizard, member of the Phantom Five

Taliesin Ostoroth – Dark Elf Cleric of the Silk Weaver, from Berenzia in the Deep Hollows, last location was the guard gates near Vesper

Teshuva – Coatl and worshipper of the Silver Dancer, traveling with Unolé

Therond – High Elf royal advisor to Queen Mirandril, last seen in Somberdale on a journey to An'Ock

Tymus – Gnome Wizard of the Citadel, currently residing in Somberdale

Unatchi – Half-Fiend sister to Unolé, currently missing, last seen outside of An'Ock

Unolé – Half-Fiend Rogue and member of the Shadow Guild, from An'Ock

Vicrum Grodstrum – Dwarf King of Soleia

Viscera Dante – High Elf founder of the Citadel, went missing after investigating a planar portal, presumed deceased

Whitney – Half-Fiend priestess of the Holy Dragon, lived in Somberdale, last location was Soleia

Zayra – Dark Elf smuggler currently working in Eleste'si

Zok – Half-Elf Paladin of the Holy Dragon, from Sunspire, currently living in Somberdale, member of the Phantom Five

Afterward

Thread of Souls is inspired by our *Dungeons and Dragons* campaign that began in 2015. After watching *Critical Role* and falling quickly for the game, I started creating the home brewed world of Corventos. It all began with Somberdale and grew into this crazy and amazing fantasy world I think of as a second home. Our game originally had three players and none of us knew what we were really getting into. We now have four players and me as the DM. We learned quickly that the important thing is telling a great story, laughing, and having fun.

Dig deep and keep on trekking.

Scott Roepel

ABOUT THE AUTHOR

Ashley Roepel has been writing ever since she could pick up a pencil. When she isn't crafting a fantasy world, she is writing about video games, movies, and *Dungeons and Dragons* for a nerd news website. She and her husband love to travel, but they also enjoy staying at home with their two cats.

52649324R00214